THE SEABORNE

The first book of the Seaborne Trilogy

A. G. RIVETT

Pantolwen
Press

First edition published 2019 by Wordcatcher
Second edition published 2022 by Pantolwen Press

ISBNs
Hardback: 978-1-80227-511-7
Paperback: 978-1-80227-512-4
eBook: 978-1-80227-516-2

Body text typeset in Charter 10.5 pt

To my grandchildren and their generation

CO SINNI CÀCH DOMNU CÀCH

as we unite, the worlds unite[†]

Contents

Author's note

The Island in this novel exists in a world both like and unlike our own. Were it to be found in our world, it would be somewhere far to the west of Scotland and well north of Ireland, and Celtic legend does speak of such a land, though it is beneath the waves. Nonetheless, this island shares some of our history. On the mainland, the Romans have been and gone. The story of Christ has reached here – and been assimilated in ways that are, in important regards, more similar to the ancient Celtic church than to modern Christianity. The Norsemen have plundered and raided – and been shipwrecked. And the language is clearly of the same family as modern Gaelic, although identical neither with that nor with any other tongue of this world.

In an English-language novel where most of the characters are speaking another tongue, language presents a particular challenge. The names of places and people must work in English at the same time as being suggestive of a Celtic world. So I have retained Caerpadraig – although were there such a place in Scotland or Ireland, the Gaelic name would no doubt be Cairphadraig, or even Dunphadraig. And I acknowledge that the name of the fishing village of Fisherhame is positively Saxon. In both instances, we can understand these names as Anglicisations of whatever the Island inhabitants called them, and at least in the case of the fishing village, evocative, I hope, of its salty tang. With both people and places, I have tried throughout to keep the English text readable, while also keeping an authentic flavour. Where I have failed, I ask those who understand the Celtic world better to forgive me.

Preface to the Second Edition

When my publisher, Wordcatcher, announced the closure of business at the end of 2021, the second book of the *The Seaborne* trilogy was already written, awaiting editing, and I had readers asking when it would be out. Responding to this situation, my wife and editor, Gillian Paschkes-Bell suggested that the only way forward to ensure *The Seaborne* would remain in print, and that the wait for *The Priest's Wife* would not be drawn out any further than need be, was for her to launch a small new imprint. It would begin by carrying the books of the trilogy, together with one by another author similarly affected. That required a second edition of *The Seaborne*, which gave an opportunity for corrections, revisions, maps and a character list – and the reappearance of one piece of text I had always regretted never made it into the first edition. I offer it here, this time in paperback, hardback and e-book, through the new imprint of Pantolwen Press.

A. G. Rivett

Pantolwen Press is a publishing imprint of Bryn Glas Books
www.brynglasbooks.com

The People of the Story

I've grouped these names first by their home, and secondly by their family relations. Where people are also referred to by another name – for example, as *son of*, or as *wife of* – I've included that. *A.G.R.*

Pronunciation:
As a general rule, *ch* is pronounced as in *loch*; never as in *church*.
Bh and *Mh* both sound like our *v*. *Dh* is just *h*.
Gh is silent (or it's a glottal stop). But *ph* is like our *ph*.
C and g are hard, so *Briged* is pronounced **Bri**-*ged*, not **Bri**-*jed*.

John Finlay *also* Dhion (*H'yawn*) and
Ingleeshe (*In-**gleesh**-eh*): the Seaborne
Helen: formerly, his girlfriend

At Fisherhame

Dael *also* Ma'Hinto: fisherman and head of
Fisherhame: the son of Intoch
Maureen *also* A'Dhael (*A'**Hale***): wife of Dael
Fengoelan: a fisherman, head after Dael
Shelagh *also* A'Fengoel: wife of Fengoelan, sister of
Fineenh
Targud: a fisherman, son of Fengoelan and Shelagh
Benrish: a fisherman
Mairie *also* A'Bhenrish (*A'**Ven**rish*): wife of Benrish
Dermot *also* Ma'Bhenrish (*Ma'**Ven**rish*): a fisherman,
son of Benrish
Siobhan (*Sh'**vaun***), Eilidh (***Ellie***): sisters of Dermot
Callen: a fisherman

Múireann (*Meer-**ahn***): daughter of Callen

Euan, Ronal: young fishermen, sons of Callen

A'Mhagus (*A'**Vag**-ush*): a visiting storyteller

Kenneth: a visiting fisherman – her escort

At Caerpadraig

Micheil: shareg, Caerpadraig

Aileen *also* A'Shar'g: wife of Micheil

Hugh *also* Father: priest

Morag *also* A'Phadr: wife of the Father

Shean (***She**-an*) also Ma'Ronal: blacksmith, son of Ronal

Fineenh (*Fin-**een***) also A'Shean: wife of Shean

Shinane *also* Mi'Shean or Mish Ma'Ronal: their daughter

Leighan (***Lee**-an*) *also* Ma'Challen: Carpenter

Catrean: wife of Leighan

Olan: their son

Donal: a paelht (***pahl**-t*), sentenced to work for Leighan

Shareen: widow of Andy

Padragh (***Pah**-drah*): potter

Rhona: wife of Padragh

Doughael (*Doo-**eel***): weaver

Duigheal (*Dee-**ile***): shepherd

Moira: Shinane's friend and Olan's betrothed

Arleen, Briged: young women of the township

Murdogh: a labourer

Tearlach (***Tchear**-lach*): a leather-worker

Others

Aengas (*Angus*) *also* Ma'Haengas (*Ma'**Hen**-gas*): High Shareg

Kefn: shareg, Dundiamharan (*Dun-d'ya-**var**an*)

Coghlane (*Co-**lane***): a wisewoman

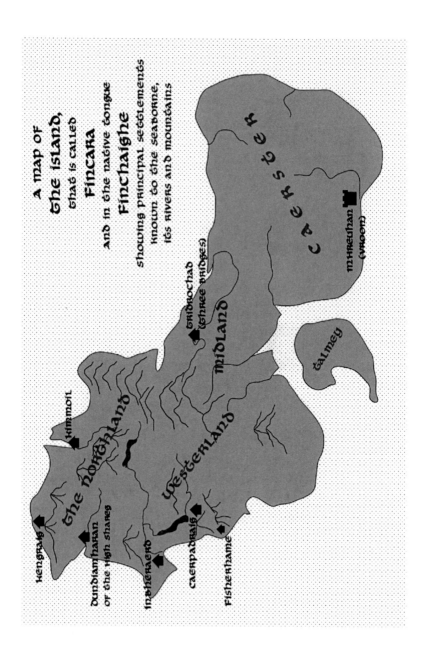

A map of
the island,
that is called
Fincara
and in the native tongue
Finchaighe
showing principal settlements
known to the seaborne,
its rivers and mountains

Caerster

Mhreithan
(Vhooi)

Galmey

Gribrochad
(three bridges)

Midland

Westerland

Kimmoil

the Northland
or the High Shaweg

Dundlamhahan

Hengraig

Insheraerd

Caerpadraig

Fisherhame

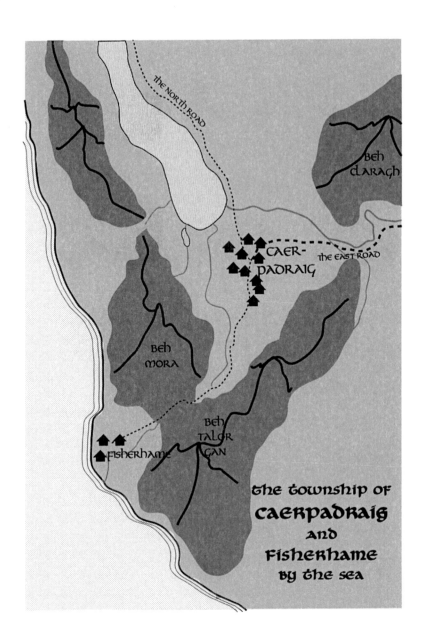

THE NORTH ROAD

BEh
CLARACH

CAER-
PADRAIG

THE EAST ROAD

BEh
MORA

BEh
TALOR
GAN

FISHERHAME

the township of
CAERPADRAIG
and
FISHERHAME
by the sea

THE FIRST PART:
CASTAWAY

Prologue

He didn't want to run away. He knew that now. The mounting debts, the creditors, no longer merely insistent, now threatening. The relationship that had failed under the strains of other failures. If only life were simpler! He felt he was not fitted for this world. Again and again he told himself: he had no choice.

What friends did he have now? What resources? Only the remaining strength of his body, the skills of mind and hand that no-one could take away from him, the credit card that could still, just, be persuaded to spew out the cash he needed to get away.

From his workshops in Vauxhall it was a short walk across the Thames into central London. He boarded the train at Euston. Glasgow Central, and another short walk to Queen Street Station. A book in the window of Waterstones caught his eye: *The Hebrides in Myth and Legend*. On an impulse he bought it.

That same evening he stepped out onto the streets of Fort William, with a ticket in his hand for the morning train to Mallaig. And then? To the harbour. To find the boat that would take him – make him – disappear. At the harbour, as he knew he must, he found that boat. He offered his services as a deck-hand and set sail into the Atlantic.

The men of the crew were from the Isles, and spoke among themselves in what was to him a foreign language. Yet something in him resonated to its sounds – rich, earthy, elemental: utterly other than anything he had heard before.

1

A raven soared on ragged wings high above the low cliff and the sea. With eyes that could spot a stranded crab half a thousand feet below, she watched. A boat drew near the shore. The bird kept her distance from men, but was interested in what they might leave behind. The westerly breeze lifted over the braes. She slid away down the coast, riding the up-currents of air. She turned, glided back, hung in the void, watching.

Dermot, in the bows holding the foresheet, was watching Fengoelan's hand on the tiller. As soon as the old man turned the boat into the wind he let go the rope and, as the brown sail shook, leapt over the gunwale and splashed into the little breakers. He grabbed the high prow and heaved the tiny craft into the shallows. Targud joined him in the water as soon as the mainsail was down and the hull beached on the sand. Fengoelan clambered out carefully from his seat at the helm, and together they hauled their boat with its strange catch across the ripple-marked shore.

As soon as they were above the high-water mark Fengoelan touched his shoulder. 'Dermot – run to your mother and tell her we're back so soon. And tell her to bring one or two sensible women with her: Dael's wife – she's wise with sickness.'

Dermot looked back at the old man's blue eyes. Did he mean it? The answer was brief: 'Go on – be quick, now.'

Surely there was no point. What could anyone do now? Still, Dermot clattered across the shingle, his bare feet scarcely feeling the hard stones. He clambered up the little gully in the low sandstone cliff, and arrived breathless among the roundhouses of his home.

'Mam…' He burst through the door. His mother was sitting with his two sisters, a pot and a pile of peelings between them. She jumped up, startled.

'Dermot – what're you doing here? Why're you back so soon?'

'We – we're just in now. Fengoelan asks that you come quickly.'

She grasped his shoulders. 'What's happened, Dermot? Is someone hurt?'

'No – no-one's hurt. We found him in the sea, out in the west.'

'Who, Dermot? Who?'

'I – I don't know. A stranger. He's –'

'Go round to Dael, Dermot. Ask that his wife come. I'll be along as soon as I've sorted out your good-for-nothing sisters.'

He turned, out of the door and back into the sunlight. Across a few strides of trampled grass and wan weeds.

Dael looked up from his bench where he sat, stitching a piece of sailcloth. Dermot addressed him respectfully, as befitted the elder of the hamlet. 'Is the wife within? There's a man – we found him in the sea – Fengoelan asks that she come.'

Dael turned and called through the half-open door. 'Maureen – the son of Benrish is here – your skills are needed.' Then, turning back to him, 'Sit you down, boy. She won't be a moment.'

Boy: the title rankled with him, but he would not show it before Dael. Had no-one noticed he'd grown up? He had a beard – red and fiery, if still a bit straggly. Give him a chance, and he would show them he was no boy.

The wife appeared in the doorway. Her dark hair, well streaked with grey, framed her wrinkled cheeks. Dermot jumped up from the bench. Her husband might call her Maureen, but he could not. For him it must always be A'Dhael – wife of Dael. He told her about the man. He ended, 'I think he's dead anyway.'

6

Dermot ran down to the shore, the women following, hitching their skirts in their slow haste. He could see Targud and Fengoelan labouring up towards the houses, the cold body slumped between them. A'Dhael had them stop. Looking carefully into the wan face, she turned to Dermot.

'You'd better go for the priest.'

Dermot gaped.

'Father Hugh – across the hill in Caerpadraig. Go on, now – quick as you can.'

A stab of indignation. He fought it down.

'If you say.'

He turned and ran once more, but kicked at the stones under his feet. He had to do as the wife of the elder told him; but it chafed him – more than he could bear. Was he at everyone's beck and call?

He was still wearing his sealskin apron and bib from fishing. Slamming open the door of his home, he shouted at his sister. 'Siobhan – take my bib, will you?' He untied the apron and pulled it impatiently over his head. Underneath was his leine – his woollen tunic hitched with a belt to above the knee.

Siobhan came, her sister on her heels.

'What is it, Dermot? Who is he?'

'I don't know. I don't think anyone knows. He looks dead to me.' He thrust the wet sealskin into her hands. 'But A'Dhael wants me to go for the priest.'

'You must go quick, then.'

He gave her a look, and was off. He ran barefoot, unhindered.

The path east across the pass to Caerpadraig was familiar to him – every First-Day the villagers would take it together, men, women, children old enough to walk the distance and sit quiet through the Tollagh, where they chanted to God and Ghea, and Father Hugh read them the old stories from the big book in the rondal.

For Dermot, God and Ghea were really no more than words you used when you greeted someone, when you left them. He knew that God was the Sky Father who shone down from on high, while Ghea was the Earth Mother, the ground you stood on. But God was what his mother used to threaten him with as a child when he was wayward. She said that God looked down on you and saw what you were doing. Now he had put away such childishness.

It was a steep scramble up this side of the pass, and he was breathless as he reached the moss at the top. Here the path was shingled for firm footing. It wandered like a grey snail-track through the dull green morass. Slabs of stone were laid for bridges across the little brooks that drained the wetland. The water gleamed in the warm spring sunshine.

Then he saw that he was not alone. As he took a chestful of mountain air, a figure detached itself from a grey rock on the far side of the moss. Sometimes his mother or one of the other women would take a load of smoked and salted fish over to Caerpadraig, and return with grain and butter and maybe a little meat. But this wasn't a Fisherhame woman. With sudden recognition – the long black hair tied back, the flash of linen at her throat – he went forward, his feet splashing through the little hollows.

She had seen him. She was waiting, as custom demanded, for him to approach. He drew nearer, caught his breath, quickened his pace, halted beside her.

'Shinane! What're you doing here?'

'Father sent me across with some things from the smithy. But Dermot, I'd have thought you were out fishing with Uncle Fengoelan. Where are you going in such haste?'

'I'm to fetch the priest,' he blurted. 'Must hurry.'

A shadow crossed her face.

'What is it? Is someone hurt?'

'Nobody you know. Some stranger. We found him – in the sea.'

'Then go quickly. Go with God, Dermot. The Father's in the rondal with the children.'

For a moment Dermot paused, watching her face. Then he nodded. Without another word, he was away.

The rondal was the big roundhouse next to where the priest lived. He was panting hard when he flung the door wide and called, leaning to support himself on the doorpost.

'Father!'

A sudden silence. A dozen young eyes turned towards him. Father Hugh stood among them, tall and thin, his brown cassock belted with a white cord, his brown beard seeming, as so often, to hide an amused smile. Dermot never knew how to read him.

Breathless, he approached and gave his message.

The priest reached out and touched his shoulder. 'I'm coming straight away,' he said.

Dermot heard the Father's voice, calm, quiet, ordering the children for his absence. In a few moments the priest was shepherding him towards his own house, fastening a small scrip to his belt.

'Come along, lad. Rest you here while I find someone to come to look after the children.' He pushed open the door.

'Morag,' Father Hugh called.

The priest's wife was another like him. Tall, with clever, blue-grey eyes. Dermot didn't trust a clever woman.

'Morag, this young man has run from Fisherhame with important news. Give him something to slake his thirst while I ask Aileen to take the children. Then I must go back with him as soon as we can. There's a man may need shriving.'

Dermot had never been inside the priest's house. He took in the space. His own home, the home he had

known all his life, was like the others in Fisherhame:
a couple of benches on the rammed earth floor, raised
narrow platforms set into the thick walls for sleeping,
and the smoke swirling around the roof timbers from
the fire that smouldered in the middle. Here, there were
carved chairs by the hearth and a wooden stand with a
book on it, over by an unshuttered window, open to the
fresh air and light outside. He was amazed by the light
in the house. A large frame filled with woven threads
drew his eye. He went over to look. So many colours:
soft greens and greys, little flecks picked out in scar-
let and orange and brown. And a border of blue and
grey, flecked with white. He had never seen the like. No
familiar shapes or patterns that his mind could hold on
to. He wondered what it was, what it was for.

'Do you like it?' said a voice behind him.

He span round, feeling the heat rise to his face. The
priest's wife was standing with a beaker and a pewter
plate.

'Uh… aye.' He hesitated. He felt the difference in
standing between them. 'But…'

She seemed to sense his question. 'It's a map,
Dermot. As if you look down on the whole island from
on high – higher than an eagle – and you see it laid out
below you.'

'Like the eye of God, then?'

She gave him an odd, searching look. She was a
foreigner, they said, from away in the Northlands, and
he never felt at ease when she looked his way. Then she
softened. 'Come outside, Dermot. Surely you'd rather be
in the fresh air on a morning like this, not stuck under
a roof. Come and sit on the bench outside.' She turned.
Her long, dark hair hung down her back, tied with a
simple twist of twine. No other woman did that.

'Thank you, A'Phadr.' That was her name: the wife
of the Father.

She sat quietly on the other end of the bench, while he ate and drank. She made good bannocks, he reflected. He washed them down with the beer.

When he had done, she asked, 'What has happened?'

Dermot told her. 'He's not from hereabouts. You can tell that from the way he's dressed. Strange.'

'How, strange?'

'His clothes were all cut close to his own shape,' he told her. 'And such a strange feel to them. But what we saw first,' he went on, 'was this red thing around him. Red as blood, it was, floating on the water. I've never seen the like!' He did not say how Fengoelan forbade him stopping to take the red thing on board. 'We must get this man in without delay,' he had said.

A light footfall approached.

'Have you had your fill?' Father Hugh had returned. 'We must be on our way – but at my pace, not yours, I fear.'

His wife took the beaker and the plate. 'Dermot has told me the news. You mustn't delay. God speed.'

'Rest in Ghea,' her man replied. Dermot noticed him give her hand a squeeze.

2

Down the steep, seaward side of the pass Dermot hastened, the priest following after, his feet slipping in the screes. Eventually the ground levelled and the smells of the fishing hamlet rose to greet them – woodsmoke, and fish, and seaweed. There was a cluster of men standing outside Fengoelan's house: Fengoelan himself with Targud, who was his son; Callen, who often fished with them. Even old Dael had left his stitching. Some were still in their sealskin aprons and bibs. But he saw his Da was with them too, dressed in his more homely leine: Benrish had stayed on shore that day to fettle his gear. That was before the calm passage of the day had been turned upside down.

They all rose as they saw the priest approach. Dael came towards them, his hand outstretched. Dermot hovered behind, uncertain where he should stand.

'Father, welcome in God's name.'

'In the name of Ghea and in peace. You have someone in need of me?'

Fengoelan came forward. 'Aye, Father, we brought him to my house. He's within. The wife's with him, and Maureen A'Dhael.'

'How is he?'

'To tell truth, Father, when we brought him in his face was pale as mist. I didn't know whether he would live or die. It was A'Dhael sent for you.'

'She did well. Whether or not he needs my ministrations, it's good that a stranger be welcomed. Has this man told you anything about himself?'

'Not a word, Father,' Dael replied. 'I'll call the wife, and she can tell you how it is.' Turning, he thrust his head round the door and called, 'Maureen.'

A moment's pause, and the old woman appeared. She dropped a curtsey to the priest.

'Father. You're welcome.'

'God's blessing on you, Mother. You have a patient again, I hear.'

'Aye, Father. He's very poorly, but now I think he may live. He's just taken the wee'est sip of broth.'

'Has he said anything? Can you tell where he's from, who his people are?'

'Och, he's too weak to say a word yet, Father.'

'Dermot here says he's not from these parts. He's dressed strangely?'

Dermot nodded, importantly. 'Aye. The coat.'

'Oh, the coat, aye.' Fengoelan turned and called through the door to his wife. 'Shelagh – the Father's here. Bring the coat – show the Father.'

They waited: not long, but in the awkward tension it seemed so.

'He was wearing this as well, Father. On his wrist.' A'Dhael opened her hand to reveal a sturdy bracelet.

Her husband drew in his breath as he saw it. 'It's silver,' he whispered. Dermot craned to get a better look.

'Father, I don't like to carry such a thing. Will you take it – look after it, until he can claim it again?'

The priest took the precious object and held it up. Dermot stared. Everyone stared. Dermot, for one, was not impressed. Silver it might be, but not at all fine. Give a silversmith such a quantity and ask him to make a wrist-band, and he would work it in intricate knot-work and richly crafted patterns. This was unbelievably plain: as plain, Dermot thought, as his own knife. But now the priest was peering closely at something on the band. Everyone waited, but Father Hugh shook his head.

'There is something here,' he commented. 'It is surely writing, though in a style I have never seen. The words mean little to me.' Gently, he placed it back in A'Dhael's hand. 'Let it stay beside him. Such a precious thing will be quite safe in Fengoelan's home.'

Now Shelagh A'Fengoel came from her house, a dark bundle in her arms. She spread it out on the ground before the door. Dermot recognised it: that was indeed the coat the man had been wearing. He peered at it more closely. It was made of a stuff he could not have imagined possible.

'We had such a trouble taking it off him,' A'Fengoel was saying. 'You see all these tiny…' She pointed to two rows of minute metal teeth, one down each side of the front opening. 'These… hook-things here. They were all joined together and for the life of me we couldn't see how to undo them. Then – I don't know – there's this tassel thing. We pulled it down the way and there they were, all undone. Have you ever seen the like, Father?'

The Father had not. The men gathered round had not. Dermot, peering over the shoulders of the others, understood.

It was Fengoelan who voiced his thought. 'He's a stranger from far away, isn't he?' he said. 'Do you think he could be from beyond the Island, Father?'

Father Hugh touched the little metal teeth, ran his hand over the smooth fabric. 'I'd be surprised if he's from anywhere near the Island. I've been as far as Sharilland across the water, and I've never seen anything like this.' He straightened up. He turned to A'Dhael. 'Now would you take me to see the man,' he said.

The Father disappeared into the house after the women.

'We'd better hang it to dry.' Dael stooped down and picked up the coat. He spread it out on the drying frame that every house had for hanging the nets or the wet clothes when the men came in from the sea. The sun was pale now, behind thin cloud, but the wind was still warm.

He glanced at Dermot. 'He's a seaborne, then.'

Seaborne. The word echoed in Dermot's mind while the men sat in silence. Washed up from who knew where, with no people to belong to, no clan to speak for

14

him: a man alone in the world. He looked at them all, at their sealskins, leinte and plaids. He thought about the man, and the tough trews of some blue stuff he had been wearing and the coat of that strange smooth cloth. If this man lived, what would he turn out to be? What might he bring among them? The thought gave him an uneasy feeling.

'But if he's not from the Island, then where?'

'I don't know,' said Fengoelan. 'But while he's in my house he will be my guest and I will speak for him. Maybe in God's time he will be able to tell us himself who he is and where he has come from. But look at these again.' The fisherman rose, a little stiffly, and bade them come with him to where the coat hung. He pulled out the hem, where one edge joined to the other at the front, and ran a finger down the tiny teeth. 'Look at the workmanship on them.'

Dermot peered more closely. Each one was made to exactly the same shape.

Callen fingered the metal teeth. 'It would take a really skilled craftsman all day to make one of these – and look how many there are.'

'You're right, Callen,' Fengoelan answered. 'No disrespect to our smith, but I doubt he could make something like that. I tell you, that man in there is someone of standing. Only an important chieftain could command such craftsmanship. Just look at the stitch-work on the seams, too. So small and even and fine.'

An awed silence fell on them.

'We'd better look after him, then.'

'Of course we'll look after him,' rumbled Fengoelan. 'Whoever he is – chieftain or serving man.'

Shinane appeared in the doorway, a wooden tray in her hands. Dermot looked up. For the second time that day – there she was.

Fengoelan rose and took the tray from her.

15

'Aunt sends these out to the men,' she announced. There were mugs of ale, and a small pile of smoked fish and bread.

'Aye, you're a good girl. I'll hold this while you take the ale around.'

She took the mugs, two by two. Dermot stretched out his hands and waited for her to put the beaker in them. For a moment their eyes met.

'Niece, I think we can look at the pieces your father sent you with.' Fengoelan's deep voice rumbled from his chest. 'Now we have a little time to sit together.'

She bobbed a quick curtsey, disappeared around the side of the house, and soon returned with the bundle Dermot had seen her with at the pass. She began the words that custom required. 'The smith your brother sends you greeting, and bids you receive these, the work of his hands.'

'Is it well with him and his?'

'It is well. And he asks whether it be well with you and with yours.'

'It is indeed well. We thank him for his labour, and will send him by you the fruit of our toil.'

Formalities over, Shinane lowered her pack to the ground and carefully opened it. Everyone gathered round. Dermot was quick to see. It was what they expected: fish-hooks, a pair of rowlocks, various boat gear. And a couple of new hinges to replace the rusty remains that held Dael's door in place.

'You'll have had to be careful with those,' chafed Callen. 'Ye'd have had a beating if ye'd lost those.'

'My father's a fair man.' Though she held her eyes down and kept her voice low, Dermot caught a hint of fire in her reply.

'Aye,' Callen went on, 'and I recall when he had a shelf of his work cooling outside and some boys came by throwing stones. Not one of them got away wi'out a remembrance on his back.

'You should have seen him,' he continued, turning to the others. 'He may be a little man, but he fair swelled wi' wrath and bellowed like a bull!'

Dermot grinned. Fengoelan gently pushed the girl towards the door. 'Go you inside, girl, and get yourself a bite.'

She disappeared into the darkness. Dermot watched her go. He helped himself to a fish.

He waited. They all waited. Dermot speared a morsel of bread with his knife.

The priest came out at last. Dermot hurriedly brushed crumbs from his moustache as the Father sat down among them. They watched. For several moments he was silent, looking at the ground beyond his hands, knit together between his knees. None of them broke the silence. It was for the priest to speak first.

'Well,' he began. 'I am little wiser than you.' He looked around at them all. 'You noticed his face, of course.' Dermot nodded with the rest of them. A man's clean-shaven face was never seen in the township, but on this stranger's chin and lip was no more than three or four days' growth of stubble. 'Did you feel his hands?'

Dermot leaned forward. He listened keenly.

Father Hugh continued. 'His hands are smooth. That man in there is surely not used to working with his hands.'

The thought sank into them. Fengoelan cleared his throat. Dermot glanced across at him.

'If I may say, Father – we've been talking together while you've been within. We've been looking at that coat of his yonder.' The fisherman leaned his head towards where the sodden garment hung outstretched. 'Would you say that only a man of some importance would wear cloth like that?'

'I have been thinking the same, Fengoelan. His coat is of a piece with his smooth hands and his silver. He has an intelligent face. I feel that he may be a leader of men.'

Another silence held them.

'But Father,' Targud began, 'how did he get into the sea?' That was a good question, Dermot thought. What had a leader of men, not used to much handwork, been doing at sea? And where was his ship now, and the men of his crew? Surely such a man had not sailed alone.

'We saw no sign – no ship, no wreckage, no...' Targud paused. 'No bodies. Just him.'

'Aye, we see them,' joined in Callen. 'When a boat's gone down in a storm. It's not long before the bodies are washed up. Maybe they're yet to come.'

'But there hasn't been a storm – not for weeks now.'

'Maybe we will have to wait until he can tell us himself,' said the Father.

Benrish broke in: 'Where do you think he's from, Father? If it's further than Sharilland?'

They looked to the shareg, the head of the township, for justice and leadership, but to the priest for wisdom and knowledge. Few of them had ever been to the other side of the Island, two days' walk away, and such ideas as what lay beyond the horizon seldom concerned them. Dermot sat up.

Father Hugh was silent for a while. 'You have heard,' he began slowly. 'You have heard tales of what might be beyond our seas. Of lands where people have strange customs and strange clothes. We want to know answers, but for now there are few. It would seem that he does come from a place beyond our knowing.' He looked up and glanced around at them all. 'But more than that we cannot say. Fengoelan has brought him to his house. When the man is well enough, he may answer for himself. As for now we can at least call him by his name. For he managed one word as I was talking to him, and though it sounds outlandish to us, I do not doubt it is his name. It is Ingleeshe.'

3

Dermot sat beside his father on the rough wooden benches at the back of the rondal. His sisters sat with their mother; he could see their backs a few rows ahead. At last Father Hugh ended the Tollagh.

There was a stirring to his right, along the bench of fishermen. Fengoelan stood up in his place, stooped yet still powerful, his white hair framing a face that seemed always lined into a kindly smile. Weakness, thought Dermot.

'My brothers, my sisters,' the older man began. 'We have a stranger lodging with us, taken from the sea, and still very poorly.' He told them in his deep voice about the seaborne man, how they had found him, how goodwife A'Dhael was caring for him, how none knew yet his people nor his land.

Dermot sensed a heaving, like a small mountain pushing itself out of the ground. The shareg was rising to his feet. Shareg Micheil always gave Dermot that feeling, as of something quite unstoppable.

The shareg took a pace forward from his bench at the front, turned, and faced them all. Black and stocky like his cattle, black-browed, black-bearded, his plaid pinned at the shoulder with a large brooch, his presence was enough to command attention.

'We welcome in God's name the stranger Ingleeshe, as a brother among us.'

Dermot looked around. Most of these people had no real idea who the shareg was talking about. He, Dermot, knew. He had been a part of it, had brought in the man from the sea. He had been there.

He joined the others, climbing the path back up to the Pass of the Sea and his home beyond. No work to do on this First-Day; maybe he would fetch down some cut

19

peat, if he was asked. For a while, Dermot was free to suit his fancy. He would spend the afternoon with the other unmarried lads of the hamlet, lounging on the sea shore, out of sight of home.

He strode ahead, stopping, turning, waiting impatiently. Memories of the last time he was there rose up in him: the frantic running, the panting for breath. Shinane – unexpected, waiting at that rock for him to pass. On an impulse he took leave of his father and started up a small and vague path to the left. It wound between rocks and boggy pools onto the slopes of Talor Gan. What was he doing? Why? He pushed the questions out of his mind. They returned.

Shinane. Should he be calling her Mi'Shean now – daughter of Shean? The little bright-eyed girl of memory who used to tag along with her mother on visits to her aunt A'Fengoel. Shinane of childhood explorations while their elders talked, poking about in rock pools, hunting for treasures washed up by the sea. His one-time playmate, now a young woman. Familiar. Unfamiliar. Unsettling.

He'd seen Shinane after Tollagh that morning, with her mother, the smith's wife. Mother and daughter had kissed, and when A'Shean turned and plodded home, the girl had run lightly away up one of the little tracks that the shepherds used, the hunters used, up into the mountain that hung to the south-west. Maybe… He was a hunter, sometimes, up in the hills. He could become the hunter now. Where would she be?

He gained a shoulder of high ground. The land opened before him, spread out at his feet, the paths meandering both up and over, and down the way. On one of them there was movement. She was there, below. He judged the direction of the wind and planned his path. Keep downwind – keep off the skyline – keep to the firm ground.

He was closing on her. Not far now. But he didn't want to startle her. Deliberately, he made to slip, to splash in a brown peaty pool.

She turned at the sound and saw him. She smiled. 'Dermot! What brings you here?'

What *did* bring him here? He didn't hunt on First-Day. On First-Day he put his knife away and left it at home – not for choice. He felt a man should always carry a knife; but his father forbade it.

'I... I don't know,' he said, awkwardly. He added, 'I wondered if I'd see you.' He felt a hotness in his face.

She looked at him, then down at her hands before glancing back to where the town lay below. She put her head on one side. 'I know Father wouldn't like us to meet alone.'

For a moment she hesitated. Then she turned back to him, a playful light in her eyes. She skipped further along the path. He followed, uncertainly.

A gust of wind blew a sound up to them from the valley below.

'Listen, Dermot. Isn't that the Father playing? I love to hear him.'

'Aye, I think it is.'

They both looked back to where the town lay. The Father often sat outside after Tollagh and played on his pipe, and sometimes his wife sang.

'Do you know the tune? I don't think I've heard it. Perhaps it's one of A'Phadr's songs.'

Her easy, everyday chatter soothed him, and he found his words more readily. 'It sounds foreign to me,' he said. 'She comes from north-away. Maybe it's one from away there.'

His eyes slewed round, up to the ridges of the mountain before him. His feet followed. Shinane stood for a second as the sound faded again. Then she ran after.

Dermot continued, without looking round. 'She's making a needlework. I saw it when I went for the Father the day we brought in the seaborne man. She says it's like the eye of God. I can't see it myself – it's the wrong colours for an eye. It's all green and brown and russet. Did you ever see a russet eye?'

'But your eyes are green. And brown.' Shinane came and stood before him, so they were level. He didn't like a woman to be as tall as he. The hot feeling in his face rushed back. He steadied himself, to make sure he gave as good as he got. He stared right at her, and saw.

'Yours are... they're like grey, and blue. They're the colours of the sea, Shinane.'

She laughed, and span around him in a kind of playful delight he found confusing.

'So the fisherman's eyes are earth-colour, and the sea is in the eyes of the blacksmith's daughter!'

Dermot walked on across the short, wiry grass that sloped upward to the mountain-top. Shinane was a good girl, and would never let you down. It was exciting to be with her, but the way she went off into things – things you'd never thought of – was sometimes too much. Sometimes... he just didn't understand her.

Her voice broke in to his thoughts.

'I must go, Dermot. Mother will want my help.' He felt her searching him with her eyes. He looked away. He had found her, tracked her down, but now... Now he felt her slipping away from him. What would a hunter do? What would a man do?

She half-turned. He still felt her sea-grey eyes on him. Indecisive, he took a step. Stood between her and her path.

For a moment he saw her flinch. Then she lifted her chin. 'Please to let me pass,' she said. She held her head high.

As he hesitated, she slipped by.

'Go with Ghea.' he heard. It was almost a whisper.

He looked after her.

'Aye. Go wi' G'd.'

Dermot woke in the middle of the night. Someone was calling at the door. He heard his father grumble, then a rustle of bed-clothes and the sound of his feet, scuffing across the floor. The door creaked open. A cold draught of night air sneaked up to him. He could hear his father's voice talking low with another man. Surely that was Fengoelan speaking.

Padding footsteps crossed the floor towards him.

'Get you up, son. It's the man again. The Seaborne. He's got a fever, and A'Dhael – She'd like you to fetch the Father.'

He'd had to drag himself from his bed, and this time he bound his feet in skins for running in the dark. Now, he looked up at the black bulk of the mountain, at the dimly-seen scoop in the skyline where the pass was, where the path was. As he bent his steps to it through the darkness, the thought entered his soul that here he was, running again for this stranger. Was he always at his bidding?

There and back again. This time by starlight, for it was the dark of the moon. The priest, even slower than before, picking his way in the shadows.

Another doorway. Then:

'Father, it's good that you've come. Dermot, come you in too and rest yourself a while.' A'Fengoel greeted them at the door. Fengoelan stooped by the wall with a rushlight. More lights flickered by the dull glow of the fire. Dermot could see another figure, squatting beside the pallet that was laid there. The woman rose stiffly at the priest's presence, turned and reverenced him: A'Dhael, of course.

'It's glad I am that you've come, Father. He's bad tonight, and I fear...'

'Tell me,' said the priest.

'It was yester-eve, just before the men came back from the boats. I've seen others pulled from the sea. Most in time return well to their homes, but it's the fever that follows that takes those who don't.'

'Have you given him your draught?'

Dermot wondered how she had come by her knowledge of herbs and how to make medicine from them. He'd heard tell she steeped willow-bark in the spirit that the men of Midland distilled from their barley brew.

'Father, that can help to bring the fever down, and that's as much as I can do. As for the ill that causes it, if they're strong they'll ride it; I canna help those who're not.'

The man on the pallet suddenly writhed. Fengoelan at once thrust the light into Dermot's hands and dropped beside his charge, ready to hold him away from the fire. The man cried out, shouted something. Dermot felt the hairs rise on the back of his neck. It was sounds without meaning.

No-one spoke. The spasm passed.

'That's how it started, Father.' A'Fengoel broke the silence. 'I was sitting by the fire, peeling the neeps for the evening meal. I was singing quietly to myself, the way we do. My mind was all on my work.'

She told how the man had suddenly jerked awake, and stared around him at the walls of the house as if he'd never seen such a thing; how he'd half-risen on his pallet – where he had found the strength amazed her – and cried out with terror, something strange and wild and foreign; how she'd jumped at his sudden shout and dropped a piece of the root in the fire, where it had hissed and crackled. Seeing his staring eyes and flushed face, she'd hurriedly put down her knife and gone to him with soothing words. Her hand on his brow felt the fever. She'd gently pushed him back down onto the pallet, pulling the cloaks up to his chin. It was then that she'd gone for A'Dhael.

24

Father Hugh approached their patient and squatted beside him. He too placed a hand on his forehead. He turned. 'Hot – and dry. Dermot.' Startled at the sudden summons, Dermot jumped. 'Come and hold your light over here,' said the Father. 'There. Look at his face.'

The stranger's eyes were staring back at the priest, rims of bloodshot white around the grey centres. The man made another sound, but weaker. Dermot had seen young bullocks being slaughtered. So had they looked, and sounded, as death came upon them.

The priest also was looking into the face of the Seaborne. 'Ingleeshe... Ingleeshe... Can you hear me?' He reached at his waist for the little leather bag he had tied there. He fumbled inside and brought something out. Dermot saw the yellow lamplight flash: a little flask of something, clear as ice. He hadn't known that such a thing could be made.

'Shelagh – a drop of water, if you please.'

The sound of water tinkling into a small stoup: she had been ready. She brought it to the Father.

'Ingleeshe, I baptise you into the One.'

He tipped a little water onto the man's lank, dark hair.

'Father... Mother... Spirit... Son.'

His finger found the flask. Oil gleamed. He brought his finger to the man's brow.

'In the name of the One,
'Without beginning, without ending,
'The All-Present One.'

4

In the long silence of the hills there was freedom. Shinane was glad of every opportunity to enter it, whatever time she could wrest from the endless circle of spinning and cooking and washing which hardened her hands and dulled her mind; away from the talk of the circle of women around the shareg's wife – a circle her mother would always try to nudge her further into, but one she did not feel drawn to engage with; not now, not yet. Their study of every detail of the community and its doings was not what held her interest. But what did? Whatever it might be – and surely it was something – she felt she had not found it yet. The nearest she could get was in the emptiness of the hills.

She broke off a reed as she wandered down the mountain path. Her mind was full of the meeting she had just had with Dermot: excited that he had sought her out up there on the moor, and at the same time, somehow disappointed. And wasn't there something about it? A tiny germ of some impulse in him that wanted to entrap her? She pulled the brown flowers one by one from where they clustered half-way up the round green stem, and one by one dropped them on the path. She'd had a feeling that he might have held on to her, up there on the mountain, used his bodily strength to keep her from leaving him. But... She turned her mind round, went back to her familiar view: dear Dermot – so solid, so known, but so... locked up. There was fire there, she reflected; it went with his red hair. There was an impetuousness that only wanted a touch of imagination. But there was danger also. Not the danger that brings a thrill to life – she was not one to fear that. She turned over the uneasy feeling she had, and tasted it again: a sense of some kind of dumb, destructive force that burned dully within him.

Sheep turned and stared disdainfully at her as she walked. The women said that if a sheep on the mountain called your name, you would die before the year was out. But she had often heard them call, 'Shinane,' and she was still here in her nineteenth summer. They would stalk a few steps off as she made her way home, and the lambs, strong now from six weeks' growing, would shake their tails and butt at the udder until their dam's hindquarters were almost lifted from the ground. She turned, to look back and enjoy again the wildness of the hills. The broad shoulder of the mountain swept down from the south before rising steeply to the next summit. Between them was the scooped neck of the low pass separating the little hamlet of Fisherhame from the town: the Pass of the Sea. High above, against the watery blue, a single buzzard circled, a speck against the sky, and a few shreds of cloud formed themselves over the mountain-top, only to be lost again as the wind carried them easily down the lee slope.

She joined the main path. The burn had cut a long cleft, and tumbled down in so many steps – a little fall into a brown pool shaded by mountain ash and willow, then another cascade into another pool. Sunlight sparkled from the splashing stream where wagtails and dippers ran and pried between the wet stones.

Then she was among the houses of the town: first, the big stone house of the shareg. There were the two paelchte, sitting outside. On First-Days they were released from their bondage, and Shareg Micheil and his little, sparrow-like wife would have their care for the day. Big Donal she knew – he worked for the carpenter – but she kept her eyes on the ground as she passed him. It would not do for a young girl alone to greet a man outside her kin: not here in the town, where someone might see.

Father Hugh was another matter. Priests seemed to be excepted from every rule. He and his wife were still sitting outside their house next to the rondal, enjoying their midday meal in the sun.

'Peace of Ghea, Father – A'Phadr,' she called out.

'God's peace, Shinane,' replied the priest's wife. She was in her long woven dress of blue-grey wool, gathered at the waist with a plaited belt. She never wore the undyed leinte the other women of the town dressed in, a shawl around their shoulders.

The other side of the rondal was Leighan's house, and behind it the saw-pit. Today it was empty, but often, glancing through the gap between the buildings, she had seen Leighan's eldest, Olan, with Donal working the big two-man saw on a bough. Sometimes when her mother sent her on an errand to the shareg's wife, she had stopped and watched them, where she felt they wouldn't notice her. There would be a shout of triumph as the two halves fell apart, and Donal would emerge from the pit covered in sawdust and grinning from ear to ear. Once he had seen her watching. He had winked.

She walked on into the town. It was barely forty dwellings, with byres and workshops and sheep-pens, at the head of the lough where the burn ran down into the strath. Built in no order, it had grown like a lump of leaven. Shinane knew no other.

She passed the house of Shareen, widowed only last year and with a young family.

'Peace of Ghea, A'De.'

'God's peace, love.'

It struck her again how strange it was to address a widow as A'De – wife of God. As if God could bring home milk from the cattle or meat from the sheep-pens. As if God could take the children off your hands for a while, or keep you warm in bed.

28

A chant that the Father had taught them in the story days came into her head. She sang it quietly to herself as she walked:

> *In the beginning is the One. All comes from the*
> *   One.*
> *We honour Ghea, our Mother, Soul of the Living*
> *   Earth*
> *We honour God, our Father, Spirit of the Shining*
> *   Stars.*
> *When God and Ghea come together, everything*
> *   is born.*
> *When God and Ghea dwell in our hearts*
> *Chrisht is born in us anew.*
> *When Chrisht is born indeed,*
> *Then we are one with the One*
> *From whom all comes.*

She wondered how easy it was for Shareen to see the One, struggling to raise her brood. Yet, the township provided for her, just. Was that the One?

She was still wondering as she reached home.

It was clear her father was not best pleased.

'Where've ye been, girl? Your mother's had to do all the meal hersel'.'

'I've been walking. Up in the hills. I asked Mother.'

'Hmm.' He looked past her from the bench where he was sitting outside the door. Then, 'Did you see anyone on the mountain?'

She suspected her father had started to think about Dermot as a possible son-in-law. So he might not mind. She answered directly, 'I saw Dermot on the hills. We –'

He swung his head round to fix her, his black brows making deep wrinkles. 'Dermot? I've told you before, Shinane. Ye're no to go walking alone with a man. You know that.'

She knew better than to answer him. She bowed her head and went quietly to join her mother inside, a turmoil of emotion hidden beneath her submissive show. Why had she thought the mention of Dermot might please him? Did she want to move her father's thoughts in that direction?

Her mother was like her husband in build. But where Shean the smith was stocky like a bull and his anger was not to be lightly stirred, her mother was comfortable in her ampleness and canny within her circle. She would know, when her only child came quietly to help her with the meal, that a cross word had been said at the threshold. Shinane felt the need of comfort.

'And how is the son of Benrish?'

Shinane felt herself colour a little as she stood with her face down. She looked sideways at her mother. How did she always know what was going on?

The questioning face melted into a softness. Fineenh put her arms around her and held her. In the warmth of her mother's embrace, Shinane felt herself relax. Suddenly, she bowed her head and buried it gratefully in her mother's shoulder.

'You know your father's right, though.'

'Oh, I know.' She hid her deeper thoughts.

'But how is he, anyway?'

'Oh, he's – he's Dermot. He's solid, and strong, but...' For a moment, the unease she had sensed on the mountain sought to come out: a fear of being seen as something to be grasped and held, captured. She pushed it down and ran on. 'But he's...' She sought for words, and the one she chose was not wholly what she meant. 'He's just *dull!* Oh, Mother – I used to enjoy playing with him when we were children. I don't know what's happened. Perhaps I've grown up, and he hasn't. Now he just...' Her words petered into nothingness.

Her mother paused. Then, slowly,

'He doesn't sparkle, does he? And you, my jewel, want someone to shine on you and light up the fire within you. And Dermot doesn't.'

There was another pause as they both digested the truth of what had been said.

It was her mother who took up the thread of the talk again. 'But that's not everything.'

She turned away and went to a small wooden chest against the wall. 'Look at your father and me,' she said, reaching inside the chest and withdrawing a neat bundle of sacking. 'Your father's a fine craftsman, and he's been a good husband to me. But he knows he has no art. So I had to learn to find one or two friends among the women who I can talk with, and we can draw the fire from each other. Look at this.'

She unfolded the bundle and held up a linen cloth. Threads of brilliant and subtle hues dangled from it, and on its face, taut in its round frame, there glowed a half-finished embroidery, intricate in the swirling, interlacing patterns of the Westerland.

'Mother!' Shinane gasped. She reached out to hold it, then took her hands back as if unworthy to touch.

'Go on – take it.'

Slowly, Shinane held the work before her.

'It's beautiful. It's… You … You're making this?' She looked wonderingly at her mother. 'When do you do it? What is it for?' The sewing she saw her mother working at in the home was all of making or mending clothes. Nothing like this.

'I work it at the times when I go to sit with A'Phadr and the shareg's wife. I sew it, but they give me ideas and point out ways of making it better. You know A'Phadr is making a tapestry? It is she who has got us all to do needlework for the rondal. This is to hang from the lectern, beneath the Book. A few are working together on a new cloth to cover the altar, one more patterned than the plain linen that hangs there now. You could learn this, if you wanted.'

'Has Father seen it? He must know – must know how wonderful it is?'

'Aye. I've shown it to him once or twice. He appreciates the work, but he knows he can't see the art of it. It's not in him. He'll make something that does the job, and he'll make it well, and there's no-one this side of the Island could make it better.' Her chin lifted a little. 'But that's all. If it doesn't work, he doesn't see the point. Still, we are friends, even when we're different. We've learned to give each other space to be different.'

'But Dermot…'

'But Dermot is a good strong lad who's proved he's got skill. He comes from a good family and he's dependable. There's none better hereabouts. So you'll try your hardest.' It was a gentle command.

Shinane's eyes flashed back at her mother.

'Won't you?'

5

As big as the sky. Above, around, below – these ideas had no meaning. And filled with light – a light that filled him. He floated in light.

No objects for the light to rest on. It shone, without reflection from any thing. Had he reached out a hand, it would not have altered the light one jot. Perhaps he did not have a hand. Perhaps he did not have a body. It was well.

Well. Welling without source, the light came from nowhere. Nothing was brighter, nothing shadow. Light. Above, around, below.

And warm. As warm as milk, milk from the breast, from the breast of the mother. He turned, turned without motion, resting in the breast of the mother.

Silence.

He was aware. There was a choice. Onward, inward, in towards a greater and greater beingness, a welling source that was nowhere and nothing; that was everything.

Or back. Out again. Back where it was cold and hard, back where things were, back where there was and was not.

He was aware of falling. Was it he who had chosen, or was it that he had been chosen? Falling – down, down. There was a down, and up was receding. Light was receding, and warmth, as if drawn up and in and away.

A pulsing, booming, slow in his mind. As of some great, slow engine. A great piston, in the darkness, pulsing, pulsing: thump-thump… thump-thump…

Waves. The sea. Cold, like he'd never been before. Dark. Tossing up and down. Around.

❧ ❧

"You may as well see what damage you can do below –
you're no bloody use on deck!"

A face veering out of the darkness. An unwashed
smell of sweat and fish and stale cigarette ash. He sought
to place it – to join it to something. To make it a thing.

The trawler skipper, an eternity ago. A throbbing
underfoot, a heaving and pitching and rolling. The
boat. He remembered the boat.

He remembered the warmth of the tiny engine-
room: the roar of the engine. The face of the engineer: his worried face smeared with oil. Something
happened. Oil and water. Water and wind. Blackness.
Cold.

Is this heaven?

A figure hovered over him. There was a dim light
all around. A womanly presence. A face, nearer. *Are
you an angel?*

Sounds. Words. Words, without sense. Questions?
What were they asking? A jumble of meaningless
sounds, and events out of order. He sensed voices coming closer. He was aware of a presence beside him. A
homely, human smell, and a quiet voice – a woman's
voice – talking in words he did not understand.

Something touched his lips. Softly. A small, hard
thing. Warm. His lips pursed around it, as thirty years
before, unremembered in his conscious mind, they
had pursed around a nipple. Something warm flowed,
warm and salty and nourishing.

The voice came and went, and came again. Another
time; another presence – a man, speaking softly. He
opened his eyes briefly against the dragging fatigue,
and for a moment he saw clearly.

A man – a long, thin face with a brown beard and
startling brown eyes. And behind him a woman. Two
women. Or was there another further in the gloom?

Black hair tied back, and something white... The man had a long garment, brown, like a monk.

This must be heaven.

The man was speaking. He could see his lips move, and heard his voice without recognising the sounds. The man was talking to him, pausing between phrases, gently questioning.

He struggled to understand. It was tiring – everything was tiring. It was tiring to breathe. He struggled to speak. 'English,' he said. 'English.' The two syllables repeated were all he could manage.

He could no longer keep his eyelids from closing, and the confusion of sounds returned. Slowly, slowly they faded and merged into the pulsing of blood in the ears: thump-thump... thump-thump...

Dark. Dark and dreamless. *Above thy dark and dreamless streets*... seamless teats... creamless treats... *The silent stars... go by...* So high... No... die.

He slept. Long, and dark, and dreamless, he slept.

He woke, into a world of terrors.

Huge masses rushed at him and smothered him in their vastnesses. Evils grinned and pried and tormented him until he cried out in dread. He felt every hair stand out from his skin. He was writhing on his pallet, tossing in an unbearable heat yet shivering with cold.

People came and went – vague, shadowy forms that were less real than the fantasies swirling around him. He wanted to grasp hold of them, feel something solid and no more than human. At times they gave him something that burned like whisky, and for a while afterwards the phantoms would retreat. Once he had been sure he saw the face of the man in brown, and there was delicious cold water on his crown and a smoothness like oil on his forehead.

Then came the sweat, that drenched him and made the bed smell like iron. Slowly, slowly, his head cleared. Slowly, he began to know that he was himself.

There was a sound. An odd little sing-song sound in a human voice. Its rise and fall repeated itself, phrase by phrase.

He turned his head where he lay. His head felt heavy; he couldn't raise it. A few feet away he could see the hem of a woman's skirt. Wool, it looked like. Barefoot on a dirt floor.

The room was dark, but there were shafts of sunlight streaked across the smoky interior. There she was, lit in a luminous cloud of motes. Her back was to him. He could see her shoulders moving as she worked at something. She was singing as she worked.

He must be lying on the floor. There was a pressure low down in his belly. A stretched sort of feeling, that he well knew the meaning of. He must get up. He moved his arms. They were heavy, too. He tried to push himself onto his side. His body must be very heavy. He collapsed back with a sigh.

'Please…'

He saw the woman start. Then she turned. A lined face, brown, framed in brown hair, whitening. A white cap drawn down over her ears. Like a Vermeer painting.

He found himself alone again, the pressure in his bladder scarcely bearable. How long could he hold out? The floor dominated his view. Hard, earth-colour, uneven. He turned his head to the other side. A rough brazier, black-and-tan with soot and rust. A slow fire, that burned with an unfamiliar smell. Peat?

He seemed to be lying on a kind of coarse material that rustled as he stirred, over which was a sheepskin. Another skin – it must be several sewn together

36

– covered him, fleece down. He was wearing – what was he wearing? A sort of woollen night-shirt, that scratched. Where were his own clothes? His bracelet, that Helen had given him? How had he got like this? How had he come here? Where was here?

There were voices. The long skirt re-entered his scope, with another. Together they helped him. He could not remember ever feeling so weak, so totally incapable, so entirely at the mercy. But oh, the relief, overcoming his embarrassment. He slept.

He woke again. Sunbeams sloped more shallowly now, dimmed to a warm orange. A fresh draught blew across the floor. There was a stamping and a clatter somewhere behind. More meaningless voices – a woman's, and a man's. He dozed.

The man's voice was right beside him. He jolted awake. A pair of stockinged feet, two knees wrapped in something like leather. A face, brown and wrinkled as oak-bark, bright blue eyes, white hair, an untidy beard. A smell of wet and fish.

And the voice, deep and resonant. The rising tone of a question.

He tried to respond. 'Speak… English?'

'*Ingleeshe*,' the man repeated. That slow, rolling cadence, almost making three syllables out of it; the woman had said something similar.

The man smiled. '*Ish Fengoelan fe.*' He said the main word again, and pointed to his chest. '*Fengoelan.*'

He grasped the man's meaning. 'John,' he replied.

'*Ish Ingleeshe thu.*'

'Yes, I'm English,' he whispered hoarsely. 'My name's John. John Fin… Finlay.'

The other stopped, his face puzzled.

'*Giorn?*' the man questioned.

'John.' With an effort he raised his arm and pointed at himself.

The man hesitated. Cautiously, he copied the sound, taking his time over it.

Then, '*Dhion*,' he said. It sounded like *Hiorn*, as if the man had taken his name and held onto it while it changed into something that sounded right to him, and had then spoken it out, in its new form. Deep furrows stood out on his brow, and he pointed at John's chest. '*Dhion?*'

John nodded, weakly.

The man turned his hand back towards himself. '*Fengoelan*,' he repeated.

John made an effort. The man's face lit with pleasure.

The woman came, bent; a hand on the old man's shoulder. More words. The man straightened his knees, still smiling down on him. His feet receded. Soon the woman returned with a bowl of soup. She helped him to half-sit and fed him with a small wooden spoon. He slept again.

He woke. From the light outside the door it must be morning. For a while he lay in a warm doze that was almost pleasant, turning over the phrases the man had said to him.

The man returned, squatted beside him.

John half-raised himself. He pointed a wavering finger at the man's chest, and said, '*Fengoelan?*'

The man smiled his ready smile, answered, '*Ish Fengoelan fe. Ish Dhion thu.*'

John paused, taking the words in. He risked it.

'*Ish* John *fe.*'

The smile of the other turned into a delighted grin.

The woman intervened again, brought him a little porridge, as Fengoelan pulled on his boots and disappeared with a last look back.

Often the other woman would come in. She would look at him carefully, ask questions that he couldn't comprehend. Sometimes others would hover by the door, talking quietly among themselves. There was a younger man who came once or twice. Their son? Couldn't anyone speak English?

Slowly John's strength returned. He could sit up, with help. Take the spoon himself. Once he tried to stand. The house went dark. He swayed, and if the woman hadn't caught him he would have fallen. He felt the strength in her arms.

Now he could look around him, take in where he was. The house was roughly circular, built of stone, the chinks packed with moss and turf. There were no windows. The light came from the half-open doorway, not high enough to pass without stooping. There was a fire in the middle of the room, and no chimney. He looked up. The roof was thatched, and blackened by the smoke that swirled lazily beneath. Surely people didn't still live like this, wherever this was? Again that question: where was here?

Fengoelan brought a strong stick. Between them, he and the woman helped John to his feet. He could not believe how weak his legs felt. He leaned heavily on the stick. Managed a few steps. Collapsed onto a rough wooden bench.

He would lie for hours on the pallet on the floor. Sometimes he dozed. Often he slept. At times he would lie awake, through the brown twilight that was day in the house, through the pitch dark of night. He no longer minded the smoky air. The smell of the sea that came in with Fengoelan set his mind back, before that nightmare dawn of consciousness. What was before? Blackness. A dense night lying over the mind for a great aeon of time. But on the far side of darkness, what was there? The boat – he remembered going on board at Mallaig; then the sounds of the working ship – the persistent pounding of the engine, the rattle of the winches, the slap and heave of a wave as it passed under her hull. Then nothing.

6

'Can you help me get up?'

He felt stronger, and something made him say the words, meaningless though he knew them to be. She was on the other side of the fire, quietly stitching. She looked across at him. Her brown eyes twinkled.

He pushed himself up with his arms. She put down her work, bustled round and knelt beside him.

'Please...' He pointed to the stick, leaning against the wall.

She rocked back on her heels, considering. She said something, and stood up. She turned, and disappeared through the door.

She was gone only a few moments. She returned with the other woman, older, greyer, more stooped. The older woman came to him, bent, hands on knees, looking into his face. She asked a question.

She appeared to make up her mind, and motioned for the stick. They placed it in his hand and each supported his shoulders. Carefully he rolled onto his side, onto his knees, knelt up. Pushed down on the stick as the two women lifted him. He stood, and felt triumphant.

He took a couple of steps towards the door. The older woman headed him off. 'Na, na,' she said, and something more. The two laughed, and turned him towards the bench.

As he sat, an idea came to him. He remembered his conversation with Fengoelan. He turned to the woman of the house, standing before him. '*Ish thu...*?'

He was more successful than he expected. She gave a little gasp and brought a hand to cover her mouth. Her other hand followed, and she turned to her companion. She was giggling like an embarrassed young girl. When she turned back to him her face had reddened.

The other seemed not so readily dismayed. She smiled, and said something. She came and sat beside him and began slowly, carefully shaping each word. *'Ish A'Fengoel shi. Ish A'Dhael fe.'*

He repeated what he had heard, savouring the long drawn-out vowels. The older woman repeated her words. She pointed to herself: *'A'Dhael,'* and to the other, *'A'Fengoel.'*

Fengoelan came in at the end of the day. John listened to the conversation between man and wife. Several times one or the other would glance towards him or motion in his direction. At length the woman went behind a curtain that screened off a doorway. Fengoelan called after her. It was unmistakable. 'Shelagh.'

He awoke the next morning as Fengoelan was getting ready to go out. Bright sunlight was streaming through the door. He sat up more easily.

Seeing him wake, the woman brought him porridge in a bowl, steaming, a little gritty, deeply satisfying. When he had finished she took his bowl and pushed aside the curtain. She returned with some clothes in her arms.

His clothes! There they were, washed, dried, neatly folded: his underclothes, his red checked shirt that he had worn in Fort William, his jeans. Only on his trainers was there still a line of white salt. She came again, bearing something in her cupped palms, a look of awe on her face. What was it? As she knelt she offered it to him, let him take it out of her hands. Carefully he picked up his silver bracelet and put it on.

'Thank you,' he said.

She said something. A question. He guessed it was either 'Do you want to put these on?' or 'Do you need help with these?' In either case the answer was the same.

'Yes,' he said, and nodded vigorously.

He had gone beyond embarrassment with this woman. She had tended to his every bodily need when he was too weak to help himself; it seemed only natural when she helped him to dress. Her firm fingers helped his still-clumsy ones with his buttons. But when he zipped up his jeans, he saw her watching him with – something he could not quite catch, but which seemed to him curious. It was the sudden intensity of her attention as he made the simple movement.

Oh, but it was good to be in his clothes again. They made him feel better, stronger. With her help he stood, leaning on the stick. She gave him her arm, and together they walked to the door. He knew her hands were hovering behind him as he passed through.

The sunlight was blinding. It poured down from an incandescent sky; it flashed around him reflected from the sighing sea. The fresh air filled his smoke-accustomed lungs. It was a resurrection. The call of gulls and of land birds dinned in his ears, his nose was filled with the reek of the sea, of the peat-smoke, of fish. The skin of his face felt the warmth of the sunlight, the cool of the breeze. He reeled as from a great gust, as from much drink, as from the heave of a ship's deck under his feet.

He looked around him. A cluster of round, thatched dwellings, low, dark. Sailing boats, hauled up on the shore. It looked – medieval. He took a long breath, and as he let it go his elation leached from him. His head sank to the arms that held his stick. Suddenly he sobbed, great sobs arising from the depths of his isolation and despair, shaking his frail body as he clung with all his feeble strength to the staff that supported him.

How long he had lain in Fengoelan's house, he had no way of knowing. Now the days were long, and if the breeze felt sometimes chill on his sickness-wasted body, at least the sun had strength to warm him. Day after day he sat on a bench looking out over the restless sea.

He would wave companionably, covering his feelings, to the men as they went about their work. They would hail him, 'Ingleeshe.' He began to accept the word as their name for him. But ceaselessly he was scanning the sea for a ship, the sky for an aircraft, that might still be searching for him.

Fengoelan and Shelagh were the only constant presences, though often the younger man looked in, the one John took to be their son. He learned his name: Targud. He would help them with this and that, and stay to eat a bite. He gave the impression of being settled in himself and his surroundings. John wondered what that felt like.

They had now given him a narrow bed in a small alcove, instead of his pallet by the brazier. He guessed that at one time, this would have been where Targud slept. He might have resented lying on the rough sacking that covered, he guessed, dried bracken, if he had not noticed that his hosts had nothing better for themselves. He had not dreamed that anywhere in the North Atlantic could be this remote. But it wouldn't be for long, he was sure. He could bear it for a while – even those crudest of sanitary arrangements. It would only be a few more days, a week, a month at the most. Surely, soon they would find him, or these people would get word back to the mainland, and he could have a bath again, a change of clothes, a phone call to his parents. Communication – that was the key. There must be someone, if not here, then not far away, who even if they didn't speak English themselves would at least recognise it. Damn it! It's an international language! There must be someone…

A few days after he first tottered outside, he was sitting again on what he was beginning to think of as his bench. It was morning. He had watched Shelagh get on with the housework, while Fengoelan stumped off to sea again. He saw others join him, heard their rough greetings, watched them haul the boat down the beach before wading in and jumping aboard; heard the scrape of timbers over shingle, the wild calling of the gulls, the sighing of the sea.

Then he heard footsteps approaching, crunching on the stones. He turned. One of the fishermen was walking towards him. A few paces behind was another figure. Not the usual rather tattered and soiled working clothes for this man. Despite his small stature he looked splendid in a kind of kilt-like, belted robe that was draped over his shoulder and held in place with a large silver brooch. And broad: like a small but sturdy rock.

They came to a halt a few feet away. The fisherman stepped to one side. He seemed to defer to the splendidly dressed man; he must be of some rank. There was a sense of occasion about this meeting. John stood.

The newcomer said something and reached out a hand. He heard again that now-familiar word they had for him: '*Ingleeshe.*' He took the proffered hand in his – it seemed a natural thing to do.

But the visitor drew his brows together – seemed to check himself. Firmly, he withdrew, then reached out again and grasped John's forearm. John got the message: this was how they greeted each other – not with a hand-hold, but a forearm hold. His mind took it in. Strange.

The man turned to him. Spoke. '*Ish Dhion thu? Ish Ingleeshe thu?*'

John marshalled the words he had spoken with Fengoelan. He felt tongue-tied. He found them, pushed them one by one through his lips. '*Ish John fe.*'

'*Dhion.*' The man seemed to be savouring the sound. He raised his head, smiled a broad, uncomplicated smile. He said something more and grasped John's forearm again. His left hand came round and landed on John's shoulder. John found himself smiling back.

Then his visitor said something to the fisherman, who nodded – or was it a little bow? – turned, and walked away. He sat on the bench, and gestured for John to join him.

Now he was talking again. Only this time he made the words slowly, turning directly to John.

'*Ish Shareg Micheil fe.*' He repeated the phrase once more.

John tried to copy.

Tried again.

Then – he'd got it. Repeated it to the man's satisfaction. They both grinned.

An irrepressible need welled up inside him. He would not let language stand in the way. This he had to say: 'Do you speak English? Do you know anyone who speaks English? Can you tell anyone that… I'm here?'

The man looked confused. '*Ingleeshe? Dhion?*' And more that he could not understand. John's hope drained away. It was frustratingly clear – the message was not getting through.

The man called Shareg Micheil also had something to say, but it seemed that he was at a loss how to say it. He said several words and pointed towards Fengoelan's house, shaking his head. Then he raised his arm and gestured inland. John followed his sign.

A steep mountainside rose above the hamlet. On his right it sloped up to a dun brown hunch against the morning sun. A small cloud hovered around its height. On his left, a rocky point needled into the sky, turned by sunlight into streaks of khaki, grey and purple. Between the two peaks, a deep dent in the skyline, beyond which he could see shadowy mountains, dulled by distance. Now he looked at it, he could make out a vague track climbing to the pass. It seemed to be this pass, this track, that Shareg was pointing out.

Before coming here, John would have enjoyed the climb up to the summit of that needle-pointed peak, as he had done a world away in Snowdonia with Helen. Helen! The sudden stab hurt. But now his fever had sapped his strength, and he was not sure even of climbing to the pass.

Shareg Micheil stood. John felt he must stand also. They shook hands – that strange forearm grasp again. Shareg said something, and smiled – his large, open smile. Then he turned, and strode away. Minutes later, John could make out his figure, shrunk by distance, climbing the track to the pass.

7

It was First-Day again. The air was warm, and as the smith and his family finished the midday meal Shinane heard a gaggle of girls making their way down through the town, chattering and laughing. As they passed the smithy one of them called out.

'Shinane! We're going to the pool.'

The Sheep Burn, beloved of herons, a broad lowland stream, wandered from under the shadow of Beh' Mora to flow into Lough Padraig from the west. A little distance above the lough-side lay the Women's Pool. Screened by willows and alder, men were not permitted to go near. Years before, as a tiny girl toddling behind her mother, Shinane had learned to swim there.

Now she looked up imploringly.

'Go on. Be off with you.' Fineenh answered the unspoken question.

She pulled her apron over her head and gave her mother a kiss. 'I'm coming,' she called.

They reached the pool. Her quick eyes spied a moorhen who, hearing their approach, paddled quietly to the further bank, disappearing between tree-roots and rushes.

The girls pulled off their clothes and splashed into the water. Shinane watched them for a moment then, unlacing her gown, she left it over a fallen tree trunk that arched like a slain dragon across the grass. She dived in after them, savouring the thrill of the cold, clear water on her skin, swimming vigorously until she no longer felt its chill.

After the first exuberance, one by one they rested on the bank, their shifts clinging wetly to them. Moira took her new bangle from where she had carefully laid it on her clothes, and showed it to them. Olan, the carpenter's son and her betrothed, had carved it for her from a piece of rowan.

'Ohh… witches' wood,' giggled Briged. 'He wants to keep you safe for himself.'

'Has your father said anything about when it's to be?' inquired Arleen.

'Next Beltane, they think,' Moira replied.

'That's a long time to wait – he might grow tired of you before then!' Briged jibed.

Moira shrugged. 'I trust him. And he's worth waiting for.'

A silence fell among the young women. Each was momentarily carried into her own world, her own private version of waiting. They were in that brief span when childhood is ended and the responsibilities of adult life are yet to come, and each mind bent itself to a reverie of hopes, fears, uncertainties, wondering.

It was Arleen who broke the silence, turning to Shinane.

'What about you?' she inquired.

'Me?'

'Yes, you, you dreamie. I've noticed Dermot Ma'Bhenrish after you whenever he gets a chance. Do you like him?'

'What? Spotty Dermot the fisherman?' Briged provoked.

Shinane coloured a little.

'Yes. I like him,' she said shortly.

There was another pause. The girls looked archly at each other.

Then Briged started chanting, 'Shinane and Dermot, Dermot and Shinane – she'll be a wife at Fisherhame!'

Shinane flushed deeply, and her eyes flashed a warning.

'I didn't say anything about that,' she said with deliberation.

'Oo-oh – you don't want to be a fishwife, then? Poor Dermot! Who do you want then?'

'I think they'll have to send for a man from another world for you,' Moira sighed. She shook her head. 'Who do I think you would like, Shinane?' she went on. 'I think you'd like – someone rather serious, and… and a little intense. Like the Father.'

'Pity he's already married,' broke in Briged. 'And he's a bit old, even for you, I think.' A wave of giggles went round the circle.

'They'll have to send from far for you. Get a priest's son from another town,' said Arleen.

'All pale and learned,' Briged put in.

Shinane stood up suddenly, turned, and, very upright, walked to the bank. Peeling off her damp shift in one lithe movement, like a cat, she sprang forward over the water. A long, shallow dive brought her to the centre of the pool, and she opened her eyes into the brown and green underwater world. Languidly she turned over and floated there, motionless, only her face above the rippling surface. The sky was far, far away. Her friends' chatter came to her faint and distorted, irrelevant. She was surrounded by an infinite world of silence.

A raven flapped slowly across her view, the only other denizen of her world. Dermot, she mused. They used to be such friends, almost from her earliest memories. Shinane the little girl had loved Dermot the little boy. And now?

Evening. In the house beside the smithy the lights were being lit as the long twilight slowly deepened around them. Behind Shinane the door to the forge let in a small draught which glided over the stone floor and round the stool where she sat, rhythmically spinning her yarn. Her father, seated on the best chair beside the fire, was quietly honing a blade, running the metal over an oil-stone, stroking it on the leather strop, gauging it with his thumb. Shinane was sitting with her thoughts. They had turned to remembrance of the week before, of the days before that, when her uncle Fengoelan had brought the Seaborne among them.

'Mother...'

Her mother looked up from the other chair, where she was working her way through a pile of darning.She turned attentively towards her.

'Did Aunt tell you anything about the seaborne man?'

Her remembrance of seeing him flashed through her mind. The cluster of low, dark little houses that made the fishing hamlet. Her uncle's home that she had known since a child. She remembered the presence of sickness in the house: A'Dhael squatting on a low stool beside a form on the floor. She had seen the half-drowned man, even taken her turn to sit and watch the deathly pale face with its strangely shaven, stubble-speckled chin, while the healing-woman straightened herself to talk with the priest.

'Did Aunt bring you news?'

Shinane knew her mother. She greatly enjoyed a gossip. And her aunt Shelagh, after more than a week of confinement in her house looking after the sick man, had at last been free to come away this First-Day. The sisters had spent the afternoon sitting together.

Now her mother carefully tucked her needle into the hose so that she could find it again, and rested her work in her lap.

'Ohh,' she began. 'Your aunt's got a handful there, and no mistake.'

'Is he very ill still, then?'

'No, no – that's the trouble. He's over his fever all right, and starting to get up and walk around. Oh but the poor thing – from what your aunt says, it seems to me he's simple. Perhaps the fever's touched him. But he can scarcely say a word, not even of the Common Tongue.'

Shinane wound the yarn onto the spindle. She drew more wool out of the batt and again flicked the spindle with practiced fingers.

'And they've had to train him as if he was a toddling child,' her mother went on. 'He doesn't know anything about looking after himself – you know. They've had to do all for him.'

Her father looked up. He growled at their talk. Her mother dropped her voice to a secret whisper.

'Poor Shelagh.' She shook her head. 'They have to mime everything… like he was a dumb thing, and he a grown man.'

She sighed.

Shinane sat still. Something held her from joining in dismissing the foreigner. She wondered what it must be like to wake up in a strange land among a strange people.

Then she ventured,

'The Father said he thinks he must be an important man – a leader, a shareg, perhaps.' Her thoughts ran on. 'Maybe even higher. He might be used to doing things in a different way from us.'

Fineenh stared, and Shinane thought her point had gone home. But it was only a moment before her mother shook her head vigorously. 'Aye, that's as may be,' she retorted. 'What he may have been only makes it so much the sadder. The poor man's simple now, though.'

Fineenh tailed off into silence. Shinane kept her thoughts to herself; the spindle hung motionless at her side.

The long evenings lengthened towards midsummer. Shinane hitched the hem of her gown to cross the Sheep Burn. The cold water on this warm, still evening was delicious on her feet. The sharp scent of new growth filled her nostrils, enlivening her step. She walked on, into a small wood of stunted oaks that hugged the western shore of the lough. Beh' Mora lifted its bulk against a green and gold sky. The eastern spur of the mountain sloped towards the water, at times edged by a small corran where the grass grew lush and the cattle grazed. The path twisted between the boles of the lichen-covered trees, pastel green in the green light. A cuckoo called, clear and strident, and was answered by another, a score of paces ahead. She knew better than to stop and search with her eyes for them among the ochre-green leaves: here under the trees on a still evening the midges swarmed.

The wood came to a sudden stop, as if cut off by a giant's hoe. The path bumped along, worn into the earth by the cowherds. A stone slab-bridge carried it across a little burn that tumbled down the hillside. She spotted the faint track climbing beside the burn, and without pausing she decided. She would take this more difficult route, up onto the mountain. Perhaps she would circle round on the heights and come down on the town once more by the little glen of the Sheep Burn.

She knew the dangers of walking on the mountain in the failing light. Once or twice her father had gone half a day's walk into the hills with a couple of men, looking for lodes where they could mine a little ore for copper or tin. He had returned with stories: the tales of their own happenings, the lore locked into their together-memory. There was the stony place where you could turn and break your leg, as did the giant who lived in these parts before time began. There were the little bluffs that would open before you and break your neck, as had happened to a not-so-wise witch in one of the old stories. And most terrible of all, there was the green bog that could suck you into its black belly, which end had been the fate of Ar, the fell Wolf-Lord. The legends played themselves in her heart. The stories were her guide, here as in everything. In their lore was her people's wisdom; in their together-memory was their strength and their life.

She came to where the burn rose from a maze of peat and heather and blaeberry. The path petered into nothingness. Above her the sky glowed green. It had lost its golden glory, and far in the east the first stars appeared. Up here on the mountain's flank there was a little breeze, and she was grateful to pause. In the distance, the hills rose high and solid, the walls of her world. As she watched, a yellow-white light grew behind their black fringe. Slowly a slim bow of gleaming silver lifted itself into her sight. A long moment more, and a half-moon of milk-white metal. Then the full and radiant globe swung clear of the peaks.

Shinane lifted her hands in prayer before her face. In a whisper she recited the hymn A'Phadr had taught her for the moon's rising.

Welcome, O Thou silver Lordling,
Brother of our Lady Earth.
Welcome, O Thou Lord of calmness,
Thrice-fold welcome be to Thee.

At Thy rising may I call Thee,
At Thy rising lift my hands.
Little Lord of night and darkness,
Grant Thy blessing on us now.

May Thy healing rays bring wholeness
On our folk, upon our cattle,
On our hearth, upon our houses,
On our people, all Thy kindness.

On the womb of sheep and cattle,
On the field, upon the furrow,
On the anvil, on the plough-share,
On the fruit of womb and soil.

53

Welcome be Thou, silver Brother,
In the name of Chrisht our Lord,
In the name of Earth our Mother,
Welcome, welcome, welcome...

Slowly, she bowed low to the Presence before her. Straightening, she washed her hands in the elven light. She washed her head, her body, her feet. She breathed in the light. She breathed its life into every street and alley of her body. She raised her hands, and circled them up and out and down, and crossing them brought them to her heart. A pause, and she turned again to her pathless path. Before her, a fading glory; behind her, a waxing faery Lord.

8

Now that he could walk a little way, John spent as much time as he could on the bench in front of Fengoelan's home. The sun between the clouds warmed him, and out on the distant skerries the long Atlantic rollers flung white plumes into the clear air. Out of the way of Shelagh's fussing, he had space to think.

Where was he, he kept asking himself. The Western Isles? Orkney? Surely this land was too big for St Kilda. But why did no-one speak English? They didn't even seem to understand the word. Who were these people?

There were concerns mounting in his mind. How long was it since he had been pulled from the sea? Two weeks? Three? The first days were confused, and he could ask no-one. When they had lost radio contact and the boat had gone down, a rescue operation would have been mounted. He could hear the news item in his mind: *The search is continuing for the missing trawler. Hope is fading that any survivors will be found...*

But there was a survivor – at least one. The others? The skipper who had taken him on – where was he? Drowned, or even now being discharged from hospital in Stornoway or Inverness and taken home by his family? And what about his own family? His parents in their comfortable Dorset home; his brother in Ealing? They would only know he had gone away, would be wondering when he would get in touch. And now he could not contact them – there seemed to be no way.

Nights were the worst time. He would lie awake in the little alcove that was his sleeping-space, separated from the only room of the house by a curtain, staring up at the turves of the coved ceiling. The deep darkness within the house seemed to reach to infinity. It was as if there were no roof-beams above him, no covering to the house, only the darkness stretching up and up to nothing and to nobody, to no answer – only questions and darkness, on and on.

What was happening back home? Would he now be considered a missing person? The police could have started from his car, left outside his work beneath the railway arches in Vauxhall. Perhaps they had traced him to Euston, and the train to Glasgow. The landlady at the little bed-and-breakfast in Fort William – could she have recognised him? He had paid by cash, everywhere, deliberately so his trail would be harder to follow. But maybe by now questions had been asked along the quayside at Mallaig.

His family must be very concerned. And Helen – what was she thinking? Had he been traced as far as that ill-fated trawler? Those dreadful three words echoed in his mind: *missing, presumed dead.*

Helen – that last night. That final argument. The last straw.

You have plenty of time for your work – you never have any time for us!

It had been more than he could take.

Did she not understand the constant strain of keeping that little engineering business afloat? It was a niche market anyway, turning out replacement parts for vintage cars and lorries. The men on his short payroll were highly skilled. But – the competition, the way rivals would undercut you…

She had been right, of course. He had put everything into that business: his money, his energy, his time. In the end, there had been little left for his girlfriend. The walks together, the films, the poetry readings they had enjoyed – one by one they had disappeared. She had written some poems herself, and valued his opinion. What had she thought when he had no more time for them and brushed them aside with frustration?

Then the final blow. A large order, lots of expensive alloy castings bought in, a big wage-bill for his machinists – employees who became your friends: people you hated to pay off with nothing more than IOUs. That was when the customer had defaulted. He was exposed, over-extended, heavily in debt. Had the whole order been a trick? Hearing that his main rival offered to take on his men fed his suspicions.

Helen – what would she think of him, running away? Good riddance? Or – and in his heart he knew it was more likely – might she be blaming herself? If only he had not been so independent, thinking he could handle everything alone. It came to him now that he had made his decisions without consulting her. If only he could get back, he would do things differently. If she would give him another chance. He had to get a message to her. But how?

Language – that was critical. If they couldn't understand English, couldn't find anyone who understood it, then he would have to learn their speech. He winced at the thought. He had struggled through French and German at school, passed his exams but was never really confident. Would it be different, hearing a language from his first waking moments to his last thoughts at night, as he listened to Fengoelan and Shelagh settling themselves not three yards away? But with no teacher, no common tongue? It must have been done before – what about Robinson Crusoe and Man Friday? How had they managed? What had Alexander Selkirk done – the real Crusoe? Maybe he hadn't even met a Man Friday out there in the South Pacific. And here he was, three centuries later – not that it felt like it – and much nearer to home. He must try.

He slept. He was riding a bicycle. The road was straight, sloping downhill. A park and trees on one side. People – lots of people – waving to him. Calling him. Shouting at him. They were calling to him to stop, but no words came through. He could not stop. There were no brakes. There was a cliff. He was going to fall over the cliff. He couldn't stop. He was falling, falling…

He jolted awake. He was aware that he cried out as he woke.

He waited until Fengoelan was away, striding out into the morning sun. As Shelagh collected the bowls from breakfast he followed her though the curtain at the back. He found himself in a ramshackle lean-to, stooping under a low roof of sagging beams and thatch. Half-empty sacks were raised off the earth floor. From a nail in the timbers hung a blackened iron griddle. A row of earthenware jugs stood on a rickety shelf. Shelagh was not to be seen, but a leather curtain swayed a little before him. He pushed it to one side. He could see her now, squatting by a small stream, singing quietly to herself one of the endless chants she used to accompany her work. Beside her were the bowls and a round-bellied pot, and she was energetically scrubbing them clean.

She started as she heard him approach; half-rose, making to shoo him away, her smile belying her action. He ignored her gestures, sat down. She straightened, looked at him, arms akimbo. Then she too sat.

After a moment he picked up one of the cleaned bowls. 'Ish…' he began, and tailed off. He looked at her, a question on his face.

She put her head on one side, looking at him. Would she understand? He repeated his gesture. She seemed to decide. Said a word in the Island speech. He repeated it. Put the new word together with what he had already learned.

Her face shone. Apparently it had worked! She repeated his phrase, with a slight alteration, correcting him.

He pointed to the pot. He splashed some water, mimicked her actions as she scrubbed, and once more put on that quizzical expression. Could he get her to teach him to say that he was washing the pots?

She said a phrase containing the new word. She seemed to understand his intention.

Again, he struggled to mimic the sounds she made. They were very different from English vowels, and there were gutterals he had no idea how to get his tongue around. He was sure his attempt seemed ridiculous to her ears, mirrored in the hint of merriment in her face.

'Na, na,' she laughed, repeating her phrase, but pointing at herself, and then saying something similar, pointing at him. What did she mean? Did men and women say things differently...?

He tried again.

She laughed again, a soft and healing laugh. Again, gently, she put him right.

John found the next days mentally exhausting as he continued his attempt to learn their language. He felt like a small child in an adult body. He longed for the relief of speaking his mind.

Shelagh took his clothes for washing, and gave him Fengoelan's best plaid; it was the only change of clothes they had from the man's working kit. John protested, but she insisted. Fengoelan helped him to dress, folding the plaid into kilt-like pleats and draping it around him, secured at the waist with John's own belt. A tail of cloth hung down behind, which John found odd at first – but soon realised its practicality when, in the cooler air, he could draw it around his head and shoulders like a cloak.

Two days later he was beginning to appreciate the kilt-like garment in a way he had not expected. It invited him to feel – what was it? A sense, tiny as it might be, of belonging. Shelagh brought his own clothes back to him. They felt strange, even after so few days.

She went back to the ancient press against the wall where they kept their clothes, and reverently returned with a dark bundle. He recognised his jacket. She laid it carefully on the bench.

There was a call at the door. A man's voice, deep and powerful. He recognised the words: 'In the peace of Ghea.' The caller did not wait for his greeting to be answered as he pushed open the door. There was Shareg again.

Fengoelan had donned his plaid himself that morning, and was wearing it pinned at the shoulder like Shareg – though not so splendidly. Now he welcomed the newcomer and had him sit, while Shelagh brought a platter of small flat cakes and a big pitcher. She poured beer for the men. John had only drunk water in their house before, and the strong brown brew tasted good in the earthenware beaker.

Then Shareg and Fengoelan both rose, and the fisherman turned to John. He picked up the jacket and put it in his hands. It seemed that they were going somewhere. John took the coat and slipped his arms inside. He was suddenly aware of the two men watching him intently. They seemed to peer even more closely as he worked the zip.

Shelagh reappeared. For a moment she raised her head to look up at him; then she looked down at her hands. He saw they were clutched tightly at her waist. 'Go with God, Dhion,' she muttered, then turned away. For a moment he saw her shoulders shaking. He understood. These were words of parting. He was leaving this house. His heart-beat quickened.

Fengoelan opened the door for Shareg, and ushered John outside as he brought up the rear. Where were they going? He remembered Shareg's visit a few days before, when he had pointed to the pass, and that track climbing the mountainside. Was that where they were going? But why? Then a ray of hope: they had found someone who could speak with him – a remote police station or army post, a lone doctor or priest working his rounds across these wild hills? A fishing station down the coast? They would have a telephone or a radio. They could send a message.

Then another thought crowded in. How well did he know these people? He had trusted them up to now – he had no choice. But what if... What? Was he to be kidnapped? Held hostage? Worse? Surely not, after the kindness he had received? Nonetheless, a suspicion remained. How far could you trust people?

He looked around him. As they passed the houses of the hamlet a scattering of children gawped. A few men rose and watched him go by. Weren't their faces too open to justify his fears? He recognised some of the words they called to him: 'Ingleeshe. Go with God.'

He found the path a struggle as they climbed up from the houses. It was steep, and often his feet would slip and his hands clawed the loose stones. His breathing was heavy before the track began to level out, while his two companions continued to talk easily to each other. Shareg led the way, calling over his shoulder. Fengoelan's deep voice rumbled from behind.

He had to stop, and Fengoelan almost collided with him. With his hands on his knees he gulped air. He straightened, and looked back. Below them were the little houses; beyond, the sea. Low rocks and broken islets, and then the ocean stretching out, deep and green and wrinkled, away to an unbroken horizon. A small sailing boat bobbed along, close inshore. Not a ship in sight; not a plane in the sky. He turned, and walked on.

As they walked through the pass, Fengoelan pointed out the peaks.

'Beh' Mora,' he said, showing him the heather-covered summit on their left that rose to that rocky crag. Then, 'Beh' Talor Gan.' He named the dark shoulder above them to the right.

A brown stream descended from Talor Gan and lost itself in a morass of peat and cotton-grass. They crossed on a bridge of flat stone slabs, passed over the col, and the land opened out before them.

A lake gleamed in the valley, surrounded by rich green pastures. The glint of water beyond showed where a sizeable river drained the lake, its course snaking away from them. Like brown-grey curtains, high mountains rose in the middle distance and lost themselves in cloud. Far below them at the head of the lake, framed between the arms of the two summits, he saw a substantial cluster of jumbled dwellings. Many of the houses seemed bigger than the ones they had left behind.

Shareg turned to him and pointed.

'Caerpadraig,' he said.

9

'You could come with me today, Shinane. Your fingers are quick and you've a good eye. Come with me.'

Shinane remembered her mother's embroidery: the glowing colours, the intricate design. Her mind's eye saw the women gathered in the shareg's house, all working on something to beautify the rondal. A'Shar'g herself holding court, her quick little frame like a dancer's, active, busy; the priest's wife, always watching, always thinking, quietly smiling, and no-one knowing what she thought; the women of the town, stitching, chatting, gossiping like finches. The shapes and colours wooed her: *you too can work us, birth us, love us into being.*

But there was another voice, still very soft, that whispered, Do this if you will, but this is not you – not in your soul: your gift is something rarer, something still hidden.

She was wooed. The shapes and colours called her. 'Thank you, Mother. I'd like that.'

They were not so many that day. Rhona, the potter's wife, was washing with her two grown-up daughters, while Mairte from one of the croft steadings was helping her man with the sheering. A'Phadr was also absent.

They worked outside, some on the bench that ran along the wall of the shareg's house, the younger ones squatting beside them. Shinane brought a stool and sat by her mother. She spread out the small square of linen pulled from their press that morning. She reached for a length of dyed wool, and began to thread her needle.

Fineenh touched her shoulder.

'Not yet, girl. Begin by choosing your colours. No more than three, I think, for your first piece. Lay the threads out. Play with them. You've got to see your beginning in the eye of your heart first. Go within. Take your time.'

She looked up at her mother, questioning.

She tried. Tried not to hear the talk that surrounded her, passing to and fro. She gazed outwards without seeing. Past the houses of the town. Across the cloud-dappled flank of Beh' Mora. Up the glen where the path ran, up towards the Pass of the Sea.

A movement caught her eye. There were figures on the path. Three men, drawing nearer. There was the shareg, with his rolling gait; her uncle Fengoelan – hale and strong, although his hair was white. And between them, a person who out-topped them both, strangely dressed in close-fitting garments that showed his form: that short coat of a peculiar flat material she had seen the day he was rescued; his legs in dull blue cloth that was plainly not the woollen hose the men would wear on First-Days.

She nudged her mother's knee. 'Mam, it's the shareg, with… with…'

Fineenh followed her daughter's gaze. 'Aileen – It's your man coming, with –'

Everyone turned to see.

'Aye,' A'Shar'g replied. 'He's roofing the seaborne man today.'

Shinane remembered twice now, when the shareg had brought her father a raw apprentice and placed him under their roof, for shelter and board and training. Both the prentices, after three or four years, moved on and found work in bigger towns down Midland way. Her father sometimes grumbled, now that he had no-one to make the fire for him in the mornings.

They were all paying attention now. 'Who's he roof-ing him to, A'Shar'g?' asked Mairie.

'To the Father,' she replied.

'Is he going to learn priesting then?' asked Eileen, the wife of Tearlach, the leather-worker. She was always one with a quick quip.

64

A'Shar'g smiled a tight smile. 'He's taking him to the Father. He's tasked with teaching him to speak.'

'To speak? What do you mean?'

'You mean the Father's going to teach him how to speak at a meeting, like a shareg?'

'No, no. He can't speak at all – not even the Common Speech. That's what my husband said.' Aileen closed her mouth firmly, and bent her head to her work.

'What, is he simple then, that he can't talk?'

'Indeed, he is, poor lamb.' It was her mother's voice. 'Shelagh told me that his words are all meaningless sounds. It must have been the fever he took, after they brought him from the sea.'

The soft voice was whispering again, deep inside Shinane. *Not this, not that,* it said.

What, then? she asked.

Wait, it replied. *Wait and listen.*

They stood as the shareg approached. Every eye was upon the ceremony that was to be played out before them.

The men passed within a few paces of them. Shinane looked at the stranger. They all stared. His hair was dark, but shorter than most men's, cut in a fashion she'd never seen. His beard was now come, but still short. An energy surrounded him that she had not tasted before, all of a piece with the strange clothes he wore. A man of some importance, she remembered. A leader of men? Yet… his clothes did not look royal to her eye. He scarcely glanced at the women as they went by.

She saw them bring the seaborne man to the priest's door. They stopped at the threshold. Father Hugh was there, waiting. He placed a hand on the man's shoulder; Fengoelan did the same. The man held himself rigidly: what must he be thinking?

Now the shareg was speaking:

'Dhion Ingleeshe, Seaborne, you are under my cloak, and I place you in the house of the Father. May he speak for you, and may you serve him faithfully –'

She brought to mind the phrase the shareg had used with their last prentice: "Until you take your place as master of your craft." What would he say now? She listened, curious.

After a breath's space he continued, '...until you take your own place among us.'

His place among us? Was he, then, going to stay?

The four men disappeared inside the priest's house. The women picked up their sewing, picked up their talk. She let it float over her. She wondered. *Dhion. What a strange name.* She turned it over in her mind. She tried wrapping her tongue round its sounds, tasting them.

The week passed, like most weeks: cooking and washing and fetching; lighting the fire and cleaning out the ashes; waiting on her father and listening to her mother. Third-day came round again. Her father had gone to Leighan's house, where his fellow craftsmen met. Her mother took the carefully-wrapped bundle from the chest. 'Come and work with A'Shar'g again,' she said.

The shareg's house had windows. Today the shutters had been taken down. Sunlight and bird-song streamed in. 'Where's A'Phadr this time?' she whispered.

Before Fineenh could answer, there was a knock, and the door was pushed open. The priest's wife stood among them, tall in her blue-grey gown, looking around the circle with her blue-grey eyes. Everyone stopped, their needles suddenly still. She spoke.

'You know how Ingleeshe, the Seaborne, has come among us. How he came from the sea with nothing. Now he is in need of clothing.'

They looked at her. She went on. 'I know you all have your families to provide for. Now that the shareg has brought Ingleeshe under our roof, and into the care of us all, I want to ask you if you would make clothes for him as well.'

Again she looked round at them. Shinane noticed Eileen catch Fineenh's gaze and lift her eyebrows. She saw Shareen cast her eyes down, and guessed what she would be thinking: *I have enough to do caring for my own bairns without spinning more for a stranger.*

A'Shar'g rose. She took her distaff from where it leaned against the wall and held it like a mace. 'The sea has given us this man. I see it as our duty to provide for him, and I for one will do it gladly.' She looked round at them all.

There was a brief pause. 'And so will I,' said Eileen.

'Thank you.' The priest's wife looked around the circle. Heads were nodding.

Her mother spoke. 'A'Phadr, is it true that the poor man's a gowk? We heard that his illness… It's left him… He canna speak?'

'You may judge for yourselves,' Morag answered. 'I shall bring him in a few moments. It is true that he can't speak our tongue, but he's not stupid. He comes from another land where they speak differently, and he's having to learn. He's learning quickly. I shall bring him.'

As she left there was a flurry of talk. Shinane noticed a thrill of excitement run through her. Now for the third time her path and that of this strange sea-borne would cross. The first time he had been ill and all but dead to what surrounded him. The second, only last week, he had been at a distance and the shareg's business had claimed all his attention. Now, he would be here – in the same house.

The door opened again. There stood A'Phadr with the Seaborne. He looked awkward. A'Shar'g jumped up and ushered them in. Shinane dropped her gaze in deference, as custom demanded.

The man spoke. His strange accent added to the dream. 'Peace of God… with you all.'

'The peace of Ghea keep you,' they chorused.

She was free to look up as they spoke. She looked straight into his face. And found him looking at her. Their eyes met. She felt it, with a shock. He smiled.

First-Day came again, and they made their way to the women's benches in the centre of the rondal, while her father took his place with the craftsmen. Shinane looked over the heads of the women around her, over to where the little windows, set deep in the stone walls, were open to the pale sunlight.

What was it? A feeling – an excitement. As if here, in this crowded space, pierced by shafts of light reaching into the enfolding darkness, she sensed something beyond. A threshold. A line, drawn in the air with the finest of knives, that separated this world from another. Separated what was known and real from what, she sensed, was even more real, yet unknown.

She loved the tales they told around the fire, by the hearth, in the rondal. She could send her dreaming into the stories and live them for a while. As she received them, so she felt that they received her and made her a part of their mystery. They threaded their way into her everyday life, as if it too were a story.

Yet the Father spoke of still another world – further beyond, yet closer than breathing.

She sensed the slightest glimmer of that world. Not in the stories and lays. Not in the words of the Tollagh – not in words at all. She sensed it in the keen mountain air, in the grass beneath her feet when she walked unshod; in the sweep of eagles soaring, the bay of breakers pounding on the stony shingle shore; in the incense-scented flavour of the rondal, when all had gone and left it silent and round with mystery.

Words washed about her. She became aware of people moving. The women were standing to leave – the men were already leaving. Her mother touched her shoulder.

'Come along, Jewel. You've been far away, haven't you?'

'I'll come in a little while, Mother. May I just stay here a bit longer?'

'You stay, my love. Only don't be long.'

The place was empty. The last sounds of people leaving for their homes slowly faded. She breathed, deeply.

Before her, over the empty benches, in its place on its wooden lectern, was the Book. From it, Father Hugh read the stories of Brede and Aengas and the children of the old gods. And stories of the coming of the Chrisht who showed the Way of Compassion, the Way to the One: the Gospel. Quietly, she rose from her place. She would look into the Book. She threaded her way between the benches and came to the edge of the sanctuary. She slipped off her shoes, put on that morning for best, and felt the woven rush mats on the soles of her feet.

A tingle of excitement, as if she was entering forbidden land. Yet it was the right of all, to come into the presence of the Unknown. Shareg or outlaw, woman or child, all could come, if they came in the right way, with humbleness and reverence.

She came to the Book and stood. It lay open before her. There it was, endless rows of marks in black ink. The characters were not completely meaningless to her – with the other children the Father had tried to teach her some letters. But their sense was beyond her. She mouthed some of their sounds.

She lifted a hand to the soft vellum pages. Carefully, reverently, she turned them.

There. Before her was a picture such as she had never seen. The brilliant colours, green and red and blue and brown, were set off by flecks and lines of bright gold. The swirling shapes were of beasts and birds, of trees and flowers. And in the centre, a man, at a book, just as she was, a woman at a book. With a long white feather in his hand. Who was he? Below, more letters, but beyond her grasp. Surely they told the story of the picture. And she could not read it.

A movement at the door. A'Phadr. With the man from the sea. A confusion rose in her. She felt a blush rising. Hurriedly she moved away from the lectern. She walked demurely towards the door, picking up her shoes.

'A'Phadr. Ingleeshe.' She bent her head, not looking at them, and hurried away.

Had they noticed? Seen her lips, trying to shape the sounds? Seen her longing? And did she fear that they might have seen? Or hope that they had?

10

John began to realise that his move to Caerpadraig was permanent. Fengoelan's home had been simple to the point of being crude, but it had become familiar to him. Even its darkness and the continual smell of peat smoke had become homely. It was the place where he first opened his eyes upon this new world. Now it was suddenly taken away. He did not know where he was, who his new hosts were, what was expected of him.

As soon as the formal handing-over was finished and Shareg and Fengoelan walked away, the tall man, monkishly-dressed, turned and tried to talk with him.

He took John's hand. He spoke earnestly, quietly. A few words, then stopped. John was blank with bewilderment.

A woman was standing there. Tall, like the man, but where he was brown, she was dark. Her eyes looked straight at him, cool, but with the cold liveliness of a mountain stream. What was their relationship? Husband and wife? Brother and sister? Priest and housekeeper? What rules applied here, in this strange and somehow ancient world?

The man in brown pointed to himself. 'An Padr,' he said.

He pointed to the woman: 'A'Phadr.'

'Morag,' she added, darting her eyes and her smile back at him.

'Hugh,' said the man, pointing to himself.

Morag put her arm around Hugh. She spoke in the Island speech, but her meaning was clear: man and wife.

It worried the Seaborne where he had seen Hugh's face before. Then it came back to him. Those days after he had been brought from the sea; that long face with the startling brown eyes, hovering in and out of the delirium that held him.

Morag was dressed in a long woollen gown of soft grey. A string of beads round her neck ended in a carved wooden cross, surrounded by a circle in the familiar Celtic style. Where Hugh was the rich brown of oak, she was the blue-grey of steel. Dark hair, with a touch of grey, most of the time tied behind her neck. Steel and oak. John could not tell whether she was the chisel shaping the wood, or if he was the haft that guided the blade.

They were clearly putting themselves out to set him at ease. Even so, he longed to talk with someone at more than the level of a two-year-old. He longed for a shower, to soak in a hot bath. He longed to clean his teeth with Colgate and an electric toothbrush, instead of chewing a bit of bark and using a bone toothpick. He had learned, with pain to his pride, about sanitary arrangements. He longed – ridiculous notion – for sausage and mash in thick dark gravy. More than anything, he longed for answers to the questions that surged through him. Where was he? How had he got here? Had anyone told his people he was here? No-one could understand his questions. Still more, he would not have been able to understand their answers.

In his first days with Hugh and Morag, John noticed the difference in this house. He had liked Fengoelan and his red-faced, homely wife. But they seemed circumscribed in their world compared with these two. Fengoelan and Shelagh had their defined positions in life, and filled them comfortably and without chafing, not seeming to mind or to notice the limitations these brought to each. But Morag and Hugh moved easily in and out of each other's role, filling in as the other's need arose. He had never seen Fengoelan do any work around the house, yet Hugh could be found cooking almost as often as his wife, while Morag took her shawl and from time to time went out into the town and beyond John's ken.

As this couple spent hours with him, helping him with more and more words of their island tongue, John began to appreciate the wit that flew between them. He sensed that they were honing and polishing a way of being that existed only in their own home.

It became clear to John that Shareg had given them the task of teaching him their language. Soon he was having faltering conversations, heavily overladen with mime. And both, in their naturally enquiring way, would pick up from him a few words of English. When Hugh discovered that he had baptised a man in the name of his language, he thoroughly enjoyed the joke. Yet the name had already stuck. John became used to the frequent visitors calling him Dhion Ingleeshe.

As a fear waned, so also a hope slowly died. There was clearly nothing to dread from these people, but neither was there any sign of contact with the outside world. Even on that first day as they had approached the town he had noticed: no telephone wires; no satellite dish; not even a radio aerial.

And now that he could no longer look out on the sea, his anxiety rose. What if a ship should pass? Would the fishermen tell him? Would they feel the importance for him? Often in quiet moments he strained his ears for the sound of a plane. Between the clouds he searched the skies for a vapour trail.

He would lie awake, sometimes for hours, the house still and dark around him. *How long?* he would ask himself. When he slept he dreamed disturbing dreams. Surrounded by the cold sea, as far as the horizon; alone, sometimes in an open boat, sometimes in the water itself. Once he was looking over the gunwale into the depths. There was Helen, lying shrouded in seaweed. His parents. His work-mates. On an impulse, he had run away from them all. He had never intended to put them beyond reach.

He jerked awake, and found himself quietly weeping. Could there really be no contact, no possibility of a message? A message... That standby, beloved of all shipwrecked mariners in the stories: the message in a bottle! He remembered a magazine article. The 'St Kilda Mail' had been used regularly by the inhabitants of that remotest of the British Isles at time of need. More often than not, the message had eventually been received and transmitted in a more conventional way, from Orkney or from Lewis or even the Norwegian coast. He would try the next morning, to get the idea across to Hugh with his few words, that he wanted to write a message.

But the next day presented no opportunity. It was a day in which the rhythm of life changed, slowed down. People seemed more at ease. John saw what seemed to be the whole community making their way towards the big round building next door, with its conical thatched roof. Hugh went as well, while Morag stayed at home with him. He felt a little inhibited in her presence, in a way he never did with Hugh.

The thought did not go away. He must write. Send the message. Even if it took weeks, months, he would know that there was the possibility it might reach – somebody.

The next morning they had their daily language lesson. Hugh took him into the big round building. As they stepped out of daylight into the sepia tones of its interior, John felt at once that he had passed a threshold, entered a place imbued with its own particular atmosphere. A sense of stillness. Of richness. Hugh showed him a marvellous book on its wooden lectern. The pages were parchment, he guessed, and it was bound with leather, held between wooden boards and closed with iron clasps. Hugh found small pictures around the beautifully penned text that showed a man in the sea, then being carried, it seemed, on a pair of dolphins; then standing on the shore, a cross in one hand, a book in the other.

What kind of place would have a book like that out on a lectern, and not in a museum?

'Rortan,' Hugh explained, naming the man in the pictures. As his teacher carefully turned the pages, John pointed to the letters. 'I want... make...' He had not yet heard a word for writing. '...like this.' He mimed with his right hand.

Hugh seemed not to understand at first. John repeated his mime show.

Hugh looked at him questioningly. 'Can you...?' He mimicked John's motions, supplying the missing word.

John nodded eagerly.

'You can write?' asked Hugh. He was looking at John intently.

'Write,' echoed John. 'Yes, I want... write.'

Hugh took his pupil back into the daylight. He ducked into their house.

'Mora,' he called, and rejoined John outside. There was fine sand at the edge of the path, ground by the passage of many feet, many hoofs. Hugh squatted and wiped it smooth with the hem of his cassock.

Morag came, and stood looking on while Hugh bent and, with his finger, slowly, carefully, wrote a word in the sand.

John saw the letters, not entirely unlike his own more prosaic script, but he could not translate them into anything Hugh had taught him. Hugh swept the sand clean again, made a gesture of invitation.

John bent, stretched out a finger, wrote in English, 'I want to write a message.' He prodded the sand vigorously to make the full stop. It was such a relief to see words of English, even if he himself had just written them.

Hugh stood up. They both stood. Hugh looked away for a moment; turned back. 'I write,' he said. He placed his hands together, opening them like the leaves of a book; said a new word that John took to mean 'read.' He went on, 'Morag writes and reads. The shareg,' he pointed at Micheil's house a few paces away, 'can read a little...' He made a tiny gap between his thumb and forefinger. 'No-one else –' he swept his down-turned palms across each other and away, '– in the whole town. How...' He tailed off, unable to find words simple enough. He held his temples between the tips of his long fingers.

'Come.' Hugh ushered him back indoors. As Morag turned to follow them, John caught her exchanging glances with her husband. His eye followed hers. He had not seen Hugh's eyebrows so raised.

Back inside, it was John who began again. 'I want... write.'

'I want to write,' Hugh helped him. 'What do you want to write?'

'I want to write... Tell people... Tell my people... I... here. Writing... in –' He looked around wildly. He had not seen a bottle since arriving on this island. That could be a problem. He saw a small fire-pot beside the hearth and mimed putting a message inside, closing it and throwing it into the water.

Hugh turned to Morag, her tall frame leaning over him as he sat. John felt that they understood, but something barred their way.

Hugh turned back, looked deeply into his eyes. He chose his words carefully. 'Dhion, we want to help you, Morag and I. We will think of a way to help you.'

John's hope collapsed. It seemed such a simple thing he was asking. Only later, when he was more familiar with the language, could Hugh explain. He had brought those books from far-away Sharilland, where he had studied at the famous School. There they could make parchment and vellum, but Hugh knew of no-one on the Island with the skill, and such products were rare and costly. Nor was this the greatest obstacle. The insuperable difficulty was to find a watertight bottle. The only bottle in Caerpadraig was the tiny glass one in which Hugh kept the holy oil for anointing the sick and the dying. This he would not sacrifice for one man, even if it would serve. They were unable to supply what John asked.

On that day, none of this could be told. Now all Hugh could say was that if there was a way, they would find it. John was left to his frustration. A piece of paper, a pen, a bottle… Was it so impossible? Like a rising tide of cold black water round his heart, he began to realise that it was.

11

Two days later Morag spoke to him. She told him that they were going visiting. He got the gist of what she said. They didn't go far. Out of their door they turned left, and walked a few yards. It was the last house in the town. Beyond, the path wound upwards to where the pass separated them from the cluster of dwellings by the sea, where Fengoelan and Shelagh lived.

Morag said to him, 'This is the shareg's house.' But he was surprised as he entered behind her. Inside was a group of a dozen or so women. They looked at him with unhidden interest before lowering their eyes for a moment, and then directing their gaze towards Morag. She was explaining something to them. He looked around. All wore long shifts with a shorter tunic over; the fabric was mostly undyed, a strangely brown and cream-coloured world. Morag's blue-grey gown stood out. There were women of various ages: some round and rosy, one or two with the puckered features of old age, a couple of younger ones. It seemed he was expected to greet them. He summoned himself, and spoke. They gave him their attention. Chorused a reply. For a moment he met the clear and curious eyes of a young woman, before she dropped her gaze back down towards the floor.

Morag took him from there into the heart of the town. John had not yet ventured this far, and he looked around him curiously at the tangled knot of buildings. He took in the various sounds and smells that met him as they walked: children playing, ordure and cooking; a variety of animals – he saw a few dogs, some hens, a couple of pigs, all wandering freely. A half-dozen grey and white geese cackled at him. Again the thought came to him that this was medieval. He heard a continuous clatter coming from a shed beside a house that was little more than a ramshackle hut. They went inside. A round-faced man, with smooth, pink skin and only a wispy fringe of beard, sat on a wide bench as he worked the treadles of an ancient loom. He flung the shuttle between the warp-threads, hammering each strand of weft home with the beam.

The man paused as Morag called a greeting, then turned to stare with undisguised curiosity towards John. The great wooden loom filled much of the work-shop, and above it, looped over poles from the rafters, were a couple of bolts of pale buff-coloured linen and more of woollen cloth, some of it dyed and woven into simple checks. On pegs protruding at angles from the wall were spools of yarn.

Morag talked with the weaver. Again the man looked at John, seeming to measure with his eyes, to ponder. He answered her in a high, piping voice. Then with a long pole he fished for a folded length of linen and showed it to Morag. As he reached it down there was a woman's voice at the door.

'In the name of Ghea, and in peace.' John recognised the greeting, if little else.

'Welcome, in God's name,' the weaver called out as he squeezed past his visitors to open the door.

John recognised the newcomer from the gathering in the shareg's house. She spoke to Morag, then turned her eyes to him. John did not know how to respond. He stared blankly back. Suddenly he saw in her eyes pity: the misplaced pity for a simpleton. A wave of anger rose in him. What had he been through? What was he trying now to accomplish? And his reward was to be dismissed in pity? He was aware of his fingers tightening, clenching. Slowly he mastered himself. He succeeded, in time to notice the weaver coming towards him, a ball of undyed wool in his hands.

Like a tailor, he stretched his wool across John's shoulders. He knotted it to length, and broke it off in his strong, bent hands. He did the same from John's neck to below his waist, and around his chest. He handed the knotted lengths to the woman.

John looked questioningly at Morag. She nodded reassurance. She understood.

The week passed, and another, each marked off by that day like a Sunday, with people gathering in the big round building. Morag took him in with them, and he found it both like and unlike church.

Another morning dawned sunny and warm. A gentle breeze blew puffy fair-weather clouds along the coast from the south. Morag sat him down at their solid table while Hugh brought the steaming pot of porridge. And once more he had to repeat: You bring the porridge. I eat the porridge. The porridge is hot. The weather is hot.

As they were finishing, there was a voice at the door. It was the woman from the weaver's shop. She stepped inside, her small, slim body moving delicately like a dancer's. She held a bundle of cloth.

Morag called John over to where she and the other woman stood, just inside the door. 'Dhion,' she said, 'This is A'Shar'g.'

John greeted her as he had been taught, remembering to use the right inflection for greeting a woman. Then he stood back in surprise. A'Shar'g held out a linen tunic for him to see. She offered it to him with a certain ceremony and stood back, awaiting his response.

Morag gently stroked the linen. 'Not everyone wears this, Dhion,' she said slowly.

He had seen what most men wore – and many women. Rough woollen cloth. He imagined how that would feel next to his skin. Perhaps they had considered his own clothes, and used their best for him. What was he in their eyes? An idiot, or a prince?

A'Shar'g turned to him. She spoke. He heard the words. 'Do you like this?'

He glanced at Morag. She gave him no help, but motioned with her hand for him to reply. He felt himself colouring.

'Yes... I like... it.'

'This is for you,' A'Shar'g explained.

'For me?' John wanted to be quite certain.

Morag nodded. 'Yes, for you. And these also.' She picked out a pair of trews of undyed wool, from the bundle, then turned again to their visitor and said something, too quick for him to follow.

Morag again whispered to John, prompting him.

'Thank you,' he said. The woman smiled generously.

The weather grew warm, and the coat that had drawn so much comment lay tucked away. However, it had to be fetched out to enable, first Doughael the weaver, then Shean the blacksmith, to come and examine the marvellous cloth and the astonishing zip-fastener. Doughael also wanted to inspect his cotton clothes. He fingered them and gazed at the stitch-work and shook his head, seeming not to know what to say. Tearlach the leather-worker came too, and John had to intervene to stop him taking his trainers apart to see how they had been made.

He saw how most people kept shoes for best. Only craftsmen who, like the smith, could injure their feet at work, would wear them habitually; or those who, like the priest, had a certain standing in the town. They gave him a pair of soft leather shoes with quaint pointed toes. He wore them as little as he could. At first his own feet were soft and tender on stony ground. But, *if they can manage, so can I,* he thought.

After this, John began to put his jeans and cotton shirt aside. In his new clothes, he felt he began to blend in a little – at least until he opened his mouth to speak.

The first moon after midsummer began to show, a thin fingernail following the setting sun into the blue-green west. The weather turned warm and clear. A gentle breeze from the south-west was sufficient to keep the midges away from open land, and John spent much of his time outside. He summoned together his few words and asked Hugh if he could walk up on the peaks surrounding them.

'Yes,' replied the priest, 'but take care. Don't go yet to Talor Gan. Beh' Mora is good for walking.'

After the evening meal he set out, up the track to the Pass of the Sea into the westering sun. He turned north off the main path, into the heather and narrow deer-tracks of the mountain. Walking near to the steep western face, he could see below him the little round houses of Fisherhame, huddling under the scarp.

Breathless with the climb, he stopped and leaned against a rock that perched on the hillside, its fissured surface orange and grey and black with lichen. He remembered other climbs – Helvellyn with his parents long ago; Moel Tryfan with Helen, only last year, when afterwards they had come down to the meadow outside the climbing hut and she had made a short poem of their climb, then and there.

He looked up into the eau-de-nil sky. The sun hung above the north-westerly horizon. It lit a few small clouds with a golden glister. Birds soared on the rising air – fulmars and skuas. And what else? Nothing else: the sky was not striped with golden-primrose vapour-trails, each headed by the tiny gleaming cross of an aeroplane surging along the great-circle routes over the Atlantic.

Where were they? John looked around. Apart from the peak rearing in the north, almost the whole sky was visible to him, arching overhead, unsullied.

He thought. He had too readily accepted the simple way these people lived. They had nothing more complex than a cart, a small sailing boat, an iron-bound wooden tub. What people on the North Atlantic coast – and surely this was the Atlantic – lived as unaffected as this by Western technology?

And no paper. On an impulse, he felt in the pockets of the jeans that he still preferred to wear, with his trainers, for hill-walking. What was this? He drew it out. A bank-note. Slowly he unfolded it, as memories flooded in of another world: a world of cars and planes, of cities and roads and rush-hours – and money. He unfolded the thin paper, creased and pressed by the movement of his body, chafed and soaked and dried by more than one wash. As he opened it out, it fell apart. The wind picked up the fragments. He watched them blow away. He turned to the glowing sunset, drew a great breath and yelled. 'Where am I? For God's sake, somebody tell me where I am!' Silently the sun sank into the sea.

He ran – back down the slope, back towards the town, towards the people among whom he perforce must live. He ran stumbling over the heather, half-blind, half-mad.

After that he ran frequently. He kept his trainers as his running shoes. It took Hugh and Morag some time to understand what he wanted; the concept of exercise for its own sake must be new to them. They needed all their energy, just for living. If you went anywhere, you walked. Only if it was urgent would you run. If you were running, it was obvious you were running to somewhere, and for something. The muscles of his legs were wasted by illness and cramped by the limits

83

of his social world, and he had nowhere to run to, and nothing to do.

So it was that John, running to stretch and mend his body, running to expand his horizon, running for the sheer need to push back the dark clouds that loomed on his mental skyline, sometimes noticed the puzzled expressions of the townsfolk as he passed. They called out in greeting, but their faces said, 'Well, he *is* a strange one.'

12

Morag was showing John how to make bread. She said to him, 'If you are to understand our language, then you must understand our life. And if you are to understand our life, it is best that you understand it from both sides: from the women's side as well as from the men's.' So she showed him where the lump of yeast was kept under a clay pot to keep it cool, fed every week with a little flour and honey. She showed him how to work it into the barley-flour and to knead it with his fists, pummelling the dough until it was well worked through. She taught him the kneading-croon, and had him repeat it in time with the kneading. And then the magic of its rising: who knew how or why?

As they washed the sticky dough from their fingers, she looked at him. 'Dhion, you are not happy.'

He paused.

'Tell me,' she prompted.

'Mora, I cannot speak. I have many thoughts in my heart, but I cannot say them.'

'But you are learning to speak well. You are learning quickly, Dhion.'

He lapsed into English in his frustration.

'I'm sorry,' he said, reverting to the Island speech. 'I cannot say enough. It troubles me all the time that I cannot tell my father, my mother, my brother, my friend, that I am here.' He looked at her.

She put her arms round him and held him close. It was not done, but she paid no heed to that – here, by her own hearth.

She released him. 'I have an idea. You remember when you told Hugh that you could write?' She paused; repeated phrases slowly. The sequence of verbs was difficult for him. 'Hugh and I have talked about it, and why you wanted to write. You know how costly writing material is?'

She explained how the few sheets of blank parchment they had, on which Hugh would write of important events that occurred among them, had come from the School on far-away Sharilland. Of course Hugh would give a fragment for Dhion to write a message, if only they could think of a way of sending it.

'You talk of sending it in a pot. But our pots would break on the rocks, and then the parchment will be lost. We cannot think of any way to send it. Can you?'

She looked at him. He turned from her, pushed open the door, gazed out moodily over the rows of beans growing behind the house. A light rain was falling. She came to him where he stood. He turned his head as her steps paused.

'Dhion, I have another idea. I have been thinking about this for a while. Your coat – the coat you were wearing. No-one here has seen anything like it – the cloth it's made of, and the shape, and those fastenings – what do you call them?'

'A zip,' said John. His voice was flat.

'*Ship*,' Morag repeated. 'Do you say that many people wear them, where you come from, these *shipion*? Surely they must be very valuable – they must take a long time to make?' John shrugged. She talked slowly, carefully. 'We can send your coat around the Island. Don't worry – it will be quite safe. Someone may see it and say, "I have heard of other people who wear such coats." Perhaps they will have met men who speak your language. And if not, at the very least your coat will come back to you.'

'Do you think it will do any good?'

'It may. Don't expect too much – do not put much hope on it – but something may come of it.'

He looked away. His eyes, his face looked as grey as the steady drizzle outside.

'It will be something,' she insisted. 'Isn't that better than doing nothing?'

They dried their hands, leaving the dough covered in its bowl beside the fire, and went to find Hugh, who was reading at the lectern in the rondal. He looked up as they entered, and closed the book.

He listened to what Morag had to say. 'It is good,' he said. Then, 'Dhion, don't hold out too much hope that we will be successful. But I think we should do it. You and I, we will go to Micheil.'

The shareg pursed his lips. After Hugh's clear and careful speech, John found Micheil harder to understand. 'I will talk with Dael.' As head of Fisherhame, Hugh explained, Dael was the one to ask a fisherman to carry the coat and its story down the coast to the next village.

Three days later, Hugh found the Seaborne. 'Micheil has spoken with Dael Fisherhame. Targud is happy to go for you. I think you must have met him with Fengoelan and Shelagh, for he is their son. And he was one of those who found you in the sea. He will be glad to do something for you. But we must take a present for his family when we go. He already knows most of the story we want him to pass along. We will teach him the last part.'

It was still a strange idea to John, to learn a story. Slowly he was beginning to see that this was how they stored memory and information. Where few people could write, then a story was a sure way of passing on news. 'Do you not have story-tellers,' asked Hugh, 'where you come from?'

After a week, Micheil knocked at the priest's house.

'Are you ready?' Morag called from the door.

John came. He had on a new tunic, recently made for him. Though still rather weak from his illness, he was looking forward to this journey, to seeing Fengoelan and Shelagh again. He had the black donkey-jacket, bundled and tied, and carried some of Morag's bread as a gift, together with a small pot of honey.

Micheil's speech, as they talked in broken phrases on the way, was difficult to follow, but when they arrived in the hamlet by the shore he could barely make out what the fishermen said at all. Yet Targud was clearly glad to see him, and seemed pleased with the few words he could now say.

Standing in the low dark doorway, Targud's wife received the bread and honey with both hands and a backward step like a half-curtsey. She invited them in, where Targud was already waiting, dandling a baby on his lap. The giving of the coat must have brought back to the fisherman memories of almost four months before. It was a strangely solemn moment.

At last they went with Targud down to the beach, with his wife and their first-born. Fengoelan and Shelagh joined the group, and a couple of young boys who were playing on the shore vied with each other to push the boat down into the waves, their tunics tucked up as they stood in the water, holding the stern until Targud gave the word.

They shoved the little boat away. John watched as the sail caught the wind and she stood out from the shore. Then off she went, sloping down towards the south, carrying the strange bundle in which were folded his hopes.

With a fair wind, Targud would be home again the next day. The coat would take much longer. They turned and retraced their steps. Shelagh gave them ale, and bannocks made with fish-oil.

It had only been a few weeks since John had lived in that small, low house, so familiar, yet already so far away in his memory, and the warmth of their greeting touched his heart as nothing else had done since his arrival in this place that he had learned to call the Island.

Time passed, and there was no word about the coat. 'Is there nothing I can do?' John asked Hugh. He did not know the word for 'bored' – indeed, whether there was such a word in their language.

'There will be plenty to do soon. The barley harvest must be brought in – and then the oats. Everybody,' said Hugh, 'lends a hand.'

They found him an old scythe, and he took it down to the smithy to be fettled. He was fascinated to meet the smith, and to watch him skilfully peen the blade for him. He came away also with a stone for whetting it. But the first day of the harvest it was plain he did not know his work.

Hugh, his cassock kilted to his knees, stood beside him in the line. He tried to imitate the movements Hugh made, to keep up with the men, their bodies swaying in time to their chant. But as the morning wore on he was overtaken again and again. Even the craftsmen, not so used to working on the land, all passed him; and each time he moved further down the line of reapers strung out across the field. Old Negus with the arthritic hands was the last one to displace him, until he lagged on the far right. By the time he finished his row, the first of the men were getting up from their rest to start on the second half. He looked back over their neat windrows, and his own disordered heaps.

They tried him with Micheil's fine black cattle in the rich lough-side pastures, until a kick lamed him for a full seven days.

Hugh asked him, 'What do you enjoy doing, Dhion?'

'I like making things,' he replied.

'What kind of things?'

How do you describe the fine engineering of motor vehicle parts to someone who has never heard of an engine; when the local smithy has hammers and tongs and an anvil, and not much more? Blacksmithing had not been a large part of John's experience; and as for a lathe, or milling or drilling a piece as he was skilled at – all this, here, was beyond imagination.

'I have made things in iron...' Those awful tenses again – John was sure he had used the wrong construction. 'But not like Shean the smith makes...' He tailed off in despair.

Hugh looked at him strangely. John reddened.

John was discovering how painful it is to be an enigma. He was slowly finding his strength again – strength of limb and of wind. He had run, not walked, up to his favourite rock on the side of Beh' Mora, the place he considered now as his thinking rock. The soreness he felt was not that of a cramp in his legs, nor a stitch in his side. There was a pain in his pride: in the confidence that says, 'I am, and I can.'

Morag had said, only the other day, how she and Hugh had met people from beyond the Island. Hugh had studied on the mainland, where people from many places passed through. 'But you,' she said, 'we can't quite place you yet.' Her voice had tailed off. Hugh finished for her. 'We find we can't fit you into our seeing of the world.'

His galling experience at harvest had hurt him deeply. He saw clearly that he could not do what was expected of him. And what he could do, there was no need for.

Those words of the trawler skipper – *You're no bloody use on deck* – echoing through his mind. How long ago? Another hammer-blow, shaking the very stuff of his self-esteem.

And now? What now? The rediscovered memory only heightened his despair. His eye scanned the sky, as it had done countless times before. It was empty of any aircraft. It looked more and more as if the journey of his jacket around the Island was his only hope: his last hope of one day facing the woes he had run from, and starting again. With Helen beside him? If she could forgive him; if he could return.

But still that insistent Now pressed itself on his consciousness. What was he to do now? He must learn new skills and begin to take his place in this new world, if only provisionally. He must make new friends. Yet language was still the barrier between himself and all around him. Without it he was alone, locked out of this old, new, world.

13

Leighan's house was the other side of the rondal from that of Hugh and Morag. And in Leighan's house served Donal the paelht. He was a huge man, yellow-haired, blond-bearded, the muscles on his shoulders and arms swelling under his shirt as he moved timber from the stack behind the house to the saw pit. His grandfather had been one of the Northmen shipwrecked off the rocks by the out-skerries, said Hugh, and might have been put to the sword for all his plundering and raiding of the people. But the shareg of those times decided to make use of him instead, and in due course he moved on and settled out Midland way.

It was clear Leighan worked Donal hard, sawing baulks of wood into planks. John would see him with Olan, Leighan's eldest and his apprentice. The sound of the saw was a frequent background to John's language lessons.

Once John heard a great commotion coming from the carpenter's house. Something had gone amiss and Leighan was shouting at Donal about the wood now being quite useless for anything better than a kennel. The wiry little man was craning his neck back to stare the giant in the face, and Donal kept an expression of abject remorse. But as Leighan turned back to his workshop still muttering, Donal looked across to where John was sitting outside. His grin suddenly cracked across his face, and he winked.

One autumn evening, as the sunset faded and a full moon began to rise, John was returning from the hills. Down from the shoulder of Beh' Mora he ran, towards the path that dropped down from the pass. Panting, he knelt by the dim shadow that was a pool. The burn cascaded and swirled. He splashed himself with the cold water, and drank a little in his cupped hands. Then at an easy pace he moved on, down the path and towards the houses. He was late coming back, and already yellow lights were appearing in the town before him, quickly to disappear again as blinds of skin or wooden shutters were pulled across. In the darkening air the smoke from the hearth-fires that lazed through the thatch could scarcely be seen.

As he reached the door of the priest's house he paused. There were noises coming from somewhere behind the carpenter's yard. Beyond the stone buildings near the rondal were smaller houses of wattle, and it was from one of these that the sounds of commotion came. One word he recognised, and it sent him running towards the disturbance.

'Fire!'

The shouts came from around the house of the widow Shareen. Morag had taken him there when she visited the family, and he knew them all by name. Now, as John passed close by Leighan's workshop, he saw Donal resting outside after the labour of the day.

He called out to him, 'Donal. Come.'

The huge man stirred. Recognising John, he jumped up. Then he gave a glance over his shoulder as if caught in sudden conflict.

'Ingleeshe, I canna.'

John stared. He heard the refusal in his voice.

'There's fire! You must help.'

'I canna.' The giant spread his open hands in a gesture of helplessness.

Invective was beyond John in the language of the Islanders. He spat out an insult in English, and ran on. Out of the corner of his eye he saw Leighan, watching.

A group of men had gathered in front of the widow's house, and Shareen herself stood hunched over at the door, her red hair wild in the angry night. A tearful little girl tugged at her knees. Shareen kept trying to re-enter but, red-eyed and retching, she fell back.

'Colin,' she called, her voice strained and hoarse. 'Colin – come out!'

'There's still her wee bairn within,' shouted one of the men who was standing there, looking at John.

John remembered his works fire training. *Don't re-enter a burning building,* he'd been taught. But that was in a land where the fire brigade could be summoned in minutes. And they had taught him how to get *out* of a smoke-filled building.

'Give me – ' He pointed urgently at the man's cloak.

The other looked at him questioningly, but he handed the garment over.

Wrapping the borrowed cloak tightly across mouth and nose, then dropping to the ground, John wriggled his way like a snake under the acrid reek. Inside it was totally dark. There were no flames to see, but his face could feel the heat. He was gagging, coughing, with the effort of drawing breath.

He kept his right hand on the roughness of the wall, until he heard before him the whimpering of a child. 'Colin,' he croaked. 'It's me – Ingleeshe.'

At the back of the house the smoke was lighter. But the child drew back in fear. John took the thin arms in his hand and, kneeling, pulled the terrified boy onto his back.

'No!' Colin cried. In his panic he resisted. But John's grip was fast. Stooping low, the little boy almost lying along his back, he ran for the door.

They burst from the smoke-filled hovel and collapsed on the ground. The child rolled off John's back. They were both retching and choking, gasping for breath. Flames suddenly spewed from the house. John broke into a cold sweat.

'I don't understand. Why wouldn't he come?'

The next morning John was still angry. Donal's refusal to come with him had galled him badly. The big man could have done anything. He could have torn a hole in the wall if necessary to rescue the child. John still felt weak and sick. He had eaten nothing. Morag had insisted that he drink.

Hugh sat him down. 'Dhion, do you know what a paelht is?'

'He is a man – who works for others,' he replied.

'Do you know why he works for other men, Dhion?'

John did not know. It had seemed strange to him that such an open and peaceable society had these apparent slaves among them.

'The paelchte are men who have done wrong. They must work for others until they have paid off their wrong.'

Hugh paused.

'Donal is a paelht, and that is why last night he could not come with you. To run away will make his time of servitude longer. There is a right way to allow a paelht to leave his master for a time. Only the man's master may do it, and it must be witnessed by a man of standing. You were not to know this.'

'But this was – ' John knew of no Island word for emergency. He broke off. Hugh continued.

'Now we have a problem. Leighan has been here to say that you insulted Donal. To insult a paelht who cannot strike a blow for himself is to insult his master. Leighan is angry.'

John sighed in frustration. Hugh gazed at him steadily. Eventually, 'I'm sorry,' John said.

'Dhion, you must go and say so to the carpenter, and then to his paelht. Come.' Hugh left behind his solemn tone. 'We will practice what you will say.'

There was a call at the door. Morag rose. She returned leading Shareen, a child trailing from each hand, her hair still unkempt, her face red and blotchy. Letting go of the children, the woman ran towards John and fell to her knees. She took his hands in hers and kissed them.

Words tumbled from her, quite beyond John to follow. But he understood her gratitude. Colin and his sister looked on, wide-eyed.

Shareen rose to her feet. Diffidently she glanced at Hugh. She took a step backward. Her hands clutched one another before her. Her reddened face turned redder. Morag took her shoulders and steered her towards the hearth. She sat beside her, and motioned to John to take the bench opposite. Hugh went to draw some small beer, and milk for the children.

They had taught John how to receive thanks with a simple formula, and this he spoke. It seemed hardly enough for such a profusion of gratitude.

He added, in English, 'I was really very glad to help.' It sounded empty to him: trite.

Shareen swallowed, and wiped her nose on a grubby sleeve. Morag put her arms around her as she wept.

'Well done,' said Hugh, when, after a little, they left. 'And now we can practice what you will say to Leighan.'

It was a simple ceremony, yet eloquent in what it expressed. Hugh went with John to Leighan's door. The carpenter received them coolly, and bade them enter. John repeated the words they had practiced, while Leighan listened, his chin in his hand. Then the carpenter led them through to his workshop where Donal had his quarters, between the workbench and the timber stack, and John said again the words of the apology. Donal sat, impassive. It was Leighan who spoke for them both.

'In the name of God, and in peace.'

Hugh nudged John. 'In the name of Ghea, and in peace.'

'I accept your words as a closing of the enmity between us,' said Leighan. 'May there be peace between your house and mine.'

Hugh prompted John with the practiced response: 'May there be peace between your house and mine.'

But it was the next day, in a break between language lessons, that John wandered the few yards to Leighan's saw-pit, where Donal was resting.

The giant rose as he saw him coming. He looked the Seaborne up and down. Then he broke into a grin. John could not follow his words, but the huge hand on the shoulder and the wink that accompanied it was a universal language. For the first time John felt he had not just a helper, but an ally here on this island.

After that, he would call to sit with Donal when he could. They had much in common. The paelht was limited by the terms of his sentence; John by his lack of understanding of the Island ways. He was tied to the priest's house; Donal to the carpenter's. And both of them were far from home and from those they loved. Donal's home and family were away east, on the northern coast of Midland, the narrow waist that joined the fertile plains of Caerster to the rocky fastnesses of Westerland and the Northland. And John's home and people? He could find not even the slightest echoes.

As the evenings shortened and life began to turn inward once more, John would sometimes cross the lank grass that grew behind the rondal to find the big man. They would talk in a kind of patois of broken speech mixed with occasional English words. And when there was nothing to say any more, sometimes Donal would produce a little bag of small, angular bones for a game of skill. Despite his massive hands, he showed far more dexterity than John in throwing and catching. So the two would relax together from time to time, holding on to the dying year, outside the carpenter's shop when work was done.

14

They heard the greeting at the doorway. Hugh rose to open, and John saw one of the young fishermen standing there.

'Dermot!' said Hugh. 'Whenever you come here there is something going on. What is it this time?'

He brought the lad in and went to fetch a beaker of ale and a bannock. Dermot stared at John. He smiled back, feeling awkward.

'The peace of God,' John tried.

For a moment, Dermot went on staring. He seemed taken aback.

'Dhion is learning our language,' explained Hugh, offering the visitor a foaming jug and a piece of cake.

'Uh… Is he?' said Dermot. 'Thanks,' he added, taking the proffered plate. He ate and drank hungrily.

'So, what brings you here today?' Hugh repeated, when their visitor had swallowed a few mouthfuls.

Dermot wiped his mouth on his sleeve.

'Coat's come back,' he announced. 'Soon as I saw the sail, I knew the boat wasn't from hereabouts. It's come back. With a storyteller. She's over by Fisherhame, and Dael asked me to go for the shareg. But he's busy with calving, and asks you to come.'

Autumn was well advanced. The rowans were red and there was a nip in the air. John borrowed Morag's cloak, and he and Hugh went back with Dermot over the pass together. Even as they slid and clattered down the last of the screes above Fisherhame, John could see a knot of folk outside Dael's house. People turned as they heard them coming. An old woman was perched on the bench outside the door, addressing a bowl of fish soup with relish. She set it down, wiped her mouth on her sleeve, and scrambled to her feet at the sight of the priest, her face overspread by a crooked grin. Beside her was a man John did not recognise, dressed like a fisherman, a pewter mug in his hand.

Hugh went to speak with the man. John watched the stranger gesture towards the woman, then at something lying beside her on the bench. But John had already seen it: his black donkey-jacket.

He listened carefully as Hugh explained what the man was saying. The woman was his town's storyteller. He remembered Hugh telling him how every community had its storyteller: someone who could recite the legends and myths of the Island and of their township. Morag said that where she came from, there was an old blind man who could recite their archives – who had married whom, who had been birthed and sired by whom – back five or more generations

'But – what's the news?' John asked.

'We must bring this lady back with us when we return,' said Hugh, nodding sideways towards the old woman, 'and she will tell us all the tale of the coat, as it has grown in its passage round the Island. That is how we will hear the news.'

'Father,' broke in the boatman, 'there is more.' He stooped and grasped a large sealskin bag on the ground beside him, untied the string, and withdrew a bundle bound up in a finely woven cloak.

'These,' he explained, 'are gifts from every town that the coat has visited.'

'Tonight,' said Hugh, 'we will gather in the rondal. You, Kenneth,' he said, turning to the boatman, 'will make a presentation of these gifts, and we will hear the story. You will be our guests.'

The sun sank lower over the long hard skyline and a chill fog arose from the sea. Father Hugh and John climbed back to the pass with the visitors from the Northland. The old woman – A'Mhagus, she told the

Father – surprised John with her agility and stamina. She held her skirts in her hands and scurried up the steep slope. From time to time he caught her stealing a glance towards him. He felt himself the object of a kind of professional curiosity, and supposed she must be considering whether he matched her expectations. He found himself hoping he did not disappoint, then rounded on himself for the thought. It did not matter what she thought of him. What mattered was whether she had news that would help him get home. Why could Hugh not ask this directly? He did not understand it. But then, what was unusual about that?

Hugh gave John the task of helping him to lay the fire in the rondal ready for the storytelling; Morag spent the afternoon in the shareg's house, helping A'Shar'g to prepare a meal for the travellers. It was both households together that gathered there in the early evening to eat with the visitors, nine in all with the shareg's nearly grown sons.

Around the fire, in the lamplight, the talking turned, from priest to shareg, shareg to fisherman, while A'Mhagus sat, her bright eyes flickering from one to the other. Words waned, paused, failed. In the fire a log slipped, sending sparks shooting.

John struggled to contain his impatience.

At last it was time to gather in the rondal. The building was full, like a First-Day. A visit from a story-teller from another town was an occasion no-one wanted to miss. When all were gathered, the shareg rose.

'Tonight we have a tale to hear,' he announced. 'The tale of the sending round of the Seaborne's coat. But before we hear it, there is a presentation of gifts to be made. For Kenneth here has brought a bundle with offerings from townships across the Island. These are gifts for the Seaborne himself. And so, Dhion Ingleeshe, please come to receive them.'

John had been given a seat at the front. Now he stood, feeling a little awkward. The Northern boatman stepped forward. He was carrying the sealskin bag, which he now opened to reveal the bundle John had seen earlier.

It contained dozens of gifts. Most were only small, but they came with a greeting from every people on the Island: anything from little parcels of oatcakes wrapped in woven reeds to a pewter quaich, neatly decorated with engraved patterns. And the finely woven cloak that had wrapped them all – who had given that?

Kenneth reached into the sealskin bag and brought out a neat linen parcel. He pressed it into John's hands and spoke. Hope leaped in John's heart. Hugh translated:

'The cloak is from the High Shareg, Aengas Ma'Haengas, from his seat in the Northland.'

The hope fluttered.

'He greets you in the name of the Island. And he gives you this' – Hugh questioned Kenneth – 'as a token.'

John opened the wrappings and withdrew a knife, its engraved blade sheathed in tooled leather. He drew it out slowly, turning it in the yellow lamplight. There was a general intake of breath.

Hugh explained carefully, a note of surprise, and even awe, in his voice. 'This knife is a traditional gift, presented to every young man on his coming of age. It is a great honour, to receive one from the Ma'Haengas himself.

'The gifts are four. They equip a warrior. The knife, the spear, the cooking pot and the shield: what a man needs to hunt and protect himself and fend for himself in the wild. There is a promise here in the knife, that the others will follow. I think you must go one day, and greet the High Shareg yourself.'

જ્જ

At last it was the turn of A'Mhagus. The storyteller sat near the flickering fire, silent. She swayed a little back and forth. A deep hush filled the rondal. Quietly she began.

The words went over John's head. Not only was the accent difficult for him, but the style was ancient, with words and forms he did not know. These are the words as Morag told them to him later.

This is the tale of the lost man, the Seaborne,
Plucked from the waters of Westerland's shore.
Plucked by the strong hand of Fengoel Ma'Fearghas,
Nursed by the wisdom of Maureen A'Dhael.
Back from the death-realms of drowning they
        dragged him.
Blessing of Rortan upon him they gave.
Into the hands of the shareg they brought him.
Into the holding of Micheil the Just.

Waking, he spake for the first time, the Seaborne,
Words of a language that no-one had heard.
Where did he come from, and where are his people?
Where is the man who could stand by him now?
He could not answer, nor hear what we asked
        him.
He could not tell where his country or town.
We could not send him, by land nor by ocean
Back to his hearth, to his home, to his kin.

Micheil Caerpadraig, from hard by the lough-side,
Called for the fisherman, come from the sea.
Send the man's clothing forth round the Island,
Send his apparel for all to behold.
Ask of the townspeople close by the sea-coast,
Ask of the villagers far from the shore.
Ask of the wise on the fair plains of Caerster,
Ask the High Shareg at home in the north.

Tell, O you weavers, you cunning of Midland,
Tell where before have you seen cloth like this.
Where are the people who wear such apparel?
Where is their homeland? Who knows their
speech?
Never before did we see cloth as this stuff.
Never before held we garments like these.
Strange to our fingers the feel of its cov'ring.
Strange must its people be, far 'cross the sea.

Borne on the fair wave to havens of Caerster
Came the swift boat with its cargo so rare;
Came to the towns of the people of Caerster,
Where sit the wise in their castles of care.
Say, O you wise men, who hear the waves speaking,
Say, O you sages who study the lore,
You who look eastward across the great water,
You who are learned in foreigners' speech.

We know not a people who wear clothes of this
kind...

John remembered that evening long afterwards: the
faces round the rondal, lit up in the firelight; the metre
of the lay rolling onward, verse upon verse, like the
endless waves of the sea itself.

'It was a fine tale,' Morag said to him, later. 'There
is hardly a town or a village that hasn't at least heard of
your coat, and she mentioned many of them in her lay.
It is important that people are remembered like this.

'But alas, Dhion, there is no news for you. The
nearest is that some seafarers of Caerster, who trade
from time to time with people the other side of the
water – where Sharilland is – they tell of a people on
the mainland far to the south, many days' sailing. They
call themselves the Aunglaicht, which, these voyagers
thought, is not so different from your Ingleeshe. But

they had heard nothing of even this people wearing anything like you. And news of something so strange – forgive me – would have carried far.'

That night John lay on the hard floor, for Kenneth had his bed, while A'Mhagus lodged with the shareg and his wife. The hope so newly fledged in the rondal had quietly folded its wings. Yet, to his surprise, he was not disconsolate. In his heart something was growing. To find himself the focus of the holding of a whole community in this way was outside his experience. He was awed, and in spite of himself, a warm feeling began to seep into his soul: a sense of acceptance – other people's, and his own. Sleep came quickly.

The storyteller had gone, and with her, the last of his ideas of finding a way to return. He didn't feel it as he would have expected. It was as if something slid into his soul from a sideways direction: something that sustained him after all. He watched A'Mhagus and Kenneth walk with Morag up the path towards the pass. The south-westerly breeze was shaking golden leaves out of the birches, and it crossed his mind that they would have good weather for their return sailing.

Night fell, and a thin crescent moon followed the sun into the west. They put out the lights. Darkness, but for the low red glow of the fire.

He was on a train, on the footplate of an old steam engine, pounding along the railway track out of the town. The buildings fell away. For a while there were roads, and cars – but they were old: veteran even. Then only the occasional cart, then nothing. They surged through a wide moorland. There were no rails. There was no train, no engine. He was compelled to walk on – to where, he did not know.

A woman – stooping low, picking up something. Gathering sticks. It was A'Mhagus, the storyteller. 'Where am I?' he asked her. She gave him her grin, her crooked grin. 'Thou'rt in the tenth hundred of the years of our Lord,' she declared.

'No!' he cried. He woke in the darkness of the house. He was sitting bolt-upright, cold and sweating.

Hugh came to him. His face, looking down, kindly, a little anxious.

'What is it, Dhion?' he asked.

John shook his head as the dream faded.

A question. A question had seeded in his heart as he held the High Shareg's knife in his hand; now it reached up towards the sought-for answer that drew it, grew it.

'Why, Hugh? Why this...' He sought for a word. 'Why these gifts? From so many people? And – Why does the High Shareg give so much, so great...' He struggled for words. '... to me?'

Hugh seemed to consider his reply. Then he said, 'Dhion, you say that where you come from you are nobody special. Nobody of importance. Yet this coat – it appears to us like the wearing of one who can command the wealth of a whole people. The Ma'Haengas greets you as befits the son of a mighty chieftain.'

John took this in.

'But... I see.'

It was all he could say.

15

Samhain came and went. The sea had turned from summer-blue to shifting grey and green. Its rollers, crashing on the beach, made launching the boats difficult when an on-shore wind was blowing. Now the waters were suddenly full of fish, and whenever they could the boats rowed out, spreading the long encircling nets which the men on the shore slowly hauled in.

Dermot trudged back to his home. It was hard work, and anyway he longed to be back on the water with the waves slapping the side of the boat. Sailing the little craft out to the deep-water fishing grounds was a skill he was learning well. Now, after standing up to his thighs in cold seawater, heaving the weed-clogged nets, he scowled as his sister called to him for help with a heavy creel of fish.

He was about to give utterance to the feeling behind the scowl, when he felt a hand laid on his shoulder. He swallowed the unspoken words. His father had come up behind him, unheard amid his discontented thoughts.

'Son. Come aside a moment.'

Dermot allowed himself to be steered away from the doorway, around the side of the house.

'Dermot, Dael is saying that he is finishing on the sea. He is an old man now, and wants to see out his days mending the nets and sitting by the smoking-house. Now that you've come of age, he wishes to pass his boat to you, and for you to take his place upon the long waves.'

The words fell on Dermot's mind like a dream. Suddenly the day was good. With a rush of feeling he cried, 'Da, I've worried about this. I know we couldn't afford to have Leighan build me a new boat, but without my own...' Without his own, if truth were told, he felt incomplete, not yet a man. Dael's boat was old and patched, but she had been made well, and was light and answered to the wind. It was an honour that the foremost man in the village should bestow his boat on him. Dael's one son had three daughters, who had all married well: hard-working hill-farmers up above Caerpadraig. They had no need of their grandfather's boat. But still, Dael could have offered it to Euan, or to Ronal. Dael had chosen him.

'Well?'

'Well, I will go and thank Dael today. An – what should I take him?'

But his father had not finished. 'And soon you'll want your own house. With your own tools of your trade you'll no longer come under my cloak. We must fettle you one, here in Fisherhame. And find a wife for you, to keep house.'

A wife! Dermot felt the heat of a flush rise to his face. He turned away from his father, to gaze unseeing across the shingle, dotted with women struggling with basket-loads of the catch.

'Now, don't tell me you haven't been looking at the smith's daughter – I know you have. You'll need a good woman when you're away at sea. As for Mi'Shean – I'm not sure. It's not everyone's life, here by the sea. Look, there's Muireann, Callen's youngest. There's no doubt she's suited to the life. I could ask him for you.'

Muireann... If ever a girl was mis-named! Rather than sea-bright, her face appeared all red and white blotches. And she had a tongue...

'Why not Shinane?' he answered. 'She's a good girl, and I like her. An – an isn't A'Fengoel her aunt? She'd have family here.'

'Aye, but would she roll up her sleeves wi' the lass-ies here and pitch in with a will? I don't know.'

'Da – If I'm to marry and have a wife an... an so on, then it's Shinane for me. I'm no marrying that Muireann anyway.'

Benrish glanced over his shoulder. 'No so loud, son. Their house is only yon.' He considered. 'Well, if it's not her, there are no other maids for you this side of the mountain. So it will have to be someone's daughter from Caerpadraig or the hills. But I think you should look around you more widely for a likely lassie who could settle to our ways.'

Dermot felt it rising in him: that feeling he got when someone tried to make him go where he did not want to follow. An angry feeling, a stubborn feeling. Let them try to push him. He'd show them he could stand firm.

'I know my mind, Da. I've no need to look further,' he muttered. He clenched his teeth.

He faced his father, his jaw jutting out a little. Stood his ground.

The older man sighed. 'Well… if you're clear, then I won't stand in your way.'

'I am clear, Da.' He raised his chin. 'She'll bring quality to my house. With the smith's daughter, an my own house an my own boat – I'll be somebody here.'

His father was slow in replying. In the end he said, 'All right. You go to the smithy when we go across to the town tomorrow. Take them a fine pair of the herring you've just brought in. See what you can tell to impress the lassie. An if it goes well, I'll see if I can get anywhere wi' Blacksmith.'

Dermot came with his father, setting off over the mountain to Caerpadraig, taking a fair load of salted and smoked fish. And he clutched something else – something a little bit special.

'I hope fortune has been kind to the hunters of the town,' said Benrish as they set out. 'It would be good to take back a little venison as well as their mutton.'

Dermot grunted. His mind was still full of what his father had talked of the night before. 'Look, son,' he'd said. 'Those fine folk over Caerpadraig way don't like to

108

marry their daughters to our lads. Although we risk our lives so that they can have the herring, we're no good enough for them. If you want to get anywhere wi' them, ye're going to have to impress them.

'Now, I know ye've had adventures at sea. But they won't understand that.'

Dermot nodded. The townsmen wouldn't know what it was like to have the Island drop beneath the skyline when a stiff nor'easter springs up. To be faced with the choice of rowing all the way home against the wind, or of tacking away to the south-east and hoping to find your way back from there – before your drinking water ran out. He had heard the tales.

Dermot pondered a moment. 'What about the goat, Da?'

His father looked at him blankly for a moment. Then he smiled.

'Aye – that was good. And it's more within their ken. Tell 'em about the goat!'

Their business was done. They had exchanged their fish for some meat and barley, and Benrish was taking his ease and a beer at the carpenter's house before turning back for home. Dermot could at last make his way to the forge.

'Ma'Bhenrish – you're welcome.' Fineenh ushered him in, and called her husband. Shean came, stripped to the waist from the forge, wrapping an old plaid around him as he entered the room, while Shinane rose from her spinning to serve them small beer and girdle-cakes.

'I came… to bring you these.' Dermot felt awkward in this unfamiliar place. He went on in a rush. 'A pair of fine herring. The biggest of the catch. They're beauties!' He thrust forward a basket containing the prize fish.

Shean admired the fish, and thanked him. He asked if he had caught them himself, and when, and commented on the fine day it had been yesterday.

What did he mean, the fine day? Hadn't he noticed that squall? What did a man like Shean know about weather anyway, working under a roof all day?

What should he say? His mind went blank. He took a gulp of beer.

Ma'Ronal gave him an unexpected opening. 'It's like we only see you but you bring us something. There's one or two in the town are still grateful to you for the goat.'

'Aye, the goat!' Dermot began, enthusiastically. 'That was a day! That was a goat!' He half-turned to the two women. He took a deep breath. 'You know Beh' Claragh away to the east?'

Shean nodded. 'Aye. I've climbed the summits in my time.'

'The top is all stubble-heather and furze among the stones,' Dermot continued. 'Not like the deep heather on the moors. You can't run at all in that. But on the summit it's short and smooth enough, and I could move quick. It's there I saw him. He was below me, grazing by himself, a big black billy – you could smell 'im.'

He looked at them. Shean, on the best chair, his eyes watchful. Shinane, seated with her distaff beside her mother, working quietly, her eyes cast down. He must get her attention. He scraped his stool a little way towards her.

'He twisted and turned, but I turned with him. Then he came to a narrow cleft and went down among the heather. But I stood on a rock and jumped, and I fell on his neck. I brought him down and killed him before he could use his horns – like that.' He made the action of pulling the goat's head up and back, to break the long supple neck. 'He was a weight to carry down, I can tell you!'

'You could be a hunter yourself,' commented Shean.

'An I will be, whenever I can get the time. But I'm a fisherman first and foremost. That's what I am. One day soon I'll have my own boat, and then we're going to fit out a new house for me. I'll make it fine. You'll see. Fit for a fine wife. An I'll have bairns to be fishermen after me...'

He had stood as he reached the climax of his tale, and now his eyes swept round the seated semi-circle. Shean looked across at his wife, and Fineenh looked around at Shinane. As he followed their gaze he felt the heat rising in his face. She looked pale. The spindle was turning well between her fingers, and the yarn was coming smoothly away from the distaff. Then she reached up, snapped the yarn, let the spindle drop on the floor. Coils of wool unravelled as it rolled in a small circle.

'Excuse me, father,' she said, and turned. Without looking at him she passed through a leather curtain and was gone.

His eyes followed her. Words dried in his throat as the curtain grew still.

16

Each morning began with their daily devotion. John sat with Hugh and Morag, for what else had he to do? But he found it difficult to join in: the words of an old dialect, the chants rising and falling with odd little quavers and grace-notes, the long silent meditation. 'The aim is to let go of thought. Don't think of anything. Only seek that which lies deepest in the chamber of your heart,' Hugh told him; but as soon as the silence fell, the memories would rise, the fantasies, the anxieties. Still, he sat it through, day by day, into the dark of the year. And in the light of the single candle, drop by drop, from some welling source, a little peace arose within him.

There was a night at the very darkest time of the year when a great gathering was held in the rondal. They had pushed the benches back, leaving a large, open space. People came together in the darkness and cold. Morag led them in chanting; and then a sitting and waiting. At last a light was lit, and from it, many lights, and Hugh set a brand to the fire. People stayed up all night and there was music and story-telling. In the end, John could not keep awake, and it was wonderful to sleep on a pile of straw, cradled in the warmth and glow and incantation.

The weeks passed. The snow melted, and came again and thawed again, and John felt his language skills improve. He was beginning to feel he could communicate.

They had come to the end of a language lesson. Hugh was sitting back and looking at him with satisfaction.

'Dhion, we think you are ready now to give an account of yourself to the shareg. I have spoken with him. He will hear you in three days.'

The sun at its highest reach was still low in the sky, though each day it climbed a little higher. It was after noon that Hugh and Morag brought John the few steps to the shareg's house.

The door stood open.

'A blessing on this house, and peace.'

Micheil's voice came rumbling from within: 'In the name of God, and in peace.'

Morag gently pushed John into the lamplit darkness, for the shutters were closed against the cold. A'Shar'g rose and greeted the priest and went to bring them ale. They had scarcely raised their beakers to their lips when another greeting sounded from the doorway: a deep and familiar voice.

'In the name of Ghea,' responded the shareg. In walked Fengoelan. His sparkling blue eyes lit up to see John.

They were interrupted by a firm rap on the open door and the sound of the customary greeting in a strong, gritty voice. He looked up as Shean Ma'Ronal, the blacksmith, rolled in. He was a small man, but John could see how powerfully built he was.

'Well,' Shareg Micheil stood. 'Now we're all here, we can begin.'

John sat on a bench between Hugh and Morag. Fengoelan and Ma'Ronal took another. He saw the blacksmith's eyes flick to Morag and then back to the shareg. Heard him clear his throat.

Micheil picked up the unspoken question. 'Morag A'Phadr is here at the Father's request and at my invitation. I know we do not usually invite a woman to such councils, but I consider that this is an unusual situation and deserves an unusual approach. I believe A'Phadr may see things in our talk that no-one else can. Does anyone here say nay?'

113

John listened intently. It was hard work following the formal speech, but becoming easier. He watched Micheil turn, deliberately, to each of the men. Ma'Ronal shifted his weight uncomfortably, but he held his peace.

'Well then.' Micheil took his chair between the two benches either side of the hearth. The firelight played on faces, beards, hair, rough clothing. 'We are here to take counsel about where and how Dhion Seaborne may take his place among us. It may be that his people will yet come for him; but after nine moons and no sign from them, we need to consider how it will be if he is with us in time to come.

'So it is needful that he has a place among us. We need to understand his family line and his connexions.'

John turned to Hugh.

'Dhion, it is important for us to know how each of us fits in to our people: who is related to whom, who would take sides with another. If a man takes a woman for his wife, her father will insist on knowing the man's ancestry before he agrees. The shareg would not agree to a betrothal until he knows to whom the man and woman are related. It is very important.'

'And so, Dhion,' Micheil took up the theme, 'first I would ask Fengoelan Fisherhame if he would tell again the story of how you came among us.'

Fengoelan rose, and recounted how they had found the Seaborne. They had all heard the story before, and Fengoelan added nothing new. But something passed between them in the recounting. And now that John could understand most of what he heard, its telling was like a deep organ note that sets a string humming.

They had spent a long time, Hugh and Morag and John, considering how he would answer the questions they knew must arise: Who were his family? Where had he come from? John told the company about his parents. He paused as he came to describe the work his

114

father had done as an industrial chemist. He realised his words made him sound like a wizard.

'And where does your father live?' The blacksmith leaned forward to ask his question.

'He lives in a town called Crewkerne. It is... in another land.'

He saw Micheil give Hugh a quizzical look. No, not even the priest had heard of it. 'Where is this... place?' asked the shareg. 'It must be very far away.'

Before John could reply, Morag spoke. 'If I may give the shareg the best answer we can? We have asked Dhion this question, and together we cannot find a clear answer. It is not that Dhion is hiding anything or will not answer. It is that with our present understanding we cannot answer it.'

Hugh joined in. 'That is so. For now, this remains a mystery.'

'Begging the Father's pardon.' The smith was looking intensely at the floor as he spoke. He jabbed his knee with his forefinger. 'It may be a mystery for the Father, for I accept that even to his knowledge there may be limits. But surely this Ingleeshe himself knows where he comes from?' His eyes under their brows darted up, to look John full in the face.

'Dhion knows where he has come from, and names his own land. But we have not heard of it. In the same way, we have told Dhion that he is on our Island, out to the west of Sharilland. But he does not know of Sharilland. When he awoke among us, he thought he knew where our Island must be. But then he did not find what he expected here. It is that his knowledge and ours do not meet.'

The smith looked down. His brows knitted as he rested his chin in his hands, but he said no more.

It was the shareg who asked the next question. 'Tell us of your trade in this other land, Dhion Ingleeshe. The Father tells us you made things from metal.'

'That's right. I worked with other men, making... metal pieces.'

'So you were a smith. And pieces of what did you make?'

'Well, where I come from, we have these...' He petered out. How could he describe a car? *It's like a covered cart, but it doesn't need a horse to pull it – it moves by itself.* How could he say that? It would sound even more like wizardry.

'We have things that move on wheels –' he began.

'There.' Shean broke in. 'You make carts. Was that so difficult to say? But tell me.' The blacksmith leaned forward, his beaker of ale in his hand. 'Did you then make all those little teeth – the ones on your coat? How did you do it?'

'The zip, you mean? No... no, I couldn't have made those. They were made in a – very big workshop, with special... tools... that make them by themselves.'

'Tools that make things by themselves?'

The blacksmith looked from the shareg to Hugh, and back again. With sinking heart, John could see how false what he was trying to describe sounded to these men. How could he give an account of anything, if everything was going to sound impossible? He lapsed into a sullen silence.

'We looked at those when first we brought him from the sea,' remarked Fengoelan. 'We said then that you must be a great man to have such workmanship on you. Is that not so, Dhion?'

Hugh must have sensed his reluctance.

'I think we have to realise that Dhion comes from a very different land from our own,' he told them. 'Would it not be right, Dhion, to say that where you come from, these *shipion* are not uncommon?'

John seized the proffered help. 'That's right. Everybody has them. I'm nobody special.'

There was another silence.

Micheil turned to the smith.

'You could do with some help at the forge, Shean?'

'Aye, ' the blacksmith replied, guardedly. 'It's been a year and more since my last prentice went back to his people in Midland. There's been no-one likely stepping forward. And I don't see the girl turning her hand to it.'

'What say you to taking Dhion Ingleeshe and trying him at the forge?'

The smith stared.

'Begging your pardon, Shareg. The forge is a dangerous place for anyone not... able. And the Seaborne has not yet proved himself.'

It was so frustrating. One minute, he was a great man; the next, an incompetent. Something stung John, and he heard himself say, quite calmly, 'I am not afraid of working with fire.'

Everyone stared at him.

'Indeed,' said Micheil, slowly, 'it was with fire at widow Shareen's house that Dhion Ingleeshe did prove himself among us. What say you, blacksmith? Will you try him? I am asking you.'

Shean frowned.

'What he says doesn't make sense to me. He's hiding something.'

John felt cold clench him. He did not deserve this. Or did he? Was this his punishment for running away?

'Tell us your thoughts.' The shareg rested his hands on his knees and turned his black brows to the smith.

'I know he doesn't speak our tongue very well yet. But he knows what a cart is, yet he finds so much difficulty in telling us he makes ironwork for them.'

Hugh interrupted. 'I believe that what Dhion is trying to describe is not a cart. Just as this *ship* is so unlike our clasps, so these things are... other than a cart.'

Shean shot a look at the priest, and continued. 'Someone else has made this *ship* for him, and must

117

have taken weeks over it, but he's nobody special?' His incredulous eyebrows soared skywards.

Micheil turned a grim face to the priest, 'What say you, Hugh, to this?'

Hugh looked first towards the shareg, then to the smith. He said, 'We have talked with Dhion day by day, as he has learned our speech. We feel him trying to tell us truth as he sees it. But it seems that his truth is not our truth.'

The smith snorted. 'The last man I heard of who had a different kind of truth was as mad as a bluebottle under the roof-beams, and he waded into the sea saying he was the Blessed Rortan and the next thing anyone saw of him was his body washed up on the shore. People like that are a danger.' He sat back, his arms folded.

'Dhion is not like that.' Morag spoke quietly, but firmly.

'Do you say the same, Father?' Shean asked.

'I do,' the priest returned. 'I say again, we trust Dhion. We do not understand. But look at what we do know: the clothes he wore when first he came to the Island are unlike anything we have. His coat went round the Island, and no-one has seen the like. What of his other garments? Doughael has never met such cloth before, nor seen clothes shaped as his were. His shoes… These things cannot lie. And they all speak together of a land very different from anything we know.'

'And where is this peculiar land?' asked Shean. 'It's nowhere I've heard of, and it seems that it's nowhere that even you, Father, have heard of.'

'And Dhion feels the same.' There was a tremor in Morag's quiet tones, and John saw her hand clench as she spoke. 'If we find his stories strange, think how he is feeling, finding himself in this place that we find familiar, but which is strange to him. The only thing that stands against his not believing in our world is that he finds himself in it.'

She sat back. 'Ma'Ronal, I think we are all of us, the Seaborne included, asked to live with not knowing, not understanding. We ask you to believe us, who know Dhion, when we say that he is not mad, and he is not lying, and he certainly is not simple.'

Like a trapped beast, Shean glanced at the priest, then at the shareg. He slowly shook his head, and rested his chin in his hand.

'Is that why you invited me here, Shareg? I see. You want me to take on a man who's come from God knows where, to take him into my house and have him sleep by my fire, on account of he seems to have made bits and pieces for carts that aren't carts? I mind how he was at harvest. There's no farmer would have him work for them, is there? Just remember, will you, I have a maiden daughter in the house, and there's all sorts of ironwork in that smithy – knives, and hammers, and... The answer's no.'

Silence.

Micheil broke the tension. 'Shean, you have heard what the Father and A'Phadr have said. Now hear what I have to say. We need to find a place to try the Seaborne. It seems that he has done metalwork before. He has been tried by fire in our midst and has succeeded where others failed. The life of young Colin is owed to him. And on top of that, you need help in the forge. I think you're the best man to take him.'

The shareg gave the smith a hard look. Then his face softened.

'Give him a try. That's all I ask.'

The smith scrutinised John from beneath furrowed brows. Then he said, 'If you command it, Shareg, I'll try him. But any nonsense, mind, and his trial stops there and then. Is that agreed?'

'Agreed, Blacksmith,' said the shareg. He turned to John. 'Agreed, Dhion Ingleeshe?'

John nodded. A sense of relief flooded through him.

'So that's settled then.' The shareg looked from face to face. Then, with a change of tone, he added, 'But before he comes to you, Shean Ma'Ronal, he has a journey before him.'

John looked intently at him. Micheil returned his gaze.

'I will take you on a journey into the Northland. You have a visit to make, do you not?'

John remembered. The High Shareg's gift: Micheil expected him to go and thank the Ma'Haengas in person. His heart leaped, and then he felt unsure. An adventure, and with Micheil whom he was coming to trust and even to admire, to meet this prestigious person whose name always made him smile – though he was careful not to show it. But was he ready for it, or would his speech let him down?

He concealed a gulp, then stumbled over his words. 'It is an honour for me to go to meet the Ma'Haengas. And to go in the company of Shareg Micheil is an honour twice over.'

'There is much he hasn't told us though.' Morag looked into Hugh's face, lying beside her in the dim yellow light of the rush-lamp. Its tiny flame gleamed from a niche above them in the little sleeping-room, whispering to her of other nights, other niches, all the way back to when she was small, a memory of a mother. Now, the light warmed the hawk-brown of her husband's eyes as she peered into them. 'I do not understand why he felt he had to leave his own town. Were there enemies whom he feared? Why did his shareg not protect him? And what of his kinsmen? Would they not stand with him?'

'Yes.' Hugh closed his eyes. She could sense him reaching into his mind to pull the right skeins of thought together. 'I am beginning to think he comes from a very different people. A people who do not stand together. Where you must fight to keep your place.'

'We must wait.' She shifted her weight, raising herself a moment on her elbow. 'And trust he will tell us in time.'

She leaned over and kissed him. She blew out the light and lay back. She stared up into the unfathomable darkness, the acrid tang of the lamp-smoke briefly in her nostrils. In a little while Hugh's breathing became gentle and smooth. She was alone with her thoughts.

17

Bride's Day passed, and the blessing of the fields, and John's speech improved fast. He knew enough to make it easy for him to learn more, and a day came when Hugh told him that Micheil would leave his cattle with his lads and the hired men, and take him into the Northland to meet the High Shareg. Ten days later the priest watched from the door of the rondal as half-a-dozen small children, coming to him for stories and to learn the lore, stopped to gawp. Two splendidly attired figures were making their way through the town to gain the lough-side path that led into the heart of the Island, and thence to the north.

The one would be well-known to the children, but only on First-Days would they see him clothed like this. Micheil's black brows and beard, his steady, imperturbable pace, were a familiar sight on his way to the pastures and his cattle. But today his great plaid was fastened with a large brooch on his shoulder. On his arm he bore a round targe, and in his hand a long spear.

The other was taller, and although now a common sight, still, Hugh knew, there hung about him an air of romance, of adventure, of foreignness. And never had those boys and girls seen the Seaborne like this, dressed as a hunter, a fine cloak on his shoulders, a good knife at his waist, the flash of the silver band ever at his wrist.

Hugh watched them out of sight, the sun throwing their long shadows across earthen wall and wattle fence. Then he called, 'Liam. Maelcolm. Hurry up – and bring those others with you.'

The sun in the fourth month warmed John as they walked beside the river that drained Lough Padraig. Catkins hung from the alder, and the soft, silver palms of pussy-willow studded the hillside. They forded the stream that flowed down from the mountains in the east. Micheil showed him how to use a long straight bough cut from the hazel to help him, thrusting its butt into the stony bed downstream and leaning on it, so that the strength of its current, swollen by early melt-water, did not wash away his foothold. As they turned north their path grew harder, along the track that few used except Leighan and his men, bringing timber down from the pine forests. The woods were busy with spring: blackbirds flew from their coming with a cackle. Above them titmice scurried around the branches, and in the distance, as steadily they climbed, black-cock clucked, until the trees gave out and the high muir rolled upward in shades of brown and purple towards the snow-line. No men lived here, and only the occasional hunter passed this way, or once or twice a year a little pack-horse train, doing the circuit of the northern and western townships. There were wolves hereabout, said Micheil, and John felt a frisson of archetypal fear. But the one they saw, on a far skyline, turned at once and slunk away.

They stopped around midday at a cluster of rocks that rose up out of the twisted heather. There they took food from their wallets – barley-bread baked that morning, smelling yeasty still, and strips of salted mutton. They had travelled almost in silence, but now Micheil began the conversation.

'You wear a bracelet, Dhion. Few would have so much silver here. Tell me about it.'

What was he to tell? 'It was a gift,' he said. He looked away, across the moor. He did not want to talk to the shareg about Helen.

He felt Micheil's eyes on him, searching. 'There are marks on it,' he said. 'What does it say?'

This was a safer line of enquiry and John answered readily, his answer pat, for of course Hugh had already put the same question. And when the sense of the marks was made clear to him, Hugh had smiled a strange smile. 'We have a chant like that,' he'd said: *'When we unite, the worlds unite.'*

Now Micheil gave him a surprised look. 'So you know that, do you?'

John shrugged. It had meant something to Helen, he knew. He had simply accepted it.

They munched for a few minutes in silence. Then: 'Who is your shareg, Dhion? What is he like?'

John considered how to reply. He must choose his words with care. 'It's not like that... Every four years or so, we choose someone to represent us, to go to a great council that we call Parliament – that is, a place where six hundred or so members discuss the affairs of the land and make decisions.'

'Six hundred?' Micheil looked incredulous.

'Yes, I'm not sure of the exact number. But something like that. There is a very large number of people living in my country.'

Again Micheil seemed to consider. Then he went on. 'So, what's he like, this man you have chosen?'

John pictured his MP. To start off with, she was a woman. But her activities seemed to have impinged little on his everyday life.

'She... seems all right. She came round to the door once. It's the only time I've seen her. I don't really know her.'

'She?' said Micheil slowly.

'Er... yes. We have women in government, as well as men.'

'In the Common Story I have heard tell of great queens,' commented Micheil reflectively. 'But none of our sharegs has been a women that I ever heard.'

He paused, considering. 'There is a wise woman who lives in the mountains over there.' He pointed

124

towards the east. 'Priests will journey to her to take counsel. Sometimes sharegs, also.'

Another pause. Then: 'But surely this woman lives in your town and you know her. You would see her in your gatherings, wouldn't you?'

'Micheil, London is very, very big, and we don't have gatherings as you do. How many people live in Caerpadraig?'

The shareg quickly counted up. 'Men, or everyone?'

'Everyone – including children.'

Micheil puffed out his cheeks. 'Including children… There are half-a-hundred and two men of age, including old Manus, but he's in his dotage… Then two-score and six wives and nine girls of marriageable age: that makes a hundred and seven. And there must be – oh, a score and twelve children… No, poor little Tilda died of fever last month. What's that? Two short of two score and a hundred, I think. Then there are the crofts, and Fisherhame –'

'Two and a half hundreds in all?' queried John. 'Micheil, just that part of London where I was living has many thousands of people. I guess…' he paused, calculating silently, 'more than two hundred Caerpadraigs. No-one can know them all – not even a tenth of them.'

Micheil paused between bites. He appeared to be looking far into the distance. As he turned his head to stare at John, his brows were furrowed.

'Dhion, I do not understand. How can that be? A town where, for every man in Caerpadraig, there are two hundred? Two *hundred*?' He brightened. 'You have your words wrong: two hundred is two tens, tenfold. You mean –'

'Yes, I mean two hundred times as big as Caerpadraig. And that is only a small part of London. In all there are…' He paused. He had not come across any word for millions. '…thousands upon thousands of people who live in London.'

Micheil turned fully to face him. He took his shoulders and looked deeply into his eyes. 'Dhion, this is not possible. You have your words wrong. A thousand thousand would be a hundred hundreds, a hundred-fold. There is no number that big.'

John had an inspiration. He plucked a sprig of heather and looked at the tiny leaves spiralling up the wiry stem. He handed it to Micheil. 'How many leaves are there?' he asked.

Micheil drew his brows together. But he counted.

'A score and sixteen – that's not counting those little brown ones at the bottom.'

'Now how many stalks of heather are there around us?'

Micheil laughed. 'I know where you're leading me – you'll ask me how many heather leaves there are on this whole moor!'

'So, in my city there's not quite so many people as that. But you see: numbers that big can exist, and often do. It's just that here you never need to count them. In my world, we really do.'

'All right,' said Micheil. 'So you do mean a very big number. But still you must be wrong. You can't have a town that big. First, how do all the people eat? You can't grow enough grain for so many people; you couldn't graze enough cattle and sheep. How do they get firewood? Or water? And – well, even at home in the heat of summer, I sometimes have to remind people to go away from the town to relieve themselves whenever possible, or…' Micheil did not enlarge on the point. 'All these problems only get bigger with more people, until the town just cannot grow any more.'

How to answer him? Maybe directness was best. He was tired of avoiding the clash.

'We bring in food from all over the world, in ships – huge ships – and lorries: like very big carts, and… other things.' John could not strain credulity too far with a description of an aeroplane. 'We have different ways of heating our homes and workplaces – which would be hard to explain – and complicated ways of dealing with... dirty things.' He knew of no word in the Island tongue for waste.

Micheil interrupted him. 'But this is my next difficulty. Surely we would have heard of it, this great city of yours. Even if it's far away, news of it would have spread throughout the world. And if you get your food – Ghea alone knows how you manage it – from all over the world, why haven't we seen these great ships off our own coasts? I know we live our own life here, but even so, Hugh and I keep our ears open for news from beyond our shores. And the High Shareg, whom you will meet tonight, makes sure he is well informed. We have not heard of a place like this.

'Dhion, you smell like an honest man. Yet what you say cannot be true. What is the answer to this riddle?' He stood, bent to pick up his pack and slung it over his shoulder.

A low, rounded, brown-grey summit stood before them, streaked with white, its hunched back to the sun, now starting to redden its western flank. To its left John made out a pass like a great bite in the skyline. They had been following a narrow trail through the heather, not always discernible to him, although the shareg seemed to know his way. Now they fell in with a broader trackway, more clearly marked, but still at other times almost losing itself in the ling and moss. And slowly the bite drew nearer. As they reached the pass it suddenly gave a view of a long wooded valley. Far away, the sea gleamed cold in the north. They descended through pine-woods where larches were putting out tufts of brilliant green along their delicate branches, and gradually the track they had been following became a clear path. The path crossed the burn beside them on a bridge of stone slabs and became a rutted road. In a stone-walled field beside the track, a man and his boy were finishing ploughing in the evening light. The man hailed them in a voice that sounded strange to John – the vowels rougher, more throaty than he was used to. Micheil answered. Then the man said something to the child, who immediately ran off down the track before them.

'We are announced,' grinned Micheil.

John looked with interest at the town. It was no bigger than Caerpadraig, but it was ringed by a sturdy fence of pine-trunks set into the ground, and so looked stronger, more determined, than the only other town John knew on the Island. Half a dozen men were at the gate, looking for their arrival. They carried spears and targets. Micheil passed his own spear into his left hand, its head downwards, and raised his right hand in greeting.

'I am Micheil, Shareg of Caerpadraig in the Westerland. I come in peace to talk with the Ma'Haengas. And this is Dhion Ingleeshe, Seaborne, of whom you may have heard.'

It seemed they had indeed heard of the Seaborne, no doubt when his coat was passed around the Island. They looked with awe, and the eldest of them gave them his hand in welcome. The others began to disperse, some looking back at them, while a young man ran onwards into the town.

Their guide walked before them along the muddy streets, his spear also reversed. The houses, John noted, were smaller but sturdier than those he had become used to. At their doors red-bearded men stared at them with undisguised curiosity.

They came to a stone house, larger than the rest, and turf-roofed. Two spearmen stood at its door. Passing between them, a man appeared: an upright man with white hair. A chair was hastily being brought for him, but he remained standing in welcome. So this was the High Shareg, of whom John had heard tell. While Micheil greeted him and presented his gift, John gave himself a moment to study this personage. He was like a fire, cheerful and warming in the hearth, but with a hidden power and danger about him. His long hair and white beard had surely once been as red and wild as he had seen on those men who had stared at the newcomer from their doorways, and still the red lingered in his thick brows.

'Micheil. It is good to see you.' Suddenly the formality dropped, as the Ma'Haengas came forward and took the newcomer's arm. 'So here is this famous stranger, this Seaborne, who wears such a coat, with fastenings that not the whole Island could command. And look at him, dressed like a shareg!' Turning to John he took his arm also.

'My cloak I owe to you, High Shareg,' replied John in the best speech he could muster, 'for which I have come to thank you.'

The Ma'Haengas turned again to Micheil. 'This foreigner has good manners,' he laughed.

'Hugh Padr has worked long with him to teach him our ways.'

'Take our thanks to him. He is a good man, Hugh, and a wise one. And this is your business, to bring the Seaborne to meet me? Ingleeshe, I hear you call him?'

'His own name is Dhion, and we indeed call him Ingleeshe,' replied Micheil.

'Good, good. We will all have a fine talk together. But now you must come in and rest yourselves from your journey. Tomorrow we have business it would be well for you to see. Now come you within, and we will find pallets to rest you, and food and drink to refresh you.'

18

John woke early the next morning. Good pallets had been laid for them that night, close to the fire in the High Shareg's house, and he felt very comfortable as he lay dozing, watching the bright morning light spilling over the threshold; breathing in the now-familiar smell of peat smoke. Aengas was already up, but the visitors were allowed to lie a while, resting after their journey. In a little, Aengas' wife came quietly into the house and started to prepare the first-food. John thought her the most beautiful old woman he had ever seen, slow and graceful in her movements, a strong face and still eyes that, he sensed, saw much. A long braid of white hair hung down her back.

It was over their meal that Aengas opened the conversation, his red eyebrows waggling.

'You have come on a good day, young man,' he said to John. 'Today you will see real High Shareg's business. Two townships are in dispute about their grazings. Kilmagas say they have always grazed their beasts on the side of the mountain. But they have become a small community. Most of their men are now old, and perhaps they haven't fully used their grazings for years. Strat'Mor say they need the land, for they have many mouths to feed and many beasts to be grazed.'

'And what have their sharegs been doing?' asked Micheil.

Aengas' green eyes flashed at him. 'A great deal of talking to much heat and no purpose,' he replied. 'So now they have decided to settle the question by battle, and have asked me to judge between them.'

'By battle?' asked John. Had he understood correctly?

'Not blood-battle,' said Aengas, with a little smile. 'Though times ago, that would have been so. This will be wood-battle.'

Micheil leaned across and explained. 'The spearheads are wooden and muffled with cloth, and the swords are wood. They hurt, but they do not wound. Each man wears an armlet of red wool; if his foe tears off his armlet, he is deemed as dead and must retire. But the result shall be held as binding by both sides.'

Aengas nodded. 'This is no game – this is serious business.'

'But why would Kilmagas agree to a battle if they are small in number and great in years?' asked John.

'Why indeed? There is a partial answer. Kilmagas wishes to put forward a champion. It will begin by single combat, not all-out fighting. But still, Strat'Mor has the pick of some fine young men, while Kilmagas has few warriors left. I expect that by this evening they will wish they had agreed to give way. But still, they are canny men, and may yet have a surprise for us.' He chuckled, almost to himself.

They finished their meal and Aengas went off to attend to some business. It was after noon that they walked out, through the stockade and up the path by which Micheil and John had come the previous evening. Instead of crossing by the bridge, they continued on the east bank of the burn. As they came out of the forest into open moorland, John saw an area marked out with flags. Two camps were there, the smoke of their fires rising into the still, grey sky.

Between the flags was about an acre of heath, where three high seats had been built on a small dais to one side, looking out across the field. 'One is for the High Shareg,' explained Micheil. 'Those on either side are for the sharegs of the two towns. They must see that all has been conducted fairly. Ma'Haengas asks that we take the other side as honoured guests. See – they are already preparing for us.' Micheil pointed to where men were lashing poles together across the field, putting up a second dais. John looked around. To him, it was a scene of confusion. He allowed his eye to be caught by a red dog, investigating something on the near side of a tent in the Strat'Mor camp. He followed the dog's progress, meandering through the melee.

At last it seemed all was ready. From behind one of the camps there suddenly erupted a frenzy of drumming: *Ba-ba-ba ba-ba-ba, Ba-ba-ba ba-ba-ba!* John's head swivelled as more thunderous drumming began in the other camp. Between them were cross-rhythms and counter-currents as each side tried to outdo the other. A din of shouting burst out. The men walked onto the field, two grim bands facing each other, bare-chested, all carrying spear and shield, a wooden sword or stick at their side. Some wore leather helmets; most were bare-headed.

Micheil turned to John.

'Although they are putting forward champions, still all the fighting men come out. One is chosen from among them,' he explained.

The Ma'Haengas stood between the opposing armies, and it was very clear which was the more numerous. The two sharegs flanked him on either side, the hubbub all around them. A loud barking took hold of John's attention. The red dog had stopped his meandering progress, and was now standing foursquare a little distance behind the sharegs. John smiled.

The High Shareg raised his arm, and a hush fell. The dog gave a last bark and fell silent. All human eyes were on the Ma'Haengas.

In the tense silence that followed, John watched as a single figure detached himself from the Kilmagas side. His muscles stood out like steel wires and his face looked as hard as flint. But his beard was grey, and he could barely have been five feet tall. When a champion came out from the other town to meet him, the younger man towered over him by a full head.

Aengas' arm dropped. The two men sprang at each other. But before John had a chance to see what was happening, it was already over. The little man had his opponent disarmed and thrown on the ground, with a Kilmagas boot on his head.

'That will have shamed them,' said Micheil.

The Kilmagas man stood his ground before his enemies. A flood of language poured from the little Islander towards the host of men from the other town. He seemed to be goading his foes to put out another champion. Micheil turned to John.

'The rules are that either side may put up as many as three for single combat. If all three are undefeated, the contest is won. But if any of them is overcome, he must leave the field, and is lost to the battle that will then follow.

'Generally, each champion engages in single combat once only. That keeps them fresh. But Kilmagas don't have so many to choose from. It looks as if they are keeping their man.'

The Strat'Mor ranks appeared in some confusion after this easy defeat of their first champion. They were still conferring when Aengas stood and raised his right arm. At once a man lifted a horn to his lips and blew a single note. Like an echo, the red dog howled.

'They are taking too long to decide,' said Micheil. 'They will have to choose a man now, or concede defeat.'

At last, another giant came out.

This time all could see that the strategy was different. Strat'Mor knew his work, and his aim was clearly to tire the older man; he would dance just within the other's reach, then dodge each stroke and swiftly step back out of range. At first he offered almost no attacking strokes at all. The crowd was all but silent, so that John could plainly hear the grunts and sharp inbreaths of the two fighting men.

Strat'Mor chose his moment, and struck. But quick as a snake, Kilmagas turned the blow on his shield, dropped his sword and grabbed the man's arm with his right hand. John had seen the occasional Judo contest, and the throw that followed would not have been out of place at one of those.

Kilmagas had won two combats in succession; but he was breathing heavily now, his hands on his knees. Still, he straightened up. His chest swelled, and again a stream of abuse flooded towards the ranks of his foes.

Strat'Mor were not so long this time in finding his opponent. They must hope to get rid of this startlingly effective little man now he was tired. If they did, John understood, there would be open battle. He had noticed women in the tents, waiting to tend the broken and bruised.

Now a man of middle height was walking out, very upright in his bearing, and a cheer went up from his townsmen. He looked an experienced fighter, strong and tenacious.

This time there was no dancing. Immediately Strat'Mor closed with his opponent, and the silence from the watching towns was complete. The only sounds were the gasping breath of the two, and the thwack of wooden sword on leather shield, again and again.

Kilmagas was down on one knee and holding up his targe to cover his head. Strat'Mor raised his arm for the stroke that must break the other's shield-arm.

And yet again, before John could see what had happened, it was suddenly over. The scene of battle was all but hidden by the surge of townsmen rushing forward. Micheil was standing in his swaying high seat, clapping his hands above his head.

'What happened? What happened?' shouted John, caught up in the excitement.

At first Micheil did not answer. Then he turned a red and beaming face to the Seaborne. Water rolled down his cheeks.

'Brilliant – it was brilliant! Didn't you see? He's slippery as a seal, that Kilmagas champion. Didn't you see how he rolled out of the way? He kicked the Strat'Mor man's legs from under him before he knew what was happening. Look at Kilmagas now, waving the red armlet in the air like a madman!'

A group of men from each camp was walking across the battlefield and standing at the Ma'Haengas' feet, the two sharegs either side. Aengas called upon Micheil to come and witness. John wandered off without any particular aim, and found himself facing the red dog, who sniffed at his shoes as if noticing something unusual there.

'Hello, boy,' said John, in English, bending towards the dog. 'You think I'm a bit strange too, don't you?' The dog looked up at him with an intelligent stare, and John gave him a pat before walking on.

The grey day was darkening into dusk when a big fire was kindled in the middle of what had been set aside as a battleground. The two towns, those who had earlier that day been ready to hack each other into submission, sat down to drink and to eat together like the best of friends. The women served.

John turned to Micheil, who had returned from the parley. 'I am surprised that these two peoples can sit down together after nearly facing each other in battle. Are they really friends now, after all this?'

Micheil raised his bushy eyebrows. 'Of course. Fighting is good and exciting, but it's a great waste of energy and useful farming time. We can't afford to harbour grudges here.'

It seemed that Strat'Mor, having lost the champions' battle, knew that they had to negotiate. Kilmagas seized the opportunity to bring aid to their ageing village, and established a grazing rent. Now they had struck an agreement: Strat'Mor would graze the Kilmagas land for a fifth part of its produce.

The feasting began.

John was silent. Tales from the land, song and fable, surrounded him. He found he could follow some of it. The red dog was still nosing around, looking for scraps. John sneaked him a morsel. They asked John to tell his story, and he stood and repeated the main points: his shipwreck, the debt he owed to the people of Fisherhame and Caerpadraig, his inability to find his way back home.

'It seems I was blown so far off course that the place I came from is unknown here,' he concluded. It was easier to find his words now, though to speak like this to a throng was a challenge. Never, ever, had he been called upon to do so before, and here he was, speaking in what had become his second language. He began to find a new confidence, buoyed by the goodwill around him. One or two called to see the coat again. Aengas intervened.

'You have all seen the coat. Do not trouble the Ingleeshe more.'

They walked back to the town in darkness. Men lit torches from the fire to carry before them. Aengas, evidently pleased with the day, talked ceaselessly, while Micheil nodded and made occasional comments. John was quiet, allowing what he had seen and heard to sink into him. Gently, an unseen rain, soft and fine, enfolded them.

19

'Well, well. And now we can attend to this other matter, eh?' Aengas the son of Aengas looked at the stranger from beneath his red brows. Aengas' wife, tall and upright, had served them their first-food. John sweetened his porridge with honey, from an earthenware jar. 'The bees are working hard again,' she said. John had seen the skeps behind the house.

The town's shareg, Kefn, joined the three men as they sat outside the door. Aengas had his chair brought out, but his long shanks seemed unwilling to be folded up in sitting for long. It was barely a surprise to John when their conversation was punctuated again and again by the High Shareg springing to his feet as he strode back and forth, swinging his spare and powerful arms.

Micheil began with an account of John's appearing among them.

'Yes, yes, we know about this. Stories like this reach even here, you know.' The High Shareg smiled a smile that pressed his thin lips together, yet lit up his eyes. He turned to John. 'I'd like to hear from this Seaborne about where he has come from. What is your country like, eh, Dhion Ingleeshe?'

It was the question John now dreaded. Since their discussion in the shareg's house, since his conversation with Micheil on the way only two days before, he knew he could not avoid being disbelieved. Aengas' eyes searched him. He saw Kefn, fair-haired, big-boned, lean forward, one hand cupping his chin, the other resting on the pommel of his sword.

Before these men he could only be honest. 'Whenever I try to describe where I come from, I find it so different from your own land, High Shareg, that I'm in danger of being thought a liar, or mad. When I look around me for signs of my own world and can't find them, then I begin to wonder if I *am* mad.'

'We have seen madmen, Ingleeshe. They do not ask if they are mad.'

Those searching green eyes began to have a reassurance in their depths. John was emboldened to press on. Where to begin? He thought back to the most recent conundrum.

'I was talking with Shareg Micheil as we journeyed here about how many people live in my city. It is a number so large that he could not imagine it.'

The green eyes darted towards Micheil. 'It is true, Aengas. Dhion had me wonder how many heather leaves there are on the whole moor.'

Out of the corner of his eye John saw Kefn fix him with a questioning stare. But the High Shareg only tilted his head on one side as he considered this.

'Then your city must be the greatest city in the whole world.'

'Well, no.' John felt suddenly reckless with his truth. 'There are quite a few cities as big as London in my world – even bigger.'

He stopped, uncomfortably. The two sharegs said nothing. They waited for the High Shareg's lead.

'We have heard of a city called Lughndain,' said Aengas slowly, 'But it is not at all as you describe. The greatest city we know is called Rhuomè. Though for some six hundreds of years she has not been so powerful as she was, yet still she is great. She used to send her warriors even as far as the lands to the south of Sharilland.'

John paused. Rhuomè: could the High Shareg mean...? Aengas was watching him. John replied. 'Where I come from there is a city called Rome. But Rome ceased to be such a great power a lot more than six hundred years ago. There are many cities in my world now that are greater than Rome.'

Aengas sat back, a hand on his hip, the other cradling his chin. 'Hm. Greater than Rhuomè? We know of no cities like that. And many, you say?' He paused, thoughtfully. They all watched him. Then he raised his head and, in an even tone, continued. 'Something in the way you answered interests me particularly. You said, "In my world." Perhaps...' Another pause. He pursed his lips, then resumed evenly. 'Perhaps we should consider whether your world and this world that we are in now are... worlds apart.' The High Shareg looked at John, searchingly. 'Have you considered that?'

The words fell on John's ears like the slap of a wave. They drenched him with an import he had not dared to admit. Yet he knew it had been lurking under the surface of his thoughts. He found himself mentally reeling.

'I... I have not let myself think about that.'

He looked from the High Shareg to Micheil, whose face was unusually blank, empty. He sneaked a glance at Kefn. He was staring, his mouth open.

'Well – can anyone think of a better answer that fits with what we know?' The astonishing old man looked quizzically from one shareg to the other, back to John. 'Let's remind ourselves of what we *do* know. A man is found in the sea, barely alive. There is no sign of his boat, nor of others of his crew. He is wearing clothes the like of which have never been seen. As he recovers, he cannot understand a word of our speech, while he himself speaks a language no-one has heard of. In the wisdom of Father Hugh his coat is sent round the Island; quite besides the cloth it is made of, its fastenings alone are beyond the skill of the finest of our smiths. Now he talks of cities far larger than anything we have seen, or heard of.'

'If I may add to this, High Shareg?' John took a breath and plunged in. 'I've been looking out for – we call them aeroplanes. Like boats that fly in the air –' he felt himself blush '– all over the world. And over

139

this last year I've seen no sign of them.' Micheil and Kefn were visibly taken aback; Aengas did no more than raise his eyebrows a little. At this encouragement, John rushed, breathless, on. 'And – something that's puzzled me –' It came out in a surge: 'Father Hugh tells me that the Blessed Rortan came to this Island four hundred years ago, and told of the Chrisht who had lived six hundred years before that. Yet we hold that our Christ lived around twenty hundreds of years ago.'

He looked anxiously across at those penetrating eyes. He let out a sigh. 'I do not understand how this can be.'

'Well,' Aengas repeated. Was there, John wondered, the slightest smile on his lips? 'Can anyone answer this?'

Kefn's mouth was still open, but he did not speak. Nor did Micheil attempt to answer the question.

'If we speak of other worlds,' the High Shareg continued, 'you must understand, it is no more than a way of speaking. Another way would be to say that Dhion's knowledge of life does not flow into our own.'

'Father Hugh and his wife said the same,' John remembered.

'Did they?' said Aengas. 'Then they and I are thinking alike. Well, I do not understand it any better than you do. Does that matter? I am constantly surrounded by things I do not understand, even if I have grown used to them.'

He rocked back in his chair, then forward again.

'Who would try to invent such a story? What would they have to gain by it?' He looked round the circle. Suddenly John felt the silent presence of Aengas' wife, sitting in the doorway of the house, a little withdrawn into the shadows. She gave no sign, but John sensed that she heard, and wished to hear, and that she thought about what she heard.

'Let us imagine for a moment that what you say is truth, and see where that takes us,' Aengas continued. 'Let us imagine that your world is not our world.'

140

He turned fully towards John. 'If what you say is true, it seems to me that you are coming from a time that, for us, is yet to come.'

John stared at the High Shareg. Was this the solution to the puzzle he had lived with these last months? It seemed so impossible, and yet everything was impossible, and at least this was some way of speaking of his experience that could include all that he had seen and lived. A door had been shut fast in his mind and he had at last found a key that turned in its lock. But could he face what was within?

Kefn leaped to his feet. 'Aengas!' He faltered. 'High Shareg, this is not possible. No-one can believe it. There must be...' He hesitated, reddened, his lips quivering.

Aengas looked up, smiling, undisturbed. 'Well, do we have another answer? Come, sit down, Kefn. When we are faced with impossible facts, must we not look for impossible explanations? If you can find a better answer, we would be glad to hear it.'

He smiled. He laid a hand on Kefn's arm, giving it a squeeze. Then he turned back to John.

'But I have two more questions for you today, Dhion Seaborne.'

John wondered what he would say.

'You who have lived in this time to come, and have lived nigh a year with us now, can you say: is it a better world that you have come from?'

John had no ready answer. Was his a better world? It was a lot more comfortable – for him. He used to hear of countless others on the news every day for whom this was not so. It was a world that contained modern medicine. Delicious cuisine. Sprung mattresses, sofas and showers. Television. Trains and planes. Computers and phones. Power stations... Automation... Toilet paper. It was also a world where there was soil depletion, species extinction, unemployment, over-population, nuclear accidents, and oceans of plastic waste. He remembered

141

seeing a photograph of the remains of an albatross chick, its stomach full of nothing but plastic. Was his world better? As he struggled to find an answer, he was aware of a sense of the depth and simplicity of the life he had been living on the Island that tasted good; a deep honesty.

In the end, 'I don't know,' was his only answer.

Aengas smiled.

'My last question I do not expect you to answer either, but still I ask it. If indeed your world exists in a time to come, is it necessarily our time to come? Or might we go another way from here? And is there something we can learn from you that will help us to direct our steps?'

John wondered how to reply, but the High Shareg rose and turned towards his door. As he passed, he rested a hand on John's shoulder. 'Keep your speech for now. You will have plenty of time to ponder these things.'

The extraordinary old man looked around at them all. He smiled again. As he passed through the doorway, his wife rose.

20

After the midday meal Aengas took John aside. While Micheil and Kefn turned to sharegs' talk, the Ma'Haengas stretched his long limbs and led the way through the north gate and down the glen. It was a track John had not seen before, stretching seaward to the north. The path threaded between small fields, sheltered from the east wind by dark pine forests and watered by the burn, now almost a frothing and swirling river.

As they walked, the Ma'Haengas asked searching questions about that other world from which John had come. Now that they had faced the impossibility of his story, he found it easier to tell. Still, John thought, to Aengas it must have been like listening to a fairy-tale. Whether he believed or disbelieved, John could not tell. The question of belief seemed simply set aside. He felt he was being listened to, was being heard, while the High Shareg asked questions that amazed John with their vision.

Still, always, somewhere in the background, walking a few paces behind them, was that question: the question Aengas had closed their morning conversation with. Is this a better world, or just – different?

A huge rock thrust out from the valley side, forcing the burn to rush around its feet. A ford carried the path to the further bank, and they splashed through it together. Suddenly from beyond the rock a long and wide view opened out as the glen broadened and ran gently down to the hard grey sea. Boats and fishermen's huts dotted the shore.

They stood on the beach, looking out across the limitless ocean.

'There is much out there – more than I can guess – that I have no idea about.' The old man gave a sweep of his long arm. He laughed, short, hard, intense. 'I would have it no other way.'

He paused. 'You know you are by no means the first stranger to come among us.'

A flame of hope kindled in John, only to fade again as Aengas continued.

'I recall my grandfather telling me about the Northmen who would come raiding from time to time. Once, he told me, two longships were blown in a storm to the Island. They foundered on the out-skerries, not far from where you were picked up.' Aengas gazed into John's face.

'The wrecks were plundered, of course. They found some very strange things there.' The old man furrowed his brow. Then said, surprisingly, 'I wonder if you might be able to tell us more about them.'

What was coming? John's knowledge of Vikings was no more than sketchy.

'They had two stones. They floated them on wee rafts in bowls of water, and the stones would always point to the north. Have you ever heard the like?'

John smiled. How to begin to explain magnetism?

'Those who survived the wreck,' Aengas added, 'told us how the stones helped them sail the seas. They called them waystones – lodestones in their language. Well, no Islander wanted to sail so far, and the stones stayed in the shareg's keeping. Micheil has them now. You must ask him if you may see them.'

'I would like to see them,' said John. 'All our ships and planes use something like that.'

Aengas was quiet for a space, his hand stroking his long beard. 'Come.' He turned, and grasped John's shoulder firmly. 'I have something for you. A gift from my world to yours, if you like. Or perhaps it is more like a welcoming gift, as you come to dwell in our world.'

They turned again up the path; passed once more through the gate. They found Kefn and Micheil outside

144

Kefn's house. Small children played under the watchful eye of an older girl. At the sight of their coming, the two sharegs sprang to their feet. 'It is time,' Aengas said, and nodded to Kefn as if with a pre-arranged signal. The big man went ahead, the High Shareg following after, flanked by John and Micheil. Men came out of their houses or rose from benches as they passed, and followed behind, while women stood in their doorways and watched, silent, children hushed at their knees. What was the occasion?

They came again to the house of the High Shareg. Kefn went in while the others waited. A semicircle of men formed, keeping a respectful distance. John looked around. He might have been frightened, but over these two days he had grown to trust this old man with the long white beard and the most remarkable depth of perception. Still, he ran his tongue over dry lips.

'Dhion Ingleeshe, Seaborne, stranger from across the worlds, I welcome you among us. I place you under the cloak of Micheil, Shareg Caerpadraig. May you find your place among us here, and be faithful and brave to serve your shareg.'

John learned later that Aengas was uttering something very like the words used to welcome youths coming of age. The men present knew how to respond. There was a roar from the crowd. 'May it be!'

Now Kefn came forward. He carried a small black cooking pot. 'These are the gifts I was telling you about,' Micheil whispered in John's ear. The pot's little wrought-iron handles were threaded by a strong woven band, and the whole could be tied onto a man's back for ease of carrying. The High Shareg presented it to John.

Kefn returned to the house, and reappeared. In his left hand was a spear: seven feet of straight ash, set well into the socket of its iron head. In his right, a target of polished leather, studded with bronze in the intricate swirling and over-and-under patterning of the

Celt. Aengas took them. He presented the back of the shield to John. Micheil was at his side. 'Pass your left arm through the sling, and grasp the loop in your hand – that's right.'

Aengas placed the spear in John's right hand. 'Hunt well, fight well. Be brave, be wise.'

Micheil whispered again. 'Go down on one knee, and give your thanks.'

'My spear is yours to command, High Shareg.'

The old man took John's shoulders and raised him. He stepped back and surveyed him, and John was filled with the warmth of his regard.

John lay on his pallet near the fire on the pounded earth floor of the High Shareg's house. But for the dull glow of the embers, it was dark. Micheil's deep, regular breathing a few feet away was broken at intervals by a quiet snore. He stared sleepless up into the dark of the roof above. He could still feel the solidity of the spear in his hand, the weight of the targe on his forearm; still smell the tang of new leather, feel the emotion in his heart.

He turned over and over the words of the High Shareg: was his a world apart? But which *was* his world now? It was a hard life, here in this brave new world that seemed so old, where children died and old men must work hard to live, and women feared childbirth. Yet it was a world where everything was done for a reason you could understand; where you could see the connexions between things. By a miracle, he found himself here. And it seemed that this world would receive him. A voice from that other world drifted through his mind: Nicodemus ironically questioning, 'Can a man enter the womb again and be born a second time?'

John was dying. Perhaps he had started to die from the moment he awoke in Fengoelan's house nearly a year before. Perhaps he had not noticed until this night how inch by inch another being was growing within him. In the place of that frightened London engineer called John Finlay there was, slowly forming, another man. Not yet an Islander – that was clear whenever he spoke. But someone who seemed to occupy a world between worlds, journeying out of one, and into another. A being, still forming, still untried, who was even now making his uncertain way from the safe and restricting comfort of the care bestowed on him, through a difficult and painful passage, before emerging into a bright and cold and dangerous world. A world where so much could be possible.

John slept. By the morning, another being arose from his pallet. A being who would walk with him, sometimes content to stay in the background, but more and more confident as the months went by to ease the old John aside and speak in his place. A man called Dhion.

They left after a hearty breakfast of porridge, this time filled with lumps of mutton and neeps to strengthen them for the journey. By now, he had become accustomed to such fare, and had all but lost the craving for potatoes, pasta or rice, that used to assail him. The fine grey drizzle that darkened their cloaks as they left slowly eased, and before they stopped for their midday meal the sun was shining bravely between the clouds. Late in the afternoon of the fourth day from their setting out, they walked back into Caerpadraig. Aileen received them with a welcome beaker of ale, and brought in a plate of hot bannocks straight from the griddle, filling the house with the warm fragrance of baking.

Hugh joined them soon, and he and Micheil spoke long over what the High Shareg had said. At last Hugh rose, and tapped Dhion's shoulder. The priest turned, glancing back towards the shareg. 'We will talk again about this, Micheil.'

As Dhion took his leave of the shareg he felt how much had passed, how much had changed, in his feeling towards him.

'He's become someone I'd fight for,' he said to Hugh, when they were back in the familiar house that was, for now, his home.

'I hope these fine gifts of yours aren't giving you… ideas?' Hugh returned. 'Are you learning how to use them? For that's an art I can't much help with.'

'Well – I've learned how to cross a river.'

'You didn't stand upon your targe and let it bear you across the flood?' Hugh exchanged a gleam with his wife. 'That's an act ascribed to the Blessed Rortan.'

'Rather more ordinary than that,' rejoined Dhion, 'and wetter. But as we were returning today, Micheil showed me how to stalk the deer. We never caught one, but –'

'But a rather more useful skill for everyday than what some of the young men imagine they'll use their weaponry for.'

Dhion gazed into the fire, while the crackling of the flames filled the silence. 'Do you never, then, have any…' He sought for the phrase that Aengas had used, two days before and so far away. 'Any – blood-battles here?'

Hugh sighed. 'Long ago, when the High Sharegs were weak and no-one respected them, and the shareg of each township was law in himself, then there were from time to time real wars between towns, and men would go out and kill each other in the name of their God, squabbling over this patch of moorland or the fishing along that stretch of coastline. Even today, a town may believe its cause to be so right that they ignore the High Shareg's ruling. Then the High Shareg will take men from every town and village, except those in dispute, and bring a force against them. But I don't remember the last time that ended in bloodshed.'

Morag looked up. 'Years ago, men would come from another land, across the sea. They came in dragon-ships, with a shield at every oar-port. They would come at harvest and raid along the coast – especially down Caerster way. Then men would fight for their lives, and the lives of their families. Still today they train and practice. There is a need for it – though not as much as the young men would like.

'But the evening grows late,' she went on, 'and we should not close on a note of bloodshed and separation. See what I've been doing while you've been away.'

She rose and, taking a light, led Dhion across the room to where her work was stretched on its wooden frame. Gently, as Hugh came up behind them, she removed the sailcloth cover.

The Island glowed, in colours of heather and moor-land, crop-field and pasture, lough and ocean, seeming to float above the sea of rough linen which held it. The yellow light of the lamp brought out its earth-tones and rock-hues, flickering like fitful sunlight upon the hills.

'Here is your Island,' she whispered.

For a long moment Dhion could say nothing. 'Is it finished?'

'Not yet,' she replied. 'There is much of the sea to complete yet, and the waves and the boats and the fishes. But yesterday I finished the Island itself. Look – this is where we are: here.' She pointed to a spot, high on the left side, where she had woven a cluster of tiny houses into the fabric.

'Here is our home.'

THE SECOND PART:
APPRENTICE

21

The kernstones growled, one upon the other. Morag heard the familiar sound as she paused at Shareen's door. Since the fire, Shareen had been living with her dead husband's parents, and within a week the men of the town had built a side chamber to the modest dwelling to house her and her two children.

Morag called the greeting. Ducking her head to step into the low room, she saw the young widow with Fineenh, sitting on the floor, the stones between them. Shareen was working the handstone while the older woman fed barley grain into the mill. It was good, she thought, that Fineenh kept the widow company.

Morag sat beside them. As they worked they chatted about this and that: about the weather turning warmer, the children and their doings, the health of the grandparents who were now becoming frail.

'The town is looking after all of us,' said Shareen. She frowned, and shook her head. 'I do all I can.'

'And it's hard work,' said Morag. 'We know.'

The talk turned back to the fire that had taken so much from her; and from there to the Seaborne, who had burst so dramatically into Shareen's life.

'How he went in and saved my Colin I don't know.'

Fineenh took up this thread with energy. 'The things my man told me he said, there with the shareg and the Father. And you were there too, A'Phadr, I hear?' Fineenh shot Morag a curious glance. 'He said he used to work things in iron to make wheels for things that they have instead of carts, and where he lived there are no carts, but only these things, and no horses to pull them… I'm sure I don't know how it will be when he is roofed with us.'

Shareen stared, wide-eyed. Morag was silent. She sensed she should not risk adding to the young woman's amazement. She could not understand it herself.

Shareen had stopped grinding, the wooden peg clutched in her hand. 'Do you think…?' she began. 'He's so tall and strange – and the way he went into all that smoke when no-one else could – not even Murdogh, and you know what he's like. You don't think he could be one of the elder ones, do you? One of the fey-folk, come among us?'

'Och, get away with you, girl. Of course he's not. You heard what he was like at harvest. You don't believe the *Sidhe* would wave a scythe about the way he did, do you?'

'No, of course not.' Shareen turned her gaze down to her task, slipped the peg back in its hole and started the stone turning again. 'But still…'

Morag walked slowly down to the lough. A fitful wind had sprung up in the east, pushing back the first warmth of spring. She thought how nothing she could do would stop its sweep. Nothing she could say about Dhion's stories of his land would make things right in people's minds. On the water, sharp little waves chased each other, breaking noisily on the shore.

It was agreed that Dhion would be roofed with the smith after Easter. In the few weeks that remained, Morag told him the tales of their own land: how each different kind of tree and flower had its place, and its lesson to be learned. How the clouds spoke of what weather was to come. How one sort of land could be trusted, but where the cotton-grass grew and the moss was yellow was where you durstn't tread.

She took him some nights into the rondal, when Aileen would take her harp, and, drawing a long chord from the strings, begin to sing. It was more a chant, slow and solemn, and the words, though known to

Dhion, sounded strange. And indeed they were in the speech of generations past. Aileen sang of the Time before Time, and of the Tuatha Dé Danann, the children of Danu, who came among the Beings of Chaos and brought order and beauty to the world.

Dhion commented afterwards, 'We tell a different story out of our... Book.'

Another night Aileen told the lay of Broha and his wooing of Choidhleena, she who was enthralled to the wolf-lord, Ar. And how Ar, finding them together one summer's night, had pursued Broha long days across the mountains, until they stood together on Beh' Talor Gan, looking out across the sea. Then Ar, in a rush of anger, came at Broha across the moss, not heeding the Hag of the Mountain: she who draws men down into her ever-hungry throat with toothless jaws. To this day, when people see small white clouds form over the brow of Talor Gan, they say they are the spirits of them who went to meet the Hag. And when a strong wind blows from across the sea, a fell cloud takes shape and rushes down into the valley of Caerpadraig. That, they say, is the wolf-lord, still hunting for Broha.

They told him other tales – of the testing of Goel, son of Broha and Choidhleena, and of Padraig's wanderings in Westerland, and how he set down his pack on a rock and founded there the town that bears his name.

But it was at Shean's house that Morag taught him the tale of Callen-Barg the silver-haired. She had taken Dhion to meet the family, as a preparation for the time when he would be roofed with them. When she mentioned that he was learning the old tales, Fineenh asked, 'Have you told him my own name-tale?'

'Not yet,' said Morag.

'Then may we not hear it now?'

So Morag began to tell: how Callen had been a prince in a far country, and leaving his own land and his father's house, after long travels he came to the western shore, ever driven by a restlessness of heart. Taking ship, he was wrecked here upon the Island. Still he journeyed on, and came to the westernmost part of the Island, and said, 'Now is my heart at rest, for I have found the place of my soul.' Morag told of the love that sprang up between Callen and Fineenh, the freckled and club-footed maid, and of how the people of that place, knowing him for a stranger, would not let him have her. So her father said, 'Let the ocean decide.' They took him to the seashore, and put him in a boat, with oars and sail, and towed him far out beyond sight of land, and set him forth. Fineenh saw all this from the clifftop, and there she stayed, waiting and watching.

Now the sea rose, and Callen-Barg spoke to the sea. 'Lord, I am upon thee as a babe upon its mother, but my deep desire is to return and be with Fineenh again, until the deep earth welcome us.'

Then the sea replied, 'What will you give me, if I take thee back to her?'

'See,' said Callen, 'I will give thee these fine oars.' The sea took the oars.

Then the wind rose, and asked, 'What will you give me?' and Callen-Barg spoke with the wind, and offered his sail. And the wind took the sail.

Then came fire from the sky, and lit up the sea and the boat and all around. He spoke with the fire. And the fire took the boat.

Now Fineenh had not left the cliff-top, but stood standing there and weeping, while the wind blew and the rain fell upon her. Three days she waited, ever looking out to sea, hoping to see the white sail returning. And as she looked, she saw a man on the shore, cast up by the waves. And she ran and took up Callen-Barg in her arms and brought him once more into her father's house.

When the people came before him, Fineenh's father spoke: 'The ocean has decided.'

'The ocean has decided,' the people said, and they welcomed Callen-Barg among them.

He and Fineenh had many children, and the people made him shareg over them. He became High Shareg, the first who ever reached out his cloak over the whole Island.

'That is the tale of Callen-Barg the silver-haired, and of Fineenh, mother of sharegs,' Morag ended.

'And it's after this Fineenh that I'm named. And all your father ever gave me was one good-for-nothing daughter.' Fineenh pushed playfully at Shinane, sitting beside her, very quiet; then rose, smoothing out her skirts, and went to replenish their cups. Morag looked across at the young woman. A memory rose, of the day she had seen her at the lectern in the rondal, gazing at the Book. Shyly, the girl raised her eyes. Morag smiled.

'What do you think of the stories you are learning?'

Morag was polishing the woodwork in the rondal, rubbing warmed candle-wax into a deep shine. She had instructed Dhion to hold the Book, which must never rest in any lowly place, while she finished the lectern, and now he watched her as her shoulders worked.

Dhion hesitated. 'I enjoy them,' he said, guardedly. Then, 'They are strange to me, Mora. I can understand testing a man by making him go out on the sea alone. But I don't understand why that man would give up his means of getting back – and I can't believe that, after all that, he'd survive anyway. Still, I do enjoy them,' he finished, as if to reassure her.

Morag did not lift her head from her work. 'We do it for more than enjoyment. The tales are important. They carry meaning.' Her voice, without her face and smile to mellow it, sounded almost tart.

She straightened herself and beckoned Dhion to place the Book back on its rest, reverently, as he had been shown. She met his eye. 'The tales hold us together, and they hold our wisdom. Without them we would know our world less well, understand one another not so closely. Do you not have such tales in your own land? What tales does your Book hold?'

'Well, yes, we do tell stories,' said Dhion. He hesitated. 'And when Hugh tells the tales that Rortan brought, about the life of Ioshu – I do recognise some of those. But, Morag, there are no stories any more that everyone has to know, the way you tell me everyone here knows these.'

'So what guides your lives?' She was watching him.

He looked down at the carefully woven rush mats beneath their feet. 'We each have to find our own way,' he answered. He raised his eyes to meet hers. 'And, in truth, not all of us manage. I think I myself was not managing when the accident happened that has brought me among you.'

She paused, letting his words settle. Then she said,

'It seems to me that when you hear these stories, you do not know how to take them into yourself. All you take in is the bare thing that happened to you yesterday or the day before. So you learn on one level how to be among us. But on a deeper level, you remain ignorant.'

Still her eyes were upon him. He felt uncomfortable, and answered nothing.

'Dhion,' she said.

He looked back at her.

'What do you think about the story of the Blessed Rortan, when he came to the Island borne on the backs of whales?'

Slowly, he shook his head.

'You dismiss the story. I feel it in you. You don't consider that this picture may carry meaning that does not appear on the surface.'

He frowned.

'So will you hear me when I tell you that for us, the whale is the Keeper of the Deep. And when we hear of Rortan brought on the backs of these Guardians, we know that what he brings us rises from the deepest source, and we pay attention to it from the depths of our own being. Deep calling to deep. If you dismiss the story, you deny yourself this understanding. What we are doing when we tell the stories – when we remember them between their telling – gives to each man and woman and child among us a space in which to join with something we could never find with our chattering minds. This gives value to our lives.'

Morag grasped his shoulders, looked into his eyes. 'Dhion, I have sensed this in you. You lack a steering oar. We are trying to give you one, but you have to take hold of it.'

She stepped back.

'I'm all right, Morag. Really.'

'No, you're not!' Dhion felt the strength and passion in her reply. 'The way you go running over the hills as you do! If, just on an outward level, you don't heed those stories, then you don't know what dangers to be careful of. Nor how to avoid them. Do you not remember the Hag of the Mountain?'

Dhion nodded. 'Yes, *She who draws men down with her toothless jaws*. It's a frightful story, and –'

'And you need to believe it, as all our men do. For she is very real. It hasn't happened for a long time now – not while Hugh and I have been here. But now and then a hunter may forget, in the excitement or the weariness of the chase. He will never come home. These stories matter for you, here and now.'

She smiled, breaking the tension. 'Come. It must be midday. You deserve some food.'

He watched her as she stood. Against the curve of the wall a great outcrop of granite bulged out of the ground. They called it the Mother. The cross – the only cross in the rondal, equal-armed, encircled – lay upon it. She bowed deeply to the cross. She knelt on the rushes and leaned forward to kiss the rock. She straightened, turned, and led him out.

159

22

Mother Coghlane had forgotten how old she was. It was an irrelevance, and it did not concern her. She was grateful to have lived enough years on this earth to acquire wisdom, and some left over to use it. She stood before the door of her solitary home and called. One by one the sheep answered. They came, from brakes of fern or from behind boulders, their full udders swinging, their voices as individual and their faces as distinctive to the old woman as any human's. She sat on a rock, while they jostled for position then stood patiently while she pulled on their dugs, the white milk hissing and frothing into the leather pail.

The last one raised her head. Then shaking her tail she took a few steps, listening. All five sheep were standing alert, their faces turned down the valley. Now Coghlane heard it too. Footsteps. The alternate splash and suck and clatter of a man's feet as he trod, now in the edge of the stream, now in the peat mire or on loose stone, climbing up to the tarn.

Few people came this way, and nobody passed through. Those who climbed the high path to her lodge in the arms of the mountain had her as their destination, or they were well lost.

A face appeared over the dull green lip of the land, and the sheep cantered away up the hill a little, to turn and stand and see what kind of intruder this would be. As the figure rose into view Coghlane recognised the brown cloak covering the cassock of a priest, kilted for the rough journey. From time to time a priest, or even a shareg, would visit her from any of a dozen settlements, to spend a day or two or sometimes more, in the bothy that perched beneath the mountain wall up above her house. They would wrestle with their thoughts, seek new insights, or simply rest in the silence. She knew this tall thin shape. She went forward to meet him.

'Father – you are welcome.'

'Mother, a blessing,' said Hugh. 'It's a long climb.'

'You're getting old and lazy from your lowland ways.' She embraced him and they kissed. 'Come inside.'

He entered and sat quietly as she brought in the frothing pail and carefully covered it. She moved without hurry, bending now to light the lamp.

'Come – rest a while. We can talk later. There is nothing that can't wait until you've eaten.'

She set a wooden plate on the board, with girdle-cakes and sheep's-milk cheese, hard and strong and yellow. Hugh gave her the small sack of oats he had brought with him, and a clay pot sealed with wax.

Coghlane raised her eyebrows and shot him a glance. 'Honey?'

She asked after the townsfolk. 'How is Micheil? And Aileen? How is Morag?' Only she knew the tug of her heart as she asked after Morag. 'Is she getting on with her tapestry, that wife of yours?'

Hugh seemed content to share the small-talk of the town as he finished his meal. She set a beaker of warm milk beside him. He drained the cup while she tidied away the wooden platters. Then she gathered her shawl about her and sat.

'Now. What is on your mind?'

Hugh told her of Dhion: of his arriving and his recovery, of his quick intelligence but complete ignorance of their way of life, of what he said about his own land. Then he told her what Micheil had reported of the High Shareg's words.

'I have known some who have come through sickness who for a time could not remember where they were or what had happened,' he concluded. 'But Dhion remembers. It is *what* he remembers that is the puzzle.

And, to my mind, the High Shareg's answer raises as many questions as it solves.'

'It is strange,' Coghlane agreed. She looked down at her apron, considering. Then, with a quick movement, she raised her head and looked directly at her visitor. 'But strange things, if true, are no different from the commonplace. Usually we can tell if it is madness or lies. Sometimes what we think we know must be re-thought and re-wrought.'

She paused. 'When he tells you his story – how does he seem?'

Hugh shook his head. 'He has not told me everything – but who does? Much, I feel, is because he does not yet have the words. But what he has told me… Well, in my heart as he is telling it – I believe him. I believe in the man, you understand?' He looked at her earnestly. 'His words are strange. But he… *he* is not false.'

They talked on, into the evening, while the sky deepened into star-speckled blackness.

'Sleep here by the fire this night and rest, and tomorrow I will send you to your bothy,' said Coghlane. 'We must both think on these things.'

She set down a pallet for Hugh while he washed at the edge of the tarn, then left him settling himself for sleep. Alone with the deep sky she sat, silent, gazing out into the vastness.

The next morning, they sat together on low stools just within the door, looking out over the fall of land beyond the tarn. A grey veil of rain dimmed and smudged the horizon, while beyond, yellow morning light was beginning to seep round the edges of the cloud-mass. Hugh had come to the end of his telling. He had laid out the perplexities that the strange visitor had brought into his life. The many roads of thought, each ending in a blind alley. And this last road that Dhion had brought back from his visit to the High Shareg: had the man come from another world altogether? Or a future time?

Or both? And what could that mean? They had spoken of it among themselves, he and Morag and Micheil, turning it over and over. But it was not a thought that could be shared more generally, for no-one, not Hugh, certainly not Micheil, could understand it.

Coghlane watched the face of her visitor, saw the trouble in his eyes. What was it that his soul needed?

In the silence of her mind she scanned the worlds. A thought came to her. She took breath.

'Where did the Blessed Rortan come from?' she asked him.

He stared at her. 'Why do you ask me that? Of course I know the answer: I catechise the town children with such questions. We say, it is a mystery.'

'Yes. That is what you say. And you are content to leave it there?'

She watched him take a breath. 'The story that he rode on the backs of whales. That is a tale that speaks of the closeness of the saint to the other worlds of being among us. It may have taken birth from an everyday truth – I have heard stories of whales and dolphins nosing drowning fishermen closer into shore until they can stagger to the beach. I have always found it strange, though, that a story never grew around where he came from. I do not know. And I admit, that disturbs me.'

He fixed her with those penetrating eyes, and she noticed the skin around his mouth tighten, pucker. Gently, she returned his gaze. Then, 'Why does it disturb you?' she inquired.

Hugh's fingers tapped against each other. His eyes strayed out over the sheep as they grazed in the grey morning, while Coghlane leaned back, her hands in her lap, watching him. She felt the lightest shimmer of mischief pass through her.

At last Hugh spoke. 'He came from another land, that no-one had ever heard about. I cannot say more.'

'And that disturbs you, that you cannot say more?'

'Yes, it does. Yes, partly because people look to me, for answers, for knowledge, for wisdom. And I have to admit there are limits to my knowledge and wisdom; boundaries that are in fact not so far beyond other people's as they think. But also because I want to know. I am not content with mysteries. A mystery may be a humble response in our lack of knowledge, but it only serves us for a time: it awaits knowledge.'

Coghlane let this settle between them. Then she commented, 'So when the people realise that even you do not have all the answers, they grow a little, and do not remain as children. I too do not have all the answers, Hugh. We face the Mystery together.'

She watched Hugh sit back; felt herself tighten with the tension in him; deliberately relaxed her own body.

'Mother – if Dhion really comes from another world, as the High Shareg thought – how did he get from there into our world?'

She paused. Tilted her head to one side, musing. An idea was coming in on the edge of her inner seeing. It did not taste like an Island thought. But that was not so unusual for her. She was no longer a person who felt strongly the limitations of time or place.

'Was there ever a moment when you knew that a different choice would have made you a different man?' she asked.

Hugh frowned. 'I could have stayed in comfort with my wealthy family and married a woman of standing there, instead of coming to dwell in an out-of-the-way place with the woman of my heart, who never knew her parents.'

Coghlane shifted, ever so slightly.

'I've never regretted my choice.'

The moment passed, and Coghlane let out her breath. She said, 'Could it be that every time we make a choice, two worlds part company and go their separate ways – the world we chose, and the world that might have been?'

She watched him. She felt his discomfort.

There was silence for a while. 'Mother,' he began, slowly, 'why are we talking like this? We began with Dhion, and then you asked me about Rortan. Now we have got on to mysteries, and other worlds that multiply themselves without bound.' With a sudden gesture, he reached for a wooden bowl that lay beside them on the strewn herb. He picked it up, waved it in the air, placed it firmly again on the ground. 'This is real. This world where I pick up a bowl. And I know where it comes from and what it is for. In the same way, I know that you and I are sitting here together now. There is no world in which I stayed at home.'

He looked into her eyes. She felt his desire for an answer like a physical force, hanging in the air between them. She looked down, unable to give him what he longed for. 'Perhaps you are right,' she murmured. 'You see what winding paths we stray down when we try to think about what is beyond our seeing. And so, I don't know.'

She waited.

'Do you mean, then, that Rortan, and maybe Dhion as well, have come from another world, which is like ours but different because of its different history?'

'World, or worlds. History, or histories. It may sound unlikely, but is it impossible? I do not know that.'

'All right. But in any case, I still ask, how did they get out of that world, and into this?'

She felt his force, almost as a glare.

She looked up again, this time with new energy. 'In the end,' she told him, 'I wonder how much this *how* matters. How does this *how* make a difference to what we need to do now – to what is being called forth?'

'Well,' Hugh began. Then he stopped.

'Do you intend to go travelling to new worlds your-self, that you need to know how?' she demanded. The space between them was taut, tense.

Her voice softened. 'Is the desire to understand *how* anything more than a wish for all to be ordered? For all to be within our power to direct?' she asked, gently.

Their eyes met.

'We all wish for such power,' she said.

Her little body suddenly uncoiled and she touched his shoulder as she straightened. Passing further into the dwelling, where the walls were the living rock of the mountain itself, she took a pot from under a big unglazed bowl, its upturned rim in water. She poured milk into two beakers, and balanced an oatcake on the rim of each.

'That is enough for one day,' she told him. 'There's plenty to be pondering. You know how you will spend your time?'

'I have much to think over. But I think better on my feet. I expect I will walk far over the mountain. You see – the rain is over.'

'Then be careful how you walk. Walk with God in your heart. Think with God and fast with God, and at the day's end rest in Ghea.'

'Come back tomorrow,' she told him, 'in the morn-ing. We will talk further, and then I will send you on your way.'

He stooped to kiss her. She watched him set off, trudging along the side of the tarn, stepping carefully among the stones as he scaled the sloping wall of the corrie. Then she turned. There was work to be done.

'Mother,' began Hugh, 'I know less about God today than I did ten years ago. Every time I come here, it seems I uncover more that I did not know of my ignor-ance.'

Coghlane nodded. She had given him a good breakfast to prepare him for his return, a porridge filled with roots and seeds. 'That is as it should be,' she said, and waited.

She watched sunlight touch the tops of the few trees that could be seen from the house, small and stunted and gnarled. Watched Hugh, who seemed not to be noticing anything outside himself. Saw him stiffen, fix her with an intense stare:

'These boundless worlds of possibilities,' he insisted. 'Can God be in all of them, and still be the same God?'

'Perhaps not the same God in the thoughts of those who live in different places and times. But those are only thoughts. There is an Is-ness that makes any place or time possible, and what can we say about that? Again, do we not find ourselves standing before Mystery?'

'Oh Mother,' exclaimed Hugh, 'tell me what you think. Where do you think Dhion has come from – another land in this world, or from another world altogether?'

She looked at him for a long heart's breath. 'Hugh, you know that I cannot tell you where this man has come from. So my question to you is, can you stop worrying about it? Go away now. Listen to what he says, and listen with respect. Then get on with what is to be done now. That is all. Can you let it be all?'

She looked up into anxious eyes. She made a little rueful grimace. Then, as she watched the tall priest, his face relaxed. She felt he had let something go.

23

Cloud after soft grey cloud rolled in from the ocean and brushed the top of Beh' Mora. The drizzle filled the air and pearled the fleeces of the sheep on the hillside. In the town, smoke seeping through thatch mingled with the water in the air and brought the tang of burning peat down to the ground. In the house by the rondal, Dhion helped Morag clear away the midday meal. Hugh was away in the north. 'He goes from time to time, when something is troubling him,' Morag told him. Without Hugh, life was quiet.

Now, for want of anything better to do, Dhion was leaning against the jamb of the door, watching the rain make endless interlacing circles in the puddles pooling on the ground. To his right, the stone wall of the rondal glistened wetly. The saw-pit was silent. The wattle dwellings behind were a dejected huddle. And beyond, the strath disappeared into distance under the cloud-laden sky.

'Dhion.' The sound of Morag's clear voice cut into his mood. 'You could call again on the smith today if you want. You could ask to watch him at work. If you're to be his prentice, it would be good for you to know each other better before he takes you on. You don't hear him easily, do you?'

'His voice sounds rough, and sometimes I find it difficult to know his words.'

'Then the practice will do you good. What do you think?'

'I think I would like to know him better. Still, is there nothing I can help you with here?'

'Oh yes. You can help me carry the tapestry frame across to Aileen's. Then you can sit down and talk with the women all afternoon and get in the way.' She grinned. 'Go on – go and learn some smithing, and then you can tell me how it's done. But help with the frame before you go would be welcome.'

He took his cloak – the same that had wrapped his gifts from the people of the Island. Reluctantly, he strapped on the wooden platforms he was growing accustomed to for keeping his shoes out of the mud, and set out, glad of the cloak's enfolding heaviness as he splashed between the houses of the town. When he reached the forge, he put his head round the big door and called the greeting. The smith was drawing a dawn-red billet of hot metal from the fire. Shean answered without looking round.

'Welcome in God's name, Ingleeshe.' He rested the metal, and turned. 'It's a grey day you've brought with you. Come in and dry yourself.'

Dhion stood gratefully with his back to the forge-fire, while steam rose from the woollen cloak. If the smith was still suspicious of him, he gave no sign. As if understanding the purpose of his visit, Shean talked as he worked.

'It must be that red, no less, before you quench it.' The iron in his tongs hissed viciously as the water seethed around it. 'And then you must return it to the fire and watch its colour change. Make it too hot, or not hot enough, and it won't hold its edge.'

Dhion watched Shean working. He clearly knew his business, and Dhion appreciated the skill with which he forged a bit of hot metal into shape with a few strokes of the hammer. He saw that the work needed strength as well as craft, and that he would not find Shean's power in his own body for a good while. He hoped the smith would be willing to break him in gradually.

After a little, Dhion went to inspect the range of work on the shelf by the forge door. There were brackets and hinges and nails ready for the carpenter, a pair of sconces of iron basket-work for a well-to-do cowman in the town, and a good range of boat furniture to go over the hill to Fisherhame.

'Do you not turn any work on a...' Dhion knew no word for lathe. He mimed a spinning piece of metal and brought a finger of his other hand against it like a cutter.

The smith chuckled. 'They may turn wood in Midland, and away in Caerster. But iron? Iron's too hard. You couldn't spin it fast enough, or evenly enough. No, Ingleeshe, lathes are for wood, not iron.'

Shean wiped his hands on a rag, and pulled a leather jerkin around him. 'Come through and have a bite,' he said.

So for the second time, Dhion entered the house adjoining the forge. It was like so many others in the town. They were bigger, and better-built than the round-houses of Fisherhame. The single room was warmed by a small fire, and around the walls hung three thick curtains that Dhion supposed covered alcoves or side chambers.

Shean's rosy-cheeked wife was sitting by the fire, cutting neeps for their meal. Dhion greeted her as he had been taught: 'God's peace to you, A'Shean.'

She rose. 'The peace of Ghea with you, Ingleeshe,' she replied, settling down again to her work. 'Ye'll for-give me if I go on wi' the neeps.' She turned her head and called, 'Shinane – leave that and take off your apron. We have company.'

The tall, slim girl who had sat so quietly during his first visit with Morag now entered from behind one of the curtains. Dhion remembered the times he had seen her before: the girl outside the shareg's house, the girl in the rondal. The girl who looked him in the eye.

'Shinane – bring some girdle-cakes – and a little butter.' The mother fussed and flustered. Her daugh-ter kept her eyes down as she served food to the men. Dhion looked at her face. For a moment the sea-grey eyes flashed at him with curiosity.

Shean munched a cake. Through the crumbs he began, 'Is it so that among your people, not only are there carts that go by themselves, but also there are boats that move without sails? And no oars either?' Shean leaned forward with his question, and fixed Dhion doubtfully. 'Now, how can that be?'

How could it be, indeed, to explain this to a man who had never seen an engine?

Dhion looked about him for inspiration. Beside him, A'Shean was attacking a large turnip. 'If I may,' he asked, and picked up a half. With his knife he pared off a thin slice and cut it almost to the centre three times. He bent each segment like the blades of a propeller, holding the angle in place with his fingers. 'This turns in the water and drives the boat forward.' He tried to demonstrate twisting and forward-movement at the same time. He dropped the slice of turnip.

Shean furrowed his brow. He cupped his hand, trying to mimic the turning of the screw. 'But what turns the...' He looked up, his face a picture of puzzlement. 'Och, come on man! Tell me, then – how do you turn the turnip?'

There was a small commotion from across the room. Shean's daughter appeared to be choking. Her hand was across her mouth and her shoulders shook. Her mother turned attentively to her. But Dhion could see that the girl's eyes were streaming, not with pain, but with frantically suppressed laughter.

Hugh returned. Easter came, and the township gathered for the great celebration. It was the time, Hugh said, to welcome new life from seed, from womb and egg; new life from the tomb. The next day, Micheil took Dhion, and Hugh with him, to Shean's door. He handed him over to the smith as his apprentice.

The work-day started early. The morning after Dhion was roofed, he was still lying on his pallet near the great forge-fire, warm from the last day's work, when the door from the house creaked open and Shean stamped in. Towering over him, he kicked him with his leather boot. Not hard, but Dhion felt the strength of the man shake his chest and he leapt up, clutching his cloak about him.

'Right. Your first lesson,' glowered the smith. 'You rise betimes, and light the fire. That's your first task, every day, unless I tell you in the evening that we won't be needing it. Is that clear?' Slowly he relented. 'Come. Put your clothes on while I find some wood, and I'll show you how I want it done.'

As Shean came in laden with small wood and a few logs, Dhion reached for the leather apron the smith had given him the night before.

'No, no. Not the apron. Not yet. The apron's for smithing work. This is bairns' stuff.'

He showed Dhion how to lay the fire, with two logs side by side, a tunnel between them filled with shavings from Leighan's pit, and kindling laid over as a kind of roof; then small roundwood, and finally larger logs; how to blow up the embers to catch a flame onto the shavings, and to nurture the infant fire as it grew.

'You must be like a mother to a bairn – talk to it, help it, love it. And don't tell the wife I said that.' He winked.

'Now – while the fire's drawing, I want you to sweep the floor, and tidy everything ready for the day's work. While I see if the porridge is ready.'

The fire was beginning to warm the workshop, and Shean put his head round the door.

'Come on, come on. Your first-food's getting cold.'

They sat, the two of them on stools in the middle of the house with steaming bowls of gritty brown porridge, while the wife and her daughter clattered behind the curtain.

'You've done ironwork for horses' tackle before, I take it?' began Shean.

'No, I haven't. We don't… we don't see many horses where I come from.'

'No, nor round here. Not like down Caerster way. They say down there that the smiths do nothing but make tackle for the fine folk's horses. But the shareg has a pair, and there are a few ponies up in some of the hill crofts. Well, Micheil has a new horse ready for working. I measured him a couple of days ago, and this morning we must get the billet ready and forged.'

They talked over their first-food of what was to be done that day. But when the smith asked him about his own previous work and Dhion tried to describe it, he noticed Shean's eyes soon glaze over.

'Come on,' he said, cutting across Dhion's attempted explanation. 'There's work to be done.' He rose with a sudden surge, placing his bowl on his stool, and strode out of the door. Hurriedly, Dhion gulped the last of his porridge and followed his new master to the forge.

At last the night came, and Dhion was alone in the cavernous warmth of the workshop. He looked back over the long day; back to the previous day's Roofing. It was the same simple ceremony that he remembered from a year before when he had left Fengoelan's house. Then, in his own mind, he had been going from one temporary place of shelter to another; somewhere for the time being, until he would be rescued and returned to the life he knew. Now, it was a different matter. That hope was all but dead within him; and the man who had clung to it was becoming a fading memory, while the new man grew, fed every moment by the world he met daily. So far as his present life was concerned, he was now leaving the one place that had become to him a home and a haven, where he had felt himself held by people who believed in him, even if they could not understand his story. His sense of present loss underlined the sense of separation from that impossibly distant home he had run away from, still ever in the background of his thoughts.

And the place he had come to? At once he missed the grace of Hugh and Morag's way of being. His pallet would now lie in no living space with a tapestry frame in one corner and a book-stand in another, but in a workplace, surrounded by the tools of a hard trade. Here, among the bellows and tongs, the hammers and rivets, would he lie down at night and wake in the morning. Helen used to complain that he lived on his job. Now, he really was going to. But even as he felt the desolation of these thoughts seeping into him, they were chased by another.

There was a part of him – and this too was a part that was still John Finlay – that, for the first time since he had come among these people, sensed recognition, familiarity of a kind in his new surroundings of iron, and of iron tools. These might not be such as he was used to, but still, they were tools. Something in him sensed that he was in a place where, in time – and maybe not a very long time – he would be able to show that he could be more than a grown-up child in need of constant help. He sensed that, indeed, he could have something to give back. He might even have something to teach them.

He turned over, felt the warmth that the hearth still held. He slept.

24

That first week at the forge, Dhion found himself using his body and mind in new ways. He was glad to be back with the smell and sound of metal, the feeling of making something he could hold. But under-used muscles were aching by nightfall. In the evenings, left to his own thoughts, memories of his past pushed to the fore, unresolved. They would turn over and over, snatching away his sleep. By the time First-Day came again, he was more than ready for the rest. So it was with a sense of relief that, after Tollagh, he accepted Hugh and Morag's invitation to walk with them. The year was warm and dry. The grass along the lough-side was growing strong, and the fat black cattle contentedly chewed the cud. The air was full of the scent of their breath.

'I have been piecing together what happened to me, and what I did, in the time before Fengoelan Fisherhame found me.' Dhion made that distinction now, between what the world gave him and what he gave back. He felt the quiet realism of the Island seeping into his speech, into his blood.

'Much of what I could tell I have no words for in the speech of the Island, and that doesn't matter. I can find words for what I do want to speak of.' He was walking between them, his head down, scarecely noticing the sun on the white rowan flowers. 'What matters is what I did. And what I didn't do.'

'And you need to talk about it.' Hugh's words sounded small and dry.

'Husband, I shall return to the house. I sense you are entering into priest's work.'

Dhion remonstrated. 'No, Mora, please stay. I feel… I don't really know what you mean by priest's work, but to me you and Hugh are both priest together.'

He saw Hugh dart a glance towards his wife. With a shock he realised that, as much as they were changing him, so he was changing them.

'Tell us,' Hugh said.

For maybe ten paces there was silence between them. Searching for words, haltingly, Dhion began.

'I have told you that once I ran away. I have not told you that when I did, I let people down. When I ran away, of course, I was not thinking about going back. But without thinking about it, I believed I could, if I wanted to; that one day, I would want to. Now that I know of no way back, it weighs upon me that I let people down, and now I cannot make amends.'

He looked at the ground, at their feet pacing on the track, folded in the soft leather shoes of common use. Morag with her firm but elegant steps, Hugh's soft, silent tread, and his own familiar feet, now shod in shoes like theirs, stepping between them. The pain of what he had just told welled up in him, dragged him down towards the ground he gazed at. Once more, but in a different way, he felt at the mercy.

Now Hugh spoke quietly: 'Whom have you wronged?'

It was such hard work to find words for this. He forced himself.

'I wronged my family. And – a friend… I can't imagine what they must be feeling, to have me disappear without a trace, with no news.'

'You left them without telling them you were going.'

It was not a question. After a short pause, Hugh went on:

'What was in your mind, when you left?'

'Only, to get away. I didn't think about anything else. But if I had, I would have thought I'd get to some place and write to them, or phone…' he broke off, realising that in the strength of his imagination, he was back there, lacing his speech with English words.

'You didn't think about it,' Hugh repeated.

'I didn't think,' agreed Dhion. The feeling that arose in him was unfamiliar.

They paced on silently. Dhion found himself wondering with an amazed disbelief at that far-away self, who looked on things so differently from how he saw them now. Hugh was speaking again.

'Did you, at that time, mean anyone any harm?'

'I – no. Well –' The thought of the man who had been his contact in the company that failed to pay him flashed into his memory. *That bland, smarmy…* 'I would have liked to have hurt the man who let me down.' Dhion stopped. Then slowly added, 'But he was only a front for – for a group of people. I never knew who it was who ruined me. Whoever it was, they gave me no choice but to let down the men who worked for me.'

'So one scree-stone on the mountain starts another rolling, and that another,' said Hugh. He seemed thoughtful. 'Who knows which was the first stone,' he added. He shot a look straight into Dhion's eyes. 'But you were caught in it. You were wronged, and who knows the story of the man who wronged you? How little, indeed, do we know of other people's stories.'

He shook his head, paced on. 'You have said you did not think. It seems, then, that through lack of thought you became a victim. Without you wanting it, other people became your victims.'

It was like a cautery applied to his skin. Dhion writhed inwardly at Hugh's words.

'What can I do?' he begged. 'I cannot undo what I have done.'

There was silence. A chaffinch called from the branch of an alder tree and Dhion looked up. High above them on outstretched wings two eagles soared, their flight-circles interlacing in the air.

Hugh sighed. Was there a kind of relief in that sigh? 'What do you want of us?' he asked.

Dhion hesitated. He had not thought of wanting anything, except to speak out the turmoil he felt. He said, 'I think I need forgiveness.' He raised his head and looked full into the priest's eyes.

'Forgiveness I cannot give you. That belongs with those whom you have wronged.'

Dhion felt a clammy pall of dismay spread out at the words, and settle in his belly. In an instant, he knew that depression would follow. Then Hugh said, 'But there is something I can give, and it has a name you do not know. I even wonder if you know it in your own tongue.' Dhion felt Hugh's eyes on him, searching. The priest went on, 'I can speak on behalf of the All, of that together-weaving of all that we call the One. You will have to learn to live with the knowledge of the pain you caused. You are by no means alone in this. What you can do now is to come before the All, acknowledging your weakness, recognising how it let you be caught, like a stone in an avalanche, and surrender yourself to the only Power that can begin to mend the rift.'

Steadily, they paced on.

'Are you ready to receive this medicine, and allow it to change you? The weft cannot be mended while the warp is pulled out of true.'

Dhion looked up again where the eagles were still wheeling. He stopped. They all stopped. Then he said, 'I have come to a place where I cannot run any further. If you have a medicine for me, I will take it.'

Morag smiled. 'Dear Dhion. The warp longs to be true again, doesn't it? It will be. You can hardly say that you have come here. You have been brought, almost against your will – it would seem even across the borders of the worlds. How, we cannot say. All that must be to some purpose.'

༄ ༄

178

Inside the rondal it was dark. Only here and there did weak shafts of light filter through the shutters. From the western wall, woven rush mats covered the floor, marking out the sanctuary. One bright patch of sun played upon the great stone, the Mother, striking a single glint from crystal caught in its red-grey rock.

Dhion knelt between Hugh and Morag. They slowly chanted in that more ancient tongue that Dhion now recognised. He could understand only a few of the words, but the rhythm of them sank into his body. A thin blue smoke arose from the dried herbs they had sprinkled on the glowing charcoal. It wrapped him round.

Their chanting stopped. There was silence. Only the wind whispered a little, softly through the thatch.

Hugh spoke from beside him. 'Dhion, be freed of your stain.'

Morag echoed from his other side. 'Dhion, be healed of your pain.'

They raised him to his feet, and walked him to the altar. Once they circled it, twice, and a third time. Morag took the charcoal burner and raised it to her lips. She blew the blue smoke across his face. Hugh moistened his finger in oil, and blackened the tip in the warm and fragrant ashes of the herbs. He smudged the Seaborne's forehead.

'Carry this mark upon your brow to bear witness that you are changing.'

In the stilling of his mind, a sudden whiplash thought cut through: the voice of John Finlay demanding:, *'Why should this mumbo-jumbo make a shred of difference to anything?'* Dhion heard the voice, but he did not attend to it. Instead, he placed his attention on the settled feeling that was kindling within him. It was not that his fault was in any way altered. It could not be. But something was changing. A simple recognition that things were as they were, but that did not prevent

179

love from being present. He would continue to live with the knowledge and memory of these things; but instead of their being a burning brand on his conscience, he would carry the remembrance of them softly, a gentle sorrow in his heart.

The weeks passed. Dhion learned quickly, and, as quickly, his strength grew. It felt good to be in his skin. As hay harvest approached there was the annual rush for scythe blades to be peened, sickles to have new handles fitted, the tackle of Micheil's cart, a vital resource for the whole community, to be re-fettled. It was hard work, and the smith worked him hard; and then there were long days, after all the hurry, when he did nothing but sit outside the smithy with Shean and maybe another man who was walking by, and pass the time of day.

The grass was starred with little orchids, rich purple and pale and creamy white. Long, warm, transparent evenings deepened into indigo, and never darkened into winter black. Shean would release his apprentice as work allowed, and more often than not Dhion would run up the slopes of Beh' Mora. There was a ridge of raw rock, fissured, and painted with lichens; it was a place where he would pause and look out over the long waves to where the slow Atlantic rollers broke in sudden white plumes on the far skerries.

A year. A whole year and more had passed since that confused awakening in the dark of Fengoelan's house. A year in which he had learned a new language from nothing. He could continue a surprisingly complicated conversation: accented, no doubt, and with the occasional rather strange phrase, but completely understandable; and he could hear all but the rough dialects of the shepherds who spent the whole summer on the high grazings with their flocks. But even Micheil had to listen carefully to them.

A year, in which he had slowly absorbed a culture at once foreign to him, but also strangely familiar, as if it had lain deep below his awareness, like a long-forgotten song learned in childhood, re-awoken in an accidental chord, an unintended cadence. No, he reflected, it wasn't perfect; what people was? He saw the limitations that women were under – even such adventurous women as Morag. Most seemed content to live within those bounds; but likely, he thought, not all.

He was still learning how to behave in this new world. He knew he sometimes appeared awkward, clumsy, rude. He felt people's willingness to overlook his blunders with maybe a word or two here and there; a subtle covering-over of his mistake.

Yet he was still a foreigner here. He caught himself pausing, staring into his bowl of broth and wondering what *they* were doing at that moment – those others, whom he had left behind. Whom he had loved, cared for, respected, and could see no more. Where were they? When were they? Did such questions even make sense?

He missed them. He missed even the noise and bustle of the rush-hour traffic; missed standing on a high green field on a still evening and looking out across the great city, swaddled in a cloak of brown exhaust. He missed them. Yet he had found something he had been looking for, without knowing it.

A hollow place inside him was being filled by a way of life lived close to the earth, governed by the simplicity of everyday need.

25

Leaving behind the reek of iron and wood-smoke in the forge, Dhion took deep breaths of fresh air before entering the house, with its homelier cooking smells. His hands were still red and dripping from the tub where he had washed them. Leighan was building a new cart. The carpenter himself had fitted the spokes and felloes of two of the wheels and Shean had shown Dhion how to forge the iron tyres that would hold the whole together. This morning they had hammered the hot metal onto the wheels, and quenched them quickly so that steam rose in clouds around the three men.

He found Hugh waiting in the house. The tall priest rose as Dhion entered, and stretched out his hands in greeting.

'Dhion – look at you! If I'd come from a strange town, I'd have thought you were the smith himself, and been born to the craft.'

Shean, coming in at that moment, must have caught his words. He furrowed his dark brows, but Hugh was quick. 'Here *is* the smith himself,' he declared. 'The blessing of Ghea on your work, Ma'Ronal.'

'God's blessing on you, Father.'

The priest went on: 'Dhion, tomorrow is mid-summer. We would like you to come with us to our celebration.'

'Gladly,' said Dhion, 'if my master allows.'

'We'll be going, along with everyone,' Shean returned. 'You go with the Father and A'Phadr if you want. You can learn smithing from me, but for story-telling an such-like ye'll have to go to another's house.'

Dhion looked up. He saw Fineenh standing, the other side of the hearth. He caught her for a moment staring down at the earth floor, her fingers entwining. Abruptly, she turned away.

The next evening, Dhion thought he would be led down into the town; but instead they turned past the shareg's house, where Aileen joined them, carrying her harp. They followed a small stream and soon their path ran in a deepening cleft, where ash and rowan entwined above their heads. A ring-ouzel sang, clear and sharp, high in a tall larch. Ahead Dhion heard the sound of falling water; then, seeming to arise out of the cascade, a drum-beat.

The cleft widened and Dhion found himself at the threshold of a wide, round space, a bowl in the rock, floored with a smooth green lawn and surrounded by trees, so that all seemed washed with a green light. Behind the lawn a cliff rose thirty or forty feet, dark and dripping, covered in moss and fern. Little rowan trees clung impossibly to its tiny ledges. And, from a high lip on the rim of the rock-wall, the stream fell: a torrent of white, plummeting to a deep pool below. In the centre of the grass a fire spurted and spat, while to one side, beneath a spire of blue smoke, two men tended a spit. The smell of roasting meat wafted towards his nostrils, and his appetite rose with an inner shout, for now he did not taste such fare often.

People stood in groups, or sat on rocks around the grass. Every face was now familiar, though he could not yet name all. One of the crofters, a wiry, red-haired man, held a round wooden frame stretched with a tight skin. The stick he held in his other hand was, to Dhion, a dark blur as he made the drum sing with a complex rhythm. Another man had a pipe, held in readiness.

Others followed them from the narrow path. Bit by bit, soon most of the township was there, and more still arriving, children standing close to their parents, strangely hushed. Dhion recognised Shareen, and beside her little Colin with his sister.

Aileen settled herself near the drummer. Hugh walked across to the other piper. They were joined by a woman with some kind of fiddle. At first hesitant, but quickly gathering in confidence and pace, the group of musicians broke into a melody both wild and sweet that caught at Dhion's heart. Then Morag stepped forward and stood, poised and still, her head slightly inclined towards the musicians, a hand extended to one side in apparent invitation. Dhion saw Rhona, the potter's wife, take her hand. Within a few seconds a half-circle had formed. Then Morag nodded her head, and slowly they began to dance. A minute more, and there was a full circle, dancing barefoot, with delicate steps, to the swirling music. Dhion watched in wonder. All were gaily dressed, with flowers pinned to their clothes or laced in their hair. The song changed, and the step, and the dancers became for Dhion an image of a complex whole. As he watched, something seemed to knit itself together within his soul.

At length they were done, and they sat on the grass. The singers and players joined them, and more wood was piled on the fire. Beer was brought in skins and pitchers, with meat, and bread dipped in the hot fat.

Light began to fade from the sky; the embers glowed red as Morag began a low chant. The thought formed itself in Dhion's mind that it was not the meaning of the words that mattered, but the sounds themselves, their pattern and their cadence. It was as if a soft light filled the air, coming from nowhere, and a faint perfume that was neither woodbine nor rose. They stood upon the supple grass, and danced again the ring around the dying fire. Only now the dance was a slow step, in time with the slowly rising perfume, and the shape they made seemed to Dhion a reflection of the light.

Gradually the glade grew dark beside the pool under the waterfall. Now they tended the fire again. And round the circle Dhion found eyes turning towards himself.

'Ingleeshe – tell us your story. It will be good to hear your tale. Tell us, please.'

Morag whispered encouragement, and Dhion stood up. His heart beat faster. Was it the magic of the dance, the music, the place? – he felt a peculiar inner stillness. He had not prepared a speech, but now he found himself taking his time, scanning an inner organ he had not known he possessed, to find what it would be most fitting to tell.

'One night, at sea in a great storm,' he began, 'I was thrown from my boat into the waves, and I fell out of my world, and into yours.'

It seemed to him the simplest thing to say, but also the truest. As he spoke, warming to his tale, he noticed that he believed in what he was saying.

'It has not been easy to learn your language and your ways,' he told them at last. 'I am still learning. But with your patience and kindness, I will succeed.'

He finished, and there was a hush round the circle. Then Leighan, with whom he had been working the day before, spoke up in his penetrating voice.

'We thank you for your tale, Ingleeshe. It is all most interesting, even if I do not understand it. But I find m'sel' wondering, as I hear of you tumbling out of another world – why is it that you cannot find the way to turn y'sel' about, and go back whence ye came?'

It was a bit abrupt. Dhion heard a few subdued gasps from around the circle, but he found he was not shaken. His answer flowed from him:

'I don't know how I came. If longing could have taken me back, I would have been away long months ago. Now the longing has faded. And I find… that I am here.' He looked around the circle. 'I am content.'

'A good answer, friend.' It was Fengoelan's deep, reassuring, voice. 'But peace. Tonight is a night for stories, not for questions. It is a time to listen and to wonder. Now look – the night draws on.'

The man with the drum began again. A single beat; then the off-beat between, and slowly the rhythm grew more complex. Always there was that first clear tap: a summons.

People began following the drum, up a narrow path climbing the side of the defile, then out onto the moor. There the light surprised Dhion. It must be late – past midnight, he guessed. The sky to the north was bright – a luminous clear green. The path wound between tussocks of grass and sedge into the deep heather, but always climbing towards a low peak, towards the north.

They stood on the summit. The rocky outcrops, swept clean by rain and wind and veined with the frozen blood of the earth, lifted low between woolly masses of pale green lichen.

Dhion looked around. All the while, more and more people were coming, breasting the top of the defile, and gathering on the bald summit. The whole town was there: Leighan Carpenter stood, dwarfed by his paelht Donal, and surrounded by his sons and sharp-faced wife. There was Shean, with Fineenh and Shinane, slender and bright-eyed. And the fishermen from the other side of the hill – Fengoelan and Shelagh, who had first cared for him; A'Dhael, standing by her husband, and near them, Targud with his young family. He recognised Dermot Ma'Bhenrish who, he knew, had run three times over the mountain on his account. And many whose names he did not yet know.

They all looked out, toward the north. They looked where the sky was brightest, low on the horizon. Then Dhion saw what they were watching for. Where the sky-line bent round gradually towards the east, there in a low gap between the hills a line of dazzling radiance appeared. A red-gold wire of light, and at its appearing the men raised a shout.

All stood, their arms extended towards the brightness, moving as one to a slow chant. The rhythm prompted them, as they brought their hands back to their bellies, their hearts, their brows, in threefold repetitions, until the chant was done.

In a minute the sun's edge had disappeared again, sliding behind the more easterly peak. The sky had changed. Now ever brighter it swelled towards the midsummer morning, and the short dusk began to drain away.

First it was the children who were shepherded or carried fast asleep down the mountain. Their parents followed, and their bigger brothers and sisters and cousins – they who had seen many midsummer sunrises. The elders, for whom perhaps the wonder of each sun-staying was growing and deepening yet further, lingered a while. Then they too turned down the homeward path.

Dhion turned to Morag, who stood beside him.

'I have never seen anything more beautiful, or more wonderful.'

Morag turned her face towards him.

'Do you not greet the sun in your land in summer, when she is so restless she hardly sleeps?'

26

Lammas came and the barley fields turned yellow. There was a week of hot sunshine, and one day when the hardest of the housework was over Shinane asked leave of her mother. She took the path to Fisherhame at first, but at the pass she turned to the south, around the seaward skirts of Beh' Talor Gan. The grass was warm under her bare feet, and blue harebells and scabious, yellow hawkweed and sea-pinks shone in the sun. It was a good step to the place she knew, where the rocks, running out to sea across the white sand like the ribs of some long-dead monster, formed deep pools of green and turquoise. She was warm when she had scrambled down onto the sand, and her anticipation of the cool water beckoned her eagerly.

She clambered over the rocks to a broad shelf to seaward, where she judged she could not be seen and, leaving her clothes on the sun-warmed ledge, stepped into the pool, her feet gripping the sandy floor. The water was delicious on her calves, and sent goose-pimples up her legs. With the water up to her hips she leaned into it and kicked off, a long lunge, embracing the fluid world. Taking a breath, she duck-dived into its depths, and with eyes open explored the rocky walls. Sea-anemones put out their dumpy arms, each with a glowing blue spot at its base. She touched one with her finger-tip and felt the tentacles converge onto her skin with a strange stickiness. Surfacing for another gulp of air, she plunged again. There were shells on the bottom – little iridescent top-shells and chunky matter-of-fact winkles; shells like butterfly wings, and shells like angels' wings. Here one was crossing the underwater sand with short, ungainly movements, quite unlike the smooth glide of the shell-fish on a rock. She picked it up and saw the neat claws of a little crab retreating inside.

Emerging at last, she waded round to her shelf and opened her hand. Out tumbled small pieces of pink coralline, deep red seaweed and shells of all colours from nut-brown to soft buttermilk yellow. She lay down in her shift to let the sun dry her.

She woke to the sound of a splash. Then the rhythmic water-sounds of someone swimming. Someone was swimming in her pool: and a man, from what she could hear. She stiffened, listening intently. A sucking sound as he dived, and a brief respite until he surfaced, and again the noise of his arms churning the water.

She reached for her clothes, and began pulling them on as quickly as she could. Any moment the man might come to the end of the pool alongside her shelf and see her. Even now she could see the wavelets chaotically slapping the rock.

Well – she was at least decent, if rather dishevelled. She cautiously put her head over the ridge of rock that hid her from view.

The man was standing now, up to his waist in the water, his back to her. She could see the muscles of his shoulders moving under his skin as he scooped water in both hands and poured it over his head. She felt a shock run through her. It was the Ingleeshe.

What was she to do? Custom demanded that she should not tarry with a man alone in such a place. But how was she to get past him? Was she to wait, hidden, while the tide came in? Or swim fully-clothed round to the next bay? Custom forbade that she draw attention to herself. But Custom was not made for a situation like this.

She decided that Custom must give place to common sense. She took an in-breath and called out to him. 'Ingleeshe – it's me: Shinane.'

She saw him start, then turn his head towards her voice.

'Mi'Shean?'

'I'm going to wait here,' she called, 'behind this rock.' Then she heard herself say, 'When you've dressed you can come here and join me, if you like.'

'All right. I will.'

She ducked her head down, and leaned her back against the rock, gazing up at the cloudless sky. An agitation coursed through her: what had she said? She heard a splashing. Then a short pause. In a little while a tousled head appeared. He swung down and perched on a ledge above her. He smiled.

'What are you doing here?' he asked.

She looked up at him, narrowing her eyes against the sun. She searched his face. To her surprise she saw there a relaxed friendliness that she knew no man of the Island could find in such a situation.

She held herself steady. 'The same as you, I expect,' she replied, with a little defiant rise of her chin. 'Women like to swim too, you know.'

'I'm sorry. I had no idea.'

'Listen,' she went on hastily. 'Father would be angry if he knew we were here together. No-one can see us in this hidden place, but we must leave separately. You never know who might be out on Beh' Talor Gan and look down at the wrong moment.'

'I do understand. I didn't come here yesterday, you know.'

'No... The day before yesterday, wasn't it?'

Had she really said that? She giggled. He laughed. They both laughed.

'Look,' he said. 'We don't have to leave at once, do we? I mean, since we're here anyway. We have a saying where I come from: *May as well be hanged for a sheep as for a lamb.*'

'Hanged?' she questioned. 'How do you mean?'

'It means… let's not talk about it now.' He paused a moment. 'So what shall we talk about?' He tilted his head. 'I'd like to know – what's it like… to be you? To be a woman here?'

She hesitated, again uncertain. Then, resolute, she said, 'No. First, I need to know. How did you come here? How did you find this place? Did you know I come here? Did you follow me?'

She pinned him with a searching stare. He was still smiling. He shook his head.

'No – no! I wouldn't do that. Even if I wanted to. I run out this way from time to time. I've swum here before.'

His reassurance relaxed her. Emboldened, she said, 'I love to come here. When it's warm and Mother lets me. That's not often, but it *is* wonderful' – she gauged how far she could go – 'being free of all this.' She plucked impatiently at her skirts. 'You don't know how lucky you are, you men.'

She looked at him, sitting above her, bare-legged, clad in his linen leine. The sun was behind him, its glare shielded by the rock that rose higher. Perhaps she had over-stepped; she blushed suddenly, deeply, felt the heat pour down her throat and over her collar-bones, where the top lace had been hastily tied. Quickly, she raised a hand and covered the place.

'I really didn't know you would come here,' he added. 'I didn't suppose you would be so free to roam away from… the protection of your family.'

She looked up at the outline of his face. It seemed to her finer than that of other men. As she watched the Adam's apple that rose and fell as he spoke, she felt a sudden stab – of compassion for this castaway, now living under their roof. Now with her, in this secluded place. She looked away. She stared out to sea.

'Of course,' she replied. 'We do have some freedom.' Then quickly, 'But I'm under my mother until I marry a man, and then I'm under him.'

He clambered down and sat beside her at a little distance. 'I see that's how it is –. Does it have to be?'

She pulled herself up, facing him. A flash of sunlight caught her eye, glancing off silver: the bracelet she remembered from the day he was found, glinting against his sun-browned skin. Who had given him that, she wondered? Could she trust him, as she trusted one or two of her girl-friends and shared with them? She judged him at least more trustworthy than gossiping Briged.

'It would be good to be like Morag A'Phadr. She and the Father – you can't tell who's under whom.'

She surprised herself with the energy of her declaration.

He nodded agreement. 'Yes. Does one have to be under another? Why can't two be side by side – as we are now?'

At his words, she felt a thrill of alarm and delight, the heat of another blush running through her.

He reached out, showing her the upturned palm of his outstretched hand, that silver bracelet on his wrist.

She tensed. For a moment she felt exposed, vulnerable. Then her very fear changed itself: in its place an exultation. Her hand gripped his. She surprised herself at her sudden strength.

She faced him again, and laughed.

'Yes – Why can't they be?'

27

Mother Coghlane was worried. There was a thought that needed her attention. As she bent her mind to the milking of her ewes, it was there. Not demanding; the present moment, as always, had her eye, and each animal that came to her stool, black-faced or brindled, full-uddered and trusting, felt her familiar hand. But she knew the thought was there and waiting, though still submissive to her will.

Thoughts of such persistence did not come often to her simple home. She knew that hers was one of the few voices of prophecy on the Island, so hers was the duty to know and understand such thoughts, and it may be to make them known. As the sun sank behind the western peaks and the moon rose big and yellow in the east, and the fire in the hearth burned down to glowing ruby embers, she began, layer by layer, to prepare herself, mind and body, fully to receive this newcomer.

She took from the wooden press a long, simple linen gown, and laying aside her other clothes pulled it over her head and tied the laces on the shoulders in neat bows. Then barefoot she opened the door. She walked across the dew-cool grass and, without flinching, the shard-sharp shingle.

The tarn lay darkly before her. Its water was smooth and deepest blue. Stars shone faintly in its depths, immeasurable distances deep. She stopped at the very rim, her heels on stone that still held the day's warmth, her toes lapped in chill water. Her mind went to her breath, the flowing in and out, the filling and emptying, the coursing through every channel of her body, and the ebbing again. After a while she took a slow step forward, and another. She waded into the tarn. She began slowly to sink into the welcoming water, and felt its touch on her skin. Smoothly, calmly, she changed her mind, her body following after. For now, she no longer felt any need of air or light. The water no longer made her want to gasp but lovingly embraced her, and as she lay back and let it close above her face she felt no fear, no panic of how or when she was to breathe. She knew that for now she had no need of breathing. Her body would look after itself in this womby world, and it was not her concern.

She listened – not to the roaring of water in her ears nor to the so slow pulsing of blood in her brain. She listened, not to the silent stillness of her mind, but only to that which was deepest within her, where she and the surrounding water were one. She began to hear the voices of the water, and the voices it had gathered to itself.

She heard the voice of the tarn, like a complex chord, and the thin, high voices of the peaty rills that fed it from the mountain. She heard the shouting of the burn as it leaped down the hillside, as it joined the churning northward-flowing river and emptied itself at last in the sea. She heard the whispering air-sounds of the breezes that blew in across the shore, of the clouds that formed and floated about the peaks. And she heard the mumbling voices of the earth: of root and moss, of rock and shale and stone, of deep-bedded mountain-roots. At last she heard even this: the distant fierce and burning fire-voices that muttered to each other, intoning from the depths.

And there was the thought. It mingled in the polyphony of the spirit-sounds around her. She listened long, and received and understood and listened more. Then she knew that she had heard. It evoked no feeling in her yet. In that state of being it was neither fearful nor dreadful nor ominous. It only was. Within the womb of the water she thanked the voices and slowly rose.

Her face broke the surface. The first scent of air in her nostrils seemed strange, a sharp sensation. She let in at first only little wavelets of air, which one by one ran deeper into her being while the water receded. She opened her eyes and saw the stars.

As the quick air ran free through her body, she stood, turned and paced back to the shore. Untying the wet linen and leaving it on the stones, she wrapped herself in a goat-hair cloak and blew up the embers of the fire. She knew herself now to be cold – bone-cold. It was the thought that chilled her.

In the priest's house Hugh opened his eyes to a pearly dawn. He woke from a restless sleep. Kissing his wife he rose and dressed and softly went out. The sun was a long way from rising above the bulk of the Island, but its light had already awoken the birds. He turned to the left, away from the village, and slowly walked past the shareg's house and up into the little glen where the path began its climb over the hill to Fisherhame. Finding a familiar stone, he folded his long cassock under him as he sat. A thin drift of grey smoke rose from the smith's forge, and he thought of Dhion, who must now be rising to do his apprentice's duty in the lighting of the fire.

He thought of the night just past. He was used to recalling his dreams and listening to them, but this morning they were fragmentary, elusive. Mountains – he saw mountains. The hills above Caerpadraig? No. And there was an urgency – what was it he was looking for? Why did a feeling of breathlessness come to him, and deep grief? He knew that the hills of his dream were not the hills of home: they were in the north, near Morag's country. But this was not her dark sea-lough and narrow coastal plain, but an upland moor and a shingly burn. Why was that little tarn familiar? Then he knew. Mother Coghlane – those were her folds, her tiny house.

He remembered now her face in his dreams, her look, her beckoning. He must go to her.

He stood up. There was now some movement in the town below him: cattle returning to their pasture, Niall the dairyman pacing smoothly from the stalls, pails brimming. As he opened his door, Morag greeted him, a shawl about her shoulders.

She listened as he told her, stirring the porridge over the new-lit fire. After they had eaten she took down his travelling cloak and set out his boots, while he prepared his pack.

Hugh took the forest path that Micheil and Dhion had taken, more than four moons earlier; that he himself had taken, soon after. As the sun crossed the dappled sky, Hugh walked the moors, until he saw the pass between the two peaks. Again the sheep were startled at the sound of approaching steps. An unseasonable wind tugged at his cloak and at his kilted cassock.

They sat each side of the fire. She had been neither surprised to see him, nor complacent at his coming. She handed him a bowl of warmed ewes' milk flavoured with myrtle. Then they talked, and after a time she told him what was in her heart as, behind the scudding clouds, the sun set due west, touching their edges with faded yellow.

The night darkened around them.

'There is a great challenge coming to our way of life.' She held her chin in her hands, her elbows on her knees. 'I do not know how we will meet it. I do not know which is the better course, or whether every way is neither good nor evil. For good and evil are only in how we meet the happenings of this world. That is the question: how will the challenge be met? I admit, it fears me, Hugh.'

She turned to look him in the face. For a moment a line burned in the air between them. Then, feeling the force of her words, Hugh dropped his gaze.

There was silence.

Hugh spoke. 'What kind of a challenge?' he asked. 'Do you speak of an invader? Of sickness? Of what? Speak clearly to me, Mother. For surely the matter you speak of is shareg's business. What am I to say to Micheil?'

Mother Coghlane looked very old in the dull red light of the fire.

'No. Not sickness. Not an invader. A change. Nothing is clear, as yet. So there is nothing more to be said. Except that there is another matter entangled with this. Concerning a young man, who bears a crushing weight. If he cannot find a way to set down his burden, there will be a death. Maybe more than one.'

'Do you know who, Mother?'

She turned her head away a little, as if regretting the interruption.

'I have told you what I have heard. Earth speaks what she wishes, and no more, even though we crave it. For now, wait, and watch. Be ready to speak when the time comes. But take care not to be over-close. A priest must speak of Spirit, both to people and to shareg. Priest may sometimes even have to oppose shareg for Spirit's sake.'

'What do you mean, Mother?'

'Just that. I do not say oppose him. I say: be true.'

There was silence in the house. A spider ran across the floor, into the circle of lamplight. It paused, stock-still, poised on the tips of its eight legs. Then it continued, finding sanctuary under the imperturbable hem of the old woman's skirt.

'You speak,' Hugh began slowly, steepling his fingers under his chin. 'You speak of new things, of changes that may have great effect. I cannot tell what these things are, nor whether they will be good or bad. Again, you give me wisdom that I cannot use. What am I to make of these things now?'

197

'Do not confuse wisdom and knowledge. I have passed on to you a little knowledge that I have heard Earth and Sky say in passing. Now it is for you to hold that in your own wisdom, to inform your sight. For these three always dance together: wisdom, and knowledge, and sight. None rules supreme. But at the centre of their dance sits truth. That is what you must listen to. When you cannot follow the steps of their dance, and their music sounds discordant, then seek truth in the stillness of your heart. Go deep within – have I not taught you? – and listen. Let truth speak, and when it is time, you will understand.'

Hugh sighed.

The old woman smiled. She rose. Laying her hand on his shoulder, she gave it a reassuring squeeze.

'All things come, with waiting,' she commented. 'Now go. Get you to bed, Hugh. You must be rested for the morrow and your journey home.'

28

Dhion was getting used to the early rising. He knew how to light the forge-fire the way the smith wanted it, and his body had recovered its former strength, even beginning to surpass it. He enjoyed the freedom given him by his evening runs over the hills. Occasionally he ran over to Fisherhame to visit Fengoelan and Shelagh. He knew he was assured a welcome, but it was a special pleasure to be able to speak freely with them now, remembering those days when everything had to be mimed. No longer did his exercise evoke a grin or an alarmed stare; it was all a part with his strange ways and his peculiar accent. People had come to accept that that was what the Seaborne did.

The fire was building well as Shean came stamping round from the house, his working leine roughly tucked over his belt. Dhion knew now the rhythm of the day. First they would work at fettling and cleaning the pieces, now cold, that they had forged the previous afternoon, and maybe assemble some work and hammer the rivets together. By mid-morning the fire would be hot. They would strip off down to the long drawers Dhion had grown used to working in, and take the billets of raw metal in the great black tongs, and hold them in the fire until they emerged glowing red and ready for the anvil.

Today Shean turned instead to a shelf at the back of the shop and reached down some small ingots of copper. He cradled one in his hands as he told Dhion of his smelting it.

'I admit,' he began, 'I was wary of you at first. Your story didn't make sense – it still doesn't, man. But I don't think you're as bad as I feared.

'Look,' he went on. He seemed uncharacteristically awkward. 'I've no son to pass my knowledge to. My father learned his skill from his father, and he showed me. Now where's it to go? Not to the girl, that's for certain. So...' He hesitated; then hurried on in a rush. 'I don't know why, but I'm minded, after all, to trust you.'

Dhion listened as he filed a fishing gaff to sharpness, wondering where this uncommon speech was leading.

'My father showed me where there are rocks in the hills. In the spring I will show you, and how you should pray the hills to take their treasure. I shall show you how to build a smelter there and fire it, and to run the bright metal into the ingot-moulds. And you must teach your son, and keep the wisdom living.'

Dhion looked at him. He knew he must make his life on the Island for the present, but still he had not considered how long that might be. Did he still assume, below the thoughts and feelings of which he was daily aware, that some day, somehow, he would return to the world he had known? Or was the smith right, that here was his only future and his children's, and his whole family line on into time?

'Look,' said Shean, 'I'll show you how to work copper. For it's different from iron. It has little strength, and no sharpness worth using. But you can hammer it and draw it much finer. You can make jewellery from it and with a small polished stone it's quite pretty enough for hereabouts.'

Shean explained that the fire need not be as hot as for iron, so they could work it now. He took the billet in tongs and drew it out into a thin rod, then beat it flat around the beak of the anvil.

'There,' he said, beaming. 'You can make this into a fine bracelet for your lady-love.'

His lady-love?

Dhion's mind had started along another tack.

'How thin can you draw it out?' he asked. 'Can you make it into...' He didn't have a word for 'wire'. He imitated with his fingers the fineness of the metal.

200

'Like this, you mean?' chuckled Shean, finding a small coil on the shelf. 'I see you really do mean to impress, eh?'

'Yes, that's right. How do you call it?' He imitated the word. 'And yes, I suppose I do want to impress.'

The thought would not leave him all morning, and after the midday meal he excused himself briefly to scratch some ideas on a wooden shingle with a charred stick.

'Shean,' he said, 'there's an idea with me, but I'd need your help. One day when we're not too pressed...'

The smith looked at him, a question on his face. 'What's this idea, then? What's it for?'

'I want to try something out.' He hesitated. Then, 'Is it still true, that Micheil has a pair of waystones somewhere?'

'A pair of what?'

'The Ma'Haengas told me. Stones from the Northmen's shipwreck. If you float them, they always point north. Have you heard about them? Because, if I could borrow them, I might be able to show you a little something from my world.'

He stopped speaking and looked at the smith. Watched the man's face, where puzzlement, resistance and curiosity converged. It was curiosity that came out on top.

'Well, I think I know what you're talking of,' Shean said slowly. 'They must be somewhere about. We'll have to ask. But I don't get it.'

Dhion remembered trying to use a turnip to explain the movement of a boat without oars or a sail. 'Would you ask the shareg for me?' he said. 'Then – wait and see. Let's see if it works first, and then I'll try to answer your questions.'

The apples were gathered and stored, and the first frosts starred the stones with crystal, giving the houses a white shadow that lagged a little behind the dark shadow as the sun rose lower each day.

Hugh had called for Dhion at the smithy. It was not a busy time, and Shean had been happy to let him go. Now he entered the priest's house, warming himself after his walk in the icy air. Morag, Hugh said, was with the children in the rondal.

'You know tonight we celebrate Samhain,' he told Dhion. 'Last year we did not think you ready, and you stayed at home. Now is different, and I would like to invite you. It is a time when the borders between the worlds grow thin. I don't know if you have anything like it in your country.'

Dhion's mind swept briefly across memories of Hallowe'en, and silly-spooky ghosts and pumpkin-faces, and children trick-or-treating.

'Umm, maybe, in a way,' he said non-committally.

'Come and sit down. There.' Hugh gathered his cassock neatly beneath him on the bench beside the fire, and motioned Dhion to the space across from him.

'You'll be aware that the year is turning now, quickly, from the light to the dark, from growing to resting. The seed needs to rest in the dark and cold before it sends forth its shoot in the spring. And so we say this is the beginning of the new year. We will not see sign of it until the first shoots. But the promise is now. And it is at this time, when we too begin to rest from the labour of the bright months, that we are most open to the spirit-world, where dwell the *Sidhe* and those who have died. We here, we see nothing clearly in that world – there is a veil between us. At Samhain the veil draws thin and perhaps we can peer through a little. This is a threshold time.

'Tonight people will come here, to the rondal. A few will choose to spend the night in a watch. The Tollagh is directed towards helping us in peering through, and seeing, and safely returning.'

'You speak as if it were dangerous.'

'It can be dangerous, for those who take it too lightly and do not show respect.'

'Respect?'

'For the *Sidhe*, the elder ones, who are still powerful, and for the dead – to whom we are grateful. And also for ourselves, as guardians of the wonderful and many-faceted jewel that even the dullest of us is.'

Hugh took Dhion through the chants and practices that he would need to know for the ceremony. He was finishing as Morag came through the door.

'They're a handful and no mistake, those children.' She hung up her cloak, crossed the floor and kissed Hugh's forehead. She moved smoothly and quickly, without haste, as she began to set out the meal. 'You'll join us?' Her eyes questioned Dhion.

Dhion always relaxed when he visited Hugh and Morag. He felt he was at home, and he sensed they liked to have him there, like the son they'd never had.

As they ate, he took the opportunity to ask about the waystones.

'Why, yes,' said Hugh at once. 'They remain under the shareg's cloak, but we keep them in a chest in the rondal. Would you like to see them?'

'Very much,' said Dhion. 'I'd even like to take them away for a time. Would that be allowed me?'

'As they are in the shareg's keeping, we would have to ask Micheil. I expect he would allow it, now he knows you. But what do you want them for?'

'I want to try to make something,' said Dhion. 'Call it a toy if you like. Something that could show you a little of my world.'

Morag glanced at her husband, a wry smile flitting across her face, and then at Dhion.

The talk moved on, and she asked Dhion how he was settling at the smith's house.

'Well, I'm only in the house for meals,' he answered. 'Now the days are drawing in and I can't go out on the hills after work, I spend too much time in the forge. At least it's warm. And some nights I look in on Donal. But it's all right. They're all kind to me. Even Shean's softened now.'

She shot Dhion one of her penetrating looks. Then she said, 'And how do you find Mi'Shean, Dhion?'

Dhion opened his mouth to reply, then closed it again. The truth was that since their encounter at the rock-pool, away from the strict etiquette of Caerpadraig, whenever his mind was not taken up with his work in the smithy, nor engaged with his new idea, it was full of her. She continually danced before his curiosity, provoking more questions than answers. For it seemed impossible to engage her in conversation within the family circle. That moment when she grasped his extended hand returned constantly to his mind. It had come naturally at the time, yet seemed so out of place in the context of their daily lives. In the end, he said simply, 'I like her. I would like to get to know her better.'

'You know she's all but spoken for?' Hugh cut in. 'Dermot, the son of Benrish from Fisherhame.'

'Aye, but that's a poor match,' put in Morag. 'I wish you'd say something to Shean, Hugh. Dermot's fine, but he wants a woman who's fitted to his life and temper. That's not Shinane.'

'Doesn't a woman have any say in whom she's going to marry?' Dhion asked.

Hugh steepled his fingers. 'That depends on her father. Quite a few parents would ask their daughter what they think of a young man; but Shean likes the old ways. That's how he's learned the art of smithing, and that's how he sees the world. Fineenh's different, and perhaps she understands her daughter better. But she will not seek to overrule her husband.'

'Still, I think Shean himself must have a question in his mind about the match,' said Morag. 'Or they would have been betrothed by now.'

Turning to Dhion, she went on, 'You want to find a way of knowing the girl better. But it's vital you do not overstep the mark. So it's strictly Mi'Shean for you. And wait and watch for an opportunity. I cannot tell you how. If it's right, it will come.'

That night a fire burned in an iron brazier in the rondal, but otherwise it was dark. People came, through the moonlight, some carrying horn lanterns, others shielding small rush-lamps from the wind. They put them out at the door, and silently sat around the matting of the sanctuary.

It was yet another new experience. It left Dhion quiet, thoughtful as he made his way back to the forge. Shinane and her parents were before him as they passed the dark houses. They, too, were silent.

Dhion lay on his pallet and stared up, past the rows of tools hanging on their hooks, the shelves of work in progress, past the thatch, past anything he could see. He felt, as it were, in a place between worlds, a place where all his worlds met. *When we unite, the worlds unite.* They had chanted it, in the darkness. He touched his bracelet.

In the house, Shinane lay in her alcove. Her mind was still full of the Tollagh. There had been darkness – heavy, oppressive darkness. But always a thin thread of light had led her onward, deeper into Otherworld. Then it, too, had failed, suffocated by the heavy air. She felt herself lost, bereft, exiled. Or was there still a glow, far away and above her? Fire on the mountain, drawing her up, drawing her through. She hugged her blanket, and slept.

ôôôôô

Hugh did not sleep. He kept watch in the sanctuary. In the Tollagh his sight had been filled by Mother Coghlane's words. And in the changed state of his own journey into Otherworld, the young man of whom she had spoken he had both seen and recognised. He had sensed the burden of the weight he bore.

29

The moon waned, and waxed again, and waned. Dhion learned the trade that Shean taught him, and he learned it well. But often when the smith gave him leisure, it was to the ingots of copper that he turned. Shean cast an indulgent eye over his efforts, knowing that in the end all could be recast without too much trouble.

Slowly he learned, to heat the metal to the right redness, to draw it out between tongs, then carefully – keeping both the heat and the tension just right – to wind the wire onto a wooden spindle that smoked and blackened as the hot copper cooled around it.

Eventually even Shean had to admit that the Seaborne could make wire at least as well as he. Thick or thin, he could make it even and constant as he wished. Where once there had been billets of red-brown metal, now there were coils and coils of copper wire on their wooden formers. Dhion taught himself how to run the wire through molten tallow and harden it in cold water; but not so much that it cracked when he bent it round an iron cylinder.

He had to persuade Micheil to lend him the way-stones, assuring him they would come to no harm. He went to Leighan for a bit of timber, and to Tearlach for a leather strip. Then he made a couple of housings and a pair of wooden wheels, one small, one large with a peg to serve as handle, and both grooved round their rims to hold the band of supple leather.

At last there it stood. It was a strange device: two standing structures connected by lengths of copper wire, each with a coil of more wire gleaming palely through its tallow coat.

Dhion slept restlessly beside his creation. All was now ready, and he'd given the handle a few turns to make sure it span smoothly. He was certain that if it worked it could not fail to impress: first Shean, of course, but eventually, he hoped, even Shareg Micheil, and with him, the whole township. But would it work? There were too many imponderables where he'd had to guess and hope, and add a few more loops of wire. He slept uneasily, and woke early.

As they finished their first-food and returned to the forge, the smith came to the subject that was on Dhion's mind.

'So you'd like to give your wee toy a try, would you? And what d'you want me to do?'

Dhion positioned his patron beside one of the structures, where a lodestone floated on a tiny raft of wood in a bowl of water, surrounded by a coil of wire. He himself moved to the other structure, where the second stone joined two iron pole-pieces. Between them, on an axle, a block of iron was wrapped round and round with wire. He placed a restraining hand on the wooden frame, and with the other grasped the handle.

'I'd like you to watch that stone, and see if it moves. It should turn, so that it points away from north.'

'All right, I'll do that. But I don't see how it's going to move.'

Dhion began to turn the handle. Slowly at first, then faster, spinning the cylinder wrapped in wire.

The older man gave a gasp.

The stone was moving.

Slowly it turned, through nor-nor-west and north-west, until it settled just short of west-nor-west.

Dhion released the handle, and the spindle whirred to a stand. Slowly, the stone swung back: north-west, nor-nor-west, due north again.

The smith gaped at his apprentice.

'How... How did that happen? Did you...? You can't have... Did you... make it happen?'

208

Dhion's eyes glittered. 'No – I didn't make it happen. It was the machine.' He used the English word for want of any other. 'It works – it really works!'

He sat on the bench outside the smithy, a group of men around him. As soon as Shean had seen the wonder, he had gone out and collected whom he could – mostly craftsmen from their workshops, for the farmers were out on the field. There was Leighan, with Murdogh, who was helping him that day; also Tearlach, and Padragh the potter and a couple of others looked on. Dhion had shown them his toy, and had whirled the handle again and again, until the leather band broke. Now he had the task of explaining to them what had happened – and, more difficult still, how.

'I don't believe it.' Murdogh spoke for most of them. 'Those wires are far too small for anything to flow down inside them. How can you make a hole down wire that small? Why, Aengas himself couldn't have done it.'

The craftsmen all nodded at such a picture: the artificer of the gods attempting the feat.

'No,' Dhion essayed, 'you have to think of the copper itself as the hole.'

They gazed at him blankly. It was Leighan who spoke:

'Are you mad, man? Wire is one thing, and a hole's another. The hole's empty and the wire's solid. You can take it in your hand. So how can we think of wire like a hole?'

There was laughter. Dhion flushed.

'I know it seems strange, but in my world…' He cast about him for a way of saying it: they had no scientists. 'In my world … ah … learned men' – it would have to do – 'have found that even the most solid object is full of empty space.'

A stony silence. And Leighan again: 'Are you asking us not to believe our eyes and ears and what we can feel?'

Dhion had no answer.

'And anyway,' Leighan ran on, 'where does this stuff that you can't see or hear flow in, and where does it come out? I've heard that down Caerster way they make wheels that turn when the water flows over them, but if you don't let the water out, then nothing flows.'

'It doesn't flow out, or in. It just goes round and round, so long as there's something to power it.' He finished lamely.

'But it happened!' The smith jumped up. 'However it worked, we all saw it happen. You have to admit that.'

'Aye, as for that... I dare say he blew on it, or he banged the bench when we were all watching the way-stone. I'm sorry, Ingleeshe, it's a good trick and I thank you for the amusement, but I don't believe it for an instant.' Leighan folded his arms in finality, and the subject of conversation turned towards the supply of firewood for the winter.

'Why is this so important to you?' asked Shean, when they were sitting down in the house for the midday meal. Fineenh and Shinane sat a little apart. 'When all's said and done, it's only a toy, and whether it works by your magic stuff or whether it's just a trick doesn't matter much, does it?'

Dhion looked down, uncertain where to begin. 'Yes, this is just a toy, to show that it works. But it's real – I wasn't tricking anyone, and I feel... What Leighan said belittled it – and me.'

'Oh, as for that, don't worry about it. He meant no harm by it. You see, people who don't know you still find you more than a little strange, and I don't think he can take you altogether seriously.'

'But you do.'

'Oh aye. I've seen what you can do. You're good with your hands, and you've got a good head on your shoulders, and... I doubted you at first, but your heart's in the right place. You've got one or two strange ideas, I don't deny, but you're all right by me, and I don't mind saying so.'

'You know,' Dhion began slowly, 'my strange ideas could change this place. This force I've shown you… There are so many things we use it for in my land.' He glanced over to the fire where the women were unusually quiet. He caught Shinane's eye. She looked down into her bowl. Suddenly, he felt very alone. Then he saw her raise her eyes, deliberately, and look back into his.

Shean was speaking. 'Maybe, Dhion. And maybe we don't want to be changed. Maybe we're happy with things the way they are. Change is a tricky thing. You never know whether you're going to like what's new, just as you realise that you've lost the old.'

'So you're happy with children being burned by rolling into the fire, are you? And old men spending their last days coughing their lungs out from the smoke they've breathed all their lives, and fishermen finding that the wind has changed and they're too tired to row against the waves?'

'Heesht now. I don't say I'm happy with it – of course I'm not. Life is hard; at times it's harder than we can bear. But we've grown with life's hardness and we accept it. Change one thing, and you change everything.' The smith rose and headed for the forge door. 'Can you do that and be sure it's for the best?'

Dhion raised his head. His master was disappearing through the door. Before he rose to follow him he looked again towards Shinane. Under his breath he muttered, 'Yes. I can.'

She met his eyes directly this time. He could see that she had heard.

30

'Have you heard what your pupil has been up to?'

Hugh cocked a quizzical eyebrow back at Micheil. He had many pupils, for every child came to sit in his school. But he knew whom the shareg meant – the man who had spent nine months in their house with them, learning their tongue and their ways; who often returned to them when Shean had no work for him: the Seaborne, Dhion.

Micheil continued. 'Those waystones I lent him – he's made a magic toy with them.'

Hugh looked archly at Morag as they sat together in the shareg's house on a dark winter's evening. The tallow candles smoked and threw shadows on the walls, distorted by the uneven stones. What Micheil spoke of was not news to them.

Their host continued, 'The one stone was there…' He gestured at the ground before him. 'And he turned a wheel over there.' He pointed at a spot a long pace distant. 'It turned! And there was nothing between them, but a couple of thin wires.'

Aileen brought them cups of warmed ale mixed with honey and flavoured with myrtle. She sat beside them, wrapping her shawl around her.

'We know,' said Hugh, smiling. 'Dhion came to the house and we had to follow him back to the smithy for him to show us too.'

'So you've seen it?' said Micheil.

'Ye…es,' Hugh replied.

'And what d'you make of it? How does he do it?'

'As for how he does it, I have to say I don't know that. He tried to explain it, and I'm sure he understood what he was saying, but I couldn't grasp it.'

'Leighan says it's just a trick, like a pedlar might do.'

'Dhion's not that sort of man.'

'He himself believes in what he is doing,' said Morag. 'This is clear from the way he talks about it with us, who know him.'

'I'll tell you what it's like,' said Hugh, taking a sip from his cup. ' – Aileen, this ale is wonderful! Thank you.'

He turned back to Micheil. 'Have you listened to Shean telling how his grandfather used to find lodes of ore in the hills? He would go out with a forked stick in his hands – he said alder was good, but he could use oak or hazel as well – and where the stick moved, that was where he dug.

'How did the stick move? I don't know. But if it was nothing but a trick, how was it that he found the ore? When you think about it, most of what surrounds us we don't understand. We accept things because they are usual. Dhion has shown us something unusual to us – but by his account it's usual where he comes from.'

'Dhion was trying to explain to us,' put in Morag. 'He was saying that where he comes from, they use this sort of thing all the time. It lights their houses, it cooks their food, it even pulls their carts. He wanted to say that he could make that happen here as well.'

'I don't know,' said the shareg. 'He tells wonderful tales of where he comes from. I still don't know what to make of them. As for the townsfolk – the easiest way is to refuse to give these things any time at all.'

'Aye,' said Aileen, 'who wants to have to turn a wheel like that so fast to light your home, when all you need do is pull a stick from the fire and light a candle?'

'Micheil,' Hugh began again, 'I've been meaning to talk with you this while back now. It's something that Coghlane said to me. It was shortly before Samhain when she summoned me. You know she's a canny woman. She had seen something that she said concerns us all. It was not very clear, but she saw new things – new ways of doing things – that she said would challenge our way of life.' He forbore to talk of the other matter she had spoken of and that now he himself had seen. 'She always says there is nothing that is either good or bad in itself: only in how we hold it. I wonder whether Dhion holds in his hand that which has the power to change much – very much. But I wonder too if we are ready to hold such change well.'

The shareg looked sharply across at his friend in the dim candle-light. There was no smile now on the brown-framed face.

'Hugh, he's only an apprentice who's made a toy. That's all it is.'

'I don't think that is all it is. He told us he could build a wheel that the water of the burn could move, to do the self-same thing, but with all the force of the water behind it. Aileen, you wouldn't have to sit there turning the wheel – the stream could do it.'

'You make me uneasy, Hugh. How many generations have we lived like this? Father has passed skill and knowledge down to son, and mother down to daughter – does anyone know how long? Why should we have to change things? A wheel's place is on a cart. When a wheel starts – what? Making stuff you can't see that runs through wires without holes in them... there's something – something not right. What do we do?'

'Watch and wait, Micheil. Welcome what is helpful, and bid good day to what is not. It falls to you first, but also to me, to lead the people in our response to what comes. It will be better if we two work together.'

'I shall watch and wait for now. But I will not stand by and allow a foreigner to change who we are. We are a people, and I have vowed to defend my people.'

'Indeed. But every people changes. The saws that Shean makes for Leighan, that his father taught him how to make, are better than those his great-great-grandsires made for their carpenters. We learn new things all the time. The glory is to have the wisdom to know which things to keep, and which to forget. Up to now, our changes came little by little. What Dhion speaks of is a great step, all at once. I doubt that our people are ready for such a giant's leap. Yet their fathers and mothers knew a great change. I think of the time when the Blessed Rortan came.'

The fire crackled and they sipped their ale. At last, Micheil spoke again.

'Hugh, this man is become almost as a son to you, and you are a dear friend to me. But our friendship will not stand against my doing what is right for our people.'

'What you say is as it should be. In the same way, our friendship must not stand against my speaking what I see to be true. So may I speak true indeed. And may what you do *be* right.'

First-Day, and Tollagh was over, and Hugh watched the fisherfolk climbing the seaward path. There was Benrish and his son – they hadn't left the town yet. He had been wanting to speak with the lad. He strolled across.

'Well, Dermot, I've heard all about your new boat. Is she all you hoped for?'

The lad kept his eyes on the ground. 'Aye.'

Benrish broke in. 'Aye, he's right proud of it, aren't you, son?'

Dermot would not be drawn. He stood, sullen, silent.

'They go out together, Dermot and Callen's lad,' said Benrish, covering his son's rudeness. 'They brought back a fine catch the other day.'

Dermot had never been one for words, Hugh thought. But this?

'I shall walk across to Fisherhame as soon as I can,' Hugh told Morag as they sat together. 'I have some visiting to do.'

215

'Then you must be gone straight away,' she replied. 'You don't want to be coming back in the dark.'

It was a fine day, cold and clear, and Hugh took enjoyment from the walk over the pass. But he wondered what he would find on the other side. He gave the greeting at the door of Benrish's house.

'The man's at Callen's just now.' Mairie A'Bhenrish brought him in and sat him by the fire. Eilidh and Siobhan dropped their sewing and scurried to bring him refreshment. 'You'll find him there.'

'Thank you,' said Hugh. 'And Dermot? Where's he this fine day?'

'Well...' Mairie glanced at the door. 'He's gone to sea, Father.'

'Today? Who's he sailing with?'

'No-one... Just hisself.' She paused, then hurriedly added, 'He's no taken his gear with him. I'm no happy about it.'

Hugh knew that Dael would make sure there was no fishing on First-Day. Still, to be out at sea alone...

'I saw him this morning after Tollagh. How is he?'

'Father...' She paused. 'He keeps going on about the girl.'

Hugh raised his eyebrows in a question, as if he didn't know.

'The blacksmith's girl, Mi'Shean, you know. He even went to the Ma'Hinto the other day. He demanded leave to start building a house, as if they were like to be married. It's worried about him I am.'

The Ma'Hinto – it was like her to give Dael his proper title as the son of Intoch. Perhaps Hugh should go on to his house before he left.

'What does your man say?'

'He's going to see the smith this coming week – talk with him. But really – he can see the poor girl's no a fishwife, for all that her aunt's here with us. You know

216

they've always been friends, but friends is one thing – marriage is another.'

Hugh glanced across at her two daughters, sitting on the other side of the fire. They dropped their eyes at once.

'Can ye no talk with him yerself, Father? Tell him…'

'I'd like to say I would, Mairie.' He remembered his attempt at conversation that morning. 'I'd hoped to see him just now. I'll try again.'

His heart was full of foreboding as he climbed back to the pass. Dael had added little more to Mairie's tale. Into his heart had come Coghlane's words, and his own vision at Samhain. Dusk was falling, and before the sea was lost to sight he turned. There below him, tiny in the distance, a boat was winging towards the shore, a single figure in the stern. Hugh breathed again, and walked on.

31

The second moon from Samhain was swelling towards the full, and after the clear night the sun had risen on the little garden behind the smith's house, making the frost on the kale glitter among the dark green leaves. Shinane pulled on boots of sheepskin and covered her shawl with a hooded cloak. She wound cloths round her hands to keep out the worst of the cold, and dropped a sharp knife into her basket. Her mother was at A'Shar'g's house, leaving her to do all that was needed at home.

'Peace to you, Mi'Shean,' a passing shepherd called over the wattle fence as he led his little flock in from pasture.

'Peace with you, Duigheal,' she answered. 'There are clouds rising yon, away over the mountain. Do you think it might snow?'

The shepherd stopped and turned, conning the weather with practiced eyes. 'Aye – I'm folding my little ones now, an I expect I'll be bringing out the hay tomorrow. God go with you.'

'Ghea keep you,' she called after him. She thought. A heavy fall of snow could break the kale heads, bury the neeps. She cut the leaves she had come for, filling her basket. She could dig out a few neeps and lay them by. Even if they were not needed, they would come to no harm. She went for the spade, where it stood in a corner of the workshop.

In the sudden warmth of the forge, there was Dhion alone, at the anvil. Despite the cold outside, he had stripped to the waist. As she saw him, she remembered how thin and fragile he had looked when he first came to them. Now his strength, the muscles of his arms,

218

though not like the wiry, knotted sinews of her father, caught her attention as she entered behind him, softly as was right, not to disturb his work.

The spade was there, sharing the corner with a crow-bar, a heavy spike and a sledge-hammer. He would not hear over his hammering. Then the tools chinked together just as Dhion's blows stopped. He glanced over his shoulder.

'Mi'Shean – can I help you?' He laid his work carefully on the flat of the anvil and turned, wiping his hands on his apron.

Shinane noticed the formality, but also the warmth of the greeting. She looked down.

'Where's father?' she asked.

'With the carpenter and a few others.'

'I came for the spade.' She told him of the shepherd's words, and how she thought to bring in a store of vegetables before the weather turned.

'The ground will be hard this morning. It'll be heavy work. Let me help you.'

He took his plaid, wrapping it round his shoulders as she watched. He picked up the spike – four feet of iron, a point at one end, a blunt chisel-edge at the other – and motioned to her to lead the way back to the kale-yard.

She showed him which leaves hid the neep-tops, purple and yellow, pushing out of the frozen ground. He took aim and drove the chisel-end deep beside the first root and pulled, splitting the hard earth.

'There,' he panted. 'You can dig that one up.'

They worked along the row.

As they came to the end, he said, softly, 'Do you remember… Do you think, ever, of the time we met at the rock-pool?'

She looked hastily around her. She could see no-one. 'I thought you would never say anything about that,' she muttered.

'I've not had the chance.' In went the spike again. Then he said, 'You remember I asked you what sort of a person you wanted to be?'

Her hands trembled. She gripped the spade. Yet she felt dazed as well. She waited dumbly on what would come next.

'I think you feel you're being trapped,' she heard him say. 'You see a future for yourself that you fear, and you can't see your way out.'

She looked up at him from her digging. His tall form sharp in the cold winter light, his face bent towards hers, a question in his eyes. She opened her mouth to reply, and then closed it. His words had unlocked a room hidden inside her. The door had swung open, revealing a chamber of such barrenness that dismay washed through her.

'What can I do?' she whispered.

'What would you like to do?'

She paused. Then, in a rush, as she cast off caution it came out. 'What would I like? I'd like to be able to read the Book in the rondal. I'd like to talk with the Father and A'Phadr about what it holds. That's what I'd like. But that can never happen. Instead, I fear… I fear…' She tailed off.

'What?' he urged her.

'Father is holding back for now,' she whispered. 'But unless he can see another way, he will not hold back for ever. In only a little time, he will have me betrothed. But I cannot… I cannot…'

They faced each other across the cold ground.

'I could teach you to read,' said Dhion.

Shinane stared at him. His words made no sense to her.

'Would you like that?'

Within, opposing voices rising up, hope strangled by custom, a chaos of noise.

'How…?'

'Well,' said Dhion, 'you know that the Father and A'Phadr are like a father and mother to me. I think they would welcome you into their home, where they have a few books. I could teach you there. I think your own father could not mind, in the Father's house.'

'But – you can read?' Her exclamation came louder than she intended. Her heart leaped. 'You mean, like the Father?'

'His books are written in different letters from the ones I know; but I was starting to read them when I was living there.'

'I've so longed to read a book! The Father let me hold one once, when I went to his story days. He read some of it to us. The tales in there! It's like magic how they come out of those marks. But – can you teach me? Really?' She clenched her hands, realised what she was doing, dropped them again; then determinedly, she clasped them together. 'Oh, please!'

'Will you let me talk to your father? I think he would need a bit of convincing, but if your mother was there, I feel she would be on your side.'

'Yes, she would, she would – I hope. I'm sure… She must – Oh…'

A snowflake drifted silently down. It touched her nose with a cold kiss, bringing her back to the task at hand.

'We must get in the neeps…'

He held out his apron and she piled them in. There were more there than she had intended. Oh, well… She picked up her basket of kale and followed him back to the house. Together they stacked the roots against the stony wall of the store.

'When?' she whispered.

'Leave it with me. I'll see what I can do.'

ॐॐ

Shinane was sitting spinning by the fire. The snow had come, but Shean was still away across the town when Dhion came in from the forge. Fineenh rose and brought him a cup of ale with bread and cheese. Quietly, Shinane got on with her work.

'A'Shean, thank you,' said Dhion as he settled himself. 'How are A'Shar'g and the women at her house?'

Fineenh hesitated. 'Oh, you don't want me to talk about that.'

With a flash of annoyance, Shinane wondered why her mother was always so ready to turn the talk away from what she loved most.

'I hear from A'Phadr that when you get together you do some wonderful needlework. Anything people make with their hands interests me.'

'The tapestry that A'Phadr is making is beautiful, right enough. You'll have seen that. I don't know how she makes all her dyes, or where she gets them from. I think the Father's family must send them to her.' Fineenh's voice tailed off.

'For sure, I've seen the tapestry many times. I've seen it growing, and it is indeed lovely. But what are you making?'

'Oh, it doesn't compare…' She looked down, fiddling with a knife. Shinane wanted to call out, *Your embroidery is beautiful, mother!* But custom told her she must not gainsay her mother's word before one who was not kin.

'Can I cut you more cheese?' Fineenh was saying. 'Oh, and… thank you for helping the girl with the roots. She mentioned you had. You shouldn't, you know – that's her work.'

'The ground was hard and I was glad to help.'

Dhion finished his hunk of bread and cheese. 'She was telling me this morning…' He took his knife and cut himself another piece of bread. 'She was telling me how she'd like to learn to read.'

Shinane's heart began to pound. She kept her eyes down. She held her breath.

'Oh, that one... Half the time she has her head in the clouds. I don't know how she'll get on in Fisherhame, I really don't.'

'It's just that I could teach her,' she heard Dhion say, 'if she'd like. I could ask the Father if we could work at his house, where he has one or two books.'

He paused. From under her lashes, Shinane watched him watching her mother, playing with the knife in her lap. She felt cold with tension.

Fineenh spoke: 'I know she'd like. But I don't know about her father. He'd say, *What does a fisherman's wife want with reading?* I suppose he'd be right. But...'

'Forgive me for saying this, A'Shean. Is it certain your daughter's to be betrothed to a fisherman? I wonder how happy she'd be as a fisherman's wife.'

Shinane bit her lip. One who was not kin should never have presumed to make such a remark.

Fineenh opened her mouth, but no word came out. For a long moment the three froze, the spindle still, the crackling flames in the hearth the only movement, the only sound.

Then Dhion got up. 'Excuse me,' he said, turned, and went back through the forge door. As it closed behind him, Shinane rose from her stool and knelt before her mother.

'Please, mother. I want it more than anything. Will you speak to Father? Please?'

Her mother looked at her. Shinane saw in her gaze a curious mixture of pity and hope.

Her father came home at last, stamping the snow off his boots at the door. She watched her mother shake out his cloak and hang it; bring him a steaming cup of ale. At that moment, Dhion came in from the forge.

'You're the talk of the town, and no mistake,' Shean grumbled. 'Leighan's telling everyone your toy is a trick, and it doesn't improve your standing. I stick up for you, and say it works, although I don't know how. I think some folk listen to me. But Doughael the weaver, who hears all the women's talk – he says you women are getting carried away with ideas of all your work being done for you by magic.'

He glowered at his wife. 'Well, woman? What do you say? What are all you squawking gulls chattering about?'

Shinane's heart sank. With all this talk about the Seaborne, her father would hardly be willing to add to it. Not now.

32

It was that raw time that follows the festival of the Rebirth of the Sun, when the earth is at her coldest and the promise of longer days is still not seen. Dhion was walking back from the priest's house. He had been looking at the book of stories collected by Hugh, mastering the script and questioning its scribe about some of the words. As he returned to the smithy, he passed Shareen, toiling to her new-built home, a load of peat on her back.

'The peace of Rortan upon you, Ingleeshe. A blessing, I pray.'

He turned. It was an unusual greeting. He had not heard it before.

'God's peace upon you, A'De,' he replied. Then, politely, 'Can I help you with that?'

He looked at her – the frayed hems of neck and skirt, her hardened hands. Caring for two young children alone, without a man to do the heavy work, was leaving its impression. He saw it in the lines of her still young face that was growing old before its time. She looked at him. The hunger in her gaze knocked him back. But he had made his offer, and now he must take her burden and carry it, at least as far as her door. *Where I can put it down,* he thought, *and she is left with it.*

The next morning, Dhion guessed that words had passed between husband and wife. He noticed how Fineenh kept out of the way. She could well read the signs, he thought to himself. The smith had no pressing work, but he took Dhion into the forge with him and made him ply the bellows until the fire roared and the iron glowed yellow-white. And he took the bar of metal in the long black tongs and smote it again and again on the flat of the anvil.

His speech came broken, between the hammer-blows. 'Women. If only they'd keep to their own bloody business and leave the men's talk to the men.'

Dhion, stripped to the waist and sweating from the nearness of the fire and his pumping the long bellows-sleeves, said nothing.

'I have only one daughter, and no sons to learn my trade and follow after me. I do the best for her that I can. I've known Benrish a long time and I know him for an honest man. Hard-working. Good with his wife. Well, there he was, only yesterday, after me about his boy.

'What could I say to him? The lad is like him. He's been brought up well. A good fisherman – he brings home the catch. And he can hunt – with his bare hands, too. That's the sort of son I'd have wanted.

'But he's not good enough for my lady. Give her a scrap of linen to wear, and what does she want? She wants to read! What for? Does reading help her cook the food? Will it help her suckle the bairns? Will it wash her clothes for her?

'And where's my lady going to get books to read, I'd like to know? The Father's long married, and he's no sons, so there's no looking there.

'Then my own apprentice,' Shean raised his voice an octave. 'The Blessed bloody Rortan himself come back to us.' He shot Dhion a piercing glance. 'He goes and offers to teach her. Teach her!' Sparks flew from the white-hot metal. They stung Dhion's shoulder as he knelt beside the forge. 'What for?'

'Come on – grab that end so I can fold it. Are you dim-witted or something?'

Dhion quickly dropped the bellows and leaped to the other tongs.

'Hell's teeth, man – now you're letting the fire go down!'

The many-layered metal slowly cooled, and Shean sat on the bench. He signalled his apprentice to join him.

'What do I do, man? What do I do? I can't hold out against all of you. Just tell me it's not that you're trying to take her.'

He looked searchingly at his apprentice. Then added, unexpectedly, 'Not that you wouldn't be a bad match, in your way.'

The moment passed. He resumed, fiercely: 'But you're no one of us, are you? We don't know anything of your people. We don't know you.'

Dhion looked down at his fingers, locked together in his apron. He looked up at the dark roof. He turned his head towards the door that led back into the house. He sighed.

'Ma'Ronal, I don't know. I don't even know myself any more. Where I came from seems like a dream. Then sometimes I think this must be the dream, and one day I'll wake up and find I've never been away. And… if, tomorrow, a ship sails round the headland and invites me to go back – I know that won't happen – but would I? I don't know – I just don't know any more.

'And your daughter? There's no denying I like her very much. But how can I even think of taking her from you, when I have nowhere to take her to, and I don't even know for sure where I'll be next year – what I'll be? All the same, I do think – may I say? – I can't imagine her happy as a wife of Fisherhame.'

'There – you have it. You speak a true word. But I see no other way forward.' The little man sighed, then he jumped up and strode over to the forge. He turned, and paced to the outer door. He pulled it open, and stared out into the white and blue afternoon. He stamped moodily on the piled snow. Dhion looked down at his empty hands. He could offer so little – and so much.

Then the smith turned again. Dhion felt the man's long stare, and looked across at him as he stood in the open doorway between the warmth of the forge and the deepening chill outside. It was a curiously still moment.

'That girl – she's so like her grandfather. A tall man, God rest him. Proud. Stubborn. Do you know what he said when I asked him for her mother? He said, "D'ye think ye're worthy of her?"' The blacksmith paused, then he added:

'Go on, do it, if you will. Teach her if you must. Make her read. Then we'll have to see whether I can marry her off to some moping bloody priest a day's journey hence.'

Dhion rose from the bench, and walked slowly over to join his master. They both looked out into the snow-covered town, the dirty footprints, the yellow hoof-prints. Dhion leaned against the door jamb. 'All right,' he said. 'I will.'

'I'll tell you one thing, though.' He added it, an afterthought. He looked down at the other. 'I'm not the Blessed bloody Rortan.'

The smith looked sharply up at him. For a moment Dhion thought he had overstepped. Then, suddenly, Shean cracked with laughter.

He approached it as he would any engineering problem back in the old days, in his workshops under the railway arches in Vauxhall. How do you teach someone to read, when you have books but nothing to write on?

He lay in the dim, red glow of the smithy, his hands under his head, staring up into the darkness of the roof. Paper? It was unheard-of. That scrap he had found in his pocket – the folded bank-note that had fallen apart and blown away even as he had opened it out – that had been the last he had seen.

Hugh had a few treasured parchment books that had come from overseas. Parchment. Dried animal skins. Carefully prepared, scraped, stretched – it was a long and skilful process. Could he get more of the stuff? Dhion remembered the priest's reply. *If you sent a messenger across the Island to Caerster, and then across the*

sea to the School at Sharilland; and if you'd had the fore-
sight to provide your messenger with a consideration – a
very sizeable consideration – for the toil of those crafts-
men, then, perhaps, you might get a little. After all that,
you certainly wouldn't use it to scribble a few exercises
on and then throw it away.

Slate? He had seen none. Maybe there was some,
somewhere. But what could you write on it with? They
had no chalk. Charcoal? It wouldn't show up.

What about clay? There had been people –
Mesopotamians, was it, or Sumerians – who had written on clay tablets. How would you make them? Could
he ask the potter – Padragh? How would he go about it?

It would be easy to make simple scribers in the
smithy. Soft clay, in wooden formers – he could make
those – and you could wet them and wipe them over
and use them again.

But Padragh. Dhion had not had much to do with
him, and the little he had seen did not encourage him.
Good at his work, but deep in his tradition. He sensed
he wouldn't like anything out of the ordinary. Well, he
could try. At least ask him where he could dig for clay.

With Shean's blessing, Dhion spent a further day with
Hugh and Morag, going through their few and precious
books. He had seen them, of course, when he had stayed
at the priest's house; now he studied them closely – the
script, the shape of the letters, the spelling of the words.
Most precious of all was the great Book that rested on
its stand in the rondal: thin-planed hardwood boards
covered with deer-skin; every page of well-worked vellum hand-written and hand-painted by some long-dead
monk of Sharilland. Hugh kept three or four others in
their house with them: one of legends and tales that he
himself had collected and written down. Here the shaping of the letters was less elaborate, more homely. The
script was not so different from the everyday Roman

229

letters that Dhion was used to – recognisable, at least – and soon he was able to read it fluently, even if occasionally he had to ask one or other of them what a particular word meant.

So began a brief, happy and relaxed time for Dhion. He made a larger version of what people called his 'toy.' By stretching a fine linen thread between wires and baking it carefully on the griddle, much to Fineenh's amusement, he could make a fragile carbon filament. Spinning both Shean's lodestones in a bigger coil, he was able to generate enough current to make the blackened thread glow red for a moment, before it burned and fell in dust. There was no suspicion now that he was tricking anyone.

And Shinane was an able learner. She understood the idea from the Father's schooling, and was soon putting together the sounds and slowly reading words. She was deft with her fingers, quickly picking up the little scribers he had made to copy the symbols and starting to write. It was immensely satisfying to watch her.

33

Cold drove the wolves out of their mountain fastness, down into the valleys, following the deer. And as near as they dared to the dwellings of men, where sometimes they could find a scrap or two to eat: a well-picked bone or a piece of hide. A pair stopped on the shoulder of Beh' Claragh.

The snow was ahead of them in its coming to the lowlands. It spread before them in the cold, thin sunlight, a winter pelt, like that of the hares. Ice fringed the black waters of the lough, and spread in flimsy, treacherous skins out over its depths. And there, crouching by the headwaters of the lough, huddling together against the cold, were the man-lairs.

Cautiously they stalked down to the valley floor. They smelt the smoke, the smells of people, of cattle, of sheep – the thought tightened the pangs of their empty bellies. They heard the hammering, clear on the still, frozen air.

One evening, after their meal, Hugh mentioned, 'Micheil has asked me to meet him tomorrow morning. Him, and Leighan.'

'Oh?' Morag inquired.

'Yes,' said Hugh, and sighed. He muttered, half to himself, 'I wonder where this will lead.'

A shadow was rising in his heart. Hugh had the feeling that the good time was coming to a close.

The next morning was sharp and frosty. Hugh's breath hung in clouds as he made his way to the shareg's house.

'Is Micheil within?' he asked Aileen.

'Aye, he's here, waiting for you, and Carpenter also. Come in from the cold.'

231

Micheil was talking with his sons – growing lads, who still attended Hugh's story days, when they could be spared from the field. They were as like as twins could be. As their father brought the priest to the fireside, they pulled on their boots and ran out into the clear air. Now Micheil turned to Leighan with polite enquiry.

'And how is your eldest,' he began. 'His marriage won't be long now?'

'Oh, it's a while yet. Let me see – it must be two moons still, and more. He's looking forward to it. We've mended his grandfather's house for him since he passed on last winter.'

'And Donal? I mind that he'll be returning to his own at summer's end.'

'Aye, he works well when he does what he's told. I shall find it hard to replace him when he goes – and with Olan newly-wed as well.'

Aileen brought them warmed ale, the mulling iron still in Leighan's beaker. It steamed as she withdrew it. The carpenter sipped appreciatively. Then he wiped his mouth, and said, 'But I came to you on another matter, Shareg.'

Hugh noticed that Leighan had not looked at him since his arrival. So far, he had directed all his words past him, to Micheil. He watched the craftsman attentively.

'I'll come straight to the point,' Leighan began. 'I've come about the trouble this apprentice of Shean's is causing.'

'I know Dhion Ingleeshe. I am not aware that he is causing trouble.'

'Shareg, people are talking. There are these – things – he keeps making, that do strange… things.' A pause, then it came out in a rush. 'And I say that he's seeing too much of his master's daughter.'

For the first time the carpenter looked at Hugh: a hard, straight look.

It was Micheil who responded. 'Leighan, what do you mean?'

'I've seen them – more than two or three times – walking to the priest's door. They don't walk together, I admit, but they are both in the priest's house together. At the same time. Isn't that so? By your leave, Father, I have to ask you. What good thing are they doing there?'

Hugh let the man's question settle in the air between them, considering his reply. In the end, he said, simply, 'He is teaching her to read.'

'To *read?*' The carpenter wore a look of astonishment. Hugh saw a thought cross his face. 'I see… That's why…' With indignation he cried, 'Padragh told me more than a moon back that the Ingleeshe was asking him for clay. He was reluctant, but in the end he showed him where he dug it. You know how kindly he is. He asked him what he wanted it for. And the man said it was for writing on. Well, Padragh was amazed by that. But – you know what he's like. If he'd thought for a moment the man was intending to inveigle a maid… He would never have… He's duped him!'

Hugh glanced across at Micheil. The shareg was leaning forward in his chair, a frown on his brows.

Micheil spoke. 'That is a serious charge, Carpenter.'

Leighan was not to be put down.

'What does the daughter of Blacksmith want wi' reading?' he demanded. 'And – who is this stranger to teach her anything at all?'

He glared at them, turning from one to the other.

'*If* she is to read,' he resumed, 'and I think that's a very big *if* – wouldn't it come better –' He swung to face the priest '– for your wife to teach her?'

The words were acid.

Again, Hugh paused before making his reply. 'Well, in truth, A'Phadr *is* teaching her, for, as you know, she is far better versed in the old stories than the Ingleeshe could possibly be. And she sees to how the girl shapes her letters. Dhion's writing seems to have been somewhat different.

'As things fell out, it was the Ingleeshe who first learned of the girl's wish to read. He offered his help. We have seen no reason – and nor, it seems, has her own father – to refuse it.'

Micheil sat back, his hands on his knees. 'I don't see that there's anything in particular that's wrong with teaching someone to read.'

'Shareg, I'm sorry to labour the matter, but I feel I have to point out that it's Shean's daughter he's teaching. It's a woman! I have two objections to that.' He held up two calloused fingers of his right hand, ticking them off with the left, one by one. 'First, if all the young women of the town can suddenly read, what ideas will they have of themselves, eh? And what thoughts will enter their heads? Who will they want to marry? Not my sons, and not your sons.'

The carpenter gave his shareg a keen look.

'And second,' he went on grimly, 'on the subject of marriage, many of us had expected that by now Blacksmith's daughter would be betrothed to a fine young man who has been known to us all his life. Not spending her time with a stranger who is in no place to offer her anything but mad notions to make her useless.

'Shareg, I'm concerned for our people and for our way of life. If this foreigner brings in outlandish ways and ideas, then there's no knowing where it will end. What exactly are these toys he's making, and why does he do it? There's something very un-Island-like about it all.'

'Leighan, I hear your words, and they weigh with me.' The shareg paused, then he went on, 'You will agree with me that nothing I have heard requires justice.' It seemed to Hugh that the carpenter fought down a scowl. 'But I hear – and not only from you – that there is unrest concerning these matters that you tell me about. Leave this with me, I ask you. The Father and I will discuss it. Come back to me here in three days and I will tell you what I shall do. Are you content?'

The other looked at him. There was a pause. His eyes flitted across Hugh's face. Then he spoke. 'I am content – for now,' he said.

'Well then,' said the shareg, leaning back. 'Drink your ale – it must be cold, man. Aileen,' he called. 'Do you have another iron in the fire for Carpenter's ale?'

Hugh spent a long time with Micheil discussing together what was best. He and the shareg looked up every pathway, every twist or turn of the situation that faced them, to the best of their sight. Together, the two of them hammered out what they should do. In the end, they agreed to listen to the people in an open meeting, to be held seven days hence. In the meantime, Micheil would speak with Dhion.

Hugh did not forget Mother Coghlane's prophecy. The shadow in his mind grew and began to shape itself.

The third moon after mid-winter, and the wolves waited for the first of the lambs to be born. Still the storms could sweep down from the mountains and bring hail and sleet and murderous cold in their jaws. But sometimes a weak and sickly scrag would come too early, while the dam's milk was still thin from the wan grass.

The crows would take the afterbirth, alighting on their ragged wings in the daylight when the wolves dared not be seen in the town meadows. But the wolves were hungry too. The deer had not begun calving yet, and the she-wolf was carrying her cubs. During the nights they could come lower, to the edges of the pastures where the smell of peat-smoke set the hairs on their backs on end. This was their opportunity, while the ewe was still recovering from the birth and the little

235

one was wobbly on its legs. Although little more than skin and bone and not yet fat on the first rich milk, it was still good warm blood.

They waited. Drew nearer. Faced down the angry ewe stamping her forefeet. Seized, and carried off.

34

The promise of spring was in the air. Then the weather turned bitter. The snow came roaring back from the hills in the north-east. Shinane watched the sheep scraping to find the poor grass beneath and Duigheal raking together the last of his hay.

The wan sun was well past the noon when, stepping outside to take in what was left of the fading light, she saw the shareg treading a path through the freezing slush towards them. Her mother was away across the town. It must fall to her to welcome him.

'Shareg – may your coming be in peace.' She knew it was the right thing to say. Hearing the household greeting to such a personage in her own voice sounded strange.

'In peace, and with God, Mi'Shean,' he replied.

She felt his eyes on her. Stepping back to let him in, taking his heavy cloak from him, cold from the winter air, she gestured towards the chair beside the hearth.

'I will fetch my father,' she told him. But the shareg stopped her as she turned.

'It is his prentice in particular that I wish to speak with.'

Shinane withdrew to prepare food for them. But she listened keenly to the men's talk. First they spoke of the cold weather and its effects on the townsfolk. She knew her father had little feeling for them: his work at the forge kept him warm. Then the shareg asked how his prentice was shaping. From there they went on to the *things* that he had made. Then the *thing* had to be fetched, so that he could see it again. There they stood, two wooden towers. Carefully, Dhion placed a waystone on its stand in a basin of water. Yet again, he wound the handle. And the stone moved.

She heard the shareg's deep rumble. 'You say... that this *stuff* can change how we do things... All right, I want you to try to make me understand. What is this *stuff* that nobody can see?'

There was a pause. Into it Shinane carried her laden tray, setting down the bannocks and beakers before them.

'I'll try,' said Dhion.

It was now her place, she knew, to retire. But she did not find it in her to leave them. Instead of taking up the tray, she waited on his words. No-one seemed to mind. Their attention was all on Dhion.

'Where I come from,' he started slowly, 'we say that the world is held together by four... I'll call them powers, though that's not really the right word.' He looked around at them all. 'These powers hold things together that would otherwise fly apart. We see one of them at work every time we drop something.'

He picked up a small wooden plate, raised it, and let it fall, catching it with his free hand.

'Why does it fall?' asked Dhion. 'We all know that it does. Where I come from, we say that... the earth herself sends out a power that draws it to her. You could say, it is being drawn towards the bosom of the Mother.'

Shinane started. Just the day before, in their reading together in the Father's house, 'the bosom of the Mother' had been in their text.

'There are other powers,' Dhion continued. 'One you may have seen in the waystones you lent me, Shareg. Have you seen how, if you put small metal bits near one, they leap towards it?'

He looked around at them, but nobody stirred.

'Can I show you?'

Dhion took the waystone from the basin, and set it on the board. He went into the forge and came back with a handful of iron filings. He scattered them near the stone.

Shinane gasped. They seemed to take on a life of their own, for they leaped and clung to the stone.

There was a stunned silence.

Then, 'How did you do that?' asked Micheil. She heard a warning note in his voice.

'The stone did it,' said Dhion, quietly. 'You can try it yourself.'

Shean went to get more filings. Shinane watched first her father, then the shareg, scattering the iron bits, and the pieces leaping up and covering the stone like fur.

At last they sat back. The shareg said, 'Then tell us, Dhion Ingleeshe, what is going on.'

'It's one of the powers of the earth,' said Dhion, simply. 'It's in some special stones, and those are the ones the Northmen chose to guide their ships. The Northmen knew about this power.'

He looked around at them, his eyes finally meeting her own. He looked back at the men.

'We see the other two powers at work without knowing that there is anything happening at all,' he went on, quietly. 'So we do not know they are working. But where I come from, we say that this dish' – he returned the plate to the board – 'and everything else, is made up of a very great number of tiny… specks, so small we cannot see them. These are held together by those other powers. They seem quite solid. But if those powers were not working – there would be no solid thing. Just a chaos of… We call them *particles*. And in among these *particles* – there is empty space. That is how there is a hole in the copper wire.'

Again, he paused. Shinane looked at the shareg. He was watching Dhion.

'If what you say of the dish, Ingleeshe, or of the wire, is true,' said Micheil, slowly, 'what does it mean for this board? Or this house? Or for our very selves sitting under this roof?'

There was silence.

'I think you understand me,' replied Dhion, equally slowly. 'Everything is made up of these tiny – specks. Our own bodies are like all things in this.' Again he looked around, then added. 'I can tell you that we too, where I come from, find this a strange thought. Strange, because it's not how things seem, to any of us. But we have managed to make… *machines'* – the unfamiliar-sounding word jarred on her ear – *'maseenen,'* he went on, repeating the strange word in a more Island-like way. 'These *maseenen* help us see more than we can with our eyes. They tell us much. And beyond what they tell us, a few rare people, ah… see in their minds, and prove what they see, using… the language of numbers.'

Somewhere in the storehouse of her memory, what Dhion was saying was connecting with a story the Father had told in the rondal, a story about how everything came into being when the One sent angels into a world of chaos, each with a power to shape and to form… Shivers ran through her body.

'Anyway,' Dhion resumed. 'The toy that I made works because of another of the four powers. We see this power in lightning. This… er… lightning-power brings light. But when you… find a way of putting it together with the power of the waystone, it can also bring movement. It is this that is making the toy move.'

Dhion stopped speaking. She held her breath. Although she knew there was much that she could not fathom, his words made sense in her heart. Did they make sense to the men? She saw her father, looking towards the shareg; the shareg, studying Dhion. He seemed to be considering. Then he spoke again.

'Dhion Ingleeshe, I will be frank with you, and tell you simply that I do not understand what you are say-ing. We all know there are powers at work in the world, and most of us are content to leave it there. You speak of this *lightning-power*, of *the power of the waystone*. I don't know what to make of this. But I see you believe what

240

you say. And this *toy* of yours… Well, I have seen it and, like your words, I do not understand it. So now, tell us. How did you come to know these things?'

There was a silence. Shinane held her breath.

'I was taught a lot of this in school,' he said, simply. 'And it was a part of my studies later on. But where I come from, everyone uses the power you see in the toy. It's not… It's nothing unusual.'

The shareg stared at him. He put his head in his hands. For a long moment he was silent.

Shinane felt indignation welling up in her. Why were people so stupid? Why could they not see the Seaborne as she saw him, simply, clearly? He was a man like any of them, yet unlike. He had different knowledge, different ways, yet he was straightforward, direct, struggling to be with them, to answer their questions in words they could hear and understand.

Then the shareg looked up. At last he noticed her, standing where she should not be. He met her eyes and frowned. 'Mi'Shean, we thank you for your service.'

She stood her ground.

Her father looked round. 'Be off with you, girl! What're you thinking of?'

She spoke. Quietly, demurely even, but without an apology. 'Father. Shareg.' She dropped a little curtsey in addressing him. 'I beg your leave to stay.'

'What d'you mean, girl?' Her father made to rise.

The shareg held out a restraining hand towards him. 'Mi'Shean. Please explain yourself. You may speak.'

She stood, unmoving, among them, her head inclined down. Then she raised her chin. She found her voice. It flowed out of her, quiet, yet filling the silence like the sea.

'I know Dhion Ingleeshe to be honest and true. Why do you keep questioning him? Do you put him on trial for ever? When will you make an end?'

241

She watched the effect of her words on them: her father, making again to rise with his hot temper, restrained once more by the shareg's hand; Dhion, looking straight at her, an expression of wonder on his face.

The shareg spoke. He kept his voice level, even if it dropped a tone.

'Mi'Shean, I have given you the right to speak. But I am perplexed by what you say. By what right do you take it upon yourself to speak for your father's apprentice?'

'Shareg.' Again the little curtsey. 'Dhion is under our roof and my father's protection. I see him day by day. With my father's blessing he has become my teacher and I have come to know him well. And I stand before the One to tell you the truth that I see. I beg your leave to say this. A woman may have opinions, as a man does.'

A silence deeper than night filled the house. Shinane could feel her heart thudding in her chest, but in a deep place within she felt perfectly calm.

Then, the creak of an outer door closing, and in a moment the curtain of the lean-to was tweaked aside, and her mother's round face appeared. She was still removing her shawl.

The company all stared in her direction. Shinane saw her mother's face redden, watched her bobbing up and down in confusion before the shareg: such a contrast with her own new-found feeling in which, for the first time, she was delivered of all doubt. She stood free, clear.

'Shinane – what are you doing, standing there? You know this is no place for a chit like you. Come away at once! What are you thinking of?'

She felt her mother's hand on her arm, pulling her back into the shadows, away from the men. Her body went; it had to. But with her eyes she declared defiance. Her new-found freedom brought her peace.

35

Tramping back to his home through the dark and the snow, Micheil turned over what he had witnessed. Dhion's account of hidden powers was beyond him, and how he was going to handle it he did not yet know. But now there was another matter pressing, and one he felt more capable of thinking about.

So this is the girl who would learn to read, he thought. She was good-looking, and carried herself well. She could have turned a head or two, even in Caerster. What had the smith been thinking of, to consider marrying her into Fisherhame? Everyone had seemed to take the match as a thing that was to be. But – especially now that he had spoken with her – could he imagine this girl with young Dermot? He could not. Now matters were not clear there, and they should be. It left a bad smell in the air.

Leighan's words echoed in his mind. *If all the young women of the town can suddenly read, what ideas will they have of themselves? Who will they want to marry? Not my sons, and not your sons.* Only once before had he witnessed any woman voice an opinion in a council of men. That was the priest's wife, a few moons before. But this girl – such an opinion! And on behalf of an outsider.

The apprentice and the master's daughter? Of course, that had happened before. Or was he really no more than teaching her to read? But a smith's apprentice who could read? How many people did he know who could read? He rehearsed the list. Still, Hugh had been quite clear. Micheil had checked with him on this very matter, and what had the priest said? *Oh yes – he reads better than I do.* Better than the Father? Would that not have been beyond belief if it hadn't been the Father himself who'd said it?

243

And what about all this rumour of the Blessed One being returned and in their midst? Hugh said Dhion denied it. He must ask the Seaborne himself. Difficult enough to be clever; but to be clever and mad enough to call yourself a returned saint – that would be positively dangerous. Yet he liked the man. Had they not spent four days together on their journey across country to greet the High Shareg? You got to know a man in such times. Had he not roofed him with the smith in order to find him a place among them? From all he had seen, that was going well.

And if he was to have a place among them, was it not natural that, in time, he would marry one of their girls?

The wind turned once more, and the recent snow was melting fast. In the meadows green patches appeared between the white, and in the town the yellow slush turned to mud, leaving snow only where it was piled up in the shadows of the houses.

The promised council was held on the third day of the week. The shepherds and cowmen from the hills wouldn't bother to come down – it was a busy and worrying time of year for them – but as he sat in his chair, at the front with Hugh behind his shoulder, and watched the men coming into the rondal, Micheil saw that everyone who could be present was there.

At last there were no new arrivals. Micheil rose, and the low murmur of voices ceased.

'Men of the township of Caerpadraig, I thank you for coming to this council. I have called you together over an unusual matter. You all know of Dhion Ingleeshe Seaborne, now apprenticed to Shean Ma'Ronal Blacksmith. Some of you know him well.'

He looked at Dhion, seated beside the smith in the front row. As heads turned toward the Seaborne, he saw the colour rise in his face.

He continued. 'Leighan Carpenter has told me of his concerns. The first is, that the Seaborne is making strange things that work by unseen powers. I have spoken with Dhion Ingleeshe about the powers he uses. He tells me that they are not magical, but natural. He tells me that where he comes from, they know rather more of the hidden powers of Earth than we do here on the Island. More than this, he tells me that this knowledge could change the way we do things here, to the benefit of us all.

'I ask for your wisdom in how we should receive these new ideas: whether we welcome them and test them, to see if we think they may indeed be good for us; or whether we hold that we do not want change at this time. So I put it to you, are we a people ready to test what is new to us, or not? This is what we are gathered to consider today.'

There was an interruption. He scanned the upturned faces. Doughael the weaver had risen from where he sat on a bench near the back. His round pink face bobbed above the sea of men. His high voice piped across the rondal.

'Shareg, is it not so that a pair of white dolphins brought us the man Ingleeshe? Did he not come to us in the way that the Blessed One came to this isle?'

Men's voices were raised. A few tried to shout the weaver down. Several, Leighan among them, jumped to their feet. Micheil saw Dhion himself half rising, until the smith held him down with a muttered word in his ear. Fengoelan, mountain-like, stood still and spread out his arms, his palms downward. As the noise subsided his deep voice rumbled. 'Shareg, by your leave.' There was a hush. 'I saw no dolphins, nor whales. Did you, Targud?'

His son shook his head where he sat.

Micheil brought the meeting to order, and Hugh spoke of Dhion's learning of their language and ways, and of their discovering that he could read. Micheil thanked him, and the priest once more took his seat. Then the shareg called upon Shean to speak of Dhion's roofing and apprenticeship.

'And I have to say, he is shaping very well, so far,' the smith concluded.

Now the shareg spoke: 'We have heard how the Seaborne, Ingleeshe, has started to take his place among us. He has applied himself with a will, and shown effort. Let no-one underestimate how great an effort it must have been. In years gone by, others have come, lost on the sea.' He looked across the crowded space to where Doughael sat. 'I see nothing so very remarkable, except for the mystery of *where* he has come from. It seems that neither he, nor any of us, can cast more light on that for now.

'But Dhion, disturbance seems to follow you as a bull follows a heifer in season. So now it is your turn. You may have your say first, before I ask Leighan Ma'Challen Carpenter to tell us of his concern.'

Never had he had to hold the reins of a meeting so firmly. Dhion had repeated the explanation he had given in the smith's house. He had shown the assembled council his *maseen*. He had even gone and stood outside the rondal, after inviting anybody to turn the handle that span the stone. Fengoelan was the first to volunteer, followed by Targud, then several of the younger men. All who wished came and looked closely at it from every angle. Micheil felt that things were going well.

Then a voice rose from the midst of the melee. 'All right, Shareg. If it's no a trick, then it's worse.' In a moment, Micheil was alert, had the man in his sight. He was a big man, heavy jowled, with a deep voice. It was Murdogh. 'What the Ingleeshe tells us of how it works doesn't add up. It's no canny, and I'll have no part in it. And neither will anyone who has any sense.'

246

Micheil held back his anger. 'Murdogh. Do you know why the rainbow appears after the rain? Do you know why the lights of the Quick-men dance in the northern sky on a winter's night? You have all heard the Ingleeshe tell us that the things he has made work by natural means. If we cannot fully grasp how, that doesn't make it wrong.'

Murdogh looked back at him stubbornly.

'Shareg, I've grown up wi' rainbows. But this – who's seen the like of this before, eh? Whatever he says, I say it's no natural, and it's no canny, and I'm having now't to do wi' it.' He sat down, and folded his arms. A few men behind him nodded.

Micheil paused to weigh his words. Before he had found them, another, younger voice broke through:

'Aye, and why can't he tell us where he comes from? What's so secret about that?'

Micheil scanned the bearded faces. He found the red-haired young fisherman beside his father.

'Ma'Bhenrish, you are to follow custom and ask leave to speak. But I say to you, and to all of you, I am going to declare that matter closed,' he announced. 'There is nothing more of benefit to be said about it.'

Still the young man did not desist. 'We don't want foreigners here. They take our land, they take our food, they take our womenfolk. Don't they, Ingleeshe?'

Before the last word was spat out, Micheil was on his feet. 'Dermot Ma'Bhenrish. You will speak civilly to this gathering, and before me.'

But Dermot seemed unable to stop himself.

'What you say is a lie, foreigner! Go back where you came from. And if you come near me, I'll help you. I'll send you back to your own land all right!'

'Silence!' Micheil's voice roared out. 'Ma'Bhenrish, you will leave this council. I have spoken.'

For a moment the young man stood, glowering. Micheil held his gaze, as in a vice. Suddenly, Dermot turned and stormed out of the rondal. Benrish rose in confusion. 'Shareg, I apologise for my son. He's young, hot-headed…'

Micheil had to call for order. It was clear that Dermot had the support of quite a few. Most, he knew, would always back one of their own people against the stranger with the foreign accent.

Fengoelan raised his hand and his voice. 'Shareg.'

'Let Fengoelan Fisherhame speak.'

'Shareg, Father, my brothers.' Micheil watched the old fisherman's clear blue eyes sweep the assembly. 'I have been ashamed to sit here and witness this council. It is not the hasty words of a hot-headed youngster that trouble me. It is that I see men and fathers and heads of families nodding in agreement with him.

'I mind what I would want to happen if it had been, not this Dhion Ingleeshe near to death in the sea that day, but me.'

A stir of voices rose in protest, but Fengoelan stilled them with his hand.

'If I found myself washed up in a foreign land, and my ways seemed strange to the people there, then I would look to them for guidance for the best way to be among them. I would be sorry indeed if they took against my ways and my knowledge, only because they are strange to them. Perhaps I might have gifts to bring them from my own land, if only they were willing to receive them.

'Now it may be that Dhion here has been a little unwise in how he has tried to bring us his ways…' Micheil saw men nodding, too vehemently for his liking. 'I say, he may have been unwise, but only a little. We do not understand his *maseenen*, and as for reading, well, we look to the Father to be learned in books, and not to our smiths. That has taken us by surprise.'

There was a sudden interruption, quietly spoken, but distinct. 'And Mi'Shean. He's teaching a girl to read.' It was Leighan's voice.

Micheil stiffened. 'Order!' he cried.

The fisherman turned to face the carpenter.

'Here we have A'Phadr among us. She reads, and she is a woman and respected among us.'

He turned back to the gathering at large.

'So I say this to you, my brothers. I say I have been ashamed to sit here and hear voices raised in fear and rejection. I ask that the people I live amongst, whom I am proud to call my people, will always find a home in their midst for the stranger and the foreigner. And I ask that we look openly at what this stranger, who has been among us now for nigh on two years, has to bring. I do not say let us change. I do say, let us look. And, above all, let us treat one another with respect.

'For my own part I say, Welcome, Dhion Ingleeshe. May you find your home among us, and may you long be numbered in our midst.'

He sat. There was silence. Then began a single slow, solid hand-clap. It was the smith.

Micheil watched to see what would happen. He stilled his anxiety. Above all things, he had to keep calm. The clapping was taken up, and spread around the rondal. But not by everyone: as Micheil looked out across his people, he saw a number of men sit unmoved, their arms folded. Among them was Benrish.

It was clear the gathering was divided. He saw this. Saw that he had to give them more time.

He rose and spoke. 'Men of Caerpadraig, Fengoelan Fisherhame has spoken fair words, and, in my opinion, wise ones. Nonetheless, I see that we are not yet of one mind.

'Strong feelings have been expressed, and are not yet settled. I put it to you that we meet again at the waxing of the next moon. In the meantime, Dhion Ingleeshe will make no more *maseenen*, but will try to explain further how they work. And you will hold him as you would hold a man born and bred here, as one of yourselves and in your honour and protection. Until we meet again.'

'What about the reading?' It was Leighan, calling out again.

This time he must say something. 'Leighan Carpenter, I remind you to abide by our rule, and ask leave before you speak.'

Micheil paused, then added, 'Leighan, though your speaking was out of order, I will answer it. Mi'Shean is a maid not betrothed to any man, and under her father. What passes between a man's daughter and a man's apprentice, that offends neither law nor decency, is entirely in the hands of her father. Shean Blacksmith is a respected craftsman among us, and is worthy of our trust in this matter.'

Micheil looked around the circle, silently daring anyone to defy him. Nobody did.

'A month's time. Until then, talk with one another. I charge you to talk, not only with those who agree with you, but also with those who see this matter differently. If you have formed a firm opinion, ask yourself this question: how do you know that what you believe is right and true?'

He paused to let his words sink in.

'You have until the next moon's waxing. Are we agreed?'

Although some were slow in signalling their consent, Micheil stood, waiting until he had them all; until, so far at least, they were agreed.

Back in his own house, telling Aileen of what had passed, he muttered, 'What happens in this month will decide much, one way or another.'

That night as he lay, the candle snuffed, scenes from the meeting repeating themselves in his mind, he felt deeply uneasy. Never before had he faced such a split within his people. He asked himself what must happen to make the wound whole again.

On a pallet by the forge, Dhion's rest was no easier than the shareg's. Things had seemed to be turning in his favour, going well, and then – did Murdogh really think him some kind of sorcerer? Did half the rest of them think so too? How little they knew him; how little he knew them. Yet this, deeply unsettling though it was, seemed less grave than the current of pure hatred he had sensed pouring towards him from Dermot. Never had he known the like. He, who had at one time been amazed by the welcome he had received in this community, realised he no longer felt safe.

36

Slowly, moment by cold, clear moment, the year turned. The short, hard days were lengthening. Off the coast the fish were waking from their deep-water hiding places, where they sat out the cold months on the never-changing plains of the sea floor. It was time to take the boats out again.

Dermot had his upside-down on the shingle, where he was giving her a last check-over. He had re-caulked her timbers and cleaned her bottom again and again. He and Ronal and Euan, together young and unmarried in the hamlet, now lit a fire and hung a tar-pot above it to warm.

'Poor Dermot, then. They're saying you've lost her.' Tall and fair-haired and blue-eyed, even Dermot recognised Euan as their leader. 'Turned you down, have they? And you with your own boat and all! What're you going to do about that, then?'

The words were scalding.

Ronal moved in quickly. He was the youngest, and his beard was still straggly. 'It's because of that stranger, the smith's apprentice. You saved him yourself, didn't you? I bet you wish you'd left him to drown. They say he's a wonder man. I reckon he's bewitched her with his magic.'

Dermot poked morosely at the fire with a long stick. 'Aye, it was him all right. Talked the smith round to giving her to him, I don't doubt. And what prospects does he have? Nobody knows where he comes from; nobody knows if one day he'll just disappear back to his own land, that nobody's heard of. Who are his people, eh?'

'I heard he made a magic toy,' Euan commented. 'Bits of copper wire. I'm surprised the shareg allowed it. We don't want strangers doing magic.'

Dermot pulled the stick out of the fire. It flared in the cold wind, a little jet of flame shooting from its end. 'I'll give him magic. I'll run him over the hills, I will. I'll show him that he doesn't come here from nowhere and take our women with his fancy tricks. We're men, aren't we? I'm a man of the West, and I'll show him.' He drove the burning end into the ground. The stick snapped into three. A little pile of charcoal smoked bitterly.

'He's a good runner, though,' put in Ronal. 'They say he runs over the moors just because he likes it.'

'Aye, I've seen him.' Dermot raised his chin defiantly. 'And I'm better. Remember the goat of Beh' Claragh? I broke his neck, didn't I? I'll do the same to him. You see if I don't.'

'Go on, you Fineenh Freckle-Face. That old goat was half lame anyway.'

The taunt was unbearable.

'He was not, too! You'll see. You'll just see.' Dermot leapt up and turned away, grabbing the tar-pot. A black stickiness slopped over the rim into the fire. Flames suddenly sprang upwards, red and blackly smoking.

The next day dawned, and a light on-shore wind blew a thin rain in from the sea. The thought of the smith and his daughter was like a burning brand. Dermot thrust it aside. He found, behind it, the nuisance-thought of the Father who, every now and then, tried to catch him and talk to him. He did not want to talk to the Father. He certainly didn't want to hear what the Father might have to say to him.

The men were to meet in Fengoelan's house that morning. Dermot came with Benrish. Callen was there with his two sons. Targud brought the seal knuckle-bones, and gave them to Fengoelan. They all gathered, damp and steaming, their shadows in the lamplit room massive on walls and eaves.

The knuckle-bones were for casting lots: who would take to the boats and hold the seals onshore, and who, alone, would clamber the rocks and have the honour of the kill. For this day, it had been decided, would be the day of the seal hunt.

They all deferred to Fengoelan. Since Dael had given over the sea, he was the elder among them and presided when they gathered. Dermot watched the older man take the bones in their ancient clay beaker, worn smooth and shining from years of use. Then he threw. The knuckle-bones were scattered. To Dermot, it all seemed a jumble. But Fengoelan's eyes raised from studying them, and looked straight into his own. He felt his heart begin to race as a sudden desire arose within him. Fengoelan gathered up the bones into their pot again. A second time he threw. Dermot waited. This time not only Fengoelan, but also his father and Targud turned their heads his way, a strange look in their eyes. Fengoelan gathered and threw a third time.

The men drew in their breath. 'Well – have ye ever seen the like? Three in a row.' Callen voiced the thoughts of them all. 'Dermot – it seems that ye're chosen for the land!'

Dermot knew the seal rocks, a good step to the north of Fisherhame, as he knew every feature of the land that made up his world. The rocks shelved smoothly down to the water. Sea-pink and golden lichen decked their fissures above the tide-line, and year after year, as the spring warmed the air again and the storms of winter ceased, the seals would return to rear their pups, until the young, grown quickly fat on rich warm milk and half-chewed mackerel, were ready to take to the sea and catch their own.

Each year the men of Fisherhame would come and take maybe a dozen of the pups. They took them with respect, for they recognised fellow spirits in the seals;

fisherfolk also, and, like them, more comfortable on the waves than on the land. They took them for meat, and fat for lamps, but most especially for their skins – fine, flexible, and water-shedding, indispensable in their work in a way that neither wool nor leather could come near.

Dermot took the iron-bound club that Callen handed him. It was the first time he had been old enough to be chosen, and he knew it was an honour that he had been picked. His father slapped his back. 'Do well, son. Mind you don't turn an ankle on those rocks. Off ye go – and mind you stay hidden and upwind until we're in position.'

A flash of irritation passed through Dermot's heart. He didn't need to be told, he thought. He kept his silence. Carrying the club easily in one hand, at its balance-point just below the head, he ran down towards the sea. He turned along the margin of sand and shingle, where little derrits of water oozed out from under the stones to spill across the beach, back towards the sea whence they came.

In five-score paces the flat beach ended abruptly in a low rock wall. To the quick eye there were footholds – uneven, irregular, sloping, but offering a way over the dark stone. He knew to tread warily on the sea-weed-slippery patches of dull greens and browns that trailed their tassels into the long and shallow pools; but he could have confidence where grey barnacles encrusted the rock, taking the skin off knee and shin if you were unwary, but offering good grip for the hard soles of Dermot's feet.

Under the looming flanks of Beh' Mora was a tumble of great boulders. Between them were crevices, some as deep as a man was tall, where a slip could mean a broken shinbone, or worse. He paused a moment at the sight of the green bones of a long-dead goat. But he had known these rocks ever since he could walk by himself; he knew which he could trust, and which would wobble and turn treacherously, and they slowed him but a little.

In a while he knew he was drawing near to the seal rocks. He slowed, and turned up the shore. Above the tideline he found his way cautiously into the heather and bog-myrtle that clothed the slopes of the mountain. Now he could see the seal colony below him, and beyond, the open sea, the line of skerries breaking the worst of the Atlantic swells and offering protection to the welcoming shore. Here he would lie up; the onshore wind would blow his scent away from his prey's keen noses, and when he lay quiet and low, they would neither see him nor hear him. It was vital that they see the boats first, and then, with their attention directed seaward, he could be amongst them almost before they knew it.

The sound of the colony came faintly up to him. The few new babes, still in their white coats, he wanted to avoid: their mothers could be fierce in defence, and he had witnessed a man lose a chunk of flesh from his calf to a seal-bite. Most of the pups were now older, their hides becoming the sleek dark grey of their parents. He could see them now, their mottled colour showing where the wet fur had come away.

The sweat he had worked up started to dry, and he felt cold. Would the boats never come? What was keeping them? He looked across the rocks to the long lines of breakers, green against the grey sea. He noted the slender branches of the birches near him, swaying in the breeze. If this drizzle would ease, the weather would be just right – a little difficult getting the boats out against the wind, but then an easy passage up the coast.

And the drizzle wasn't bad. If his hair was now lank and clinging around his face, his plaid was keeping his body dry. Dermot wondered how well Euan could be trusted with his boat. That boat underscored what he was. The Seaborne owed his life to their boats. *Damn him,* he thought with a sudden fierceness, and gripped the club's haft. *Why didn't we leave him in the sea?*

Why did they have to be so damned kind? Fengoelan – his grand words; but he didn't have to live with the outworkings. He, Dermot, did. Well, since he had been part of the man's saving, could he not undo that work as well? He could… He would. He looked along the shaft of the club, to where its head lay nestled comfortably in his left hand.

There were the boats! Now they were taking up position between the two low rocky heads either side of the seal rocks. The seals had seen them. Heads were being raised, mothers were shuffling together, shepherding their few-day-old pups between them. The yearlings were already heading for the safety of the sea, knowing they could under-swim the boats with ease. He must be quick.

Dermot burst from his hiding. He leapt down the brae and onto the foreshore. There were seals in the water, seals on the rocks. There was barking all around. Now he gripped his club at its haft's end, raised over his shoulder, ready to strike. He overtook one and swung the heavy wood. Another. A seal rose up on his right, waist high, its mouth open, teeth threatening. He struck at its head and it sank down, its bloodied skull on his foot. He kicked the body away. There was no seal before him. Stretched upon the rocks was the body of the Seaborne, that day they had brought him from the sea. He raised his club again and brought it down with violence. Again and again he struck, while a fine spray surrounded him, of water from his hair, and blood and spittle and tears.

'Dermot – what're ye doing?' It was Callen. Two of the boats had landed, and the men had jumped ashore to take the carcasses.

Damn him. Damn them all!

He felt a restraining hand on his arm as he swung the club upwards, and a voice in his ear. 'That's enough, man. She's well dead.'

He turned, staring at the newcomer.

'Dermot – are ye all right?' Dermot stared, unseeing, into Callen's eyes.

He heard Targud's voice, and then his father's. 'Where are they? Did ye only get two?'

'There's another here,' Callen called. 'But it's a mother with her whiteling.'

'A mother?' Benrish hurried up. 'Dermot, you know we don't…' He stopped. He had seen the mess of blood and blubber at his feet. The pup bleating a few yards away. 'Son, what've ye done?'

Dermot turned on him in fierce anger. 'It's dead, isn't it? You wanted them dead. Well, it is. What more do you want?' He broke away from them. He gripped the club and ran blindly up the shore. He was done with words.

37

Now the winter was truly behind them, the towns-people could start looking forward to Easter. Buds on birch and the grey-blue buds of alder swelled and burst. In sheltered places above the lough-side meadows, blackthorn began to bloom. 'The time of the singing of birds is come,' said Hugh.

Morag woke early from a fitful sleep, and rose from beside her husband. The sun was not yet up, but the sky was lightening, a ruddy glow behind the eastern hills. Dressing was a simple matter, and she left the house as quietly as she could.

Primroses were beginning to show between tree-roots and on the steep little banks of the rills that fed the lough. Every year that she could remember she had been glad, with an uncomplicated, childlike joy, to see their pale yellow faces. But today something clouded that happiness. *Go back,* she told them in her heart. *This world is too cruel for you.*

Why did she say that? Spring was here, and the sun was about to burst over the mountain. Yet there was a heaviness within her that was at odds with the new life around her; a feeling in her belly that was laying cold fingers on her bowels.

A small dark shape caught her eye beside the path. She stooped, squatted to look. Half covered by last year's brown leaves lay a brown bird. A dunnock. Its feathers, once a rich chestnut and grey, were in disar-ray, its head twisted back, its eyes dark pits.

She covered it again with leaves, and as she sprin-kled a pinch of earth upon the little corpse, muttered a prayer for its soul.

Death. The world was full of life, and within her heart was death. The sense of foreboding strengthened within her as she turned back to the town. The sky reddened over the mountain. She hardly noticed Dhion as he passed the rondal at a steady jog, heading up to the Pass of the Sea.

As he came from the smoking house a little while later, Dermot did notice the runner. His eyes were sore from lighting the slow fire and then, as the flames took hold, almost dowsing them with wet leaves and bark, so that smoke rose in wreathes to envelope the rows of gutted fish hanging from their poles across the narrow chamber.

Stepping outside, he took a great breath of refreshingly clean air and, looking up, saw the running figure for a moment against the sky at the head of the steep path that clambered down from the pass. There was no-one else it could be. No-one else was strange enough to run for no reason.

So the Seaborne was alone on the mountain. What was to stop him, Dermot, from following after? A fire that had never died since the council meeting flared up in him. His father's hard words when, at last, he came home after the hunt, only added more fuel. And then there was Targud, who'd called three times, his mam said, trying to take him aside with his soft talk, telling him he'd got to put things behind him and walk away. He'd show them who'd got to walk away. He saw his chance.

He looked down at his clothes. His leine would be sufficient on this mild morning. He unwrapped his working plaid and threw it down outside the smokehouse. His knife was in his belt, where he kept it through the working day. It was sharp. He always kept his knife sharp. His boat would have to wait this morning: he had other work to do. He set off, wolf-pace, up into the rising redness of the sun.

৯৯

Morag could not concentrate all through their morning devotion. Hugh knelt there, so calmly, his face unmoving whenever she glanced from under her eyelids towards him, while within her own mind there was turmoil. Had not Coghlane told them of a death? That was months ago, but now it came to her afresh. Death could come in a thousand guises: gentle and kindly to the old and tired. That would not be what Coghlane meant. Or sudden and cruel – the spotted sickness, the stupid accident. Even that would not be a matter for prophecy, unless it concerned one of the great ones, whose lives affected all. The angry knife or spear? Today? Was that what her distress meant? Was that how her intuition was melding with the Book of Nature? Was there nothing to be done?

She could not eat her morning meal, and Hugh looked with concern at her. She rose and kissed him, and went out, back to the rondal. Not even there could she settle. After only a short time she rose from her knees and went to the door.

Suddenly the air was filled with a scream. A seabird twisted and veered in its flight, as the eagle stooped upon it. She heard the wing-beats as they passed above her and disappeared behind the larches that marked the path to Fisherhame.

She hesitated no longer but, dressed as she was, set off up the path.

The hunt was easy from the start. At first the sheep-track leading up towards Talor Gan was soft, and the foreigner's strange shoes left clear impressions in the dark ground. Even later on, when Dermot came out onto the moorland which lay in the lap of the mountain, there were enough clues: the damp, dark underside of a stone upturned by a passing foot, a branch of heather or a reed recently bent.

261

Then he saw him. Once more he was silhouetted, in the nick between the rising shoulder of the summit and a low rocky ridge, black against the sky. Now Dermot was sure of him; it was only a matter of time.

Dhion paused, and rested on a rock. The wind blew fresh and steady from the sea, chasing in clouds that formed on the upper slopes behind him. Around the dark pools that dotted the moorland it bent the little flags of cotton-grass. The land stretched out before him, dun and brown and red, until it steepened down towards the broad and fertile valley of Strath Padraig. His eye swept westward. He could see the sea, framed in the wide cleft he had passed through. Lights on the waves shone, reflected back to him with a hard, metallic sheen.

A movement caught his eye. A man – running. There, in that same cleft. He was coming this way. Few people came up here. There were peat workings further round, but here, only the occasional hunter. And no-one beyond the age of children ever ran, except in case of need. This must be an emergency. He waited.

A sudden ray of sunshine caught the runner in its light. A red-haired man dressed, like himself, in working leine, hitched over the belt for ease of movement.

Dermot. In an instant his words, the look that he had given him at the council, came back to Dhion, and a dark intuition entered his mind. Not here. Not away up here, where there was no-one else, no other voices to temper him, no other hands to restrain him.

Pride was his first impulse. Pride told him to stand. Fight it out.

Discretion told him to run. Run without fear, without shame. The man might well be armed, unlike himself. In any case, how could a fight end well, up here, in the raw elemental world of predator and prey?

Consciously he took charge of himself, of the situation. He would meet the man on his own terms, not those of a headstrong youth. He ran.

Once in a while he would look over his shoulder. His pursuer was always there, neither gaining nor losing. He wondered: who would have the longer wind? He had the advantage. He still wore the trainers that protected his feet. And he could choose his ground, though here there was little to choose between. This was the wild, where there were no clear paths. A narrow track would at times open before him, made perhaps by deer or wild goat, and as suddenly disappear again. Running here was testing – that was why he had chosen it – but it was testing for both of them. Despite the situation, he began to smile.

By now he knew the country well, and chose the quickest way towards the town. He would have to detour round some soft ground that lay across the direct line, but then he could pick up a fairly well-marked path downward, that descended from the peat-diggings further round the ridge.

The bog now lay on his left, a long strip of sickly yellow-green moss filling what looked to be no more than a slight hollow. Skirting round its edge, he jumped its headwaters and gained the path.

Again, a backward look. What he saw brought him to a halt. Dermot, spurning the detour, was making straight for him, towards the treacherous waste.

Time out of mind there had been a deep cleft here from the ancient ice days, carved into the tortured bones of the earth. Its lower end blocked by boulders, silt and roots, it had slowly filled with water. So slowly, that the growth of water plants, of moss and slime, had kept pace with its filling. Generation upon generation had sprouted, grown up towards the sunlight and died here, filling the cleft with their loose tangle of rotten stems and roots. Filled with its own slow, in-turned life, it was a place that seemed to hate all life other than its own – hated the quickness of animal intrusion, of hasty step of hoof or claw. Hated, and sucked it in; held on to it in its own slow way, hiding it for ever in the oblivion of its own deep darkness.

Dhion stood. He turned to face his pursuer. Barely forty paces separated the two. He looked across at the fresh and freckled fisherman, who returned his gaze with one of utter intent. Dhion felt it as a spear aimed at him. Mentally he put up his guard. They were now so close; so separate.

'Dermot. What's the matter?'

'You are,' came the snarled reply.

'Why? What have I done to you?'

'You lied to the council. You took her from me. You belittled me.'

'I have not lied. I spoke truly to the shareg, and to you. I'm sorry if you could not hear it. As for taking her away, I would not take anyone where they did not wish to go.'

'I don't want your nice words. Come and meet me here, and we'll have it out. Once and for all.'

'Dermot, I won't fight you. Come down to –' He was not allowed to finish.

'But *I* will fight *you*. And I'll show you what it means to belittle a man of the West.'

Then, to Dhion's fascinated horror, he began to cross the bog. Suddenly it was clear to Dhion that this was a man who knew exactly what he was doing. He stepped with poise and care, never taking his eyes off his prey, yet moving steadily out over the wetland, finding firmness in the forbidden mire. Dhion watched, entranced. It was as if a glamour was upon him and, forgetting his flight, he hesitated.

Then he awoke. He cried out, 'Dermot – for God's sake, don't! Go back!'

'You don't tell me what to do. Stay there, and I'll break your neck as I broke the neck of the goat.'

Like a cat stalking an unwary bird, Dhion could see Dermot trembling in every limb with the tension, the exhilaration of his skill. He was going to succeed, he was actually going to cross the bog. But still Dhion stayed, watching. The skilful step; the unwonted mastery of this element.

Then, all of a sudden, something changed. Where there had been wet and quaking ground, suddenly there was opaque black liquid. Before Dhion's eyes Dermot sank, almost to his knees. It was as if a presence deep within the bog itself, in the cold wet darkness, had woken like a huge predatory insect at the vibration of an alien tread. Woken, and sprung its watery trap. He could see a flash of consternation on the fisherman's face before it set again with concentrated rage.

'Dermot – I'm going for help. I'll be back – as soon as I can. You'd better stay completely still.'

The man was trying, trying to raise one foot and lift it out of the morass. But at every movement he only sank lower. Suddenly his face twisted into a contorted mask of hatred and fear.

'I'll go and bring help.'

Dhion turned and ran. The path took a gentle route downhill, curving away to the east. He took a risk and cut across a rocky chasm, following the stream that drained the bog as it leaped over six-foot, twelve-foot steps of stone. Some he scrambled down, some he slid, scraping the skin of the backs of his thighs. He jumped, fell, picked himself up, went on, blood trickling from his knee.

The path again. The town. The sawyer's pit.

'Donal! Is the master at home?'

The giant looked up at him. 'Aye. He's within.'

He burst into Leighan's house. All Morag's careful rehearsing of how to enter another's home was put aside.

'Heesht, man! Have ye got the wolf-lord after you?'

'Dermot... Dermot Ma'Bhenrish... He's...' He gasped for breath, doubled up, hands on knees.

As his story came out, Leighan looked across the hearth to where his eldest was sitting. 'Olan. Go round the back and sort out a pair of long planks. Ingleeshe, come with me.'

The carpenter carefully set down his ale. He gave a deep sigh, and walked out.

Dhion's mind was racing. *Hurry! For God's sake, hurry!*

Leighan called curtly to the paelht: 'Donal. Come.' He spoke over his shoulder to Dhion. '*This* is how it's done.'

The three of them came to the priest's house next door. Hugh was clearly surprised to see Leighan with Donal and Dhion.

'Father, I release this paelht for this day into the charge of Dhion Ingleeshe Seaborne, that he may deliver him back before nightfall. I call on you, a man of good standing, to witness.'

Hugh replied. 'Leighan Ma'Challen Carpenter, I witness.'

Leighan turned to Dhion. 'Take him. Go round to the back of the house. Olan is finding some boards for you. You may as well try.'

Donal took a long pole in his hand, and he and Dhion shouldered the planks and set off. Dhion was grateful that the big man took most of the weight: his own calves were screaming with cramp. He made to turn off the path.

'Why that way?' They were the first words the giant had spoken since leaving the town.

'That was the way I came. It's the quickest way.'

'Quickest bloody way down isn't always quickest way up.' He grinned good-naturedly. 'Quickest way down's too often quickest way to break yer bloody neck!'

They rounded the ridge that bordered the bog, and saw it lying there, livid green and black, surreally smooth. There was no sign of Dermot.

'He's gone,' Dhion exclaimed. 'I... I can't see him. But... he was there!'

'Thought so.' It was all the other would say.

He had Dhion direct him to where he had last seen Dermot. It meant going round to the far side of the expanse. It was eerily quiet. Donal laid the boards across the treacherous surface, and crawled on his belly out along them. With his pole he probed into the depths.

He wriggled back onto firm ground. 'He's gone.'

'Gone? He got out?' Dhion's mind could register nothing, take nothing in.

'The others'll be along soon,' said Donal flatly. 'We'll go and meet them.' Dhion heard the words, and did not hear; stood, stupidly, not finding an impulse to move, to do, to think anything. Donal added, 'I can't go alone. You'll have to come with me.'

They came to the place where Dhion had stood when he had pleaded with Dermot to go back. There was a figure away on the hillside above them. A woman in a grey gown. It was Morag. Here?

'Come on,' said Donal.

THE THIRD PART: SACRIFICE

38

They met the men half way up the path. Micheil was leading a good number from the town. Hugh was beside him, Leighan behind him. They came, silent and empty-handed.

Donal spoke to the shareg, and Leighan, listening, signed to his son further back in the column. Olan and another youth set off back down the hill at a loping run. Donal took his own place submissively on the shareg's left as they continued on, back to where Dermot was not. The clouds, stretched across the sky, began to over-flow in fine grey rain.

Dhion heard her before he saw where she stood. A high, piping, plaintive call, like those long-legged birds of the seashore. Now Morag was standing where they had laid the planks, her face and arms raised, her mouth open in the chant. Her long hair, dark with rain, fell about her face. The sleeves of her dress had dropped back above her elbows, her white arms stretched out towards the place.

It seemed a long time before the women came. As they caught the chant they began a ragged ululation. It formed a shrill ostinato, circling, tangling, in and out of the call.

Aileen was at their head and, leaning on her shoulder, supported by her firm arm, a woman Dhion did not remember, followed by two young women.

Dhion realised he was cold. He was trembling. The feeling suddenly, sickeningly, reminded him of how Dermot had looked when he last saw him. Horror broke out in a cold sweat.

His teeth started chattering. Fineenh, unseen, was behind him. She slipped her cloak over his shoulders. Damp as it was, its warm weight was comforting.

One by one, more men and women arrived. They stood in the rain, surrounding the place, their chant, their grief, held within the lap of the hills:

The protection of God on the soul of the dead.
God of earth and fire.
God of the rushing waters and the great winds.
God of the web of life, of the shining stars.
God of the Golden Goodness.
The protection of God on the soul of the dead.

After a time beyond bearing, except that he must bear it, the chant came to an end. There was silence. Stillness throughout the throng. Then, as Morag moved, she began a new chant. Three notes repeated, constant in rhythm, changing in tone and interval.

She led the way slowly back to the path, slowly down the mountain, the chant constantly accompanying the dead pace.

Where they met the track to the pass, Dhion expected her to turn right, towards the town. But she took the other way, and they climbed down, slowly down, to gather before Benrish's home in the fishing hamlet.

The man was at sea, unaware. Aileen brought the woman, still leaning on her arm, to the door. Realisation dawned on Dhion: this was Mairie A'Bhenrish, come from witnessing her son's resting place. They took her within, her two daughters with her. Other women joined them now, some with infants on their hips. They stood silently. A child wailed.

In the distance the sound of the sea, the seabirds' cries. A boat being drawn up on the beach. The sound of footsteps trudging across the shingle, stumbling into a run.

ॐॐ

Dhion watched as Morag stepped forward and stood before Benrish. She did not speak at once, but only looked at him. As Dermot's father returned her gaze, a change came over him. A stiffening. At the same time, his eyes stared, his mouth hung open, as if to receive.

She spoke to him quietly, personally. But in the silence kept by all, Dhion could hear her words.

'Your son is lost,' she told him. 'I was with him. I saw him go. And in spirit, I held him.'

The fisherman did not move. Then, 'Where?' was the single word.

'On the mountain. In the Corrie of the Deep Moss.'

Never had Dhion seen, never imagined, such pain as appeared in the face of the bereaved father. The man shrank; aged and stooped before his eyes.

'I have stayed with him since the morning,' she went on, softly. 'I can tell you that, soon after he disappeared, a curlew rose from the marsh and flew. Straight out, towards the western sea.'

Micheil turned to Dhion. 'Go to your house, and stay there. I will come to you.' His face was grim.

It was Fineenh who directed him away from the cluster of roundhouses and sheds and drying-frames that was the hamlet, and back towards the pass. Shean was already on the path, impatient to be off. As they trudged slowly up the stair, Dhion was aware of other men silently joining, and following behind them.

He began to understand the meaning behind the shareg's words. This was the sheriff's posse, come to ensure that their man fulfilled his house arrest.

The hearth had burned down to a few glowing coals, although deep down there was still fire in the peat. Shinane at once began to mend it, bringing more fuel and blowing up the embers. Once only she looked towards him. It was a look of helplessness that left him feeling yet more deeply alone. Shean retired to his forge, silently.

Fineenh sat Dhion down, took the damp cloak from his shoulders, and brought his own dry plaid from his pallet in the smithy. She hurried to fetch him a hot drink. He looked across at Shinane's bent back as she knelt to tend the fire. There was silence.

The moments dragged. He could not bear to look at Shinane. She knelt, working the bellows as if nothing else mattered. Fineenh came at last with a steaming cup in one hand, a bannock in the other. She sat down, facing him.

'Dhion, you understand the shareg's words? You must stay here, not leave this house, until he comes and hears your story. This is important. Do you hear me?'

He nodded, glumly. There was nothing to be said. The weight of death, and of such a death, was upon everyone. He knew it was too early to protest his innocence.

She continued. 'He will come as soon as he can. But it may not be today. He will have other people to speak with, and first he will talk with Benrish and his wife.'

Shinane rose, and took the damp cloak to hang it by the fire. The silence hung like a heavy curtain between every sentence, over every word. Dhion pulled it aside with an effort. 'I would like to talk with Hugh and Morag. Is it allowed me?'

Fineenh sighed. 'The Father and A'Phadr will be up by the Hag all tonight, keeping vigil. I do not know when they will return. They will not forget you.'

'The Hag?' Dhion looked up at the woman, her habitually rosy cheeks strangely grey. 'That bog – the Corrie of the Deep Moss – that is the Hag of the Mountain?'

Fineenh nodded. There were tears in her eyes. She turned away.

There was movement behind her. Shinane appeared again at the doorway. She brushed down her skirts and came across. Her back to the rekindled fire, she knelt before him. At last the girl, looking steadily at Dhion, reached for his hands as they lay, clasped in the furrow of his plaid, and took them in her own.

Dhion felt a hand on his head. He knew it was Fineenh's. Her other hand she laid on her daughter's head. She held them there. He felt the three of them, connected, a trinity.

Night fell, long and dark and sad. Dhion lay on his pallet in the smithy. The forge-fire was long cold. At Shean's instruction he had not lit it that morning – so long ago. If they had been going to do forge work that day, he would have had to stay and see to the fire. He would not have run up in the hills. Dermot would not lie sunken in his undug grave. He shivered at the thought. He turned over and pulled his cloak more tightly around him.

It was a long time before rest came. He slept fitfully.

Alone, he stood on a high cliff, looking down. Below him, people were coming and going, going about their ordinary lives, talking and working. He stood alone, clouds drifting between them and him. He could only dimly see them. In the cloud, Dermot's face. Dermot's hands, reaching out at him; falling, falling into darkness.

It was not until the middle of the next morning that the shareg appeared. The rain had cleared, but a warm and gentle south wind had met the still-cold waters of the northern sea, and a thick grey fog enveloped all.

Dhion watched Shean usher Micheil to the good chair by the hearth, and himself take the lower chair. Dhion brought a stool and sat. He felt the focus of the two men bearing down on him. Shinane stood near. Fineenh bustled to bring them refreshment, then retired to the shadows and her distaff. As she went, he looked after her and saw her take Shinane's hand.

'Come away, Jewel.'

The young woman shook off her mother's hand. 'I will stay.'

She stood very straight, very still.

But Micheil's voice, commanding, cut across her: 'Mish'Ma'Ronal.' At her title, so grimly announced, she dropped a deferential curtsey. 'Once before you asked to stay in a council of men, and I allowed it. I will not allow it now.'

Far away across the town, down by the lough-side, a cow bellowed.

For a moment Dhion thought she would defy them. Her eyes flashed dangerously. She stood still. No-one moved. Then she bowed her head, bent her knee gracefully to the shareg. She turned, retreated to the shadows at the edge of the chamber, and sank down beside her mother.

The shareg turned back to his interrupted task.

'Dhion, before we begin I must warn you. You must speak truth in everything. Even to your hurt.'

'I have no need to do else.'

'I am glad to hear it. But if you are found false, if we find that even in a detail you have set forth to mislead us, then there will be no place for you here amongst us. And,' Micheil leaned forward, his dark brows furrowed, 'since you are a stranger, a foreigner, if we cast you out, there is no township on the Island that will receive you.'

The outer door creaked open, and a familiar brown-framed face appeared. 'Shareg. Forgive me. I came as soon as I could.'

'Father, you are welcome. Do you speak to this matter?'

'I speak for truth, and for compassion.'

'Then we are of one voice. We have only just begun.'

The priest came and sat on a bench near Dhion. He folded his cassock neatly around his spare frame, and exchanged glances with the Seaborne.

The shareg turned back to Dhion. 'I want you to tell us, in your own words, what happened. Start from when you left your master's house, and finish when you arrived at Leighan Carpenter's. As for the rest, we have others can speak.'

Dhion found it difficult to recount his tale of the day before. Time and again he had to stop, collect himself, go on once more in answer to Micheil's probing questions. At length he finished.

'Dhion, did you provoke Dermot to anger against you?'

Dhion paused. 'I did not intend to provoke Dermot. He was provoked. But that was not my wish.'

'When you saw Dermot, did you think to bring him to the Corrie of the Deep Moss?'

'I saw him at a distance, running towards me, and thought it not good to meet him there in the wild. I was up under the Crag of the White Rocks, and the most direct way back to the town lies past the Corrie of the Deep Moss. I did not imagine he would try to cross it.'

'When you reached the Corrie, did you provoke him or entice him to cross it?'

'No. No, I did not.'

'Did you wish the son of Benrish dead?'

'No. I did not.'

'Thank you.' The shareg brought his interview to a close, but remained seated, his face still grave. 'I have others to talk with, and I cannot bring this before the people until the first week of mourning is completed. I will let you know. In the meantime, I will ask you to remain as much as possible within the bounds of the smithy and not to go about in the town. And on no account are you to leave the town, except on my word. I will not lightly give it. Is that clear?'

Dhion nodded. After all that had been said, he heard it with relief.

Shinane left the house by the back door and the kale-yard and the wattle fence. She wrapped her cloak about her. Soon the fog had covered it with a shimmering, jewel-like net.

For all the dignity with which she withdrew from the men's council, her heart was in turmoil. She hated men – all men, even Dhion: their arrogance, their short-sightedness, their fixity of ideas. And for a moment she hated her own sex, that she was born a woman. Until she realised the absurdity of holding both hates together, and laughed a short, bitter laugh.

She walked without knowing where she went. Down to the head of the lough, up past the women's pool, up the eastern slope of Beh' Mora.

Mish'Ma'Ronal! Why must I be the daughter of the son? she demanded of the mountain and the lough. Why could she not just be herself? And why should her word not be heard with any man's? She knew the man! She *knew* him! He would not do what some of them thought. She could see it – why couldn't they?

And why wouldn't he speak for her? She had stood by him – couldn't he have stood by her? Oh, she knew he couldn't – yet she'd wanted him to say something, to try...

She walked through the dew-laden heather and coarse upland grass. The fog enclosed her, trapped her, cut off her vision from the great spreading world around her – the limitless sea with its skirts of restless motion. All this was lost to her, unreachable, beyond the narrow confines of her own limited circle.

She sat on a dark, wet rock. A pearliness was spreading through the cloud above her, an opalescence that slowly became luminous with a warmth she could almost feel.

And suddenly the grey cloud thawed, melted, dissolved away. There was the sun, beaming down on her, a majesty of radiance bringing glory to all it touched.

Why are you sitting here, Shinane?

What are you doing, letting this greyness into your soul?

How dare you – how dare you – be less than you are?

She looked around. She looked up, and behind her. There was no-one there. She knew the voice was not from beyond her self. And yet it was. She was aware of her hands gripping the cold stone. Her throat was tight: if this was fear, then she would gladly be fearful all her life. Her whole body tingled, with much more than the sun's warmth.

She felt a strength kindling within her. Everything was possible. Beyond everything, she was still She. And beyond that, there was the light that was not light, but was Joy, bubbling up from an infinite source, that seemed – just beyond the hillcrest.

With that strength, that power, came compassion. People were, in the end, only people like her. They too had been limited in their vision, in their belief of what was possible.

The vision faded. The sun disappeared. The cold fog once more enwrapped her. But no more did it confine her. Rather, she wore it as a cloak, and as she slowly walked back to the town, so it came with her, streaming from her shoulders.

39

The following morning was First-Day. The office said, first-food dishes cleared away and Hugh gone to the rondal to prepare for Tollagh, Morag knew she was exhausted. She was about to lie down when a voice called from outside the door.

'A'Phadr.'

Morag opened. 'Shinane. Come within, love.'

It was hard to read the girl's face.

'May I talk with you, A'Phadr?'

'What is it?'

'I fear for him. I can't sleep for worry of what will happen, what they may do to him.'

Morag considered.

Slowly, she began, 'Hugh will go to him, after the Tollagh. He does not believe that Dhion has done wrong; but there is an ugly mood in the town, and even more in Fisherhame. I don't know how it will unfold.'

She looked carefully at her visitor. 'Are you brave enough for this?'

'I... I don't know.'

The sea-grey eyes looked up, and Shinane went on with a sudden rush, 'You know I did care about Dermot. He was always my friend. I just couldn't be his – his woman. I wish he hadn't taken it so very hard. He has brought about such terrible harm. And most of all to himself.'

'I am glad you consider Dermot in all this,' said Morag. 'He has indeed done very great harm. And not only to himself,' she added.

Again, a pause.

Morag studied the girl, taking in her measure. 'All I can tell you is to hold the vision of your hope steady. It is a work you must do. Doing this work will help to make hope reality. And pray. Pray for healing for all in this present time. All things are possible, and anything may happen. Shinane, I see a new wisdom in you. But walk carefully. There is a fire smouldering among us deep at the roots; if the wind should change it will spring up again, and then we shall all be burned.'

The girl looked straight at her, a long moment. Then she said, 'I must go. Mother will expect me at Tollagh.'

Morag nodded. 'Come back whenever you need to. I will help you all I can.'

The door closed. Morag stood still a moment, then she turned and went at last to her bed. She never missed the Tollagh. But now, her need for rest was overwhelming. She trusted people would understand.

The Speaking was to be held following the week of mourning, on the second day. As the light crept over the eastern skyline in greys and rose and faint apple-green, Morag and Hugh, a single candle between them at their morning office, knew that their prayers went mostly to the Seaborne.

Liquid gold ran along the rim of the world, and every hollow and rock and wall was shadowed in violet. Then the sun rose, and struck spangles of diamond-edged light from the dew, transforming each spider's web into a diadem of incalculable worth.

Morag watched her husband open the proceedings with a prayer. 'In the name of the All-Present One, the Source, the Way, the Wisdom.

'Shareg, take the sword of justice...' Hugh was standing before Micheil on the dais that had been built before the shareg's house. The sword was raised in his hand as between them they began the Speaking. This was not a council, held behind closed doors, attended by only the free men of the community. This was in the open, under a clear sky, admitting all. All who could speak to the matter were free to do so. For a man of the township had died, and the possibility of wrongdoing had been raised among them. All must understand whether wrong had been done or no.

Morag saw Shinane pressing into the inmost ring of townspeople, her mother following close behind. And in the open space at the centre of the circle, she saw Dhion, standing between Padragh and Tearlach before Micheil; saw him standing tall and strong and still.

She heard how he was cautioned to tell only the truth, on pain of banishment. She heard how he told that truth as best he could, his foreign accent and occasional strange phrases singling him out, always: different, apart.

Hugh questioned him, probing his motives, his feelings towards the dead man. The shareg asked him, why was he on the slopes of Beh' Talor Gan? How was it that he met with Dermot there?

Morag heard Leighan tell his story, how the Ingleeshe had burst in on him, appealed for help. Then came Donal's tale, his words few and blunt.

Now it was her own turn to speak. She must bear witness to those events of the early morning that had linked with her deep unease on that day; how at the last she had set off up the mountain, alone, even before the ill tidings had been brought. How she had witnessed all, approaching from afar; had seen, and had done the only thing she could: her prayer for the departing soul.

It was over. All the witnesses had spoken. She heard Micheil bringing the several voices together into one story. That Dhion Ingleeshe, the seaborne one, had been pursued by him who was dead, there on the mountain. That he had reason to fear his intent, had tried to escape from him. That the fisherman had attempted to cross the bog to come at the Seaborne, and had been lost. That there was no blame upon the Seaborne.

282

She allowed a wave of relief to wash through her.

A rough voice. It came from among the seamen of Fisherhame. It was Benrish.

'Shareg, it is not enough. My son is dead. I will not get another. We have only the word of this foreigner that that is how it happened, against the good character of a man of the Island. How can I tell that the Seaborne is not lying? How can I tell that he did not lure my son to his death for his own gain, to make his way clear to that woman there?'

He pointed a shaking finger at the smith's daughter. Morag saw the colour rise in Shinane's face and throat, then drain away. She could imagine the struggle within. She closed her eyes, and inwardly sent the girl strength. *Ghea help her. Help her.* She opened her eyes, and saw Shinane standing, pale and firm.

There was a growl of agreement from Fisherhame. Only Fengoelan with Shelagh and Targud stood silent, dark rocks amid a boiling sea.

Benrish warmed to his theme. 'Two years ago, my son was wooing Mish'Ma'Ronal. They were like to have been betrothed. Then this man appears, washed up by the sea, from no-one knows where. Not even he will tell us where he's from.'

'Aye,' came the sound again from Fisherhame: stones grinding under the wave.

'And he's placed under the smith's roof, and straightway there's no betrothal to be made. That stranger is seen with the smith's daughter far more often than is right. And what's more, he brings us these strange *maseenen* that no-one finds canny. What's going on, I want to know. What good has he brought us? My son is dead! I demand justice for my son's poor soul.'

Callen stepped into the circle. 'Aye, it's true. Only last week, the day before he died, I could see that poor Dermot was not in his right mind. As if there was a spell on him. I don't know how, but it was plain for anyone

283

to see that his heart was twisted out of true. Benrish is right: it's no canny.'

At that Shean leaped forward. 'If that's true, Callen, then it's no my prentice's doing. If Dermot's heart was twisted, then he twisted it himself.'

'Order!' roared the shareg. 'Ma'Ronal, you will address all that you say to me. I will not have men shouting at each other.'

Shean turned to him. 'Shareg, I was in the wrong with how I said my words; but the words were not wrong. If Dermot was out of his right mind, then that was his own doing. If there was jealousy, then it was his jealousy, not the Ingleeshe's. My prentice is a good man and true. I stand by him. And my daughter is a good woman too, and I will not step aside and hear her standing brought low.'

Targud raised his hand to speak. Micheil nodded to him. 'Shareg, we could see the signs. We should never have left him to go off on his own.'

But Leighan was on his feet. 'Shareg, you yourself, have said that trouble follows this man, and none worse nor greater than this last. How long do we go on believing him, that he brings no evil with him? What more must happen to us before we say that this is enough?'

A woman's voice pierced the heavy atmosphere: 'He saved my Colin!' It was the widow, Shareen.

A silence fell on the gathering. Morag searched her heart for anything she could say that could help, could mend matters. Finding nothing, she closed her eyes, and set herself to pray. *Beloved God, Sweet Ghea, send us the help that we need.*

Then into the silence rose a second voice. Clear it called, thin and piping, like a bird. Morag recognised it: the weaver, Doughael. The words she knew, but never had they sounded so chill. 'Let the ocean decide.'

Beloved God, Sweet Ghea… She saw Micheil look puzzled, Hugh's face pale. Never had Morag prayed more fervently than she did now. A low mutter of incomprehension rose from the crowd. Doughael took the pause as permission for him to enlarge.

'Remember the tale of Callen-Barg? When he wooed Fineenh Clubfoot. He was a stranger among them, and her father bade the ocean decide their fate. This stranger has come from the sea, and we cannot see the way forward. Then let the ocean decide.'

'Doughael Ma'Cholm, thank you.' Micheil's voice was strained. 'We are grateful for the old tales. We look to them for guidance. We do not look to them for law.'

He was interrupted. 'Let the ocean decide.' Benrish took up the call.

Morag saw Micheil glance with consternation at Hugh, seated beside him, then back at the grim fisherman before them, his arms folded. She could not recall hearing him speak with less assurance. 'If you are suggesting that we take this man and cast him forth upon the sea like Callen-Barg, then I tell you I will not do it. From everything we have heard, this man is not guilty, and I will not hazard his life like this.'

'Do you doubt, then, the tales we tell our children?' It was Callen who spoke. 'If the sea can't judge between the good and the evil, then we tell our children a lie. I join with Benrish – let the ocean decide.'

Surely this could not be the answer to her prayer? Not this? Micheil was looking helplessly at Hugh. Her husband rose. 'Benrish, I feel your pain in the loss of your son. We all feel it. For one of our fine young men has gone, and it grieves us all. But we need not and we must not add to this with the loss of another good man. We have heard the smith speak for his prentice.'

'Let the ocean decide. Let the ocean decide.' The chant was being taken up, not only by Fisherhame. It was breaking out all around the circle. It drowned out Hugh's voice. It was greater even than Micheil's desperate call for order. But it ceased altogether, faltering, sputtering like a fire in the rain, when – the last thing she had expected – Dhion turned to face them all and raised his hand to speak. Micheil nodded.

A silence fell. Dhion stood. Beyond expectation, his bearing was calm.

'My brothers,' he began. 'My sisters.'

An appreciative stir among the women. A scowl on the faces of some of the men. In Dhion's voice, an unfamiliar note of authority.

'I declare before you all this day, that my hands are clean of Dermot's life.'

The fishermen shifted, ready to spring.

'I say again, my hands are clean. But I cannot live among you while you do not trust me. So I will not resist. Send me out, if you must. If I do not return, you will be rid of me. But if the ocean brings me back again, then I call upon you all to accept me without reproach. I am willing for you to do this. Let it be done to me as you ask. Let the ocean decide.'

'No…' A strangled wail, like a ghost. It was Shinane. The composure she had worn when she had visited Morag seemed like a mantle slipping from her shoulders. She crumpled. Her hands hid her face, and, turning, she all but fell into her mother's arms.

Fineenh led her away amid a confusion of voices, with Micheil calling again and again for order. She stumbled on her mother's shoulder. Morag detached herself from the crowd and ran to join them.

40

'That fool of a romantic weaver. I could wring his fat neck!' Micheil slumped down on the nearest stool. They had returned to his house. 'Don't leave me alone with him, or I'd strap him to his own beam until I'd shaken some sense into him!

'I'm sorry, Father,' he added, glancing at Hugh, 'I sin. Forgive me.'

'I would,' replied the priest, 'if I were not guilty of the same feelings. The man brings out the first of the old tales that comes into his head without even considering what effect it might have. And now we're in a very great difficulty – greater even than before.'

Micheil looked keenly at Dhion, who sat silent, his arms lying deep in the folds of his plaid, his head bent. Shean stood by him, restlessly shifting from one foot to the other.

Micheil broke into the silence. 'Well, I have called the Speaking together again for the day after tomorrow. Before then, Dhion, I have to be very certain of my way. I have already said that I am not willing to pronounce this doom. I am not. Your public offer does not help me.'

Dhion looked up. But it was Shean who spoke first. His voice sounded strained.

'Shareg, by your leave, my daughter ought to be here.'

Micheil raised his eyebrows. Still the little smith went on, doggedly. 'Shinane is closer to this matter than anyone but Dhion himself. Her fate is bound up with his, and I ask that we call her now.'

Micheil stared. Was this really Shean's voice? He answered, 'Shean, you know what I have said to this –'

'Shareg,' said Hugh, quietly, 'we are not in ordinary times.'

287

At once, Shean made for the door. 'I'll fetch her,' he said.

'By your leave, Shareg.' It was Hugh's voice again. 'Let Morag accompany her.'

Micheil glanced from one to the other. So much had happened already this day, so much had taken him by surprise, so much he had not been prepared for; what more was this?

'Damn it, bring them both, Shean,' he called after the smith's departing form. 'And why don't you invite any other women who may fancy strolling by,' he added, acidly. He doubted Shean heard.

They talked of this and that, of matters of no importance. Micheil would soon be able to take his cattle out to pasture; soon he could go and inspect the summer grazing. Dhion said nothing.

Micheil heard Morag before she opened the door, talking in a low voice. But as they appeared he saw, not two women, but three. Shinane held her mother's hand. Her face looked strained, yet she stood tall and upright. As she dropped a little curtsey it was only her knees that bent, not her head. It was as if something of her strength had seeped into her mother, for as A'Shean also observed the customary courtesies, her eyes met those of the men.

Shinane let go of her mother, and crossed to kneel beside Dhion. She took his hand, and Micheil saw him hold it, strong and tight. Fineenh hovered behind like a small, fierce guardian angel.

Micheil looked around in the world of bright sunlight and deep shadow within the house; at the unaccustomed scene, the three men and three women before him. He took a breath, and began.

'Dhion, I recognise and respect your courage. We were thrown into a very difficult position, and you spoke well, and at great cost to yourself. But you must know, I cannot add my voice to what you say. I think you do not fully understand what you agree to, and so I must come against you.'

The Seaborne raised his head, but Hugh spoke first. 'Dhion, what the shareg says is right. Please understand what this means. You have, I know, been taught these tales, and you know that in the tales, Callen-Barg returns to claim Fineenh as his own. I ask you to remember why it is a story – because what it tells of, whether it really happened or no, is not what was expected. Fineenh's father expected him never to return. That is what happens to men who are cast away on the ocean with no means of reaching land. They drown, or they starve, or they die of thirst. Or they go mad from the solitude, and the sea-water never-ending around them.

'You are innocent of Dermot's death. All here –' his arm swept the whole room '– accept the truth of what you have told us. Even Benrish, in his pain at his son's death and his need for someone to blame, can say no more than *supposing*. You do not deserve what you are taking upon yourself.'

Micheil looked into the young man's face, an unfamiliar compassion rising in him.

They waited for Dhion to speak. His voice, when it came, rasped out of a dry throat. 'I see no other way,' he said. 'If I do not do this, many will never accept me. That is all.'

Dhion turned towards the priest. He spoke quietly, his voice more fluent now. 'Hugh, I know what is most likely. I have already come closer to death on the sea than any of you.'

A sudden gust of wind swung the door open. In the silence that followed, the distant murmur of the town sounded clear.

Softly, steadily, Dhion continued. 'I do not understand these things. But if, in the sea and near to death I crossed from my world into yours, then might it be that in the sea, and again near to death, I will cross back again?' He raised his head. Micheil, watching closely, found his gaze meeting that of the Seaborne; found himself out of his depth, knocked back. Dhion shook his head. 'I don't know.'

He turned back to Hugh.

'In any case,' he told them, 'I see no other way.'

'No!' The desperate cry came from the girl, crouched beside him, now staring straight into his face. 'No, Dhion. The shareg has pronounced you clean. You need not do this. Trust to the shareg's justice.'

Dhion looked back at her with an expression of deepest sorrow. The girl was shaking.

'Mi'Shean, I agree with you,' Micheil said, steadily. She swung round, and he saw the sudden hope in her anguished face. 'I will do all in my power to carry that view when we next meet.'

Dhion shook his head. 'I do not think you will change their hearts.'

Then he added, 'But what if – I know it's not likely – what if I do return after all? Do you not think they will accept me then?'

Shinane clung to him, her head now on his shoulder. In the silence they heard her sob.

'He is right.' The words sounded small and thin. Slowly, Morag continued. 'He is right. There is no other way. And Callen is right also.'

Micheil stared at her.

'He said that if we do not believe what the old stories tell us, then we teach our children a lie. What do the old stories tell us? We do not remember them only because they are unexpected, the exception. We remember them because they teach us how the world works.

'This is how the world works – do you not believe it? Dhion believes it, for he is willing to pledge his life on its truth. When one goes willingly to meet an ordeal that is unjustly thrust upon him, the All sees, and within the All lies help. The true-hearted will find it. I cannot say how that will be, for Dhion. We cannot expect the outcome will always be to our liking. Do we not walk in the footsteps of One who faced an unjust death?'

She stood there in her grey robe, a shaft of spring sunlight lighting her. A long silence gathered about her. She spoke into it.

'He must be prepared, and prepared well, to meet what he will find, out there on the ocean. He will need all the help we can give him. There is only one I know who can prepare him for such an ordeal.

'And you, Shinane, you have a foremost part in this. For you must stand and hold his life-thread. It is no light task.'

They met two days later, in the forenoon, before the shareg's house. The whole township was there.

Micheil stood to speak.

'People of Caerpadraig. You have demanded that we bid the ocean decide upon the rightness of this man, Dhion Ingleeshe Seaborne. Never have I heard such a demand. Never have I heard my brother sharegs countenance such a request.

'I find this man innocent.' He held up his hand to quell the unrest. 'Your priest believes him innocent. There is no witnessed tale against him. The evidence stands in his favour. Yet you have demanded this doom. And the Ingleeshe has accepted your demand.'

He looked around at them, and glared. 'But I have not.'

He continued, 'This demand stands against all reason and all compassion. I see no good in it.'

Thus the Speaking began again. And it went on, and on. Fengoelan spoke, Shean spoke, Targud spoke, all of them in Dhion's favour. But Micheil sensed a current running through the discourse that would not be stayed, that must have its way. Time and again he sought to divert the course of that current. When he had run out of arguments, he drew unashamedly on the loyalty of the people towards himself. But for all his effort, the current gathered strength and became a tidal surge. Then Micheil knew that if he did not give way, he would lose them, and leave them leaderless. And this he could not do. He raised a hand and stood, until he had the attention of all. He heard himself speak.

'People of Caerpadraig and Fisherhame, this man before you is braver than any I have met. For he is willing to accept your challenge. He is willing to accept the judgement of God through the ordeal of the ocean. I have questioned him and am satisfied that he understands what he is taking on, and still he is willing to do this. He does so, not to throw away his life lightly, but because you have offered him no other way. This is a truly brave man. Make no mistake, we take upon ourselves a very great responsibility.'

He paused, his gaze sweeping the assembly.

'I do not gladly agree to your demand,' he told them. 'But with the Ingleeshe's consent, I have to accede. We will put him to the ordeal of the ocean.'

Instantly a babble rose, like the bubbles thrown by a breaking wave. As the noise burst out all around, Micheil felt a sudden surge within him.

'But – ' His one word leapt out over them. To his satisfaction, they fell still.

He went on, 'If he returns –'

There was a murmur, and again he cut through, sensing the renewed strength and energy in his voice ringing out among them, calling them back.

'If, I say, he does return, I call upon you all to swear most solemnly. You will put aside all malice and evil thought against him. You will accept him as a brother among you and as one with you. He will be to you as one born and brought up amongst us all. He will stand cleared of any wrongdoing against the son of Benrish and of any wrongful part in his death. Will you so swear?'

There was silence.

'I call upon Benrish, the father of him who has died, to swear before me.'

The fisherman looked round at his fellows, then he stepped forward, newly aged and stooped as he was. He dropped to one knee. 'I do so swear.'

'And Callen Fisherhame, you also raised your voice. You will swear before me.'

That man also stepped forward and, speaking solemnly, declared, 'I do so swear.'

Micheil's eyes sought for the face he wanted. He found it in the crowd.

'And you, Doughael Ma'Cholm, Weaver Caerpadraig. You were first to raise this. I require you to swear this before me.'

Doughael looked round. His red face turned redder. Micheil wondered for a moment if the man would weep. Those standing near pushed him forward. He came before the shareg. He gathered himself.

'I d… I do so swear.'

'And all of you, men. And women.' There was a stir. 'You will all swear.'

A great rumbling voice rose from among the men of Fisherhame. It was Fengoelan. 'We do so swear.' First one, then a handful, then the whole multitude, took up the oath. 'We do so swear.'

Hugh stood. 'In the name of the One, who is in all, and over all, and beyond all. May the One, without beginning, without ending, hear you and hold you to your oath. Amen.'

As he regained his seat Micheil heard him mutter, 'And may they have cause to enact what they swear to.'

'What does it mean, to hold his life-thread?'

Shinane was in her bed, her mother bending over her. She had been sitting up, unable to find rest, her thoughts going round and round like a rat in a trap,

293

finding no way out. Then this thought: *What does it mean?*

She looked into her mother's eyes, and saw the weariness.

'Talk about it with A'Phadr. But leave it for another day.'

Shinane nodded.

'Sleep now, pet. Sleep till you wake. I won't call you, and I'll see that he...' she nodded to the bed where Shean lay slumbering, 'doesn't disturb you. You need your rest.'

She let her mother push her gently down, pull the bed-clothes up around her and kiss her good night.

41

'So this is the seaborne one, eh?'

Dhion stood, looking at the old woman about whom he had heard much, who was now looking back at him, a long and thoughtful look. Through the open door the land fell away, corrie and tarn and downfall, glen and pine forest and, far distant, a gleam of the cold northern sea.

The shareg had given Dhion two weeks in which to prepare himself. 'Long enough, but not so long that you find the wait unbearable,' he had said. Four days later Hugh had accompanied him to the high tarn where Mother Coghlane's cottage hid nestled in the mountain, with its tumble of sheep-folds and its bothy for men like himself to come and find what they needed in the stillness. That night Hugh had slept beside Coghlane's fire and she had installed Dhion in the hut.

Despite the exercise and fresh air of the day before, Dhion had not slept well. Ever since the ordeal of the ocean had been agreed he felt that he was living in an altered state, curiously apart from his everyday life. He lived, but at the same time observed himself living, as if from afar. It was as if his life was being filmed, and he was both the subject and the cameraman. This un-Islander-like thought distanced him still further from his surroundings. He had lain awake, wondering if he would be equal to the encounter to come. *She's a canny woman*, the priest had said; but the word he used was not familiar to Dhion. It seemed to imply more than simply *she knows a lot*. In the word there was something of numinence, a quality that wrong-footed the part of him that was still the engineer from Streatham. He was aware, even more than with Hugh and Morag, of setting foot on unsure ground. All the ground that lay before him now was unsure.

He rose before the sun, and explored the narrow path that threaded under the mountain wall behind his hut. With every step, he carried with him the awareness that this might be the last time he would do this, look upon that. The sheep, grey with dew, turned and stared at him before ambling a few paces further away. High above, an eagle circled.

The clatter of an old brass bell summoned him to breakfast, and he and Hugh dug in to their bowls of porridge, creamy with ewes' milk. 'Where is Mother Coghlane?' he had questioned, but with a smile Hugh had simply shaken his head as if to say, *Don't ask*.

She appeared – from where neither of them knew – soon after they had finished, as they were washing their bowls in one of the small rills that splashed down from the peak to fill the dark tarn below. As Hugh was ready to set off, a small pack, emptier than when he had come, slung on his shoulders and a stout staff in his hand, she reached up and, to Dhion's surprise, pulled his head down to her height and kissed him.

She watched as Hugh disappeared over the lip of the land below the tarn. Then she took Dhion's arm, steered him back to her tumbledown home and sat him down.

'Dhion. They call you Ingleeshe, I hear.' She smiled, as if at a private joke. 'And what do you call yourself?'

He was taken by surprise. How was he supposed to answer? He stumbled over his response. 'John... That was my given name.'

'That's your name where you have come from. Is that what you call yourself?'

He realised what she was asking. 'It's a long time now since anyone called me that. I hardly think of myself as John any more. If someone were to ask me my name, I would tell them it is Dhion.'

A flash of clarity lit up his will. 'Yes, I am Dhion. It's been a long time coming, but that's how I feel about myself now. Still, I am Dhion the Ingleeshe. I always will be.'

He looked at her. 'Just *Dhion* will do for now,' he added, smiling in spite of everything.

She returned his smile. 'You learn quickly.'

'Well, Dhion.' She leaned forward. 'What are you going to do? In a few days they will place you in a boat, and row you out until you have lost sight of land, and they will leave you there. What will you do then?'

'I... hope I will return. Most probably I will die.'

'Are you ready for that? Do you feel in the heart of your heart that it is your time to die?'

He looked down. 'No,' he answered. 'I don't. I... have too much to live for.'

'And what is that? What is it that you live for?'

Where should he begin? Shinane's face filled his vision. He said, 'I have so many ideas – I can make life easier, less hard, for people.'

'Ah – your *maseenen*. Yes, I have heard of them. Are they the most important thing?'

No, of course not. He would give up all the machines in the world – ugly, hard, unfeeling things – if he felt that would truly benefit the least of the people of Caerpadraig. Yet, if he looked deeply into his heart, it was not only for the benefit he believed he could bring that he had made his toys and presented them to the people. It was because he wanted them to know who he was. And, if he was honest, he wanted them to admire him.

But, he felt, even that was not the wholeness of what Coghlane was asking. She sat there, patient, bright-eyed as a heron, waiting for the truth to swim by.

A strange feeling came upon him. He remembered, in his other life, out on the hills above Capel Curig, he had been caught in a sudden cloudburst. Within minutes he had been soaked through. He had come to the point where he knew that he could get no wetter, and there was no point in trying to protect himself.

He could enjoy the freedom that the rain brought. He sensed now how she saw into him. He felt transparent before her. And the realisation brought a freedom: he could hide nothing, so there was no need to try to hide.

'It's Shinane. She has… unlocked something inside me that never found the light of day. I… Where I have come from, I was once with a lovely woman.' He hesitated. 'I allowed the cares of my work to come between us. I don't know what she may have been ready for, what she was capable of, but as I look back, it's clear to me that I hadn't found the depths of myself in those days. I didn't really have much to offer. But now: I want to live because of what Shinane has awoken in me.'

'Yes, you do, don't you?' He had not shocked her. Did she know of Shinane? Could she know even of Helen? Did it matter whether she knew or not?

'Can you understand that?' he asked.

She smiled. 'Perhaps it may help if I tell you a little about myself. It may help you feel less alone.' She grinned up at him.

He listened.

'I do know what it is like to love. I know all about the madness of love. I loved once, a strong young man, a little like yourself. We could not wait, we were head-strong, and our parents were unwilling. I bore him a child, a little girl. The sun was in her eyes, and the stars in her hair. But when she was weaned they took her from me, and I did not see her again.

'For whatever reason, my man could not bear it. They found him a wife, from a house in the town, who could cook and sew and spin, and he married her. I mourned for him. I grieved to sickness for my child. Then I put away mourning, for I knew I had no right to go on being sad. Life was calling me.

'So you see, I do know what it is to love, and what it is to lose love. But I don't know about your love. So I'd be glad for you to tell me.'

Where to start? How to describe something that enwraps the wholeness of you? He told her of the smithy and the rock-pool; of the kale-yard and the reading lessons; the meetings with the shareg. He found a strange freedom, in that he could talk before this woman of feelings he had not recognised fully until that moment.

She listened, her chin in her hand, her eyes almost closed. When he was done, she drew a breath and sat up. 'Well, then. What will happen to you is in the hand of the One, who dwells within you and beyond you. There we arrive at the place of surrender, for which we must be prepared. Yet what you truly want is more powerful than anything else you know. Have you ever thought that perhaps it was a deep desire of yours that brought you among us in the first place?'

She paused. He felt doors opening in his mind, blinds being pulled back from once-shuttered windows; her words, spelling out his interior landscape, so that it stood before him, seen more clearly than before.

She was continuing. 'I think that through your journey here you have touched the quick of yourself, and it is my task to help you know where you have arrived, and know how to turn what is there to your good. So that when the time comes, you have a choice.'

The afternoon spread over them like a blue mantle, bright with scudding clouds.

'Can you sing?' Mother Coghlane's bird-like eyes glittered.

Dhion's mind was too tired to wonder. 'Yes,' he answered. 'Fairly well.'

'Good. Song is a powerful tool. I will teach you a chant. It is not magic, but it works. Like your *maseenen*, eh? We don't always know how they work, but they do.'

It was in an old tongue, and he needed time to make the words to her satisfaction. She taught him how to feel the different sounds, resonating in different

299

parts of his body, echoing the different layers of being within himself, within the world around.

The sun was casting shadows that began to stretch into the east before she was done with him.

'Now go and sing it to the mountain. Sing it to the stones, to the waters, to the mosses. Sing it to the birds and the sky. They will each want to hear it in their own way, so be sure you sing it to them all. Off you go.'

She almost shooed him out. 'Go on,' she called. As he set out towards the folds and the rough country beyond, he thought he heard her mutter, 'I believe he might do.'

42

Morag found her at the washing pool, where the burn tumbles down at last to the lough. When the work that kept the women each in their own homes was done, then there was always the washing. Here the news and the gossip was passed from one to the other, circled around, snipped here and sewn onto there, until they had knitted every strand together into the story that would be remembered by all.

There were only two women there at the pool that morning. That day, only a little while before, Morag had bade goodbye to Hugh and Dhion as they left for the Northland, and immediately her thoughts had flown to the girl who was now so deeply entwined in the fate of the Seaborne. She would have much on her heart. The everyday chores of the house might even be a solace.

Who was the other woman, kneeling beside the water and pummelling the clothes? Only when she called Shinane's name and the two of them turned, did she recognise the once-beautiful face, still young, but drawn and lined by too much care, and framed by long lank hair – once the rich red that had drawn a young man to her. She first thought to call Shinane away. But perhaps Shareen's presence was a gift to be grasped.

'Shinane. I had been hoping you would come to see me.' She dropped down beside them on the fresh grass. Shareen stood, trod her washing under the sliding water, and stepped out on the far bank. She squatted to her work again.

'I wanted to. Mother has kept me busy.'

Morag could guess why. 'She means well,' she said.

'She does. But my mind keeps coming back to what you said to me in the shareg's house.'

'It was that I wanted to talk with you about.' Morag looked up, and met the shining green eyes of the young widow kneeling across the little pool. She turned again to Shinane. 'You are in the presence of one who has done this work. Although her labour did not bring about the end she hoped for, yet it was not in vain. She helped a good man on his journey onward; this I know, for I too was with him at the last. Shareen, do you mind telling us of when your Andy died? I'm sure Shinane has heard it, but maybe she missed this side of the story.'

Shareen swayed back onto her haunches and wiped her red forearms down her front. She looked at Morag, and then at Shinane, and then down, at the washing in the pool. She raised her eyes and looked questioningly into their faces. Then she spoke.

'A whole month he was ill. And he such a strong and healthy man. I mind how he used to go with Leighan Carpenter into the wild and they would choose a tree together. My Andy would cut it and lop it and have it ready for when Carpenter's men could come with the team and bring it home.

'But I seen him getting thinner and grey, and he says to me one day, "Sharie, my love, I canna go out today." And he coughs and it's red like a rusty pot, and he takes to his bed and then he never left it until they carried him out to bury him.'

Shinane looked up and away towards the near hills. Tears stood in her eyes.

Shareen continued. 'I sat with him, whenever I could, and bless her, the good Father's wife here it was made sure there was always someone to look after the bairns and see to the food and the house.'

'A'Shar'g and several of the women did that,' put in Morag.

'But while I sat with him, it was like I was holding him, here in my heart.' She raised a raw red hand to the place. 'Even when it came close to the end, and

I could see there was now't left o' his strength, still I held him... until I knew it was time to let him go. Oh, that was a moment of moments. It tore my heart out. I almost saw it – his life-thread – slide out from my breast and curl and fade like smoke. He died before the sun went down. But before he died – do you mind it, A'Phadr? – he looked around at us wi' a smile that lit up his poor, wasted face. I knew that he felt loved. And then he looked away from us, up, up, at the roof above. I think he saw beyond, for the look in his eye was of wonder, and I canna say what he was beholding.'

She fell silent. They were all silent. Shinane was kneeling, very upright.

Morag looked into the anxious young face, and smiled. 'This is what you must do, my love. Only we will hope and pray for a different outcome. Shareen can be a good teacher for you – better than I. It has been a blessing of my life not to have lost anyone close to me yet.'

Shinane turned questioning eyes to her. 'Not your mother and father?'

'My father never had much to do with me. And my mother – well, I was brought up in my grandfather's house, without her. You could say I lost them before I knew them.'

She looked away, then went on.

'Only remember this, my love. Shareen's story is not your story. You have something to learn from it, but it is not the same. For one thing, Dhion is not ill; he is strong and well. We do not know what will happen to him out upon the waves. But we trust that what will happen there will grow out of what goes on in his own heart.

'So he will need all the help we can give him. That is why you must hold that thread and never let it go – unless, as Shareen did, you come to know from inside yourself that it is his time.'

She paused. Then continued, 'There is another difference. Shareen could sit by her man's bed, close to

303

him, reading his face, hearing his every breath. You cannot do that; you will not know what Dhion will be going through – not with your earthly senses. You must learn to feel deep within you, where the two of you meet and are one, for it is only there that you will be able to know him and hold him. Once you are in that place, no distance can come between you.'

Again she read a question in Shinane's sea-grey eyes.

'Find yourself a quiet place and still yourself. Look past the chatter of your thoughts and ask to be guided to the centre. More I cannot tell you, for you must find your own way to that place.'

'How can I find my own way?' Shinane asked, her eyes anxious.

'The need of the time calls forth help,' was all Morag's answer. Then, 'When you find it, you will know it. Like the right touch that sets the harp-string thrumming. You will know it.'

Her mother was calling her. When would she be allowed some peace?

'Shinane, will you go and bring two measures of oatmeal – the middle grind will be just right. We'd better make some cakes for your father. And nearer the time we'll make more for that man of yours. Then we've got the evening meal to get ready.'

The cakes came off the griddle, hot and golden-brown, and smoking just a little. Shinane saw them, and thought of the first time she had served them to Dhion – here in her own home. She remembered her father's question, about the boats that moved with neither oar nor sail. She reached for one of the neeps she had been preparing, and took her knife from her apron pocket. Making a thin slice, she cut into it three times, almost to the centre. She twisted each segment, and held them with her fingers, as she had seen Dhion do.

'Look, mother. Do you remember? Do you remember what Father said? He asked him "What turns the turnip?"'

Her mother looked from her to the twisted root as if she did not know whether to laugh or weep. All she said was, 'Now off you go and fetch down that bolt of cloth – you know the one. We'll sew him a wallet to keep the bannocks in. You'll find a nice piece of soft leather there as well – that'll do to keep out the water. Off you go, now.'

Shinane took her thimble and a sailmaker's palm and a stout needle. She scrubbed the block with holly that pricked her hands and arms, and laid out the leather upon it. Carefully she cut it, and knocked holes for the stitches with a punch and one of her father's small hammers. Now she worked the linen thread through and through, folding the supple leather into shape. As she stitched she whispered to herself, *Ah Ghea, take my thoughts; guide me to the centre.* She repeated it rhythmically, over and over. *Ah Ghea, take my thoughts…*

She rubbed the leather with goose fat. *That'll do to keep out the water,* her mother had said. The remembrance brought a huge sob rising in her breast. She almost spoke aloud. *No. I shall not let myself. Not yet.*

With an effort of will she stilled herself. *Ah Ghea, take my thoughts.*

She fought back the tears. She bent her eyes to the task. Later. There would be a time for that later… *Guide me to the centre.*

43

'So that you may come back to us – come back to your love and the life she is opening up in you – you must learn to enter the world of dream, with awareness.'

Dhion waited, wondering at the old woman's meaning. It was now the sixth evening. He had been out walking and practising the chants she taught him. He felt self-conscious at first, singing to the sheep, to the few twisted or gnarled trees, to a rock. Bit by bit, the feeling ebbed away. He found he felt connected to the rocks, the trees, in a way he had not experienced before. It was a peaceful feeling.

As the days unfolded, he fell into a rhythm. In the mornings they sat, much as he remembered with Hugh and Morag, stilling his mind. Later, she would teach him. Chants – she had chosen just three – and other practices. Or they would talk. Or he would walk. He was no longer inclined to run. At noon, they sat together 'telling the beads,' repeating the same phrase, over and over. Rather to his surprise, he found it stilled his mind, kept at bay the anxiety that was so ready to torment him.

'I will give you this prayer circle,' she promised, when first she handed him a string of horn beads. He noticed she wore one herself.

In the afternoons he did whatever practical work she had for him, until again it was time to sit and be still. After the evening meal, he was soon ready for bed. 'Go back over the day,' she advised him. He rarely completed his review before falling asleep. At first, he craved stimulation. But after a few days he found himself dropping into a deeper and more settled space within. He found he had never been more happy.

'You must learn to enter the world of dream. Our dreams guide what we do,' she said. 'So they are quite as real as our actions – if, by reality we mean that they have power.'

He broke in. 'I don't dream very often. Most nights I just… sleep.'

'It is not only night dreams that I speak of. What about your day dreams? Where else have your *maseenen* come from, eh?' He caught her eyes, sparkling, mischievous.

She smiled. 'Some dreams are beautiful, and bring beauty to the earth; some are ugly. But make no mistake, everything that happens is foreshadowed in a dream.'

She looked at him with those keen, inquiring eyes. Dhion had been trying to follow her, but now he shook his head.

'Mother, I find this teaching hard. This is the real world to me.' His arm took in the stones and packed earth of the hut, the fire sending its smoke curling into the roof beams, the rough stools and the simple curtain that hung, he supposed, across Coghlane's sleeping place. 'To me dreams are always less real than what is here around me.'

'Yet, it is the dream of the people that is sending you to this test. And your dream that leads you to hope to return.'

He looked down. What she said was true. He was not sure how much more truth he could bear.

She was looking at him, her face shadowed in the dim lamplight. 'This, I think, is your work for tomorrow. If you are willing, I will teach you how to enter the world of dream, with will and awareness. You will see later why this is important for you – indeed, it is necessary if you wish to return. But you will have to trust me to guide you. We must go underground.'

'Underground?' he questioned.

'Yes. You will see.

'But for now, I think it is enough. You need your rest. Be off with you. Go. And sleep.'

Mother Coghlane did not indulge her guests. The hut was cold, the pallet hard, and he wrapped himself in his cloak, pulling it over his head and drawing it tight around him. Almost as soon as he had settled himself, he slept.

He was in a passage, flagged with stone. He touched the walls – they were hard and cold and damp. He looked around. He must find the door. In his grasp was a key, great and old and steel-hard in his hand. There were many doors – heavy dark oak, bound in black iron with antique locks; cheap panelled doors glazed with tawdry frosted glass, closed with tarnished Yale keyholes; doors of rough-sawn planks with clumsy rim-locks. He could discount none of them, for the key changed even as he presented it to a door. It could fit anywhere, but seemed to fit nowhere. In his frustration he sobbed. People walked past him. They all had keys; they walked through their own doors and disappeared, and he was left outside. Then he knew: he must go downstairs. A door swung open before him, and he climbed down the stone steps, spiralling downwards, dark, uneven. There was a light at the bottom – a dull red light, as of a forge-fire burning low. And something lying there. A beast; a dog, a dead dog. No. She breathed, she lifted her head, weakly. The dog tried to look at him.

'Here you are after all. I thought you were out on the mountain when I called and you did not answer.' It was Mother Coghlane, and the day was bright and busy with the bleat of sheep outside. 'Stay there, and I'll bring you your porridge. I see you've been on a journey.'

A journey? Yes, it felt like it. He felt limp, spent.

She came in, quietly, smoothly, a steaming bowl held in a cloth, and a horn spoon. She sat herself cross-legged on the floor beside him, her skirts stretched across her old knees.

'Eat,' she said. 'Then tell me.'

The porridge was mixed with a little honey and ewes' milk. It gave him strength.

She listened quietly, closely. When he was done, she said, 'Tell me more about the dog,'

'She was a big dog. You don't have them here on the Island. In my world we call them German Shepherd dogs. They are – a bit wolf-like; but they're good working dogs. We used to have one, when I was a boy.'

'A shepherd's dog. Weak, but not dead.'

'No, but... she seemed ill, or injured. She couldn't get up.'

The old woman sat, her chin in her hand.

Then, 'That is good,' she said. 'That is something to come back to.'

She rose. 'So,' she said, 'at last, it is time. I want this day to be a little different. After the noon I want to go exploring with you. But for this morning, some work. And while you work, let your mind go to the chants. Always keep them in your heart.'

Coghlane's vegetable garden was high-walled with stone, against the foraging of sheep and goats, but also to give shelter from the wind. It occupied the one small piece of land with a southward slope. All morning Dhion dug over a bed, raked it, picked out the larger stones, prepared a tilth for sowing. The dream went out of his mind. He was warm and tired when the bell summoned him for the midday meal.

They sat together in the sun afterwards. 'Now,' she said, 'are you ready to meet your dog?'

'My dog?'

'The dog of your dream.'

He had forgotten. Only now he remembered.

'I don't know how you mean,' he said. 'But... all right.'

She rose and went into the house. 'Come.'

She led him through the one room of her home. She took the light that stood in a niche against the fire and lit it from the coals. She pulled aside the curtain, where he expected her pallet to be hidden. But there was no pallet there. A heavy cloak hung a couple of feet behind the curtain, faded and holed. She thrust it aside and, to Dhion's astonishment, uncovered the entrance to a passage. Smells of earth and sounds of water greeted them. The dim lamplight showed walls of rock.

'Men dug this, many years ago, searching for the treasures of the earth.' The words slid backwards over her shoulder. 'I have found another use for it, which suits my work better.' Her bare feet made no noise on the hewn floor, except when they splashed through a shallow puddle.

Eventually the passage opened out. The lamplight barely reached the walls. The chill of the tunnel was gone, and Dhion felt the warmth of the mine.

There were boards on the floor, and skins. Even cushions – the richness of the chamber contrasted with the starkness of the hut they had left behind. 'Take off your shoes,' she said, quietly.

While he untied the laces, she placed the lamp on a little brass stand. 'Dhion, I have brought you here that we may go together into hidden places – places, I imagine, that have lain unexplored a long time. I have an idea what we shall find, but I cannot be certain. There is always some danger in these journeys. Are you willing?'

'Does the tunnel go far into the mountain, then?' he asked, speaking softly, like her.

She looked across the cavern to where a black hole could dimly be discerned. 'Oh, very far. But *that* is not the tunnel I mean. The journey that I want you to take goes into another mountain altogether.'

She looked straight at him.

He swallowed. 'Very well.'

There was a wooden screen perpendicular to the wall beside her, and hanging on it a long, linen cloth. This she took and offered to him.

'Go behind that screen and remove your outer clothes,' she said. 'You may wind this cloth about you. Then, go and lie on the skins in the middle of the floor. It will be well if you lie without covering, as much as you are willing.'

She pointed to a pile of sheep-skins, on an area of board enough for a body to stretch out on. She herself settled on a low seat near the lamp, a little distance from the boards. Her woollen gown hung loose around her. Her wrinkled skin glowed orange in the lamplight. He saw she had a small clay vessel in her hand, and charcoal in it. Holding a piece in a pair of tiny tongs, she lit it in the lamp flame.

He did as she bade, and lay down upon the skins. She threw a handful of dry leaves onto the red charcoal, and a sweet smoke filled the space. She placed the vessel on the floor, by his head.

'Breathe deeply, and slowly, and let go of your thoughts.' She reached for a tambour and held it in her hand. She beat it softly with a double-ended stick. *Bo-bom, bo-bom, bo-bom.* Regular as a heart-beat, close as the blood in his ears.

Slowly, as he breathed in the scented smoke that curled around him, a delicious warmth crept through him and filled him. He felt the fleece on which he lay against his arms, his legs. *Bo-bom, bo-bom, bo-bom.* He felt he was sinking, sinking, through the skins, through the boards, into the solid rock beneath.

Her voice came, from a distance. Softly, quietly, like the voice of moss or fern; the voice of seeping water.

He lay fathoms deep, no longer sinking, at rest on the sea-bed.

'What do you see?'

Nothing. Blankness. Void. He lay silent.

'Look around you. Without judging, tell me what you see.'

Like a black mist slowly clearing, his imagination led him further on. A green beech-wood: primroses, wood-anemones, white stitchwort. The pale scent of bluebells, the up-down song of chiffchaffs.

'I am in a wood. Bluebells. I can hear the birds.'

Bo-bom, bo-bom, bo-bom.

'Without judging, what do you see now?'

Nothing. Only the silver-grey tree-trunks, fading into the blue-green distance.

Then, 'I can see something.' A darker shape, over there between the shining grass-blades.

'Go to it. Tell me.'

It lay there, still, lifeless. Its sharp, pointed ears lax and drooping, its eyes closed, its fur lank and clogged with mud. 'A dog. The dog.' The dog of last night's dream.

'Speak to the dog. What do you want to say to the dog?'

No words came. Only tears welled up. How long had this dear creature been lying here, neglected, uncared for, because he had not known, had not been, had never chosen to spend time here, in this wood, this centre of the heart of his heart? For he knew without knowing that he looked upon himself – the other side of himself, a side unrecognised, unknown. 'I'm... sorry.'

The black nostrils twitched, opened a fraction. An ear's tip moved.

She lay, between life and death. He could not lift her, he feared to drag her. He put out a hand, and began to stroke her. Her breathing became deeper. For a long, long time he stroked her, his fingers furrowing the sleek, strong hair. He felt as if strength was seeping into her through his fingers.

'Without judging, what do you see?'

The dog raised her head, looked at him, placed her muzzle in his hand. His heart opened to receive her.

It was night. They sat under Mother Coghlane's earth-scented turf roof. She had given him a warm broth, ladled from her cauldron. A fire burned low on the hearth, red lumps of charcoal glowing where the lamplight did not reach. She took the empty bowl from him.

'Well, my love. We have gone far together, these seven days. As far as we could have gone, and not as far as we should have. Tomorrow Hugh will come for you, and the next morning, you must be away.' She looked at him in the yellow light. 'Had we been starting from the beginning, we could have taken many years and still not fully prepared you for what lies ahead.'

Her voice went softly on. 'We never start from the beginning, do we?' She paused a long moment, as if peering down the enormous perspectives of time. 'All your life you have been preparing for what you must now face, and so these days are enough. My task is to give you what tools I can, for you to use with what skill you have, when you find yourself left alone. The rest is already in you.

'But look. I have still two gifts to give.' She rose and left him, while she went to the back of the hut and pulled aside the curtain. All became very quiet. When she returned she bore a small glass bottle, its stopper of brass lined with a soft leather ring.

Dhion stared. He remembered when he had asked Hugh and Morag how he could send a message, and they had impressed upon him how rare was such a thing. He had seen the bottle that Hugh kept for the consecrated oil – a precious substance in a precious vessel.

'Take this. Do not use it lightly – only when you are on the point of need. One sip can help you go to that place where we left you – you remember, when you travelled to the wood? There is unfinished work to do there, and it may be that you have to complete it away from here, out upon the waves. When that work is finished, you will know your power. But you cannot finish it, until the worlds are come together in you.'

'What do you mean, Mother?'

'You will know. Remember: one small sip, and one only. Only if you come to that other place – and I will be praying that you come not there – where all hope has died; only then, at the very last when all is beyond your power to bear, then the remainder will ease your passing. You understand?' Her bright blue eyes pierced into him. He nodded. He understood.

She gave it to him. His hand closed around it gently; he felt humbled by an offering of such worth.

'My other gift I cannot give you yet. You will know when you have it. What do you call in your tongue that grey seabird, that flies on stiff straight wings?'

He looked at her, puzzled. 'A seagull?' Then he understood. 'A fulmar?'

'Yes. That is it. Look for the fulmar.'

44

Those days after the Speaking. A sentence of death upon a man, anywhere on the Island, was so uncommon, Micheil had never had to do it. Now he found himself needing to arrange the details of an execution he did not himself believe in. He could not see it any other way.

He and Hugh had pondered when the sending-out should be. He had given the Seaborne two weeks to be prepared. He had not thought at first how that would bring them all to the commemoration of the Death and the Rebirth. But it would be fitting, Hugh said, that he be sent out on the Day of Sacrifice.

His first duty was to have a boat made ready. He had plodded over the pass to Fisherhame, hoping to see, first Dael, and then Benrish. Returning, he closed the door wearily behind him. Aileen rose from her place. She took his cloak from his shoulders and hung it on its peg.

He looked at her. 'Well, that's done.'

'Was Benrish agreed?'

'He was,' he replied. 'It seems that the Ingleeshe is rising in his estimation, despite his loss. It's the fishermen who know better than any of us what asking the ocean to decide really means, and they are coming to respect a man who submits, despite sharing such knowledge.'

'And the boat?'

'As we hoped. He sees it as fitting, that Dermot's boat carries the man to his doom.'

Aileen brought him beer, and set a steaming bowl of stew before him.

He had passed by Fengoelan's house and found the man strangely silent.

'Not fishing today?' Micheil said, trying to break through.

The blue eyes fixed him.

'Targud was out yesterday,' he answered. 'With Callen. They caught nothing.'

His speech was deliberate; slow.

'It happens.' Micheil looked back into the fathomless eyes and, finding no help there, turned away.

Walking away from the house, he'd found Shelagh standing in his path.

'Shareg,' she greeted him. He saw her worried face.

'Shareg: why?' He knew there could only be one subject of her question. 'Why this, of all things? Why do you allow it?' Her grey eyes seemed greyer than ever, her face more lined than he could remember.

He sighed. 'I am a man,' he had told her. 'Can a man stand against the tide?'

'Husband, it troubles me.' Aileen disturbed his reverie as she cleared away the platters. 'In the story Callen-Barg goes forth in a boat with oars and sail, and he offers them to the elements. Yet here –'

'Yes. We send him forth with neither. But how else would the ocean decide? The other stories all speak of *corrachs* without oars or sail. You remember the story of Brede?' He stood up heavily.

'Oh, but it weighs on me, Aileen. It is stupidity. I keep thinking there must be another way. But I never find it.'

'So A'Phadr is right, isn't she? And the Ingleeshe is right. It is now the only way.'

'Aye.' He drained his beer in one draught. 'They're right.' He slammed the cup down on the board. 'Unfortunately.'

Micheil knocked at the priest's door. He found Hugh seated within, his feet in a bath of steaming water, and Morag kneeling before him, a cloth in her lap.

Micheil came straight to the matter that was on his mind.

'Do you think he'll return?'

Hugh's brown eyes met his gaze. 'And if he doesn't?' he asked.

Micheil brooded. 'In one way, he'd save us much trouble.'

'Indeed.'

'So what do you think, man? Do you think he will?'

'Does what I think matter?' said Hugh.

Micheil waited.

'Well, if you're asking me,' the priest went on, as Micheil knew he would, 'I think he will come back. As you've told him, no-one else will have him. And I don't see him making a life for himself running wild out on the hills.'

'He might not think of that in the moment.'

'Perhaps not. But, Micheil, he is playing for all. The dice are loaded against him, yet he has staked all on the one throw. He has to make that throw. It's the only way he might, just, win.

'And you may be forgetting that he is in very capable hands. His only way out now is through. She will see him through.'

The next day, Micheil went through the town. He felt an odd sense of listlessness upon it; he could feel Dhion's absence. Yet things were not simply as they had been before the Seaborne came among them. What were they going to lose? And by their own, deliberate, choice.

He made his way to the smithy and knew from a distance that Shean was at work. As he pushed open the heavy door the smith was raining blows upon a white-hot bar of iron.

Completing the task and red-faced from the effort, he'd said, 'I don't know why I'm doing this just now. But a man's got to do something.'

'He's due back on the eve of the Washing of Feet. By nightfall,' Micheil commented.

Shean shot a look from under his dark brows.

'In his place,' he growled, 'I wouldn't come back.'

First-day came and went, the last before they would send out the Seaborne upon the ocean. The week before Easter always seemed to Micheil a strange time. A between-time, neither ordinary, nor celebration. A pause in the current of life, when Time herself seemed to hold her breath. And never more so than now.

On third-day, Hugh had gone the long walk back over the northern hills. Now the eve of the Washing of Feet was come at last. As Micheil went down to the pasture, he saw the carpenter's paelht, sitting at ease beside the saw-pit.

'Donal, man, has your master no given you work?'

The big man gave a glance over his shoulder, where Leighan's door stood ajar. 'He has'ne. He's in a queer mood today, to be sure. I think he's forgotten that I be. And it's no for me not reminding him, either.'

Micheil sat beside him. The paelht continued.

'I'm no fretting for that, though. It's no long now that I can go home. Ye ken, my bairn was only wee when I was took from her. Whenever I'm allowed back I see her that much bigger, an it's more and more a wrench when I have to leave her again. An my missus needs me there. She's got her hands full wi' the wee one, even wi' the help o' the other two.'

Micheil nodded. 'We'll miss you, Donal. You've been good for us. And soon you'll have done your time.'

Donal sighed. 'Aye. It can only be a few weeks, an I'm home for good. An it will be for good,' he added, with sudden energy. 'I was stupid, an I let my anger get the better of me. It's no going to happen again.'

Micheil continued on his way. Two men, soon to be gone from them. But one, to his home. And the other?

Towards evening he plodded back from the pastures with Young Manas, his cowman. The cattle were grazing on the new grass, and a day-old calf lay in the warm air. They'd helped it stagger to its wobbly legs and find its dam's udder. They looked over the herd; there was a bullock ready for slaughter for the Feast of the Rebirth.

He spotted a movement on the lough-side path. Two men were walking towards the town. He recognised Hugh; and the other? So the Ingleeshe had come back from the wise-woman after all. Hugh had been right – here he was.

He watched Dhion go, quietly, towards the forge, a stillness hanging about him like a garment. Micheil felt now the separation between them: the Seaborne – a man marked out, apart.

The evening sun broke through around the grey bulk of Beh' Mora, turning the fleeing clouds a smoky red.

45

Her parents seemed unusually slow in going to bed that night. Her mother, knowing what the dawn would bring, tried to hold her close before blowing out the light. Shinane turned away. She needed to be left alone. She lay, after her mother had kissed her, where she had lain all down the years of childhood. Now the bed felt too small.

Her mind turned to the mountain. To the memory of four weeks earlier with everyone assembled around that ghastly green gash where Dermot lay. And then, that other mountain; she saw it there, fog-wreathed, sun-pierced. She heard again the voice; she felt again the power.

Then the time of waiting: those long days of Dhion's absence. She knew that he must go; that he must be prepared by one of the Wise, and that she must make her own preparation with Morag, and, strangely, with Shareen. She thought of the priest's house without the priest, the long silences with Morag, seeking to find her own way to rest in the One. And all the time, waiting, with mingled longing and dread, for his return.

And that evening, as dusk fell, there he was. The door had creaked open. He had turned in the doorway. She heard him bid goodnight to the Father. She had gone to him, wanting to hold him, and found him empty, as if himself was curled up deep within his body, unreachable. She had served him his supper, and he had eaten, but listlessly, without appetite. Her eyes could not leave him.

At last she heard her parents settle in their alcove. At last their breathing came smoothly. Her mother's soft snore crept round the curtain.

Still she waited. She did not want to waste a moment. But she must be sure they were sleeping deeply enough not to be disturbed. She tweaked a corner of her curtain aside. The house was dark. She was trembling.

She turned the covering back, and swung her legs off the bed-shelf. With her left hand she followed the wall until she felt the curtain that covered the store. Softly, so softly, she pulled it to one side and passed through. She must be careful not to upset a pot, send an empty pan tumbling to the floor. She reached the wooden door that gave onto the kale-yard. She opened it and passed through. And gasped.

There in the sky hung luminous veils, faintly shimmering in the north: blue, and green, and turquoise. Even as she watched they changed. Faint red rays grew in strength and swept the sky, and disappeared again. Again the blue and green curtains hung there, and through them she could see the stars. For long moments she stood, watching, wondering.

The smithy door was dim in the starlight. Gently she opened it. There he lay, in the dim, warm light of the embers, his eyes wide, looking at her.

'Shinane,' he said, softly. He pushed himself up on his elbows.

She stood in the doorway.

'Come,' she whispered.

He looked at her, questioning. She saw he was naked. She waited.

He slid out of the bed, wrapping his cloak about him, and followed her to the door, out into the glittering kale-yard.

They stood together, barefoot on the cold ground. His arms were about her waist.

'We say that they are warriors, running to battle. We call them the Hasty Men.'

They stood together, in silence, while the lights in the northern sky shifted and swelled and shimmered above them. She put her hands behind her and felt him, close against her, the rough cloth of his cloak, the warmth of his body.

Then she turned to him, and led him back to the smithy door and the warmth of the forge-fire, glowing low in the darkness of the night.

Loosing her hand, he lit a rush-light. On a shelf beside them it gleamed on iron. He sank onto his bed and looked up at her.

'Did you come to show me that wonder?' he said.

Something seemed different about him. She felt as if a barrier he had been putting up against her was no longer there. She slipped onto the pallet beside him. She felt him hold her close, and for a long space they lay wordless, their bodies pressed together. She felt the strength of him seeping into her; her own strength seeping into him. And in that mingled strength she felt the sweetness, the healing of all the long years of feeling herself a person apart.

'Dhion.' He looked at her. His face in shadow obscured his eyes.

'Dhion, this is the last chance we have to talk together. I want to say...' She raised herself on an elbow, and turned on her side to face him. 'If you come back... When you come back... Will you ask my father for me? Will you do that?'

She fixed him, waited for his reply. It did not come quickly. He looked away, and she sensed again that dread distance between them. If she could not bridge that gap, could not reach him now, then she knew she would not be able to find her way to the place that Morag had spoken of.

At last he looked at her. His words came slowly.

'Shinane, you know what I am, a stranger among you, washed up on your shore like – a piece of old timber from some long-forgotten shipwreck. A head full of ideas that have no place here. And tomorrow I face a trial that will take me from you.

'My head tells me I will perish. My heart hopes… But I don't see how I can return. In my wildest thoughts I even wonder… Will my old world claim me back?'

He paused. His eyes met hers. He drew a breath. Then he said,

'What can I tell you? If anyone can, it is you who will draw me back. What else could I do, if I return, but ask you to share whatever life opens up before me. If you will.'

She drank in his words greedily, as if she were the shipwrecked and starving stranger, and they were the vital nourishment she required.

Something was released within her. With a sudden, lithe movement, she rolled over onto him. She looked down into his face. Her long hair hung on either side of them. Closer her face came, and closer. She pressed her lips to his. Her arms burrowed under his neck. His arms wrapped around her waist and drew her close.

She pulled away. 'Is that how they kiss… in your world?'

'No,' he said, solemnly. 'Nothing like…' There was laughter in his eyes.

Again she lifted herself on her long arms and was grave. 'Dhion, there is another thing I want to ask of you. I long, I pray, that you will return. I don't know how you can, but I will do everything in my power while you are away to help you back.

'But if you don't – Dhion, if you can't come back… I want to be able to remember you. I want to be able to go on remembering you, until I'm an old woman with a face full of wrinkles. I want to go on loving you all my life, and if you're not there beside me, I'll still talk to you, and ask you what you think about things. I'll –'

'Shinane – you mustn't. If I don't return you must find another man. You must marry and be glad with

323

him. Raise his children, let them be with you in your old age.'

She silenced him. For a moment, still, silent beside him, she weighed again the cost, the terrible cost that could be exacted of her. If he did not return, there were few who would understand her choice.

'I don't want someone else's children. I want your children. If we can't have any more than that, I want this night to lie with you as wife with her man; and if God wills to bear your child. And if you don't come back, I'll have the memory. And maybe I will have your child. That is what I long for.'

She stopped speaking. She sat back and watched him. She waited.

He returned her gaze, long and searchingly.

'You know what that means. Your parents... Everybody...'

'Of course I know what that means! Do you think I don't know it better than you? I've weighed this.'

She rolled away from him, her eyes challenging him, searching his face.

It was after a long moment that he spoke. He seemed to be choosing his words carefully, to be speaking from his thoughts more than his feelings. 'I have no right to put you at risk,' she heard him say. 'So much of me feels I should tell you No, to protect you. But maybe that would be to treat you with contempt. And that I will never do.'

He turned towards her, with a question that seemed, this time, to arise from his heart. 'What if the years pass, and you see me no more? What if you have borne my child and lost the respect of your neighbours... What if you come to regret this choice and curse me, for pleasuring myself at your expense?'

This time it was his keen gaze that challenged her. She took in his words. She pulled herself up straight to answer him.

324

'I cannot know what will happen in the time to come, and what I will feel. But I do know that if you will not give us this, I will live in vain, for I will never have known what it is to have lived fully.

'And,' she went on, with a sudden realisation, 'unless you give us this time, I will not be able to hold you as I long to.' She felt herself beseeching him '… To hold your life-thread, while you are out there on the sea.'

She held his gaze. And saw a change come over him, like the sun breaking through clouds. His face was transfigured, shining up at her. The terrible distance into which he had been growing, day by day, since his ordeal had been set, was finally bridged.

He said nothing. His hands reached for the hem of her shift, and pulled it up and over her head.

The wave of emotion within her took her by surprise.

With him she entered a world of their own making, with confines in no way limited by the rudeness of a simple pallet in a forge.

A time began, to her sacred, when she drew near to the quick of the man who was so vividly other and now so vividly alive; in truth she lived fully, expressed herself fully, and felt herself heard.

Once she cried out, whether in the ecstasy of bliss or of pain she herself could not tell. He quieted her with a kiss, covering her quivering lips with his own.

It was still dark when she woke. The night had been too precious to waste in much sleep, but now she knew it was far gone. She must leave him.

Gently she pulled his arms away from her and reached for her shift, at their feet where it had been thrown. She sat up and pulled the white linen over her skin. She slipped out of the door. The waxing moon had set, and the men in the sky had hastened away. Through the lean-to, slowly she went, carefully, softly,

325

back to her own bed. As she settled herself, her body still throbbing, tingling, alive with the fullness of all that had passed, she sensed the faintest stirring, light as thistledown, fluttering deep in her belly. Sometimes she felt this, around the middle of the month; only this was different. Now everything was different.

He turned, half-asleep, and reached for her. But his fingers found only the stone of the floor. Sleep ebbed from him, but as he heard the cawing of a crow outside, he was at the same time aware of the warmth of the woman suffusing his being. She was joined to him. Still, a thin, cold light was beginning to seep under the door. It was morning.

46

Gradually over the wide round rim of the world the sun rose red and gold. Shadows that had been grey and ash became richer, stronger, in a world that was suddenly encoloured. An eagle floated up, up, on wide circles high in the new gleaming air, looking down. The Island laid out below, a thing of moor-green and rock-grey and fern-russet, now stirring with the movement of the beings of day.

The wolves crouched in their lairs. The hinds with their new-born fawns stalked slowly through the heather. The ptarmigan and the black-cock strutted and paraded before their hens. The wildcat, fierce and aloof, observing from afar.

And in the little towns and villages life began again as it did every morning: milking and feeding and driving to pasture; cooking and washing and giving the breast; a woman shouting at her lazy man who, senseless creature that he was, had taken too much drink the night before. Now she would be left to blow up the fire and fetch new wood from the stacks and peat from the pile. In Caerster and in Midland, in the Northland there-away it was another day like every day, while the waves beat on headland and rocky promontory and washed sighing upon shingle beach and crashed with regular roar upon the gentle sandy shores. While from the east the great wave of the tide slowly rose and bore towards them, as twice every day it did without fail, washing the shores clean of their guilt and passing on.

And for most of Westerland it was the same. Only in Caerpadraig beside the lough and in Fisherhame towards the sea, and up in the scattered hamlets and farmsteads in the hills around, was it not every day. Slowly there rose within the mind of each that this day was different: in shepherd and in cowman, in farmer's wife and craftsman's wife and unmarried maid, in raw youth and little boy. They took it in, and each in their many different ways responded. Even the babes, nuzzling and suckling at the breast, they took in something different, and whimpered in uncertainty.

There was a hush over the land. This was the Day of Sacrifice. Not the death of a living victim for appeasement, as it had been in the old times; but rather, the remembrance of an act of love.

And this morning, before the three hours' vigil, with its rhythm of reflection and silence, and chant and silence, before that they would take the Seaborne out upon the great water and leave him there. And which, wondered Morag, was it? Love, or appeasement? Or both?

The ragged procession formed and wound its way upward beside the burn. First the shareg, stolid, black-browed. Then the Seaborne, and the brown-cassocked priest and the grey-mantled wife who was his steel. The blacksmith and his wife, and behind them the long train of the townspeople, all who could spare themselves that forenoon.

Dhion felt numb. How does a man walking to his execution feel, he wondered. He came, with his cloak and a bundle wrapped in sealskin. It contained his donkey jacket and the wallet Shinane had made for him, filled with her baking. As he passed he saw the rowan trees that hid the burn, the splashing little falls where the water fell from one pool to another, as the procession climbed towards the pass. He saw them, as if he were both player and spectator. He was the central part of all that was happening. He was detached, remote; as if he were elsewhere, looking down on it all.

He raised his eyes, over the shareg's broad shoulders before him, across the green-grey grass and moorland, across the tumbled boulders: the rising land, shelf upon shelf, step upon step. There was Talor Gan, solid against the sky, dark and looming, accusing. *I go,* his heart said. *I go at your sending. I go to pay your due.* This was the price demanded of him, to put all at hazard – comfort, safety, love and life. *I go.*

Behind him followed the trailing crowd. Shean and Fineenh; all the townspeople who could. From time to time more would join – terse, tight-lipped hill-farmers from the out-steadings; shepherds from the high grazings. They crossed the moss in the cup between the hills, where the grey-shingled path wound like a snail-track across the soft ground, down the steep screes to the sea.

Between the roundhouses they went, the dark homes of the fishermen. The seafolk were there, lining the way, motionless, taciturn. From the throat of one or another came the time-worn, the homely and fitting farewell: 'Ingleeshe. Go in God's name.'

He passed them, his head down, his eyes, unfocused, on the trodden ground. He heard. And he did not hear.

Benrish. Standing there before his door, the mother who had lost her son behind him, her head covered, her daughters beside her. Watching silently.

His eyes lifted, and for a moment they looked straight into those of the stricken father. They saw there the grief, the pain, the germ of respect. It was four weeks exactly from the morning that Dermot had been lost.

'Go in God's name, Ingleeshe.' Dermot's father spoke. Dhion answered, 'In God's name, Benrish.'

The press of people moved him on.

They came to the gap in the low sandstone cliff, and passed down it onto the shingle beach. The boat was there, made ready, victualled and watered for three days, her nose pointing down towards the water, as if eager once more to breast the waves and feel the keen salt spray.

Hugh brought holy water and sprinkled it upon her timbers, pacing three times around her length. 'Go with Ghea. Be guided by God.' Morag stood, still, silent.

Dhion laid his bundle in the boat, and knelt before the priest. He anointed him with water, delicious and cool. *'An Ainm Chrisht.'*

It was not he. It was someone else who knelt, who rose, who stood alone there on the seashore. Someone else through whose eyes he peered out upon the grey and sparkling sea. His hand – the hand of this strange other – felt for his wrist. The silver bracelet that he always wore, no longer there. He had left it where Shinane would find it. A love gift, once more.

A scraping of strakes on shingle, and the hissing rub of a boat's timbers being hauled across the sand. Not the vessel that would carry the Seaborne; this was Callen's boat, putting out to sea. Callen, who had brought his voice against Dhion at the council, now undertaking the act his words required of him. Six oarsmen passed, their feet splashing in the water; younger men. Fengoelan and Targud who, with Dermot, had first found him, stood apart on the shore, silently bearing witness.

Strong hands helped the Seaborne push Dermot's boat into the water, hands gripping the empty rowlocks. As she lifted onto the waves he clambered on board, alone. The men stood, knee-deep in the sea, watching. In the other boat, the rowers bent to their work. The tow-rope sprang suddenly taut, throwing drops of salt water spraying into the air.

He did not look back. He knew that the only eyes he could bear to look upon, that he could not look upon, were not there with the crowd. They would be up on the hillside, from where she would gain the longest view. Across the cable's length of swaying water, past the down-turned faces of the oarsmen, the rising prow of Callen's boat, the long low grey-green swell, the broken skerries ringed with white water, his eyes searched towards the horizon, where the worlds meet.

They rowed him out. They pulled the little craft bouncing over the rollers, past the skerries and out into the open sea. As the sun rose to its height the land finally dropped away behind them, and, with many a 'Go with God, Ingleeshe', they let him go and bent their backs for their home.

He watched them. Soon they would disappear into the trough of a long wave, then as either they or he were lifted on a crest he would catch sight of them again, and each time smaller, less distinct in the westering sun. There came a time when he thought he could still see them, like a minute insect in the vastness of the sea. Then they were gone. He was alone, under a huge sky.

Fear encircled him. It swam beneath him, hovered above him. Fear for life, fear of loss. Certain he felt now that he would never again walk upon those flower-sparkled shorelands of the Island. Never talk and joke with those once-kindly people, who had received him, welcomed him, protected him, and who now demanded this. Certain that, for the last time, he had looked into the sea-grey eyes of the one who lay enfolded in the heart and soul he knew he had left behind him.

All was gone. Behind the all he had just lost, was the all he had already lost: the life he had been brought up to. The loss, confusingly, of the one he had not loved well enough, in the time before.

What seemed nearest to him now, in the dark rolling sea, as each wave climbed up above his head, only to lift him and let him slide down its gull-black back, was that his end would be here, alone in the vastness. He looked at the casks of water they had left him, the loaves and the dried fish they had sent with him.

Shinane's wallet. Three days' supply: that was what he had. Suppose the waves did not overwhelm him, suppose the boat was as good as they had said and it bore him faithfully. If the weather turned hot, soon after that supply ran out he would die of thirst; if it turned foul he would die of exposure before then. And his body would drift on, borne on the breast of this great ocean he called the Atlantic, until its bleached bones grounded on a far shore.

He held each loss before him. He looked each death full in the face. And slowly, there in the boat as darkness began to fall, the chant that Mother Coghlane had taught him rose up in his heart: *'Ah Ghea...'* Thin it was as it began, an act of will, but with each repetition it gained in strength, until he sang out loud its sounds. And there in the air it seemed to call out another song. Evoked from a dusty attic of his memory, back from another world, the words of St Francis:

> *And thou, most kind and gentle Death,*
> *Waiting to hush our latest breath,*
> *O praise Him, Alleluia!*
> *Thou leadest home the child of God,*
> *And Christ our Lord thy way hath trod,*
> *O praise Him, Alleluia!*
> *O praise Him, Alleluia!*
> *Alleluia!*

Behind him, a silver circle, the moon rose.

47

Empty, at last Shinane turned away from her vigil. She had not moved while the sunset deepened over the empty horizon, but finally common sense prevailed. Weary now to the core, she must sleep, renew her strength for her task. Finding her way in the dark down from the slopes of Beh' Talor Gan would be perilous. She must go at once. At first light she would return.

She pushed open the rough door that had, longer than she could remember, separated that which was home from that which was outside. There seemed little difference now.

The room was lit by the lamp and the glow of the fire. Her father looked up with a frown. Her mother reached out a hand and laid it firmly on his arm; then, rising without a word, went to the hearth, returning with a bowl of broth and a hunk of bread in her hands. She laid them on the board.

Shinane shook her head. 'No, thank you,' she whispered. 'I can't.'

Her father seemed on the point of saying something. He was silenced with a look.

She went to her bed and undressed. She lay on her side, her knees drawn up, her face staring at the darkness that was the wall. The darkness was comforting: it asked nothing of her.

A rustle behind her. The curtain was pulled aside and mellow light filled the alcove. She did not move. A warm hand pressed her shoulder. Reluctantly, she turned. Her mother looked down at her, a long, wordless look. Shinane turned away. The curtain swung back and she was alone. She lay unmoving, except for an occasional shuddering sigh.

When, at last, she stretched out, her foot encountered something small and hard and smooth. Making no sense of it – but what now did make sense? – she reached down until her hand closed round the unlooked-for object. She drew it up to her face, knowing suddenly what she held.

The bracelet. His silver bracelet. The one he always wore. It seemed to be a part of him.

Its hard reality broke in upon her numbed senses, broke through the fortress of will with which she held her focus. She clutched it to her wildly, and wept.

As soon as the grey light of morning seeped into the smithy Shinane rose. Quietly she dressed and wrapped her cloak around her and went out. The silver bracelet was on her right arm, pushed up above the wrist to where it held firm.

Fineenh woke from a poor sleep. She rose, and crossed the cold floor to her daughter's bed. It was empty. She paused, uncertain what to do. Today was the Day of the Entombment, and no-one worked more than they must. Still, there was the porridge to be made. Absently stirring the pot, her mind was all on her daughter. She saw Shinane as she had been that last night, remote, unreachable. Her eyes had lost any sparkle, and shadows had lain under her cheek-bones. She hated her neighbours, for it was they who had done this to her Jewel. With a start, she realised she had let the oats catch. Now the porridge would be lumpy.

It was after the midday meal when Shinane returned.

'Where've you been, child?' she asked; but she knew the answer.

The girl shrugged. Fineenh watched her turn to where her distaff lay propped up in a corner. Watched her pull out a thread and listlessly wind it round the spindle. Watched her spin it, more carefully, as she sat on a low stool. Then a faint sound came from her scarcely-parted lips. She keened as she sat, drooping like a rootless flower.

Fineenh opened the creaking wooden door into the workshop. Shean was standing at the bench, filing nails to a point. She crossed over to him.

'You'll be gentle with your daughter, won't you?'

He glanced back at her, his face hard.

'My lady's returned then, has she? And what's so important that takes her away from us all morning?'

'You know quite well what's so important.' There was a sharpness in her answer. She laid a hand on his forearm to stop his repetitious action.

He pulled his arm away. 'Aye,' he said. 'I know. And now we have to carry on. All of us. Her as well. Carry on with our work. I'll no have a daughter of mine traipsing off by herself half the day to God knows where.'

'Perhaps just at the moment she has other work to do,' Fineenh blazed at him. 'You'll be gentle with her for now and give her some slack. Or you'll cook your own dinner.' Their eyes met and drew fire between them. It was he who dropped his gaze first.

Shinane sat, the distaff under her arm, the spindle between her fingers. Her body felt empty, her mind numb and grey. But in her heart and in her belly something was stirring, was taking form and substance. Like the thread being drawn from the tumbled fibres of the wool, pulled, twisted, wrung into a strong skein, it lay coiled, spooling out and away, across the miles, across the worlds, to where he was upon the waves. The power of the mountain was upon her, was growing within her, was passing from her like the cord that joined mother and child. It pained her, the pain of bringing forth. It drained her. And filled her and comforted her.

Soon after the Seaborne had left her, after the morning milking, Mother Coghlane called her sheep to her. She took her strong walking-staff, and led them down the burnside, her gown whispering through the lank grasses and snagging in the heather.

She brought them down to the town at the foot of her high valley and, leaving them with a shepherd there, she crossed the moors. Finding shelter where she could on the high moor, she rested through the night. She too saw the Hasty Men come and paint the skies with sheets of coloured light, and hasten away. Much of the next day she walked, following the deer-tracks through the heather, down to the lough with the little town at its head. As they were taking the seaborne one out, she skirted the town and climbed the slopes of Beh' Mora, until she looked down upon the grey sea far below.

She knew she did not watch alone. Somewhere, she was aware, another watched, achingly. She sent her surrounding love upon her like an unseen cloud of fire.

But most her spirit was bent upon the man from another world, whose end not even she could see. She had prepared him as best she could; now he had to meet his fate himself, alone. Still, there was aid she could give him. She had still her second gift. Through that long night she watched. She saw the moon rise and reach his height, and set as the new day dawned. The moon was just past the full.

A thin washed pall spread over the sky. All day, deep in her mind, she prepared herself.

Again the sky darkened towards evening. There were no stars. She sat long into the night, and waited until she knew within herself that she was ready. It was time. She drew herself in. She rose above the cliff, seeing her body squatting there on the dark mountainside below. Then, swooping like a seabird down and across the waves, into the far west, her spirit flew towards the man. For a moment she saw the boat. She saw the man they called Dhion, Ingleeshe, the Seaborne, alone. She released her soul upon him. And with this world's eyes she saw no more.

48

Throughout the long day, the first he had spent completely alone, he drifted, he knew not in which direction. He used the tools of mind and heart that Mother Coghlane had taught him, of chant and meditation and body-prayer. He ate little, and drank no more than he needed to keep thirst away. He watched the clouds drift across and the sun break through and be hidden again. Nothing happened.

The night was worse. He slept, as Fengoelan had taught him, in the stern-sheets, but fitfully; and some time – the round moon in the gaps between clouds was at its height – he woke and knew he was afraid. He had no idea where he was; was he slowly being carried back to the Island, or further out, far into the west? Or to the north, into the cold seas below the Pole? He started the chant again, but it seemed to him weak, ineffective, useless. He was powerless to direct his course. He lay across the thwarts and stared up into the moonlight. The moon would be shining on Caerpadraig, as here. Caerpadraig? What was that? The little town by the lough was now no more than a dream.

He longed for this unknowing to be over. No – it was not a longing. It was emptier, deader, more colourless than any emotion. What was this listlessness that was overwhelming him? He began to recognise it. It was not hopelessness: it was the death of hope. He began to wish for death. That one wish began to spread over him like a grey pall. If only it could take him now and not delay. *Waiting to hush our latest breath.* What was the use of breath? Could it take him back? Could it take him anywhere? What was the meaning of this monotonous pulse that tapped behind his knee, the heartbeat that muttered in his ear? It could not give him the only thing he wanted.

He sat up and felt in his bag for the little bottle. Not all of it – not yet. A sip, she had said. That could take you into the world between the worlds, if you were careful and knew the way. Did he know the way? In his mind he saw again the pathless way across the moors of Talor Gan. He repeated to himself all she had taught him, and unstopped the flask.

He smelled it. It had a musty odour, with a strange sharpness beneath. He put the mouth to his lips, and took a little. It tasted almost unbearably dry, like sloes, and yet not like, and then a peppery fire. He swallowed.

Again he lay down, and waited. The chill of the night slowly faded, and he began to feel almost warm. His heart stilled. His mind sank. An emptiness crept over his thoughts until they ceased.

It was as if he could see, dimly, through dirty glass. A smoky red, like the forge-fire he had tended so many months. Shean's house, the street outside, the homes of the town among the arms of the hills. The sparkle of water in the burn, the sun on the lough. He floated above them all, bodiless.

The sight faded. Only a dingy deep dark grey. A cold shiver passed through him, and he shook. Slowly, another vision appeared, and little by little took on reality. He could make out moving shapes, vague forms of muddied colour. A distant cacophony at the edge of hearing. The shapes, the sounds becoming clearer. A grey London street. A red bus in a swirl of dust and diesel smoke. A street market – could he catch the very words the costermonger shouted? It was all remote, distant, but drawing nearer.

Again he could see nothing. The boat was a dream, the fitful dream of near-death. He lay in the cold sea with his jacket tightly zipped, in the encircling arms of the lifebelt. The island, the girl, his whole life since the fishing-boat had plunged him into the water, all was no more than a dream. He was shaking with the bitter cold.

Consciousness slipped from him once more. He wandered in the dream-world. A grey world, a dry and barren world, that had once been a fair woodland. Nothing moved; no wind stirred the grey skeletons of trees.

There were dim shapes. They took more form, and he saw they were walking around – aimlessly, slowly, lost. All sorts of people, all kinds of beasts, in a loose unseeing crowd.

He was looking for something, and he couldn't remember what it was. He stumbled on, blindly.

A bird flew over him, grey and white. Like a seagull, but it was not a gull. Its wings were shorter, stiffer. Its beak was thicker, darker. Dully, his mind remembered: *Look for the fulmar.* It was completely out of place in this cold desert. It circled over him, then flew on, like a grey cross in the sky. *Follow me,* it seemed to say in his heart.

He followed. It flew ahead, circled, returned to him and flew on. Shapes passed him, unseeing. The fulmar led him up a barren slope. The crowd thinned; there were fewer shapes up here, more space, and he could see further. Slowly he looked around. If only he could remember what he was looking for. Below him, where the shapes were moving, one caught his eye. The pricked ears, the alert eyes, the half-open mouth and white teeth, stood out sharply in this dull world. The dog turned her head and saw him. She lifted her dark muzzle in recognition. She paused, gathered her black-and-tan flanks, and ran towards him, determined, sure.

The noise of water was back in his ears. Slowly, beyond that, he became aware of another sound. A distant, clattering roar. Sea surrounded him again. He looked up and searched the sky. And then he saw it. The flat red of the helicopter's underside, and the shimmering circle of its rotor-blades, still some distance away.

'Here we are,' it said. 'This is where you belong. This is your world. You will be safe here: no hunger or cold or want. We have made a world for you – your world – where you can have everything you desire: everything, so long as you can pay for it. And even that we make easy for you. You need not pay the full price – not yet, not ever. Come. We are real, we are here, we offer what you want.'

Then another shape in the sky. Nearer, lower, silent. A grey-white cross in the air above, the fulmar circled close, looking down at him. 'Listen,' she said. 'There is a choice. You are between worlds, and each world is as real as any other. Two worlds have a claim on you – but you can live in only one. Choose,' she said to him. 'Choose now, or never. Choose either world; they are both good, they are both bad. Only choose.'

'What should I choose, Mother?'

'It is not for me to say. One is a world where children fall into the fire, and young men are lost at sea, and young women fear childbirth, and all is hard work and worn hands and worn-out bodies. And one is a world where sometimes people do not know who lives beside them, do not notice when an old woman dies alone; and where all is bought at a price that Earth must pay.

'Neither world is perfect,' mewed the fulmar. 'Neither is utterly lost. But you can live in only one of them. You must choose.'

'This is the only world,' clattered the helicopter. It wheeled closer. 'Look,' it said. 'We are here. Rescue. Safety. Warmth and comfort. If you do not choose this, you choose death. There is no alternative. That is what happens to people who are not rescued. Do not believe you can return to that made-up world of your fantasy. There is no boat. There is no land back there. There is no girl waiting for you on the sea-shore. There is no choice.'

He looked up. The cold numbed him, dulled his thought. Only... lift an arm... wave an arm, wave it...

'I accept, I submit, I repent. I have erred and strayed from thy ways. I come.'

'You belong to this world.' Now the helicopter hovered right above him. Its downdraught whipped up the water into a circle of spray. 'You owe us your duty, your service. You would not be a turncoat, a traitor, would you? Your parents. Your brother. Helen. Helen... Just... wave... wave...'

'I... come... I... return... I... wave...'

And the dog that was the other side of his soul rose and licked his face awake. 'Awake! We are ourself. We are free. We can choose. There is a choice.'

He reached inside – or was it beyond? – to a place where thoughts were not. A warm place. A clear place. In that place he felt joined. Joined within and without. Joined to the whole. And in that joining, she was there: the woman who had given herself to him with no holding back. Simple, and solid, and liquid, and flowing.

With shocking clarity Coghlane's words came back to him: *What is it that you call yourself?* And his answer: *I am Dhion.* In that moment of remembering he knew that his choice was already made; had been made before ever he was put to the ocean. In that moment he knew what he would do. He was no longer torn. It was the work of a moment. The work of all his life.

A glimpse, and he thought he saw a helmeted face, peering from the side of the machine. A cable snaking down. The vision faded. It was gone. He sat up, stiffly, damp and cold. He felt the timbers of the boat around him. Dermot's boat, the one they had put him in, the one on which lay Hugh's blessing. A grey light was warming to green-gold along the rim of ocean.

In his heart, with mingled sadness and joy, he said farewell to the world he had known from his birth: the world of cities and roads, of brick houses and centrally-heated rooms, of money and profit and debt. His parents, his family, the woman he had tried, not well enough, to love.

The fulmar had given him something; had broken something in him. Broken through. With a new-found clarity, and surrounded only by a seascape that could be in either world, he reached out and held to his new world: a world he could never have imagined, a world he had arrived at by some unaccountable grace that reached out, beyond the other side of desperation.

He paused. A still space. Helen – he reached back to her. Here was himself: more of him than he had managed to give her in that other world, that everyday world. He had been driven, driven by wrong priorities. He had destroyed their dreams. He had betrayed her.

A farewell, a confession; but also a benediction. Something within himself had healed. Some deep place within had been made whole. Now at last he could do it. He could entrust her – entrust them all – to: to what? To whatever it was had reached out to him.

His task completed, he turned. Inwardly he turned towards the woman who had chosen him, with whom – he felt it, like a cord coiling between their hearts – he knew himself to be joined. He turned towards a world that only now could he say Yes to with all his heart.

The morning sun lifted, and he saw two distant peaks, low on the skyline. He took off the black jacket and folded it carefully. He took his cloak and threw it round his shoulders.

He stood up, straddling his feet against the slow roll of the boat. With new-found courage he spread his arms wide and called out. In the wild Island tongue he called upon the wind and the waves. 'Take me home,' he said. 'Carry me safely, I pray, to my house and my home.'

A breeze out of the west ruffled his hair. The little boat shivered, hesitated, and slid down the face of a wave; no longer adrift, but purposeful, onward, towards the shore.

49

In the house next to the rondal, Morag woke suddenly. Something was calling her. She nudged her husband in the darkness. Together they rose and dressed, and walked out into the early half-light.

'I must light the Easter Fire,' Hugh told her. He motioned with his head towards the rondal, where already a small knot of people was gathering.

He went on. 'I feel what you are doing; I will be thinking of you through the rite.'

She squeezed his hand and left him. In silence she walked the well-trodden path of the pass, the descent towards the sea, the rise at the last up onto the cliffs above the village of Fisherhame. As she expected, Shinane was standing, wrapped in her cloak, looking out, out over the vast glimmering waters.

But the girl was not alone. In the gathering light it was not hard to recognise the shorter, older woman. Fineenh stood on the cliff-top, there with her daughter – yet not with her. She held herself back, at a respectful distance; now she turned to face Morag as she breasted the cliff path, crossed the springy turf, took up her place beside the watching mother.

Shinane did not turn. Her stillness was profound. *Ghea, give her strength.*

Below them, Morag saw a movement. From the houses by the shore two people were coming out: Fengoelan and Shelagh, toiling up the path towards them.

A wind blew softly in their faces, and ruffled the girl's dark hair. The long lines of rollers stretched away towards the horizon, broken only in the distance by the out-skerries. She waited. They all waited.

There was nothing.

And then, beyond the skerries – could she see – a tiny, dark, something?

Morag fixed her eyes on the skyline. Something was moving out there. Something so small, she was in truth not sure it was anything; sometimes there, sometimes gone. She turned to look at the other watchers. Fineenh, her anxious mother's gaze never leaving her daughter. Shelagh, between her sister and her man, her head slightly bowed. But Fengoelan had seen it, she could tell. His keen gaze held steady.

It was impossible to read Shinane, who stood, her back to them, motionless. Morag gazed out across the skerries, to the open sea beyond. Slowly the speck gained in solidity. A boat. A small boat, without a sail.

Nobody moved, and the boat grew in size. Now she could see the outline of the man who sat in the stern who, beyond reason, could be only one man. Still nobody moved. She turned her eyes to the watching girl. She was fixed, trembling, leaning forward with her eager hope.

Then, with a low moan, Shinane gathered her skirts and turned. She was running. Running down the cliff path, and they were all following after at their own pace. First Fineenh, unused to running, but hastening, ungainly, her skirts clutched in her hands to keep from falling. Fengoelan striding after, steady and even-paced. Morag fell in beside Shelagh.

As the boat came into the shallows, scraping on the shingle, the fisherman splashed into the water. Dhion leaped over the gunwale and the two men hauled the little craft in. Shinane was already wading into the shallows, her skirts dragging through the water. With a sob that tore Morag's heart, she clasped him, her arms wrapped tightly about him. Letting go the boat, Dhion held her shaking body close until at last the sobs subsided. Long, and hard, and urgent, they kissed.

࿐

It was after the midday meal that Duigheal Shepherd nervously called at the priest's door.

'Father. You'd better come.'

Morag listened with Hugh to his story. He had stumbled across an old woman's body in a hollow place in the cliff above Fisherhame: seated upright, her knees drawn up to her chin, her glassy eyes still open, still staring out towards the west. Hugh walked him across to the shareg's house.

It was not until twilight that Hugh returned. 'They're bringing her down to the rondal now,' he said.

'Who is it?' Morag asked.

He raised his eyebrows. 'It's Coghlane.'

Micheil sent out runners to all the townships of the west and the northlands. Coghlane had been a notable seer, and it was deemed right that her burial belonged to a far wider community than that in which she had died. Morag heard from Aileen how there was some dispute about where she should be laid: her local town claimed she belonged to them. But the sharegs came to agree that Coghlane had chosen her own resting place.

By the time she had been found on the slopes of Beh' Mora her limbs had stiffened. And that was how they had to bury her, sitting, still hunched up like an unborn child.

It was a big feast, and the young men competed at wrestling and running and throwing the spear, and the older men showed their skill with metal and wood and stone and leather, while the women displayed their embroidery and tapestry and weaving.

Passing through the crowd, Morag overheard Murdogh and Tearlach talking.

'D'ye ken this woman at all, Tearlach?'

'I dinna. But I heard some people from north-away sayin' she was a witch or somethin' '

'Aye. I heard the same. Why the fuss for an old witch then?'

'Aye, but, man, it's a good feast.'

Morag held her peace, and passed on.

On the third day of feasting Micheil called the people together. A dozen sharegs had come, the High Shareg among them, but this was Micheil's place and his people, and while the High Shareg was rightly honoured, it was for Micheil to preside. Manus of Kengraig, the acknowledged finest of the harpers of the north, sang the tale of Coghlane's life, and how she had died, auspiciously, on the day and in the place where the seaborne one returned among them from the dead.

'You know, when the wise die, they don't do it like everybody else,' Morag whispered in Aileen's ear. 'They choose their time and their manner of passing. There is more to this story than we have heard.'

The bard finished, and Micheil called out. 'Dhion Ingleeshe, now twice-seaborne, come and stand before us.'

All eyes turned as the Seaborne walked out into the space in the centre, where the sharegs sat in an arc. In his plaid and jerkin, and carrying the spear and target the High Shareg had bestowed on him, Morag half-expected him to come stepping like a warrior, with head held high. But he came slowly, as if seeing something beyond. What kind of man had he become? Micheil turned him to face the people, and laid a hand on his shoulder. His voice rang out.

'This is the man: Dhion Ingleeshe. He has come across the sea to us. He has faced the testing of the elements and has been returned to us. Will any man deny his place among us now?'

Micheil's eyes swept the assembled people. No-one spoke.

The High Shareg rose. 'Where is the man's father? Who speaks for him?'

Morag smiled, and glanced to where the priests sat together; waited for what she knew would come.

'I do. I am his father.'

The voice was quiet, yet it carried in the silence with a power that came not from the throat but from another place altogether.

Hugh rose from his seat and stood beside Dhion, his cassock ruffling in the light breeze. Opposite the shareg, he also laid his hand on Dhion's shoulder. Simply, he said, 'I speak for him. This day he is born anew, into my lineage.'

A murmur went through the crowd.

Again, Micheil repeated, 'Who will deny his place among us now?'

He looked about him.

And for the third time, 'Does any man deny his place among us?'

There was silence.

Now Micheil called out: 'People of Caerpadraig, and all who are under my cloak. You have sworn an oath. I call upon you this day to fulfil it.'

Morag waited. A dozen heart-beats in the silence.

Then Benrish stepped out from the crowd. He walked forward until he stood before Dhion. He reached out his hand, and took the other's arm. He spoke. 'I have sworn, and I will fulfil my oath. I am become an old man, broken by grief. But I have seen in you bravery. And truth. I welcome you among us.'

Then Callen came, and Targud after him. Old Dael hobbled out on a stick.

And Fengoelan: 'Dhion Ingleeshe, Ma'Phadr.' On the fisherman's voice the new name rose like a falcon into the bright air. 'I welcome you among us as a man of the Island.'

'We welcome you. We welcome you!' A roar went up from the crowd.

It was done.

When they fell silent, awaiting what would next come, Micheil turned to the Seaborne. 'Dhion Ingleeshe Ma'Phadr, do you have anything to say?'

At last, Dhion spoke. But this was not the voice of the man Morag had taught to speak. This was the voice of a new man. His speech no longer set him apart. He was speaking like one grounded in his place, and with authority.

'Men and women of my Island. I thank you for your welcome. My heart warms to it. I am grateful that at last I can take my place among you. I can name you as my sisters and brothers.'

A murmur went through the crowd. Into the quiet that followed, Dhion said, 'And now, there is something I must do straight away. Before you all today, and before the spirit of Coghlane to whom I owe my life, I call upon Shean Ma'Ronal, smith of this township.'

Morag looked around. She saw the blacksmith step forward, his chest swelling with pride.

'Shean Ma'Ronal, my master in our craft, will you betroth to me your daughter?'

A hush fell on the crowd. A woman's voice broke through. 'Yes, he will!' It was Fineenh.

To Morag's amazement, the little smith smiled. 'I will,' he replied. The smile became a rueful grin. 'I'll have to cook my own dinner else!'

A ripple of laughter in the crowd.

'But please to ask my lady,' he added.

The shareg smiled. 'Does the girl agree to this betrothal? Shinane Mi'Shean, you may speak.'

The slender young woman arose from among the people. Her long hair was plaited down her back. She stepped out, tall, erect, her chin raised. She curtsied before him, bowed before Hugh, and went to stand beside the one she now claimed her own. She took his hand.

She turned her head to look into his eyes. 'With all my heart,' she said, 'I agree.'

'So you did change our ways after all.'

Morag looked at her newly-adopted son in the wavering lamplight. Shean had agreed it was not seemly for a betrothed man and woman to sleep under the same roof, and his apprentice, soon to be made fellow-craft, had returned to the priest's house until the wedding.

'But not in the way you looked to do,' she continued. 'Your choice forced us to choose.' She paused. 'Why did you?'

He sat silent for a long time, his face towards the fire, his forearms deep in the folds of his plaid. Neither she nor Hugh would interrupt.

At length he replied,

'I betrayed my family and friends once. I have to live with the knowledge of this. I do not want to betray anyone more.'

'Surely, Dhion, there are things that you miss?'

'It is true. In the world of my memory, we learned how to make ourselves comfortable beyond anything you could dream. We found ways of treating sickness and injury that helped us live long.' He paused. 'Though sometimes our old age was accompanied by a frailty of body or mind that made it a suffering. And despite our bodily comfort, people's ordinary lives often brought them far more worry than I have seen here.

'In many ways it was a marvellous world,' he went on. 'But it was a world that had fallen out of balance.' She saw him searching for a picture, and finding it. '– Like a drunken man who lurches from one side of the path to another, heedless of what he's treading on. Heedless of the sick mess that he's become; thinking that, whatever's wrong, more drink will put it right.' He looked straight at her. 'I tried to bring some of that to you here, only you have the good sense to be wary of it.'

'In what way was it unbalanced?' she asked.

'Our cleverness in developing – things – together with our greed for having them. And our success! You would not be able to imagine how many we became, and all wanting to live like gods.'

'Is ours a better world, then?'

Dhion paused.

'What worries me,' he said, 'is how you women are denied your voice. Both voices are needed together, the men's and the women's, or your world will fall out of balance too, like my world of memory.'

He gave Morag a keen look. '*You* told *me* that, once.'

Morag returned his gaze. She felt the wryness, and smiled.

'Your world of memory?' She picked out the phrase. This was a new way of naming Dhion's world.

He looked up, and into her face. 'Sitting here, that world seems so far away that I doubt its reality. Only, what else do I have for the time before I came to you? And on the ocean, there it was again, so real that I had to resist with every grain of my will, in order to choose this.'

'You chose Shinane, and with her, this. In the end you did not choose those you left in your – your world of memory.'

Again he was silent.

At last: 'I chose the self I have become here. I owed it to you – you who have helped me become what I am. And it was my heart's wish,' he added.

He looked up, straight into her eyes.

'I do not know where my choice will lead. I only know that my feet feel they have found a path. Now I will stay on it, and meet whatever it may lead to.'

Epilogue

In another world and another time, a woman awoke from her dream. A dream so vivid it had seemed, if anything, more real than the familiar room that claimed her now. Reluctant to enter that everyday world, Helen closed her eyes, to be again with the presence that had seemed so real to her, of the man she had once loved, though perhaps not well enough, the one she had left in frustration, who had then run away. Now he was missing, presumed dead. But in her dream he had been very much alive. More alive than she ever remembered him.

The dream. Just his face, looking right at her, into her. No words. And yet a message. A message she could now not quite remember.

As she got up and dressed, she began to notice something different. That poisonous lump of anxiety and blame – of self-blame – was not as strong; was at last beginning to thaw. And in its place she found an unaccustomed stillness, a budding shoot of peace, that had the power to grow. She felt at ease for him. She felt, beyond reason, that in an unexplained sense he had come through to a good place. She felt he wanted her to know this; but, more than that, she felt a sense of his concern for herself, even as he faded from her sight.

There was no going back. Mysteriously, she understood that. This was not a dream to herald his return, but rather one to let her leave him, with renewed courage to go her own way.

Breakfast. It was a Saturday morning and, unusually, she had a weekend before her with no arrangements: nothing to distract her from the unresolved pain. And there was a sense of inner prompting. She would phone his parents. Perhaps she could visit them again and tell them about the dream. She did not know what they would make of it, but she sensed there might be something to be shared among them all. Slowly, uncertainly, she reached for her mobile. There they were, listed among her contacts, next to John himself. And his brother. A moment's hesitation, and she selected their number. She waited, listening to the phone ring.

Acknowledgements

I would like to thank those who have read drafts of *The Seaborne* and offered their encouragement and their creative criticism. Mary Coles, Richard Danckwerts, Natasha Hood and Simon Howell all did a complete read-through, and my working with the text developed in relation to their comments. Alexandra McNamara's enthusiastic reception of the opening chapters did much to spur me on at the beginning, and Joan and Pete Garrard's comments after reading the first edition informed the same chapters in the second. Other friends have volunteered their time in listening to the reading of a chapter here or there. To all I am grateful.

I would also like to acknowledge the expert tuition of Maggie Hamand and staff on The Complete Creative Writing Course at the Groucho Club, the inspiration and support of tutors and fellow participants of the Teifi Valley Writers group, and the archeological advice of Cathy Dagg. Any failures that may remain in either narrative competence or historical accuracy must be laid at my door. I am also grateful to Gelda MacGregor for her comments on names and language, and hope she will forgive the hybrid mix I have finally chosen.

I am grateful to David Norrington of Wordcatcher for his vision in taking the book on and publishing its first edition.

This book could not have been written without my experience of three communities of very different kinds among whom I have had the privilege of living. The communities of Scoraig and Findhorn are in Scotland, and the text is suffused with what I have learned from them. The town of Maiduguri, where I spent eighteen months as a foreigner in the 1970s, is in northern Nigeria – geographically very different from the world of my story, and yet in some ways closer to that world than the others. The influence of the Anglican Church, in which I grew up, and the late Joyce Ferne of the Coach House, Kilmuir, who gently challenged and broadened my understanding, and some of the people I have met from the One Spirit Interfaith Foundation, all come out in the telling.

The Old Irish quote on the title page is reproduced here by kind permission of Sr Fiontullach, Head of the Order of Céili Dé. I owe her, and the Order, much gratitude for my knowledge of Celtic spirituality. However, the spirituality of the Islanders is my own creation.

My greatest thanks must go to Gillian Paschkes-Bell, my partner, now my wife. She gave me the encouragement to re-awaken this book from its dormancy; read and critiqued every sentence, cut here and added there. The prologue and epilogue that bracket the entire narrative originate with her. The story has come through me, but its final telling is a work of collaboration for which I take final responsibility.

AGR